THINGS COULD GET

UGLY

A NOVEL BY
GARY REED

Top Quark Publishing Co., Union, Kentucky 41091

Copyright @ 2018 by Gary Reed

ISBN: 9781980646501

Cover:

Rob Williams – Designer

Fiverr.com/cal5086

Cover photo of Charles Schilling:

Permission by Linda Schilling Mitchell

TCGU120318KDP

THINGS COULD GET

UGLY

A NOVEL BY

GARY REED

CHAPTER 1, FRIDAY JULY 7

War had not broken out overnight, and Jack O'Brien needed a story and wanted breakfast. Tucking his reporter's notebook into his back pocket, he stepped into the Bridge Café, the little diner near the Covington end of the Roebling Suspension Bridge. An unkempt man, his own size and build but twenty years older, accompanied him. Smells of coffee, bacon grease, and cigarette smoke greeted them.

Jack scanned the breakfast crowd, looking for an empty table, but the diner was full. At some tables, business men exchanged gossip and opinions. At others, patrons who were feeling less outgoing sipped their coffees and read the morning newspapers. And at still others, preoccupied with thoughts of the day ahead, men simply hurried through their breakfasts.

As Jack took in the scene, a young man rose from a stool at the counter and moved toward him, stopping in front of the cash register. In his early twenties, the man was short, thin, and nervous.

Behind the counter, a large woman in a uniform a size too small moved to the register. "Everything okay, hon?" Her name tag identified her as "Emma."

The young man opened his jacket and pulled a gun from his waistband. "Everything'll be fine," he said, "when you give me the money in that there cash register."

"Now what's got into you?" Emma asked. "Did the cook burn your toast?"

The young man pointed at the cash register with his gun. "Just give me the money, and nobody'll get hurt."

Jack figured the guy learned that line from some radio drama. He glanced at his companion and rolled his eyes.

"How about," Emma countered, "we say your breakfast is on the house this morning? That way you won't end up in prison, and your parents won't have that shame to deal with."

"Just give me the damn money," the young man said, louder than necessary.

At the counter, the men seated closest to the confrontation stopped talking and watched the unfolding drama.

Shaking her head and muttering to herself, Emma turned away from the young man and walked to the service window where the cook was placing orders for the wait staff to pick up.

"Sam," Emma said in a loud, condescending voice, "we got ourselves a problem. I think you must have burnt this gentleman's toast."

From the other side of the opening, the cook shook his head in frustration and shouted back, "I haven't even put the roast in the oven yet!"

Emma looked back at the young guy with the gun and shrugged her shoulders. "Cook can't hear worth a damn."

A man opened the door to the diner and squeezed in, forcing Jack and his companion to move further into the diner, just a step from the young guy with the gun. The new man was about forty, short and thin, with a short, thin mustache. He wore a fedora, a double-breasted suit, dark shirt, and white tie.

Jack caught the new man's eye and turning his head, looked at the young man's gun.

The new man followed Jack's gaze, nodded, but made no effort to back out of the diner.

Turning back to the cook, Emma shouted, "Sam, you need to come out here right now and tell this gentleman why you burnt his toast. Otherwise, he's liable to up-and-shoot somebody with this gun he's waving around."

More patrons at the counter stopped eating and turned their attention to the young man with the gun.

Emma took her time walking the half dozen steps back to the cash register.

"I didn't say nothing 'bout no toast," the young man said. "You're just stallin'."

"Josef Plucking Stalin!" Jack's companion complained.

"Open that cash register right now," the young man demanded, "or I'm gonna shoot one of those big tits of yours right off."

Emma glared at the man, holding her expression for what seemed to Jack a long time. "Which one?" she asked.

"Jesus H. Christ, lady, just give me the money."

The cook pushed through the kitchen doors. He had three or four days' stubble, and a cigarette dangled from his mouth. Stains and soil discolored his apron. His right hand clenched a cast iron frying pan.

"Which tit?" Emma demanded of the young man. "I got two you know."

"Just give me the money," the young man pleaded. He used the back of the hand holding the gun to wipe sweat from his forehead.

The cook hesitated and sized up the young man. He slowed his approach but continued to move forward.

Jack saw a large, menacing man in the back of the diner stand. Like the man behind him, this man also wore a dark double-breasted suit, dark shirt, and white tie, but he was taller, beefier, and scarier. He began to move forward.

Emma shook her head, waving the big man off.

The big man—Jack would later learn his name was Gus Panzer—stopped, but put his hand inside his jacket, and held it there.

A customer at a table near the front yelled, "Emma, just give him the damn money, so nobody gets shot."

With that, the diner went quiet.

The man behind Jack unbuttoned his suit jacket and pulled a snub nose .38 from a shoulder holster. He held the gun at his side.

That put Jack between the nervous young man with a gun and a gangster with a gun. He had been thinking this incident would make for a nice little story he could sell to one of the wire services. Now, he worried about becoming part of the story. He wanted his name on the story, not in it.

The young man in front of Jack shifted what little weight he had from one foot to the other. "Give me the goddam money," he said, "before I start shooting." He pointed the gun at the cook, who was now close to the cash register. His hand shook.

The cook froze.

Jack's companion stepped forward, putting himself directly behind the young man, but a little off center to the left.

"Woody," Jack cautioned, "stay out of this."

Ignoring Jack, Woody touched the young man on the shoulder. His voice not much more than a whisper, he asked, "Horseradish?"

The young man with the gun tensed but didn't respond.

"Woody," Jack said, louder and more demanding, "stay out of this."

Tapping the young man on the shoulder again, Woody repeated his request in a more normal voice. "Horseradish?"

"What the hell is wrong with you?" the young man said over his shoulder. "Can't you see I'm busy here?"

"Horseradish!" Woody repeated, his voice stronger and more insistent.

"I don't have any damn horseradish," the young man said, turning. "Now just —"

Woody landed a hard-left jab in the young man's face, then a second jab.

The young man's face twisted away from the punches just in time to meet the backside of the cook's frying pan. He crumpled and dropped to the floor, his nose bent like a crushed cigarette. Blood poured from his nostrils and pooled on the floor.

"Jesus, Sam," Emma said. "There goes my tip."

Woody bent down and removed the pistol from the unconscious man's hand. He checked the safety and made sure there wasn't a round chambered.

The young man groaned and opened his eyes.

The short, thin gangster who had been standing behind Jack pushed forward and grabbed the young man by an arm. With surprising speed, Gus Panzer, the large, menacing gangster from the back of the diner, came forward as well and grabbed the kid's other arm. Together, the two men hustled the dazed young man from the diner.

Emma shook her head. "You didn't have to do that," she said to Woody. "You could have got yourself killed."

Woody shook his head "no."

"He might have shot you," Emma insisted. "Been me, I know I would have."

"Safety razor," Woody said.

Emma looked baffled.

For a moment, Jack was too.

"Safety razor," Woody said again, holding up the gun.

"Woody," Jack said, "are you trying to say he still had the safety on?"

"Safety razor," Woody agreed.

That's good, Jack thought, *but you didn't know that until after it was over, and you picked up the gun.*

Moving the frying pan to his left hand, the cook took the cigarette from his mouth and positioned it on the counter, the lit end extending over the edge. He reached across the counter with his free hand. "Thanks, Mister, but I need you to give me that gun."

Woody turned the gun handle toward the cook and surrendered the weapon.

The cook took the gun and handed it to Emma. "Put it in the box," he said, "with the rest of them."

Emma emptied the bullets from the gun and dropped it and the bullets into a box under the cash register. As she did, the cook picked up his cigarette again.

Pointing to the door, Jack asked Emma, "Are they taking him to the police station?"

Emma shook her head. "Not likely. They're with the Syndicate."

Jack pulled his notebook from his pocket. "Can I get a comment from you for the paper?"

Emma arched her eyebrow. "Comment about what?"

"About the man who was pointing a gun at you," Jack said, forcing a smile. "The man who just tried to rob you."

"Don't recall anything like that and wouldn't want the bad publicity if I did. Now, run along and go find a table. I'll bring you some coffee."

Jack looked at Sam.

"Don't look at me," Sam said. "I'm just the cook." He turned and headed toward the door to the kitchen. As he did, he used his apron to wipe blood from the back of the skillet.

Jack returned his notebook to his pocket. Looking around, he spotted a table with only one occupant, a businessman in a suit and tie. In his fifties, the man had the self-satisfied look of success.

Jack made his way to the table, with Woody following. "Mind if we join you?" he asked.

"Please do," the man said. He stood and extended his hand. "I'm George Hanover."

"Jack O'Brien. My friend here is Woodrow W. Whitaker the Third, but he prefers Woody."

"Pleased to meet you," the older man said. "Woody, you sure landed a solid one on that young guy's face."

Woody looked the businessman up and down and said, "Duck deodorant." He turned and wandered off toward the restroom in the rear of the diner.

"What's with your friend?" Hanover asked.

"He's a good man," Jack said. "He was a college professor before the war. They conscripted him like everybody else his age, and he did his time in the trenches. Something happened to him, not sure what. Maybe a shell exploded too close, maybe he just saw too much terrible stuff. When he came back, he wasn't right in the head."

"Shellshock," Hanover said.

"Maybe."

Emma arrived with two cups of coffee. "Where's your friend?" she asked Jack.

"Washing up."

"George," Emma said, turning to the older man, "you ready to order?"

"Same as every day, Emma. Scrambled eggs, bacon, toast."

Turning to Jack, Emma asked, "How 'bout you, hon?"

"That sounds good. My friend will have hot cakes—and sausage."

"Coming right up."

Jack turned back to the businessman. "Sorry, I guess my head's still back with the excitement. Your name's Hanover?"

"That's right but call me George."

"George, I want to take back what I said about Woody not being right in the head. I think he's just fine upstairs. It's just that he can't seem to express himself. It all comes out wrong."

"What's he do for a living?"

"Odd jobs mainly. I'd like to find him a decent job, but with so many people still looking for work, it's hard. Who wants to hire a college professor who talks nonsense?"

"I thought all college professors talked nonsense," Hanover said, chuckling at his own joke. "He lives with you?"

"No, he lives on the river."

"He's one of those shanty-boat people?"

"Yeah. When he got back from the war, he bought a shanty. He's been living there since."

"Speak of the devil," Hanover said, letting Jack know Woody was approaching.

Jack pulled back the chair next to his own, beckoning his friend to take a seat.

"You're a reporter?" Hanover asked Jack.

"Yes, sir."

"With the *Tribune*?"

"I hope to be soon, but for now, I'm a stringer, selling stories to the AP or whoever will buy 'em."

"You're not from around here?"

"I grew up here and elsewhere. Went to the University of Kentucky. Got a degree in journalism. After I graduated, with the Depression and all, the best I could do was a job with a small paper downstate."

"So, you came home and hope to land a reporting position with one of the papers here?"

"You got it." Jack downed some of his coffee. "What I'd like to do, tell you the truth, is get a job as a foreign reporter and cover what's happening in Europe–Hitler and all that. But first, I've got to get some experience under my belt, and that means getting on with a paper here or across the river in Cincinnati. You know, chase the big story and all that."

"The big story?"

"The story that makes a reporter's reputation–and gives him a chance to do the stories he wants to do."

"You married?"

"No, sir, haven't met the right girl. Besides, unless I can land steady work, who'd want me?"

Hanover said nothing.

"So, how 'bout yourself," Jack asked. "You a banker?"

"God, no! I earn my money honestly, thank you very much."

Emma arrived with a plate in each hand, and another balanced on her forearm. As she placed one of the plates on the table in front of the older man, she said to his tablemates, "Gentlemen, you're in the presence of royalty. Business royalty, anyway."

She placed a plate on the table in front of Jack and passed a plate to Woody.

"George owns the brewery. And this year, he heads up the Businessmen's Club. Thought you should know."

"You own Hanover Brewery?" Jack asked.

"That and some other things."

Woody's eyes widened. "Hand Over Brew?"

The Syndicate man who had entered the diner just in time to witness the excitement approached. He carried a cup of coffee he'd gotten at the counter and took the seat next to Hanover.

"Gentlemen," Hanover said, "this is Salvatore Rizzi. He joins me here for breakfast on Friday mornings."

"Call me Sal," Rizzi said, shaking hands with Jack and Woody. "You're the guy responsible for the chin music?" he said to Woody. "Distracted him so the cook could smack him upside the head with that skillet?"

Woody shrugged.

"Mr. O'Brien," Hanover said, pointing his fork, "is a reporter."

Rizzi folded his arms and gave Jack a hard look.

"Please call me Jack."

"Jack, you're not here for a story, are you?" Hanover asked. "We don't have to worry that you're going to write a story about something we say?"

Jack had sensed a change in the older man the moment Rizzi arrived. "No, sir, not unless you want me to. I'm off duty. Everything said here is off the record."

"I have your word on that?"

"Yes, sir, you do."

"In Sal's line of work, he can't afford to have some young reporter doing a story about him."

Jack turned to Rizzi. "You and that other man," he asked, "you turn that kid over to the police?"

"A kid like that don't need no police record," Rizzi said. "We just taught him some manners and told him the Bridge Café is off limits."

Hanover interrupted. "Jack, you understand that Sal's business associates wouldn't like it if you reported anything about him. He and his associates, if they don't like something, they don't express themselves by writing a letter to the editor, if you get my drift."

"I understand," Jack said, shooting Sal a grin. "I wouldn't want him to get upset about something I wrote and... cancel his subscription."

"And how about you, professor?" Hanover asked.

"Shut your puss, octopus!" Woody said.

"As you can see," Jack said, "my friend here couldn't say anything even if he wanted to, and I'm sure he doesn't want to get on the wrong side of Sal or his business associates."

"Good." Hanover reached into his inside jacket pocket, extracted an envelope, and put it on the table.

Rizzi picked it up and slid it into his own jacket pocket without opening it.

"Sal handles my wagers for me," Hanover said.

"You ever play the ponies?" Rizzi asked Jack.

"I've been to the track a few times, but I know next to nothing about horses or racing. So, no, I've never bet on the races, except two-dollar bets at the track."

Rizzi reached into his pocket and pulled out a pair of tickets. "These are tickets to the Latonia Race Track for the big charity day on Monday," he said. "You guys go and enjoy yourselves, and if you ever want to place bets when you can't get to the track, just remember me, and I'll help you with that."

"Tanks," Woody said and pushed the tickets to Jack.

Jack picked them up and offered his own thanks. He was betting his future on being able to break into a tough profession where every day was a race against other reporters and a deadline. In comparison, placing a $2 bet on which nag would make it across the finish line first seemed silly. Still, the Charity Day was a big deal, and he could use a little fun. "Is it true," he asked Sal, "that if a race horse breaks a leg, they shoot it?"

Sal shrugged. "Yeah, so what? A headline chaser like you messes up a story, they kill it, don't they?"

Jack shook his head. "Not the same thing."

Sal's face broke into a crooked grin. "It is, if the reporter breaks the wrong story. Then, maybe it's not his story that gets killed."

CHAPTER 2, MONDAY, JULY 10

**Thousands To See Charity Day
Event At Latonia**
Advance Sale Of Tickets
Shatters Records
*Kentucky Times Star, July 8, 1939,
About a July 10 event*

**Plants And Public Offices To Close
For Charity Race Day At Latonia**
Kentucky Times Star, July 10, 1939

Portly and perspiring, Harry Boyle, the Vice Mayor of the City of Covington, retrieved his already damp handkerchief from his pocket and patted the sweat on his forehead. He had just walked from the Courthouse at 3rd and Market Streets, where he had his office, to Front Street, where he lived. The walk was only a few blocks, but it was July, and he was wearing a suit and tie.

Boyle stopped in front of the stately Victorian house that was his home and surveyed the grounds. He insisted on orderliness and took pleasure in seeing that the grass was not creeping into the flowerbeds or the rings around the trees. Even if his own forehead was extending upwards into territory where it did not belong, at least the lawn remained within its allotted boundaries.

Two Penny Smith, the black man who maintained the yard and did odd jobs around the house, was fussing over the azaleas like they were precious jewels on special display.

"Mr. Two Penny," Boyle called out, catching the man by surprise. Boyle knew his surname was Smith, but he believed calling the colored man "Mister" was flattery enough. *One had to draw the line somewhere.*

"Good afternoon, Mr. Mayor, I didn't even hear you," Two Penny said in an even louder voice. He walked toward Boyle.

Boyle was the Vice Mayor, not the Mayor, but he didn't mind when folks gave him the salutary promotion. The fact was, he controlled all the levers of power in the city. He was in charge in every way but the title. And if anything worth knowing happened in *his* city, *he*, by God, would know about it, usually before it happened. That was how he maintained his power. Not that Two Penny would know anything about that.

"Dem azaleas sure is pretty this year," Two Penny said. "But da bugs, dey love azaleas pert-near as much as people do, mebbe more."

"You've got them looking just fine," Boyle said. "I'm sure Agnes appreciates what you do. And the neighbors, too, since they get to see the yard more than I do."

"Speaking of your wife, Mr. Mayor, I imagine she'll be surprised to see you! I ain't never seen you come home this early afore, you being the mayor and all."

"Mr. Two Penny, as I'm sure you've heard, the Latonia Race Track is having a special charity event today. It's a big deal. Anybody who's anybody will be there, so I have to put in an appearance."

"The Latonia Race Track! It's a beautiful day, and all the swell folk there. Lordy, I imagine you'll be having a fine afternoon, sir."

Boyle patted his forehead with the handkerchief again and returned it to his pocket. "That's a positive way to think about things, Mr. Two Penny, but the truth is, it's just something someone in my position has to do."

"Ain't never been there myself, of course."

Boyle felt himself growing impatient with the conversation. He had more important things to do than exchange pleasantries with a colored man who liked to talk too much. "Now, Mr. Two Penny, don't let me keep you from your business. I just wanted to say hello."

"Then, I'll just be going on about my work," Two Penny said, taking the hint. He went back to the business of studying the azaleas.

Boyle strode the last few paces to the house, climbed the front steps, and moved into the shade of the wide front porch. As he did, the front door swung open, and Reverend Jonah Breckinridge stepped out.

"Well, hello, Reverend," Boyle greeted the minister with the forced cheerfulness of the politician he was. He extended his arm to shake hands. The preacher had the anxious look of a not-quite-house-broken pup that's soiled the carpet again and expects a beating. His palm was damp.

"Here to talk with Agnes about your project?" Boyle searched his memory, trying to recall what the preacher's project was.

"Yes, indeed, and good day to you as well, Mr. Mayor. As God is my witness, I had no idea how involved fundraising would be. I sure am mighty grateful for the guidance and suggestions your wife provides."

"You're collecting food and money for hungry children?" Boyle asked. He chose to ignore the preacher's Appalachian accent and the suggestion of inbred ignorance he associated with it. He did not understand why his wife had agreed to help this preacher. *For God's sake, we're Episcopalian, and this cretin is a Bible-thumper from eastern Kentucky.*

"Yes, sir," the preacher agreed. "Except for missionary work and saving souls, I can't think of a better cause than feeding hungry children."

"Yes, well, very good, Reverend, nice to see you again."

"Going to the race track?" the minister asked.

Boyle nodded and forced a smile, but made a mental note that Agnes needed reminding not to talk about his business. "Yes, Reverend, it's a charity event, and I've got to get out among the public.

It's part of the job." Boyle assumed the preacher disapproved of the track and gambling. "So," he challenged the minister, "do you have a special verse from scripture for me?"

The minister hesitated a moment, then flashed a broad smile. "First Corinthians, 9:24, sir. 'Do you not know that in a race, all the runners run, but only one gets the prize?'"

"Apt," Boyle said. "Now, Reverend, if you'll excuse me."

"Of course, sir, and good luck."

As the preacher rushed off, Boyle glanced at his watch. He still had plenty of time to change clothes and get to the track, but he didn't want to be late. After all, he wasn't going to the track to meet the goddam Corinthians. He was going to meet some men who had come all the way from Cleveland to make a request that would put him in a difficult position.

They were important men—men who didn't run for election and whose names never appeared on any roster of city officials. But their role in a city's affairs could be decisive. Covington's sister city, Newport, was evidence of that. And they were men to whom you did not say "no."

***

When Jack could not persuade Woody to go with him to the Latonia Race Track for the Charity Day event, he called his friend and former University of Kentucky classmate, Ben Strasberg. Ben agreed to drive up from Louisville for lunch and a day at the track.

They were standing in the infield, twenty minutes before the first race. The crowd jostling around them was classier than the usual weekday-racetrack crowd. The ladies wore short-sleeved summer dresses and colorful, wide-brimmed hats. The men dressed better than the usual racetrack crowd as well. And unlike the fellows who came to the track on a weekday, these men spent more time back-slapping and glad-handing than studying the track records of the horses.

"Perfect weather," Ben said, looking around. "And an impressive crowd."

Jack followed his friend's glance around the infield crowd and clubhouse. "From the advance sales figures in the local papers, everybody who's anybody bought tickets. Most of them must be here, hobnobbing."

"By the way," Ben said, grinning. "Aren't you the picture of spiffy? Boater hat, seersucker suit, bow tie. Are you expecting to sing in a barbershop quartet?"

Jack bowed and tipped his hat. "I'm just here to mingle with the swells."

"Oh, Good Lord," Ben said. "You're hoping to meet a dame."

"Ben, I believe that falling in love is the most important thing a young man can do. That's why I make it my practice to fall in love as often as possible."

Ben laughed. "That's why you always get the girl..."

"And you get the story," Jack said, finishing the familiar exchange.

Ben looked around again. "It's a shame you don't know any of these bigshots."

Jack spotted George Hanover a short distance away, near the rail. "Ben, come with me," he said. "I want to introduce you to one of Covington's top business bigwigs."

Jack called out George Hanover's name and hurried in his direction. Ben grimaced and trudged after Jack.

Hanover smiled and said something to the woman standing next to him.

"George," Jack said when he caught up with the businessman, "this is my good friend, Ben Strasberg. He's a crack reporter for the Louisville *Courier-Journal.*"

George Hanover shook hands with Ben and said, "Gentlemen, I'd like you to meet my wife, Lillian."

Lillian Hanover appeared to be about fifty. She was attractive, with the posture and good manners instilled in the upper crust. Jack guessed she was Episcopalian, played bridge, and if she voted, was a loyal Republican.

As the two young men greeted Mrs. Hanover, an attractive young woman, about their own age, approached. She wore a hat with a wide brim that turned up on one side and a white sundress with a floral print. The dress had short, puff sleeves that revealed long, slender arms, and a fashionable wasp waist that showed off her figure.

"This is our daughter, Maggie," Mrs. Hanover said. "She just graduated from Barnard College, in New York, and it's wonderful having her home with us again."

Maggie was pretty, and she had a winning smile, but she radiated something more than that. She was one of those people who have great presence. Anywhere she went, she would be the center of attention—someone who, as the saying went, could light up a room.

"Maggie," George Hanover said to his daughter, "these impecunious young men are reporters. They know how to turn a phrase, and I don't doubt they also know how to turn a young lady's head. But in their profession, they work for space on the front page, not real money. Not that you'll listen to my advice, but I suggest you stay as far away from these headline chasers as you can."

"George!" Mrs. Hanover said. "That's positively rude. I'm sure these young men have their own plans for the day. Besides, Maggie can decide for herself who she wants to spend the afternoon with."

Maggie smiled, leaned in, and planted a kiss on her father's cheek. "I think it's sweet that father wants to protect me," Maggie said in a condescending tone. "It's *so* Victorian."

Jack noticed that George Hanover didn't smile or look the least bit mollified.

Maggie turned from her parents, and said, "Would you gentlemen be willing to show me to the paddock? You can tell me all about what you do on the way." She slid her arm through Jack's, and said to Ben, "Are you from Louisville?"

"Lexington."

"If you're from Lexington, then you *must* know all about horses. You'll have to tell me which horses to bet on."

***

After the third race, Jack, Ben, and Maggie retired to the clubhouse bar above the grandstand where they took seats around a small table and sipped Long Island Iced Teas.

"So," Maggie asked, "which of you is the better reporter?"

"I am," Jack said, "but you'd never know it because Ben gets all the breaks."

"Maggie, hold on to your hat," Ben said. "There's a big wind headed this way."

"I suspect you're right, Ben, but let's hear him out."

"In late '36 and the first half of '37," Jack said, "I'm in eastern Kentucky –"

"Writing for the *Harlan Harlot*," Ben interrupted, stealing the nickname Jack used for the Harlan County newspaper that had given Jack his first job.

Jack grinned. "Writing for the *Harlan Harlot*. And from Pittsburgh to Louisville and on south, the Ohio River floods. It may be the best damn natural disaster either Ben or I will ever see, and Ben's in Louisville, right in the middle of it, floating along in his bathtub with his Remington in his lap, pecking out stories left and right."

Ben gave a "what can I say?" gesture with his hands and shoulders.

"Meanwhile," Jack said, "I'm all the way on the other side of the state, high and dry in eastern Kentucky, where people are doing what they've always done–mining coal, reading their Bibles, eating squirrels and possum."

Maggie rolled her eyes.

"The best story I got the whole time I was there, was when someone discovered a Pentecostal preacher was doing more than ministering to his congregation. He was doing some special missionary work with the ladies of the choir."

Maggie arched an eye but didn't interrupt.

"Honest to God," Jack said. "And after they ran him out of town, they discovered he took the church's money with him."

"That sounds like an interesting story," Maggie said, letting a mischievous smile show.

"Yeah, *sure.*" Jack pretended to be in despair. "Ben gets forty days and forty nights of rain, Noah and his Ark, pestilence and pillaging, all the good stuff, and I get to write that the faithful of Last Holler, Kentucky, drove a philandering Pharisee from the temple."

"Let's toast reporters," Ben said, raising his glass. "Here's to those who know how to ride a rising tide to fame and glory, and to those who languish in the backwaters writing about ecclesiastical matters."

"Funny guy," Jack said, joining the toast. "So, then I got a position in Bowling Green and moved to western Kentucky."

"Writing for the *Bowling Green Massacre*," Ben said.

"*Bowling Green Messenger*," Jack corrected his friend.

"Never heard of it," Ben said with a sly smile.

"I get there just in time for the mid-term elections," Jack said. " 'Referendum on Roosevelt and the New Deal' and all that."

"Wasn't that a big story?" Maggie asked, putting her elbows on the table and resting her chin on her steepled hands as if hanging on Jack's every word.

"Sure, the mid-term was a big deal, if you're like Ben and you work for a *real* newspaper in a *real* city. But the *Bowling Green Massacre* has this arch-conservative editor, who goes around talking about the 'Jew Deal' and calling Roosevelt a socialist."

"Sounds like my father," Maggie said. She took a sip from her drink.

A loud cheer went up in the stands outside the clubhouse bar.

"A longshot must have won," Ben said.

Jack took a sip from his own drink. "And then I come up here to Covington, and all hell breaks loose in eastern Kentucky. The coal miners go out on strike, violence breaks out, and Governor Chandler sends troops in. That mine explodes. Meanwhile, up around Rowan County, there's horrible flooding, lots of people without homes."

"Those poor people have had it hard," Maggie said.

"Yes, it's dreadful, awful stuff," Jack agreed. "The preachers down there must be going on non-stop about the Book of Revelation, telling the faithful that the End Times are upon us. But would it have killed them to have scheduled at least some of that good stuff while I was down there begging for a story to report?"

"You're terrible!" Maggie said, shaking her head.

"I'm glad for Ben that he's in Louisville," Jack said, his tone more serious. "His paper covers anything in the state worth covering. The big Editor-in-Chief"–Jack looked with mock reverence toward the heavens– "is taking care of Ben. But if He is listening, what I'd like, what I'd give my eye teeth for, is a job as a foreign correspondent."

Maggie looked at Jack and blinked. "Really?"

"Think about it. I'm writing about an adulterous, thieving preacher in Last Holler, Kentucky, and –"

Maggie put her hand on Jack's hand to get his attention and then left it there longer than necessary. "Is there a place called 'Last Holler'?"

"No," Jack admitted. "The preacher was in Clay County, down in the southeastern corner of the state, on the Tennessee border."

"What was he like?" Maggie asked.

"Tall, good-looking guy. Curly, coal-black hair, in his thirties. They said he was good with the choir and quick with a quote from scripture."

Jack searched Maggie's face. Maggie was thinking something, but he couldn't tell what.

Maggie turned to Ben. "Does Jack always go on like this?"

"Yes, absolutely," Ben attested. "This is at least the third time I've heard Jack explain that all the good stories are happening wherever he isn't. It's a tragedy. Remember last week, when that mine exploded in Harlan, and it trapped those coal miners underground?"

Maggie nodded.

"When they were breathing their last breaths, they had tears running down their faces because they were thinking about how unfair it was that Jack wasn't still in Harlan to write about it."

"You're awful too," Maggie said, laughing. "Both of you! When something terrible happens, all you can think about is how you can get the story before someone else does."

"Maggie," Ben said, "I suspect if you were a reporter, you would beat both of us to the big story."

"Why I do declare, Mr. Strasberg," Maggie said, hamming it up. "You'll turn a girl's head."

"You've been reading *Gone with the Wind*," Ben said. "Even in Atlanta, no one really talks like that."

"You're right. I am. The book's melodramatic and awful, but I can't put it down." Maggie took a sip from her drink but kept her eyes on Ben. "What are you reading?"

"Steinbeck. *Grapes of Wrath*. It's at the top of the best-seller lists."

"And you?" Maggie asked Jack.

"Raymond Chandler, *The Big Sleep*."

"Hmm," Maggie said. "The prize goes to Ben. But you're both writers. Which of you will write the book everyone wants to read?"

"We'd both like to write that book," Ben said. "But to write it, you need to have something important to say. Neither of us has seen enough—enough of what's truly important—to write that book. Not yet, anyway."

"Ben's right," Jack said. "We're in Kentucky, and the stories we're writing wrap tonight's fish before it goes in the trash. But look at what's going on in Europe."

Jack took a quick sip from his drink. "There was that Civil War in Spain with Hitler helping Franco. Huge story! Then, Germany goosesteps into Austria, proud as can be. Another huge story. You know what I was doing when that happened? I was writing stories about county officials cutting the ribbon to open a new outhouse."

Maggie smiled.

Jack was exaggerating, but he was sure Maggie knew the type story he was talking about. "Then Hitler demands a piece of Czechoslovakia, and—when was that, last September? —that idiot Chamberlain gives in to Hitler and comes back promising 'peace in our time.'"

"Oh, come on, Jack!" Ben said, challenging his friend. "After all they went through in the last war, do you really think England and France would go to war over German-speaking Czechs?"

"I'm a reporter," Jack said. "Here's what I think: That's a terrific story. In our lifetimes, how often are either of us going to get to write a story like that?"

Ben nodded agreement but remained skeptical.

"We all know what happened next," Jack said. "In March, Hitler moved into Prague and took over the rest of the country. And now, he's demanding a piece of Poland. So much for 'peace in our time.'"

Jack realized he was no longer being funny. He took a gulp from his drink. "Sorry," he said. "What I'm trying to say is, if you're a reporter, you'd rather be covering what's happening in Europe right now than writing about what's happening at the county fair."

"Jack," Maggie asked, "do you think there will be another big war?"

Jack thought for a moment before responding. "Yes, I think so. It could happen real soon, but if it doesn't, my guess is, Hitler will keep pressing his luck until someone stands up to him. And then things could get ugly."

Jack thought he saw genuine concern flash across Maggie's face, but she recovered quickly and glanced at her watch. "Oh my gosh! I've got to get going. My parents never stay past the fifth race. If I don't get back, my father will blow a wig."

Ben looked at his own watch. "I've got a long drive back to Louisville," he said. "I need to take off too."

Jack offered to help Maggie find her parents, and the two of them gave their goodbyes to Ben.

When they located George and Lillian Hanover, Maggie stopped Jack before they got close. "Let me deal with my father," she said. "I had a wonderful time."

"Can I see you again?"

Maggie thought a moment. "Would you be willing to meet me at church?"

The question surprised Jack, but he agreed.

"You better write this down in your reporter's notebook," Maggie said. "Meet me Wednesday night at that little Pentecostal church on Garrard, around Sixth or Seventh Street. At 7:30."

Jack wrinkled his face. "I took you for an Episcopalian."

"I am," Maggie said and flashed Jack a big grin.

"Are you sure you wouldn't rather go to a movie?"

"Trust me on this," Maggie said. She gave Jack a quick peck on the cheek and hurried off to where her parents were waiting for her.

Jack was more than willing to meet Maggie for Wednesday night church services, but he was sure his heart didn't have a prayer.

CHAPTER 3, WEDNESDAY, JULY 12

**WAR TO COME
IF HITLER MOVES**

ON DANZIG, WORLD TOLD
BY CHAMBERLAIN.
The Cincinnati Enquirer,
July 11, 1939

Jack O'Brien spotted Maggie Hanover standing in front of the shabby little church and quickened his pace. She wore a yellow dress, white gloves, and a jaunty, laurel-green pillbox hat with a yellow bow on top.

"Maggie," Jack greeted her, removing his own hat. "You should have waited for me inside. I would have found you."

Maggie broke into a grin. "I wanted as many people as possible to see me. I'm hoping someone will say something to my father. He suspects I'm going to a bar or a party." Sliding her arm under his, she smiled at Jack. "He's warned me more than once to be careful not to fall under the charms of some ne'er-do-well Irishman."

"Is that why you wanted me to meet you here?" Jack asked as he followed Maggie into the little church. "Because of your father?"

"I had lunch with a friend from high school," Maggie whispered, "and she told me how wonderful the choir is. And the preacher."

Jack studied Maggie, trying to decide if she was serious, or if, as her smile suggested, she was teasing him.

"My friend says the minister spends a tremendous amount of time with the ladies of the choir to help them prepare."

Jack began to say something, but Maggie put her finger to her lips and whispered, "Shush!"

Jack followed her halfway down a side aisle and slid into a pew beside her. Moments later, Reverend Jonah Breckinridge entered, carrying a large Bible. He was a tall, ruggedly good-looking, thirty-something man, with curly black hair.

Jack had no doubt. This was the preacher from Clay County. He turned to Maggie and broke into a big grin.

Maggie put her finger to her lips.

The pianist, a plump, middle-aged woman, began a vigorous assault on the keys of the upright piano. She did this with enough energy, Jack thought, to drive the devil himself from the instrument.

Reverend Breckinridge came to the podium, laid the Bible there, and squared it just so, before turning and taking his place before the choir. When the music reached the right note, he raised his arms, and the choir sang in one voice.

The choir delivered vigorous renditions of three hymns. Jack recognized only one, "Be Glad in the Lord."

It was hard to tell, but Jack thought he detected great affection for the minister and for the opportunity to sing among some in the choir, but a hint of bitterness and scorn from others. Jack cautioned himself that he might be reading into their expressions what he expected to find.

Reverend Breckinridge strode to the podium. He pulled himself to his full height and surveyed the small congregation. After assuring himself he had everyone's attention, he thanked the choir for the blessing of its singing and for the many hours its members devoted each week to practice. Next, he thanked the congregation for coming out on such a warm and humid summer night. He assured his listeners their devotion would touch God's heart.

After a pause that signaled he was about to begin his sermon, Reverend Breckinridge picked up the Bible and opened it to the first of several places marked by ribbons. He looked around the congregation, hesitated, and returned the Bible to the podium.

"I don't need the Bible to tell you," he said, his voice smooth and quiet, like a neighbor with sad news, "that these are difficult and trying times. A depression, the likes of which none of us has ever seen, has struck our once vibrant nation low. Able-bodied men are out of work and standing in bread lines. They are riding in boxcars, hoping to find work in some other place just as bad off as where they came from.

"Brothers and sisters," Reverend Breckinridge continued, warming to his topic, "in the land of the Pharaoh, the enslaved tribes of Israel toiled under the taskmaster's whip to build the Great Pyramids. Just so, today in this nation, men by the tens of thousands are in government camps, doing work that doesn't need doing.

"These tough times try men's souls. My heart goes out to those who cannot find work, to those who have no roofs over their heads, to those who are hungry. As the Bible warns us, times like these tempt even the faithful to despair."

The congregation responded with heartfelt "amens."

"Indeed, my brothers and sisters," he said, his voice rising and falling in cadence with his message, "the Bible warns us that just such tribulations—and worse—will come before the Son of God returns and establishes his Kingdom." He looked around at the congregation, his countenance stern and foreboding.

The congregation responded with another, more muted chorus of amens.

"Brothers and sisters," Reverend Breckinridge said, "we are now at that time when the Beast is at large in the world, and the Antichrist is beckoning us to his side, deceiving us. The Bible warns of these things too."

More amens.

Jack wondered where the preacher was going with this. He glanced at Maggie, but she concentrated on the sermon. Or pretended to. Only when Jack turned his attention back to Reverend Breckinridge did Maggie sneak a look in his direction and flash a big smile.

The preacher reminded his congregation that godless Communists had taken over Russia and threatened the world with their vast hordes and atheistic philosophy. "This was foretold," he said, his voice rising. "It was foretold in the Book of Revelation, chapter fourteen."

Reverend Breckinridge lifted the Bible from the podium, turned to the Book of Revelation, and read: "And I looked and beheld a white cloud, and upon the cloud sat one like unto the Son of Man, having on his head a golden crown, and in his hand a sharp sickle."

The preacher looked up from his Bible and thundered at the congregation: "A sickle! A sickle, my brothers and sisters. The Bible warned us that Leninism, Stalinism, and Communism would come!"

The congregation responded with groans and murmurings.

Reverend Breckinridge looked down again and read the next verse: "And another angel came out of the temple, crying with a loud voice to him that sat on the cloud, 'Thrust in thy sickle, and reap: for now, is the time for thee to reap; for the harvest of the earth is ripe.'"

Once again, the preacher looked up from the text. His voice shaking now, he informed his congregation, "That second angel is the German Chancellor, Adolf Hitler."

The congregation responded with more amens, but this time, an older woman in a pew near the front interrupted, calling out, "Save us, Sweet Jesus!"

Reverend Breckinridge acknowledged the response before returning to the scripture. "And another angel came out of the temple, which is in heaven," he read in a booming voice. "He also had a sharp sickle."

Scattered amens anticipated what was to come.

Maggie turned and watched Jack's face.

"That angel, who also had a sharp sickle," Reverend Breckinridge said, lowering his voice, "was no cherub in white with little wings and the garb of an infant."

"No!" several parishioners called out.

"No, indeed!" Reverend Breckinridge said, his voice driving toward a crescendo. "That angel—that fallen angel, that follower of Satan—is the Bible's warning to us. It is warning us,"—he paused for effect — "of Franklin Delano Roosevelt."

The congregation shouted its approval with loud amens.

Stunned, Jack looked at Maggie. She was grinning ear-to-ear but hid her face from the congregation with a hymnal.

Except among certain sectors of the business community, the wealthy, and die-hard conservatives, people revered President Roosevelt. *Why in God's name*, Jack wondered, *were these people, most of whom appeared to be poor or just clinging to a thread-bare middle-class status, opposed to Roosevelt?*

Jack listened as Reverend Breckinridge launched into the heart of his sermon, telling the congregation that Roosevelt was a socialist and a deceiver and the Antichrist. Time would unmask his perfidy. Stalin and Hitler and Roosevelt would raise great armies, he foretold, and men would know the scythe. The armies of Stalin and Hitler and Roosevelt would harvest them like ripe wheat. But Christ would return, he promised, and would destroy Stalin and Hitler and Roosevelt. Christ would gather the faithful beside him, and his kingdom would last a thousand years.

As the preacher made his case, citing one verse after another, Jack scanned the congregation for dissent and saw none.

Reverend Breckinridge finished his sermon, cautioning his congregation to stay faithful during the tribulations to come. "Now, if you will," he concluded, "please give your attention to the choir."

The choir gave rousing renditions of three more hymns, and with that, the service wrapped up.

As the congregation began to stand and file out of the little church, Jack looked around again. Here and there, a congregant greeted a friend or relative. But for the most part, the faithful filed out wordlessly, weary souls headed home—saved by the grace of God to sleep, if they could, in the stagnant summer heat and to rise again at the crack of dawn, to return to soul-deadening jobs.

When the outbound tide of congregants ebbed, a short, thin man with a short, thin mustache, wearing a dark suit, dark shirt, and white tie made his way forward from the back of the church. Jack recognized him as Sal Rizzi.

The man greeted Reverend Breckinridge and moved with the preacher to a corner where they could talk.

Reverend Breckinridge handed Rizzi an envelope. Rizzi slid the envelope into the inside pocket of his suit coat.

Jack turned his attention back to Maggie but made sure not to show his face to Rizzi. "How did you know this was the same preacher I did that story on when I was in Harlan?"

"I didn't, but from what my friend said about him, I thought it might be." Maggie waved at the preacher and turned toward the back of the little church. "We can talk about it while you walk me home."

In the vestibule, Jack looked around and found a flyer that listed the names of the choir members. He slid it into his jacket pocket and pushed open the church door.

Maggie stepped into the warm summer air. Jack followed, eager to learn what other surprises Maggie might have.

CHAPTER 4, WEDNESDAY, JULY 19

**HOPE OF DANZIG PEACE GAINS
DESPITE DENIALS BY OFFICIALS**

PHONE WORKERS DRILL FOR AIR RAID
The Cincinnati Enquirer, July 19, 1939

Jack made his way through the list of choir members, interviewing as many as he could—all the while hoping the women did not compare notes. The next choir member on his list was Ruth Hill. She lived within walking distance of his boarding house and was expecting him.

On the phone, he had told Mrs. Hill he was doing a story about the choir. Jack passed a market on the way, and on impulse, bought an inexpensive bouquet. He figured he would need all the goodwill he could establish once his questions got closer to his real interest.

Five minutes later, Jack knocked on the door of the home of Mr. and Mrs. Roger Hill. It was a little wood-frame house with a tiny front yard. From its location on the east side of Covington, Jack imagined the '37 flood would have inundated the basement and covered much of the ground floor.

Mrs. Hill answered the door. She was in her mid-thirties, not unattractive, and, by appearances, a full-time housewife. "You must be the reporter," she said.

"Yes, ma'am, I'm Jack O'Brien, and these are for you."

"Oh my, isn't that thoughtful. Please, come in."

Jack stepped into the small, well-kept living room. He noticed a china case filled with knickknacks, confirming his guess that Mrs. Hill did not have children. He also noticed a Bible by what was likely her chair.

"I didn't know," Mrs. Hill said, "that reporters brought flowers. I thought you reporters were no-nonsense and hard bitten and all that. My husband will think I'm having an affair."

Jack swallowed. After a moment's hesitation, while Mrs. Hill arranged the bouquet in a vase, he decided to jump to why he was there. "Are you?"

Mrs. Hill looked up from the flowers and asked, "Am I what?"

"Having an affair? I've heard from several of the ladies in the choir," Jack said, "if you'll excuse me for being so blunt, that Reverend Breckinridge has been intimate with certain choir members, including you."

"Oh," Mrs. Hill said. She studied Jack and asked, "Would you like water?" Her voice was even, but no longer chatty and friendly.

"Only if you're having some."

Mrs. Hill turned and left the room.

It occurred to Jack that she might well return with a shotgun. He took heart when he heard water running in the kitchen, but still, he breathed easier when she reappeared with two glasses of water and no weapon. Mrs. Hill put one glass on the end table next to his chair, before taking a seat on the couch.

"Thank you," Jack said, hoping his voice revealed only gratitude for the water.

"What have you heard?" Mrs. Hill asked.

"That the Reverend can be quite charming, and that several of the ladies of the choir have succumbed to his charms."

"Why would you want to write a story like that and destroy their reputations? And their marriages?"

"If Reverend Breckinridge is posing as a man of God but is a lecherous fraud who is taking advantage of unsuspecting women, I think that's something people would want to know."

"Who told you I was having an affair with him?" Her voice

was hard and direct.

"I promised not to reveal that," Jack said. "I assume your affair with the Reverend is over now and that he's moved on to –"

Mrs. Hill waited to see if Jack finished his sentence. To see if he *could* finish his sentence.

Jack, in turn, waited to see what Mrs. Hill would say. He knew most people were uncomfortable with silence. He felt certain that if the pause hung there long enough, she would feel compelled to say something.

"You don't know who he's pursuing now," Mrs. Hill said. "Do you?"

"What I know or don't know doesn't matter," Jack countered. "I need to have a source." He was beginning to suspect that Mrs. Hill was a good deal shrewder and more calculating than he had imagined.

"What if I were to tell you whose life he's ruining now, and when you're likely to catch him at her home?"

"That'd be aces." Jack watched the woman's face for any sign of panic or retreat and saw none. Despite all the rubbish about women being the fairer sex, Jack thought this woman would make an exceptional poker player.

"What *I* think would be *aces,* as you put it, would be if you were to leave my name out of this."

Upping the stakes, Jack asked, "What time does your husband get home?"

"Late," Mrs. Hill said. "It's his poker night. Do you play poker, Mr. O'Brien?"

"Not much," Jack said.

"I didn't think so. I figured you for one of those men who'd rather spend his time and money at a whorehouse."

Where did that come from? Jack wondered.

34

"My brothers are delivery men," Mrs. Hill said. "I wonder if they might have seen you going into or coming out of one of those places. Is that something your editor might find interesting?"

Jack had never been to a brothel in his life, but he knew that wasn't the point. The point was what her brothers might be willing to accuse him of. So, he'd upped the stakes, and she had matched him chip for chip.

Jack considered what Mrs. Hill was proposing. He would get his story, and she would keep her good name. It wasn't the way they taught you to get a story in journalism school, but despite what he'd implied, none of the other women he'd interviewed had admitted to anything. He had gotten some to point the finger at someone else, but their suspicions weren't enough to base a story on.

"I see what you're getting at, Mrs. Hill," he said, flashing her a big smile. "And I see the story playing out just like you said."

"Do I have your word on that?"

"Yes, ma'am."

"Gertie—Gertrude Fulton—lives on Trevor Street, just off Scott. I think if you position yourself outside her home tomorrow afternoon, about 1:30, you just might find the Reverend making a house call."

Jack jotted the name and time into his notebook. As he did, Mrs. Hill stood and pulled the flowers from the vase. "You can take these and—"

Understanding that the interview was over, Jack stood.

Mrs. Hill hesitated, "— and give them to someone who wants them."

"Yes, ma'am," Jack said, accepting the flowers back.

The woman glared at him.

"Mrs. Hill," he said.

"Yes," she replied, daring him to press his luck any further.

"I hope your husband is as good at poker as you."

Mrs. Hill allowed a smile to show. "He's not."

CHAPTER 5, THURSDAY, JULY 20

STONES HURLED AS NEGROES
USE SWIMMING POOL
Police Stand Guard as Water Is Drained
PARK POOL
Whites Allowed to Use 5 Days A Week
Kentucky Times Star, July 17, 1939

Halfway down a residential street, across from a house indistinguishable from any other on the block, Jack O'Brien leaned against an oak tree, a big grin on his face. He was chatting with Dick Watson, the newspaper photographer he had persuaded to come with him.

"Jack, can you at least give me a hint," Watson said, "what the blazes we're doing here?"

"Sure thing, Flash," Jack said, using the nickname local reporters had given the cameraman. "Revelation, chapter sixteen, verse fifteen." Jack's grin broadened.

"So, you're not going to tell me a damn thing," Watson complained but dropped the subject when a car turned into the street.

The aging Plymouth 30U came down the lane a bit too fast and pulled to an abrupt stop in front of them. The driver leaped out of the car and hurried to the front door of the house, unlocked it, and entered. Jack figured the man was about thirty-five and the owner of the home.

"Things could get ugly real soon," Jack said, pushing himself off the tree. He crossed the street.

Watson followed.

Tall hedges surrounded the small front yard, and a black wrought-iron gate guarded the only break in the hedge. Watson opened the gate and stepped inside, positioning himself near the front step. Jack stationed himself on the sidewalk in front of the gate, blocking the exit.

The front door swung open, and a naked man bolted out.

Watson raised his camera and snapped a picture.

Startled by the flash, the naked man hesitated.

"Reverend Breckinridge," Jack called out. "Did Mr. Fulton catch you in bed with his wife?"

Watson snapped another picture.

"He's looking for his gun," the preacher said from the other side of the gate. "Get out of my way."

"Reverend," Jack persisted, blocking the gate. "I wonder if you would like to comment on the rumors that you've been sleeping with several of the ladies in the choir at your church."

A noise from inside the house startled the Reverend. He swung himself over the gate and began running, naked, down the street.

The homeowner emerged from the house, gun in hand. A woman inside yelled, "Jacob, please don't make this worse —"

The man turned and shouted, "Shut up! I'll deal with you later." When the man turned back toward the street, Watson snapped a photo.

The man raised his gun.

Jack opened the gate and stepped into the yard. "Mr. Fulton," he said, "did you just catch Reverend Breckinridge in bed with your wife?"

"Which way did he go?" Fulton asked. "I'm going to kill the S.O.B."

Fulton waved the gun this way and that, making Jack nervous.

"I'll take that as a 'yes.'" he said. "Did your wife tell you how long she and the Reverend had been sleeping together?"

"Get out of my way," Fulton said stepping toward Jack.

Jack kept his position between Fulton and the gate. He tried to keep Fulton engaged. "Will you and your wife –"

Fulton swung at Jack with the butt of the gun. Jack was taller and quicker.

"Will you and your wife," Jack repeated, "be looking for a different church?"

"You're goddam right we will."

"Your wife was in the choir?"

Fulton stepped toward Jack's left, attempting to get around him. "Yeah, but I don't see where any of this is your –"

Jack stepped in the same direction, keeping himself between Fulton and the gate. "The Reverend was sleeping with several ladies in the choir. What was your reaction when you caught him in bed with your wife?"

"What the hell do you think it was?"

Jack tried to modulate his voice, to be more conversational, less confrontational. "What made you come home in the middle of the afternoon?"

"Some woman called and said it was an emergency. Told me I needed to get home as quick as I could."

"Did she tell you why?"

"No, I thought my wife was hurt or sick or something. If that woman had told me why that preacher would be a dead man."

"Who called you?"

"I don't know. Some woman."

Jack could see that much of the steam had gone out of the man. "Did your wife tell you how long she's been sleeping with Reverend Breckinridge?" Jack asked again, his voice softer, more empathetic this time.

"Look, I don't want to talk now."

"I understand," Jack said. "Can I speak with your wife?"

Watson grinned at Jack's chutzpah but hid his face behind his bulky camera.

"No, leave us alone." Fulton began to turn, to go back inside, but Jack reached out and put his hand on the man's arm.

"Mr. Fulton, I need you to tell me that you're not going to hurt your wife, that you're not going to shoot her with that gun or do something foolish."

"Get out of my yard," Fulton said, pulling his arm away.

"Your wife wasn't the only woman this man seduced. We're going to expose him."

"Leave my wife and me out of this. If you put this in the paper, we'll never be able to show our faces again."

"I'll see what my editor says, but that preacher needs to be exposed."

"He needs to –"

"Just tell me," Jack interrupted, "that we're not going to have to come back here later, because you shot your wife, or beat her up and put her in the hospital. Just promise me that I'm not going to have to write a story about the police arresting you, and –"

Fulton shook his head. "I'm not that kind of man." He turned and walked back into the house, slamming the door.

Watson shook his head and gave Jack a knowing glance. "Did you put someone up to calling him?"

An impish grin spread across Jack's face. "What if I did?"

Watson chuckled. "You're a son of a bitch, you know that?"

"Come on, Flash, we're not done." Jack motioned for Watson to follow him. He hustled a couple houses down the street and opened the driver-side door to a Ford Cabriolet.

Watson ran around to the passenger side and got in, holding his camera in his lap. "Whose car?" he asked.

"My father's. He left it to me when he died," Jack said, pulling the car from the curb. Jack drove down the street. "Keep an eye out for the Reverend. In case Schmitty doesn't catch him."

"Schmitty, the cop?"

"There they are," Jack said, pointing down a side street. He made a sharp turn into the street and pulled the Ford to the curb, near the policeman and the naked preacher.

Watson was out of the car before it came to a full stop. He snapped several shots of the patrolman handcuffing the preacher.

His body sweat-slick, the preacher stood first on one foot, then the other on the hot pavement.

"Schmitty, what's the charge?" Jack asked.

"Public indecency," Patrolman Schmidt said.

Watson pointed to a middle-aged woman coming down the street, holding the hand of a little girl. The girl, who couldn't have been much more than five or six years old, was pointing at the naked man and giggling.

"And exposing himself," Schmidt added.

A police cruiser turned the corner and eased down the street, stopping next to Schmidt. He opened the cruiser's rear door and motioned for the preacher to get in.

Reverend Breckinridge lowered himself into the back seat.

Schmidt moved around the cruiser to the front passenger door.

Jack stopped the cop. "Let me shake your hand, officer. Thank you for protecting our community." While shaking the patrolman's hand, Jack slipped him a neatly folded dollar bill.

"Just doing my duty," the patrolman said, accepting the money.

As the cruiser pulled away, Watson sat his camera on the hood of Jack's Ford. He pulled a pack of cigarettes from his shirt pocket and offered Jack one.

Jack declined.

Watson lit a cigarette and took a drag. "Are you going to tell me how you figured this out?"

Jack decided not to mention Maggie. "People were saying how much time the Reverend spent with the ladies of the choir, rehearsing and all. I figured, if the preacher was spending *that* much time with the ladies of the choir, he was getting more than amens."

Watson took another, more skeptical, drag from his cigarette.

"So, I started talking with the choir members, one at a time."

"Now look here," Watson said. "Those ladies didn't just up and tell you they were sacking up with the preacher."

"No, of course not," Jack said, the impish grin returning. "But some of them *were* quick to point the finger at *other* members of the ladies' choir."

"In other words, some of the choir ladies were upset that the Reverend had switched his attentions to someone new?"

Jack shrugged. "I learned from one of the choir members that the preacher was spending time with Mrs. Fulton. And that the preacher might be doing missionary work with her this afternoon."

"Jack, I don't know if that was good reporting or just plain creepy. Schmitty should have arrested us for loitering."

"Revelation, chapter sixteen, verse fifteen," Jack said, opening the door to the Ford. "Blessed is he that watcheth and keepeth his garments on; he shall see the guilty man walk naked and see his shame."

"Yeah, well, you're still a crazy son-of-a-bitch, and one of these days, you're going to get someone killed."

"And if I do, Flash, are you going to want to be there to photograph it?"

"Of course, assuming I'm not the one you get killed."

CHAPTER 6, FRIDAY, JULY 21

"REGAIN DANZIG" WITHOUT FORCE

UNEQUIVOCAL REJECTION OF WAR
BY HITLER SPOKESMAN

"Führer Means Peace"

Cincinnati Times Star,
July 21, 1939

On Friday morning, when Jack and Woody arrived at the Bridge Café, George Hanover was in his usual place, reading the morning newspaper. Emma had already served him coffee and breakfast.

As Jack and Woody took their seats at his table, Hanover held up the *Tribune.* Jack's story on the preacher had made the front page, and the *Tribune* had even run Flash's shot of the preacher running buck naked down the street. To avoid offending reader sensibilities and attracting divine retribution, the paper had blacked out the preacher's posterior.

"Nice story," Hanover congratulated Jack. "No telling how long that scoundrel had been getting away with this. You show up in town and nail him right away. I'm impressed."

"Thanks, George. That means a lot coming from you." Jack knew George had schmoozed his way to election as head of the Businessmen's Club, but thought the compliment was mostly sincere.

"Yeah, well, don't let it go to your head," George said. "I still don't want you dating my daughter."

Woody pointed at Jack and announced, "Real rhubarb."

Hanover chuckled good-naturedly and asked Jack, "What's Professor Scrambled Brains here talking about?"

"The managing editor at the *Tribune* liked my story and gave me a job. I start Monday. I'm covering the courts."

"Congratulations, but if your job depends on the lawyers who hang around the courthouse, you're still chasing brass asses to get a story."

"Brassieres," Woody agreed.

"Oh, Christ," Hanover said, looking in the direction of the door. He folded his newspaper.

Jack turned to see who entered the diner. The man was a hand-some fellow, mid-to-late thirties, in a nice-looking suit, crisp white shirt, and silk tie. He was carrying a handful of flyers.

"That's Victor Morgan," Hanover said. "He's running for City Commission."

"That gives you heartburn?"

"Yes, it does. For one thing, he's trying to make it a contest between him and Vice Mayor Harry Boyle."

"What's wrong with that?"

"He's only going after Boyle because everyone knows Boyle controls things behind the scenes. Vic's looking for publicity."

"Sounds like a smart strategy. Is that really what bothers you about him?"

"No. It's his pestering me," Hanover said. "The Good Government League is backing him, and he thinks the Businessmen's Club should come out for him too. On top of that, he wants the Businessmen's Club to contribute to his campaign."

"I don't know anything about the Good Government League, but if they're backing him —"

Hanover shook his head. "First, the Businessmen's Club can't support candidates. We are not allowed to, and besides, businesses have to deal with whoever wins."

"Hoover pins!" Woody said.

Jack wasn't sure, but he thought Woody was making fun of Hanover.

Hanover ignored Woody. "And second, Vic hasn't got a chance. The public knows and trusts men like Boyle."

Jack watched for a moment as Morgan glad-handed his way around the diner, passing out flyers. "What do you know about him?"

"He's an attorney. They say he's an up-and-comer, but his politics stink."

"You're not in favor of clean government?"

"Of course, I am, but Vic is a New Dealer. He worked for Roosevelt's reelection, and rumor has it, he even tried to get a job in D.C."

"Lot of people like Roosevelt. He's done a lot of good."

"Horse puckey!" Hanover exploded. "He's a goddam socialist. He will ruin business and bankrupt the country."

"Good morning, George," Morgan said, approaching. "Somebody must have mentioned FDR."

"Good morning, Vic," Hanover replied. "This is Jack O'Brien and his friend Woody."

"Pleased to meet you both," Morgan said, handing Jack and Woody copies of his flyer.

Hannover nodded at Jack. "This young fellow wrote the article in this morning's paper about that preacher."

"You don't say? O'Brien, right?"

"Yeah, but please call me Jack."

"Listen," Morgan said, "I was about to sit down somewhere and have breakfast. Would you mind joining me for a few minutes?

I may have a story for you."

Hanover stood and picked up his check. "I'm done and have to run. You can sit here if you like."

"George, take care," Jack said.

"Can you give this to Sal when he shows up?" Hanover asked Woody.

Woody nodded, took the envelope, and put it in his own pocket. Hanover grunted something and headed to the register.

"Is your friend a reporter?" Morgan said, still standing.

"Woody?" Jack asked. "No, he's just a friend of mine. It's okay to talk in front of him. Woody minds his own business."

Woody pointed his fork at himself. "Cornstalk."

Jack said, "I think Woody's trying to say he can't talk."

Woody nodded in agreement. "Cornstalk."

"Head injury?" Morgan asked.

"Probably," Jack said. "Came back from the war that way."

Morgan slid into the chair vacated by George Hanover and asked Woody, "Is the right side of your body weak?"

Woody nodded his head. "Night tide."

"It's called 'aphasia.'" Morgan said.

"Mr. Morgan, you sound like you've picked up some medicine."

"Lot of lawyers do. But please call me Victor or Vic."

Emma arrived with coffees and took breakfast orders. She cleared away the dishes Hanover left behind.

"I'm running against the Vice Mayor, Harry Boyle," Morgan said. "Know him?"

"I grew up here," Jack said. "Here and other places. But I've been away for a long time. I don't know him or much of anything about local politics."

"You know the Syndicate runs Newport? Gambling, prostitution, the whole ball of wax—it's all out in the open."

"Sin City?" Jack said, using the name that clung to Newport. "Yeah, everyone knows that."

"A lot of us would like to keep that filth out of Covington," Morgan said. "But not everybody is on board. The Syndicate spreads a lot of money around."

"Are you saying your opponent, Vice Mayor…"

"Boyle," Morgan said, filling in the name Jack was trying to recall. "Harry Boyle."

"Are you saying the Syndicate owns him?"

"I can't prove that, but over the last six months, there have been a lot of rumors."

Emma arrived with coffees. "Your breakfasts will be up in a minute."

"Thanks, Emma," Morgan said. "You're the best."

"That's what they all tell me. But, Vic, hon, don't be chasing away my customers, or I'll have Sam come out here –"

"Won't be necessary," Morgan said. "I promise to behave myself."

When Emma left, Jack noticed that Rizzi had taken a seat at the counter. He nudged Woody with his elbow and nodded toward the counter.

Woody stood and said, "Caboose me."

"I can't write a story based on rumors," Jack told Morgan.

"I know, I know," Morgan said. "But –" Morgan looked around, then leaned in toward Jack. "Two lawyers helping with my campaign have been snooping around City Hall, going over City Commission meeting minutes, city contracts, what-have-you. Boyle has helped route three contracts to companies with Syndicate ties over the past year. They were all small contracts. In two

48

cases, the Commission rejected the low bidder and gave the contract to the company with Syndicate ties. In the third case, it was a small, no-bid contract."

"You have the details?"

Morgan sat back in his chair. "Yeah, but not with me. You work for the *Tribune?* I can have someone bring what I have to you there."

"I start Monday." Jack was wary of the offer. "I imagine the *Trib* already has someone covering City Hall and the City Commission race."

Morgan pulled a business card from his pocket and slid it across the table. "Can you stop by my office in a couple hours? I'll have the details on the contracts ready for you. If you're already working on the story when you show up at the *Tribune*, you won't be getting out of your lane. You'll just be following up on a story you were already working on."

"Have you already given this to whoever's covering City Hall for the *Tribune?*"

Emma arrived with the men's breakfast orders. Jack and Vic chatted with Emma. Woody, who had returned from his exchange with Rizzi, dug into his food like he hadn't eaten in days.

When Emma left, Vic said, "Joe Dinklehaus covers City Hall. He and I don't click. I don't know if he's burnt out, lazy, or if someone has something on him, but I don't trust him."

Jack's instincts bristled. "Have you shopped this to reporters at the other papers?"

"No, my friends just dug this up yesterday. Someone told them what to look for."

"Then why me?" Jack asked. "I'm the newest, greenest weed in the garden."

"Because you haven't been around here long enough for the Syndicate to have gotten its claws into you. Besides, if you're the new guy, you've got the most to prove."

Jack thought Morgan seemed sincere, but still, the response was the obvious answer to his question. "Boyle must have explanations for what the Commission did on those contracts. Besides, he didn't approve those contracts alone, did he? If the Commission approved something, didn't it have to follow some protocol and act by a majority vote?"

"You're right," Morgan said. "But Boyle controls things behind the scenes."

Jack took a bite of his eggs. Morgan did the same. Woody finished his pancakes and pilfered a piece of toast from Jack.

"Look," Morgan said, "here's where I'm going with this. The City just put the contract for trash collection out for bid. That's routine. It's required to do that every so many years."

Jack took out his notebook and jotted a note.

"It's one of the largest contracts the City of Covington has," Morgan said. "Aside from the utility contracts, maybe the largest. The incumbent is a local company that does a decent job and is the low bidder. The other bidder is a Cleveland company controlled by the Syndicate. Watch what Boyle does with that contract."

"That's it?" Jack asked, searching Morgan's face.

"If you're interested, and I learn more," Morgan said, "I'll let you know. But it's a lead. You will have to do some digging."

"Have you, or any of your supporters, seen Boyle with someone from the Syndicate? Or seen him at a Syndicate joint?"

"No," Morgan conceded, shaking his head. "If anyone had mentioned that I would have –"

"What?"

"I don't know," Morgan said. "But I would have done something with that. Given it to one of the papers. Maybe all of them."

"Here's what you need to do. Spread the word among your backers, campaign workers, and friends. Tell them to let you know, or better still, to let *me* know right away if they see Boyle in any of the Syndicate joints. Or even if they see him with any Syndicate men."

"You'll follow up?"

"I'll stop by your office this afternoon and look at what you have. But remember, I'm starting a new job. I'm not sure what I can do."

Woody finished his coffee. "Best goon," he said and headed off toward the restroom.

"How'd you meet your friend?" Morgan asked.

Jack hesitated and pulled his fork across his plate, dragging the scrambled eggs he hadn't eaten into a pile. "Woody prefers I not talk about it, but he's my uncle—my mother's brother."

Morgan dug into his breakfast but signaled that he was still listening.

"My parents died a month ago."

"I'm sorry," Morgan said. "That's awful."

"It was unexpected. A plane crash. But I wonder if my mother had a premonition. The last time I saw her, she said if anything ever happened to her, she wanted me to check on Woody from time-to-time."

Morgan gave Jack an empathetic look but said nothing.

"I was working downstate at the time and thought nothing of it. I didn't dream she and Dad would be dead so soon." Jack downed some of his coffee. "Woody is now the only family I have. He wants me to treat him as a friend, not a charity case, but he lets me buy him breakfast here on Friday mornings."

"Does he have a job?"

"Odd jobs, whatever he can find," Jack said. "He lives on the river in a shanty boat. Fishes when he's not working."

Emma stopped by to drop off their checks. "Anything else?" she asked.

Woody came back to the table from the rest room just as Emma arrived.

"Carry tea!" Woody said, folding his hands as if praying. He batted his eyes at Emma.

"He wants you to marry him," Jack said.

"Not a chance!" Emma said, picking up Morgan's empty plate. "I've already got enough men to pick up after."

Woody threw Emma a kiss and left, pretending to be heart-broken.

Morgan stood. "Nice work exposing that preacher. And good luck on the new job."

Jack stood and picked up his check. "Thanks."

"I'm hoping," Morgan said, "that next time, you expose a dirty politician or two."

"I've got to catch them with their pants down first," Jack said. "But if I do, how will the Syndicate react?"

Morgan shrugged. "Welcome to the big leagues, Jack."

***

Friday evening. Vice Mayor Harry Boyle ran his hand through his hair. He had been in budget meetings all day. The meetings started early, well before he usually arrived for work, and continued all day without a break. *One meeting after another, all goddam day.* The afternoon papers were out, and he hadn't even had time to read the morning papers.

Boyle stacked the morning and evening local papers in front of him on the dining room table. He would read until Agnes had supper ready, which should only be a few minutes—he could smell liver and onions frying and cornbread fresh from the oven.

He sensed it wasn't the meetings, as irritating as they were, or the unread newspapers that were bothering him. He liked to be in charge, in control, but the pressure he was getting from Cleveland was unrelenting. They came *to him* to ask him to use his influence. They could be powerful allies and give his career the boost it needed, so he'd agreed to help them—for a fee. But as soon as he'd agreed to do them a favor, their notion of who was in charge, of who was doing whom a favor, had shifted. For the moment, he couldn't do a damn thing about that.

But he could read the newspapers, and that would have to do. He skimmed the *Kentucky Post*, the evening paper, but was too agitated to concentrate. Even though he'd already had a couple drinks before heading home, he went to the sidebar and poured himself a bourbon. The bourbon tasted sweet and rough. In a few moments, it would produce a soothing warmth. He lit a cigarette.

The *Tribune* was one of the two morning papers. Boyle picked it up and scanned the front page. The picture of a naked man running down a street caught his eye. He read the headline, then the lead. A husband had come home early and caught Reverend Jonah Breckinridge in bed with his wife—a choir member, no less. When the outraged husband went to get his gun, the Reverend had run down the street naked. The article said rumors suggested Reverend Breckinridge had affairs with several of the choir members.

Harry sniggered. "Agnes," he called to his wife, who was still in the kitchen. "Did you see this article about your preacher friend?"

"Harry, you know I can't hear you when I'm in the kitchen."

Boyle walked to the kitchen, taking the newspaper with him, and repeated his question.

"How could I? You left before I got up this morning and took the papers with you."

"That preacher friend of yours was in bed with one of the choir ladies. Her husband came home and surprised them. The newspaper has a photo of him running down the street naked."

Agnes moved servings from the skillet and surrounding pots onto plates for Harry and herself.

"You have to wonder," Harry said, shaking his head, "how their husbands could have been so stupid." He snorted. "Didn't they have any idea that something was going on? You'd think they would have noticed their wives were spending too much time with…"

An unwelcome thought occurred to Boyle. As he turned the thought over, he could feel hot anger rising from his gut to his face. He watched Agnes carry their plates to the dining room as if nothing were wrong. He followed her into the dining room and moved the newspapers.

Agnes set his plate on the table. "You were saying?" she asked.

"The paper says that preacher has been sleeping with women all over town, while their husbands were out working their asses off."

Agnes stiffened, just for a second, before recovering.

Harry saw his wife's reaction. "You were sleeping with him, weren't you!"

"No, of course not. I was just –"

"How long?" Harry demanded. "How long have you been sleeping with him?"

Agnes stood, her dinner still in her hand, her back ramrod straight, her chin up, and stared at Harry. "How long have you–"

"How long, goddam it?" Harry shouted.

"How long," Agnes repeated, "have you been going to whorehouses, sleeping with every whore in town?" Her voice was cold with anger.

Without a thought, Harry swung his arm, slapping Agnes in the face, hard, with the back of his hand. She stumbled backward, lost her balance, and fell. The plate she had been holding broke in pieces. Food scattered across the floor.

Immediately, Harry regretted what he'd done. He'd never hit Agnes before. He wasn't that kind of man. "I'm sorry," he stammered. He bent over and helped Agnes up. "I don't know what came over me."

When Agnes was on her feet again, she glared at him. Her face was still red from where his hand had made contact, and blood trickled from her nose. Her eyes burned with contempt.

Harry realized—feared—that he had just done something he could not undo. Yet, that fear and contempt on Agnes' face, which should have—and did—mortify him, also kindled something warm and satisfying. Maybe, he thought, he should have taken a firmer hand with her all along. Maybe he'd been too lax, too beholden to her status and money.

Harry watched Agnes try, without success, to staunch the blood dribbling from her nose with her handkerchief. *She was pathetic.*

"I won't tolerate," Agnes said, between sniffles, "your hitting me."

"Look, I told you I'm sorry."

"I never thought you were the kind of man who would hit a woman."

Harry grunted. "And I never thought you were the kind of woman who would sleep with some hick preacher."

Agnes looked at the little handkerchief in her hand, now drenched in blood. She wiped a tear from her eye with her sleeve and glared at Harry. "Why are you going to whorehouses? Why, Harry? To impress those mobsters? To humiliate me?"

Harry's first instinct was to deny the accusation. *But what was the point? She knew.* Truth was, he hadn't made much effort to conceal his trips to Greta's Place. Besides, Agnes hadn't answered his question about the preacher.

"I haven't been going to whorehouses," he said, stressing the plural. *That was true after all. He'd only been to Greta's.* "And I haven't slept with *every* whore in town. I don't know where you get off saying I have. You're just trying to change the subject."

Agnes began crying.

"Go take care of yourself," Harry said. "Get yourself cleaned up, whatever you need to do."

Agnes walked to the bathroom. Her eyes watery, she held her arm up in front of herself to make sure she didn't walk into a door or wall.

Harry finished his bourbon and to settle himself, poured another. He knew he should make some gesture—at least clean up the mess on the floor—but he couldn't bring himself to do it. Instead, he picked up his cigarette and took a long drag.

When Agnes returned to the dining room, her eyes were red and swollen from crying. She glared at the bourbon glass and shook her head in disgust but said nothing.

Harry could tell she was forcing herself not to say what she was thinking. He exhaled a long stream of smoke.

Agnes turned and went to the kitchen.

Harry took a sip of the bourbon. He pushed his hand through his hair and cursed.

Agnes returned with a cup of coffee and sat it on the table in front of him. "Drink some coffee. And eat something. You need something on your stomach besides Jim Beam."

Harry detested it when Agnes told him what to do. He pointed to the broken plate, food, and blood on the floor. "You need to clean up that mess."

When he moved his arm to point, Agnes flinched, but refused to back down. "Harry, I had such great hopes for you—for us." She pulled back a chair, sat, and gestured for him to sit. "I thought someday you would be the Governor, or maybe a Congressman. But with your drinking and those hoodlums –"

Harry shook his head. "That's naïve, and we've been through this before. Nobody wins an election around here unless they find an accommodation with the Syndicate. You have to go along to get along. Besides, being City Commissioner doesn't pay worth a damn."

Agnes dug her glasses out of a pocket and put them on. "You are throwing away your—*our*—future."

"If I turned on those men, I wouldn't have *any* future. They'd kill me."

"And the whorehouses? Are they making you do that too? Or is that just to humiliate me?"

"This isn't getting us anywhere." Harry rubbed the business end of his cigarette into the ashtray, extinguishing it. "We both need to calm down. I'm going out. Take my plate. I'll get myself something."

Agnes stood. "Harry, you cannot compromise with those people. You cannot 'go along' with them 'to get along.' They will destroy you. I'm not going to watch that happen. If you don't stop with the mobsters and the whores, our marriage is over. I won't put up with it."

Harry stood and moved to within inches of Agnes. His eyes narrowed. "Where do you get off telling me what I can and cannot do?"

"It's just a matter of time, Harry, until some reporter catches you, just like they caught Reverend Breckinridge. Or, they arrest you. You'll end up disgraced, maybe worse, and I won't have people thinking I was part of that."

Harry turned that over in his mind, trying to decide if Agnes was making a prediction or a threat. And then it all came together. He was surprised he hadn't figured it out sooner. *The bourbon must be clouding my thinking.*

"You found out you weren't the only woman your preacher friend was bringing his Gospel to, got mad, and told that reporter about him. That's how that reporter found out, isn't it?"

"That's ridiculous, Harry. Your brain's gone soggy."

Harry found his cigarette pack and tapped one into his hand.

He lit the cigarette, breathed in the smoke, and held it a moment, before exhaling. "Have you told that reporter anything about me?"

Agnes shook her head. "No, and you're the one trying to change the subject."

Harry picked up the newspaper and found the byline on the article about the preacher. "Jack O'Brien. Have you said anything to him?"

"No, but ..."

"If you ever —"

"If *you* ever," Agnes interrupted him, "hit me again, I'll find that reporter and tell him how you're always hanging out with gangsters and how you spend every Friday night whoring."

Harry looked at her with studied contempt. He drank some coffee, looked at Agnes, and stuck out his tongue. "This coffee tastes like warm piss."

"I wouldn't know," Agnes retorted, then seemed to think better of that. "It's a new brand. Something they recommended at the grocery."

Harry took another swig of the coffee, set the cup down, and straightened his tie.

Agnes tensed but said nothing.

"Look, I'm sorry I hit you. I should never have done that. It won't happen again, I swear. But you can't talk to that reporter, to *any* reporter, about the men I'm dealing with. You'll be a dead woman, or I —"

Agnes interrupted. "You're a killer now?"

"No, of course not, but you don't know about the men I'm dealing with. And, I guarantee you, you don't want to find out."

"You're no better than they are."

Harry sneered. "And you're no better than the rest of the stupid, gullible women that son-of-bitch preacher has been schlepping it to."

The sight of his wife made him sick to his stomach. "If you haven't got that mess cleaned up when I get home, I'll —"

"Go to hell," Agnes said.

Harry moved as if to hit her. When Agnes flinched, he laughed. He removed his suit jacket from the back of the chair and put it on, maintaining eye contact with Agnes as he did.

He took a last gulp from the coffee. "Like I said, we'll sort this out when I get back."

***

Before the Syndicate moved in, Greta's Place catered mainly to locals. The building at Sixth and Philadelphia in Covington was a graceful three-story mansion, but during Prohibition, poor upkeep and fading décor gave it the air of an aristocratic lady down on her fortunes. As Prohibition came to an end, Roscoe "Fats" Mascelli, a local Syndicate "soldier" with backing from the organization, persuaded Greta to sell but kept her on to manage the girls.

Mascelli renovated the building from top to bottom and gave the first-floor lounge lots of brass trim. Most nights, a piano player entertained the drinking customers on the first floor, and on weekends, a small jazz band played, often with a singer.

As Boyle entered Greta's, he was feeling sick to his stomach. He took a seat at a corner table. Attributing his upset stomach to his concerns about how he would pull off what the Mob wanted him to do and his fight with Agnes, he ordered a double whiskey— a stiffer start on the evening than his norm.

The drink did nothing to settle his stomach, and neither did the one after that. Thirty minutes after he'd arrived, he asked for Greta and told her he was going to be sick. "Food poisoning," he explained, but he slurred his speech and spoke in a voice that was too loud. His gestures were clumsy.

Greta arranged for two Syndicate men to help Harry up the stairs to a small, third-floor bedroom. Two Penny Smith, who worked at Greta's as its janitor, arrived with a bucket, but not in time. Harry had vomited the contents of his stomach on the floor.

"Don't worry 'bout that at all," Two Penny said. "I'll take care of it." He returned minutes later with a mop and a bucket of soapy water.

Harry spent the next several hours alternately vomiting and dragging himself to the toilet. Greta returned to the little bedroom from time-to-time to check on Harry, spray perfume, and supervise Two Penny's efforts to keep the area clean. Eventually, she gave Harry something that knocked him out.

Greta employed only attractive young white women, but at Fats Mascelli's insistence, she found two buxom black prostitutes and had them strip and crawl into bed with Harry. One of the Syndicate men snapped several photos of Harry with the naked women. Harry had woken briefly, and in speech so slurred as to be unintelligible, had tried to ask what was going on, but fell back asleep.

A couple hours later, Gus Panzer and another man shook Harry awake and helped him down the stairs and into a waiting car.

At his own home, Harry unlocked the front door, but the men had to help him upstairs. He collapsed into bed and fell into a deep sleep.

CHAPTER 7, SATURDAY, JULY 22

**ANGRY THRONG WRECKS NEGRO HOME
FORMER OWNER, PURCHASERS
FLEE FROM 2 HOUSES**

Total of 3000 Mill About Place
500 Said To Have Taken Part
In Brick Hurling Episode

The Kentucky Post

Vice Mayor Harry Boyle did not get out of bed until afternoon but still felt the effects of the night before. He took what comfort he could that it was Saturday and he had not missed work. He shaved and bathed, all the while debating with himself whether to return to bed. He decided he did not want to give his wife the pleasure of seeing him spend even more time trying to recover.

As for Agnes, he was of two minds. He was sure she put something in his coffee that made him sick. He would be within his rights, he felt, if he went to her bedroom, or wherever she was, and beat her to within an inch of her life. But Agnes just might be stubborn enough to file charges. If she did, the newspapers would have a field day, and his political opponents would use that against him.

Or, he could sue for divorce, citing her own infidelity—not that she'd admitted to anything. If he did, she might well counter-sue for divorce, claiming he frequented brothels. And that would be another field day for the newspapers.

But if he filed first, his attorneys would ask the court to seal the file, and the court would likely grant that request. Courts, after all, almost always sealed the divorce files of public figures. There would be rumors but that couldn't be helped. Besides, he wasn't sure how many people gave a tinker's dam whether a politician visited a brothel now and again.

The problem was, if he divorced Agnes, she would walk away with her money. It wasn't a Rockefeller fortune, and if things continued the way he believed they would, he might one day be worth more than she was. But the timing was terrible. For the next couple years, if she left, he wouldn't be able to make ends meet. Worse, a divorce would end his chances of running for Governor or Congress.

His head ached, and his stomach was queasy. He cautioned himself that he might not be thinking clearly. He firmly believed there was always a third option. He just had to be patient enough to consider all the possibilities. It was like he had always told himself. It was his willingness to look for and find that third option that separated himself from the rest of the City Hall crowd.

But here, the third option wasn't hard to find. He could apologize, concede Agnes was right, promise never to hit her again and to give up his trips to Greta's. He could then wait until the right moment and get rid of her. His new connections could take care of that for him. For a price. And if he did that, he would inherit her fortune and keep all his options open.

He didn't like it, but that might be his best bet.

Already in his slacks and a casual shirt, he headed downstairs. His wife's bedroom door was closed but he was fine with that. If Agnes wanted to give him the silent treatment, so much the better. His head was already pounding.

Agnes had not made coffee and had not set anything out for breakfast. He didn't care. It was the middle of the afternoon anyway, and he could make coffee for himself. He wasn't sure he wanted to eat.

He set about brewing coffee, and while it percolated, he went to get the newspaper from the front yard. When he opened the front door that damn fool colored man had already picked up the papers and was heading his way.

"Good afternoon, Mr. Two Penny," Boyle called out—and immediately regretted doing so. The sound reverberated painfully inside his skull.

Two Penny handed Boyle the newspapers. "Good afternoon to you, Mister Mayor. Glad to see you're yourself again and everything."

Boyle wondered for a second how this colored man knew he had been sick. "You here to see Agnes?" he asked.

"Not today, Mr. Mayor. I was just checking to make sure you were okay and everything."

Boyle could feel the sun on his face. The fog in his brain begin to clear. Two Penny worked at Greta's. He had cleaned up after him and had helped get him into the car that brought him home.

"Thank you," Boyle said. "Worst case of food poisoning I've ever had, but I seem to have survived."

"I'm glad you did."

It occurred to Boyle that maybe Two Penny was looking for a tip. Boyle didn't know whether to take affront or consider himself fortunate that was all last night would cost him. Deciding he didn't have the energy to be angry, he reached for his wallet, extracted some cash, and offered it to Two Penny.

"That's very generous of you, Mr. Mayor, but I can't take that. You and Mrs. Boyle been too kind to me. I'm just happy you're okay and everything."

"Take it anyway and forget who gave it to you and why."

"You can trust me, I guarantee you that," Two Penny said. "A man's business is his business, and if it's *his* business, it ain't *my* business."

"Mr. Two Penny, that's a good philosophy. See that you abide by it."

"Yes, sir."

Why was this infernal man still standing there? "Now, if you'll excuse me —"

"Mr. Mayor?"

"What?" Boyle snapped.

"Will there be anything special you'll be wanting me to do while the Missus is away and everything?"

While the Missus was away?

What was he prattling about?

Oh, Christ!

***

Boyle made his apologies and closed the door. He charged up the stairs and without bothering to knock, opened the door to Agnes' bedroom. She had made her bed, and everything seemed in its usual place. But the room looked somehow empty.

Boyle went to the closet and opened it. It was empty. He pulled open several drawers, and they were empty.

Damn it!

He sat on the end of the bed and let the pounding in his head and the uneasiness in his stomach subside.

Steeling himself, he rose and made his way back to the kitchen. Realizing he still had the damn newspapers in his hand, he tossed them on the table, filled a glass with tap water and downed it. He took a couple aspirin and downed them with another glass of water. Then, he poured himself a cup of coffee and put toast in the toaster.

He took the coffee and newspaper to the dining room table and sat down. He sipped the coffee and opened the paper. The front-page headline and lead story recounted the latest developments in the growing crisis in Europe.

Boyle had trouble concentrating on that. He carried his coffee back to the kitchen counter, got the toast, and spread it with apricot jam. He took a couple bites, still standing, and waited to see if it stayed down.

Two Penny. What the hell was he doing here today? Had the folks at Greta's sent him to make sure he was okay?

Boyle took another bite of the toast and washed it down with coffee.

How the hell had that idiot known Agnes had left?

Boyle carried his coffee and toast to the dining room table and sat down. He stared at his coffee as if the answers were hiding in it.

The last time he'd seen that preacher leave the house, Boyle thought, Two Penny had been there. *How many other times had Two Penny seen that preacher come and go?*

Why didn't that black son of a bitch tell me that preacher was spending too much time with my wife?

Boyle remembered what Two Penny had just said. "A man's business is his business, and if it's his business, it ain't my business."

Was Two Penny trying to explain why he hadn't said anything about the preacher? Is that what his visit was all about?

Boyle finished the toast. He stood, walked to the kitchen sink, and dumped out what remained of his coffee.

Or was Two Penny just trying to tell me he would not tell anyone about last night?

Before that instant, it hadn't occurred to him that it might pop into Two Penny's head to talk about what he saw at Greta's. Two Penny hadn't kept his job there by speaking out of turn.

Still, Boyle kept returning to the same question: *How the hell did Agnes know he'd been going to Greta's?*

A disturbing thought occurred to him. *How many times has Two Penny seen me there?*

"Son of a bitch!" he said aloud. *That stupid son-of-a-bitch! Two Penny told Agnes. That's how she knew, and that's why she screwed that hick preacher.*

   Well, I'll make him pay.

   And then, I'll make her pay.

***

Boyle learned about the riot in Covington's Austinburg neighborhood from Deputy Police Chief Rasche. Rasche called Boyle at home to brief him.

After speaking with Rasche, Boyle called Roscoe "Fats" Mascelli at Greta's. "We need to talk," Boyle said. "I'll come to your place if you will be there."

"This about last night?" Fats asked.

"No. Something new. It's important."

"I'll be here."

Fats was five feet six inches tall, weighed at least three-hundred-fifty pounds, and had a neck that would inspire envy in a walrus. Fats' body, Boyle figured, had tried to compensate for its girth by keeping Fats' brain small and by not weighing him down with a conscience. What was worse, Fats was notoriously impatient and always carried heat.

Boyle would have preferred to deal with Fats on the phone, but that wasn't an option. Concerned that the Feds might be tapping his phone line, Fats refused to talk business on the phone.

"Give me thirty minutes," Boyle said.

"I ain't going nowhere."

Boyle thought of Fats as an incomprehensible jumble of contradictions. The man was a Southern Baptist who hated dancing and refused to sleep with whores but considered running a brothel to be "business" and therefore not a Biblical concern. He also refused to gamble or drink alcohol, yet he insisted that if others wanted to go to Hell, that wasn't his concern. He ran a business, not a church.

Instead of booze, Fats drank Coca-Cola—often, a twenty-four-bottle case of six-ounce bottles a day. Some of Fats' associates blamed the soft drinks for his impatience. But bottom line, Boyle didn't care why Fats was the way he was; he just didn't want to get on the wrong side of the overstuffed Guinea.

Fats was the local contact for the Mayfield Road Gang—the Mafia gang that ran things for the Syndicate in Cleveland. Alfred "Owl" Polizzi headed the gang. Polizzi also controlled a trash collection company, the Mayfield Disposal Company. He wanted the Covington trash collection contract for his company and had promised Boyle a good deal of money—more than his yearly salary as Vice Mayor—if Boyle steered the contract to Mayfield Disposal.

Boyle took a taxi to Greta's—his car was still there. When he arrived, he spoke to the two men at the bar. They were expecting him, and one of them escorted Boyle through two locked doors to Fats' office.

"I heard you got ahold of some bad pretzels last night," Fats said. Bad pretzels were a running joke in Covington. People blamed their hangovers not on the excessive amount of alcohol they drank the night before, but on having eaten "bad pretzels."

"Something like that." Boyle thought the joke was stale.

His patience for small talk exhausted, Fats asked, "What is it you need to talk about?"

"You heard about the ruckus in Austinburg?"

"What about it?"

"Some asshole sold a house to a Negro family. The house is a piece of crap, but it's on Byrd Street, down by St. Benedict's, and that's a white neighborhood."

Fats leaned back in his chair. "That ain't my concern."

"I know, I know, but hear me out," Boyle said, bottling up his hatred for the smug bastard. "When this colored family moved in, word spread, and next thing you know, there's a couple thousand pissed-off white people milling around outside the house. Several hundred of them found bricks and threw them."

"Like I said, not my concern."

"Of course, it's not. But here's what I was thinking," Boyle said. "What if we were to spread flyers around town saying that Silas Hamlin, the guy who owns Covington Waste Company, put up the cash for this colored family to buy that house? What if we were to spread the word that Hamlin says, if coloreds are good enough to pick up the trash on a street, they're good enough to live on the street? Blah, blah, blah."

Fats pulled a bottle of Coke from the wooden soft drink case on the credenza behind him. He used a bottle opener to pry the lid off and drank half of the soft drink. "This Hamlin guy. He said that?"

Boyle felt nothing but disgust at how dense Fats was. "Not that I know of, but once those flyers hit the streets, nobody will care. The phones at City Hall will ring off the hook. And then my colleagues on the City Commission will be a lot more sympathetic to giving the trash contract to your friend."

"You going to take care of these flyers?"

"No, Fats, I can't do that. If someone connects the flyers back to me, this whole thing goes south. I have to be reacting to this, not organizing it."

Fats let out a loud, deep belch. "Okay, how about this? How about I talk to the Owl? I'll see if he can get the flyers made up. My guys can spread them around. We'll get everybody worked up and tell them to call you muckety-mucks down at City Hall and complain about this Hamlin guy and his company."

"Like I always say, you're a smart guy," Boyle said. "Some people wouldn't know how to take advantage of something like this, but you're smart. You get it, and you know how to get things done."

Fats finished his Coke and dropped the bottle into a box under his desk. "We done?"

"One more thing," Boyle said. "And this is kinda delicate."

"You think I ain't delicate?" Fats said grinning.

"Yeah, Fats, you're the sugar plum fairy."

Fats laughed. "I like that," he said. "I'm gonna tell my kids what you said."

Boyle tried to control his own impatience.

"But listen, Harry, don't *ever* call me a fairy again. I'll slit your throat."

Boyle nodded. He could feel his body tense but forced himself to stay focused. "You've got this janitor here."

"Two Penny?" Fats said.

"Yeah, that's him. Before I knew he worked here, I hired him to take care of my yard and whatever errands my wife wanted him to do."

"So, what?" Fats looked at the clock on the wall of his office.

"Two Penny talks too much. He sees me here, and next thing I know, my wife is complaining that I'm going to whorehouses."

"We ain't never had a problem with Two Penny."

"If I'm right, that's only part of it."

Fats studied Boyle.

"Two Penny's son works for Covington Waste. If Two Penny is willing to tell my wife about me giving your girls some business, then he'll sure-as-hell share that with his son. Next thing you know, Covington Waste and its lawyers will be saying that's why I'm backing your Cleveland friends on the trash contract."

"Like I said," Fats repeated, "we ain't never had a problem with Two Penny. I'm not going to have him whacked just because you can't control your wife."

"I don't want anything to happen to him," Boyle said. "I was just thinking, maybe you could talk to somebody and have him arrested for something and locked up until we get this trash contract squared away and I get past the election."

Boyle watched Fats' face for a reaction.

Fats grimaced but didn't respond.

Boyle couldn't tell if the thug was mulling over his suggestion or just suffering from indigestion.

"I'll talk to some people," Fats said. "I'll see what we can do. But listen, Harry, we're counting on you to get this contract for the Owl. You're asking us to do all the work. That's not what we're paying you for."

Boyle felt hot and flushed. He could almost feel the sweat forming on his forehead. "I'll get it done," he promised. "But we've got to be smart about it."

"Then, maybe your wife's right," Fats said, "about you spending too much time here. Maybe we shouldn't see you here until the Owl gets the contract. Like you say, we don't need rumors that your spending time here had something to do with that."

Boyle stood to leave. He didn't like getting a lecture from Fats, but the Guinea meatball was right. The last thing he needed was for some reporter to do a story about him frequenting a brothel. The editorialists, the Good Government League, and his political opponents would be all over that.

Fats stood and came around the desk.

Boyle expected a pat on the shoulder or a handshake. Instead, Fats pulled his gun out, opened it, and spun its cylinder. "Make sure that wife of yours don't go running off at the mouth," he said. "She might not like it so much if her husband was a widower."

CHAPTER 8, MONDAY, JULY 24

**Hungary May Offer
To Exchange Jews
For Aryan Magyars**
*The Cincinnati Enquirer,
July 24, 1939*

With his first day at the paper behind him, Jack stepped out of the *Tribune* building, planning to head to the boarding house where he was staying. To his surprise, Woody was waiting for him.

"Legit fears," Woody said.

Jack had no idea what Woody was trying to say.

Woody pantomimed pouring a beer and wiping the foam off the top of a beer mug.

"Let's get beers?" Jack guessed. "You want to get a beer?"

Woody nodded.

"Okay," Jack said. "Let's go to Scrivener's."

Jack led the way to the bar and grill across Madison Avenue from the newspaper. After they found a booth and placed their drink orders, Woody pulled a flyer from his back pocket, smoothed it out, and pushed it across to Jack.

Addressed to "Dear Neighbor" and signed by the "Austinburg Neighborhood Association," the flyer asserted that Silas Hamlin, the owner of Covington Waste Company, was behind the colored couple's attempt to buy into the Austinburg neighborhood. Hamlin or his company, the flyer alleged, advanced the money for the couple to make the down payment on the house.

"Even though the Mayor sorted that situation out," the flyer continued, "Covington Waste employs over thirty Negroes. Hamlin and his company want to break up white neighborhoods and destroy their property values, so his Negro employees can buy homes cheap."

"Tell Silas Hamlin," the flyer said, "that just because you let his colored employees pick up your trash, doesn't mean you want them living on your street, near your wife and children."

In bold letters, the flyer warned, "Your Neighborhood Could Be Next!" It urged concerned citizens to contact their City Commissioners and to tell them to end the City's contract with Covington Waste. Just to be helpful, it listed the Commissioners' names and City Hall phone numbers.

"Where did you get this?" Jack asked when the waiter left.

"Bum pie."

Jack thought a moment. "Some guy?"

Woody nodded "yes."

Jack scratched his head. "Why did he give you this?"

"Jerk."

"Because he's a jerk?"

Woody shook his head "no" and banged his fist on the table in frustration.

Jack worried about Woody. Naturally gregarious, Woody delighted in being around people, but when he was, his speech problem left him frustrated and depressed. As a result, Woody spent too much time doing odd jobs by himself or alone on his boat.

Jack pulled his notebook from his back pocket, turned to a blank page, and slid it, along with his pen, across the table to Woody.

"Pranks!" Woody said. Picking up Jack's pen with his unsteady right hand, he printed: "Work! Want men to distribute. Greta's Place 7:30."

"Tonight?" Jack asked.

Woody nodded.

"Okay if I change and go?" Jack asked. "You can act like you don't know me."

Woody wrote, "Y I told U."

Jack called the waiter over and ordered sandwiches.

***

At 7:30 p.m., a line of unemployed men, maybe twenty-five in all, stretched down the street from Greta's Place.

The men in charge wore the Syndicate look—dark suits, dark shirts, and bright ties, but in the heat, they had removed their jackets and ties and had rolled up their sleeves. At the head of the line, Gus Panzer—the big, imposing guy Jack first saw in Bridge Café— chatted briefly with each man in turn.

Panzer gave each a crude little map and a big stack of flyers and directed him to a waiting car. The cars would drop the men off in the areas marked on their maps. They were to distribute the flyers to every home and business in their assigned area. When they finished, the cars would bring them back to Greta's, where they would collect their pay.

Jack looked around and didn't see Sal Rizzi. That was consistent with what old hands at the newspaper had told him. Fats Mascelli ran Greta's. He and his men also ran racketeering operations throughout Eastern and Central Kentucky, all the way down into Tennessee. But their business was separate from the Syndicate's gambling operations in Covington and Newport.

As he studied the mobsters, Jack also saw no one who looked like his nickname would be "Fats." He joined the ragtag line. "You know those guys?" he asked the man ahead of him in the line, pointing at the men running the show.

"Nobody's paying me to know who they are," the man explained. "Got a cigarette?"

"Fresh out," Jack said. Truth was, aside from Ben Strasberg, he was the only man he knew who didn't smoke, but he found that saying he was "out" created less ill will.

"Not good for much, are you?" the man said.

"Reckon not," Jack said. "How about yourself?"

"Me? I ain't worth the rotgut I'll put in my stomach after they pay us." The man spat on the pavement. "*If* they pay us."

Jack shrugged his shoulders. "It doesn't look like a scam."

"Everything's a scam."

It was a sentiment he'd heard often from men down on their luck—and nine years into the Depression, too many men were still down on their luck.

Jack shuffled forward. When he reached the front of the line, he gave a phony name, collected his little map, and accepted a stack of flyers.

"If we catch you dumping the flyers," Panzer warned, "we won't pay you." Panzer pointed over his shoulder to one of the Cleveland mobsters. "And you'll have to answer to Frankie."

Jack glanced up at Frankie. Tattoos littered the man's skin, and several of his teeth had gone missing. His left eye stared off in a different direction than his right. At the mention of his name, Frankie smirked and tapped the tire iron he held in his right hand into the palm of his left. It wasn't clear to Jack that Frankie had questions in need of answers.

Jack hurried to the curb and crowded into a Packard with three other men. The car stopped about eight blocks from his boarding house.

"What time are you picking us up?" Jack asked the driver.

"Ten," the driver said. "Give or take."

"What's your name, so I know who's picking me up?"

"Just deliver the flyers," the driver said.

Jack got out and scribbled the license number of the car on one the flyers. When the Packard disappeared around the corner, Jack headed to his boarding house with the flyers under his arm. He put all but one in the trunk of his car, then drove back to Greta's.

He parked where he could monitor the Syndicate cars coming and going. He counted six cars transporting the men around town. He was able to get the license plate numbers for all but one. Two of the plates were local. The others were from Cuyahoga County, Ohio, where Cleveland and Mayfield Disposal were.

CHAPTER 9, TUESDAY, JULY 25

**GRAND JURY WITNESS
TELLS OF NEW ASSAULT**

FORMER LOOKOUT HOUSE
EMPLOYEE SAYS HE
WAS ASSAULTED AGAIN

---

*Kentucky Times-Star,
July 22, 1939*

In the morning, Jack made his rounds of the courthouses, checking for new filings of interest and scuttlebutt that might lead to a story. After a quick stop in the newsroom for messages, he drove to the offices of Covington Waste Company.

Jack gave the receptionist his business card and asked to see the owner, Silas Hamlin.

"May I ask what this is about?" she asked.

Jack handed her one of the flyers. "Give this to Mr. Hamlin. Tell him I need his reaction for a story I'm working on about it."

Minutes later, Silas Hamlin came into the lobby and introduced himself. He was a tall, energetic man, with a deeply receding hairline and a modestly protruding waistline. His patrician jaw and thick eyebrows made for a strong face, but his dominant feature was his gaze. Beneath drooping lids that hinted at sadness, his eyes looked directly at Jack. The impression was of a man who was intelligent and forthright.

"Please come to my office," Hamlin said, "so we can talk."

Jack followed Hamlin down a hallway and into an office that

was small and unimpressive. The desk and other furniture pieces were economical and spare. Linoleum covered the floor.

Jack explained what he knew about the flyers. As he did, Hamlin's face colored, but his eyes remained focused on Jack.

"I'll start with the obvious question," Jack said. "Did you help that couple buy that house in Austinburg?"

"I had nothing to do with that." Hamlin stood. "This is just a smear campaign by that mobster and his company."

"By Mayfield Disposal?"

"Who else," Hamlin said, "would be interested in smearing me and my company?"

"The gist of what this flyer alleges," Jack said, "is that you are behind a campaign to help your Negro employees buy homes on the cheap. It implies you're doing that, so you don't have to pay them a fair wage."

Hamlin shook his head and sighed. "I pay all my employees—colored and white—the same, based on how long they've been with the company. And I'm not behind any block busting. This," – Hamlin held up the flyer– "is a pack of lies."

Jack recorded Hamlin's denial in his notebook. When he looked up, Hamlin was pacing back and forth, the flyer still in his hand.

"Let me tell you something," Hamlin said. "This is nothing but an effort by those gangsters to railroad the City Commission into giving the trash collection contract to that company from Cleveland."

Jack waited to see if Hamlin would add to that.

Hamlin picked up Jack's business card from where he'd laid it on his desk and found Jack's name. "Mr. O'Brien, if this succeeds and the City awards this contract to that gangster, it will destroy my company. It will put a lot of decent people out of work."

Jack moved in his chair. "Is Covington your company's only

customer?"

Hamlin returned to the chair behind his desk and plopped down in it. "No, we have contracts with several surrounding communities, but they're all smaller and spread out. Without the Covington contract, we won't have enough business to cover our fixed costs."

Jack watched Hamlin. The older man was working hard to contain his frustration.

"I know I should have pushed harder to expand my business," Hamlin said. "My son has been telling me that for the last two, three years. But I won't pay bribes, and that limits how much we can grow. Take Newport. I'll never get its business. Same way with a lot more places I could name."

Hamlin shook his head. "We do an excellent job, and to be frank, we don't charge as much as we should. That's why we haven't had any real competition in years. I guess I got complacent." Hamlin stared at Jack for a moment. "How do you take your coffee?" he asked.

"Black."

Hamlin pushed a button and spoke into an intercom system. "Miss Benning, can you bring us two coffees, black?"

"Yes, sir," a woman's voice said.

Turning his attention back to Jack, Hamlin said, "I'm about to see my business destroyed by the Syndicate. Look at me. I'm fifty. I'll be fifty-one by the time this plays out. What am I supposed to do then?"

Miss Benning entered with two cups of coffee.

Hamlin thanked her, and she left, closing the door behind her.

Jack felt for the guy but focused on the remaining details he needed. He questioned Hamlin about how many employees the company had.

Hamlin rattled off the number, then gave Jack an appraising

look. "You're right. I'm feeling sorry for myself, but some of those people have been with me from the beginning. This will be a damn sight harder on them than me."

Jack asked how many of his employees were white and how many colored.

Hamlin picked up his phone and had someone check the numbers.

While Hamlin did that, Jack checked his own notes and stole a glance at his watch.

Hamlin jotted down a couple numbers and hung up the phone. He gave Jack the breakdown.

Jack jotted down the numbers and then stood. "Mr. Hamlin," he said. "I appreciate all the time you've taken with me, but I've got to run. Deadlines and all that. Besides, I imagine you'll be glad to have me out of your hair."

Hamlin stood. "Listen, I'm glad you jumped on this. I appreciate your taking the time to get my side of the story. I hope it makes a difference, but…"

Jack put his notebook in this pocket. "You don't sound like you have much confidence in the City Commission."

"You know about the lunch plates, don't you?" Hamlin asked.

"No, I don't think so." Jack wasn't sure he'd understood the question.

"The Mayor and the Commissioners have lunch together at the City Hall Café before their Wednesday meetings. If there's a contract to award, the bidders put their bribes under the Mayor's and Commissioners' plates before they arrive. If three of the Commissioners take your money, you're assured of winning the contract."

Jack hadn't heard that. He wasn't sure he believed it.

"That's for your run-of-the-mill contracts," Hamlin said. "This contract was too big for that, or this Cleveland company would already have it sewn up."

"You know that for a fact?" Jack asked. "About contractors putting money under their plates?

"I've never put any money under anybody's plate," Hamlin said. "So, no, I can't say that from firsthand knowledge. But ask anybody. They'll tell you that's how it works."

***

After his interview with Silas Hamlin, Jack made another round of the courthouses before returning to the *Tribune*'s press room.

Jack dug through his desk drawer and found Vic Morgan's business card and called him for a comment. Morgan was happy to oblige. Jack also called Mayfield Disposal and Greta's Place. They were not happy and did not feel obliged to comment.

"With Decision Due on Trash Collection Contract, Mobsters Spread Flyers Accusing Local Bidder," Jack typed. His stab at a headline needed only to inform the editors and headline writers of the subject of his story. If his story made it into the next morning's paper, they would craft the actual headline—considering whether the story made the front page or appeared inside, space requirements, and other factors.

Jack typed the lead.

> With the Covington City Commission due to decide on the city's trash collection contract on Wednesday, beefy men operating out of Greta's Place paid unemployed men to distribute flyers throughout the city Monday evening.
>
> The flyers make racially charged allegations against the low bidder, Covington Waste Company, in an apparent effort to sway City Commissioners to award the contract to the Cleveland-based Mayfield Disposal, Inc.
>
> Silas Hamlin, owner of Covington

> Waste Company, denies the charges,
> which he attributes to Syndicate ef-
> forts to influence the City Commission.
> He fears loss of the contract with the
> City of Covington will destroy his com-
> pany, putting its 53 employees out of
> work.

In subsequent paragraphs, Jack detailed what the flyers alleged and Silas Hamlin's denials. He also described the men in charge, gave background information on Greta's Place, and mentioned that the license plate numbers linked several of the cars to Cleveland.

Jack loved the comment he got from Vic Morgan:

> Local attorney Victor Morgan, who is
> campaigning against Vice Mayor Harry
> Boyle, branded the flyers "the sort of
> smear campaign you would expect from
> this Cleveland company."

> Morgan also asserted that the Cov-
> ington City Commission had a history of
> rejecting low bids in favor of companies
> rumored to have Syndicate connections.
> "You'll be able to tell which City Com-
> missioners the Mob owns," Morgan said,
> "by how they vote on this contract."

Jack ended his story with details about how many employees of each race the Covington company had and how long it had held the contract.

He proofread his draft and dropped it off at the U-shaped desk where copy editors pored over the articles the reporters submitted. Sometimes they would pose questions about the support for claims made in the reporter's submission or insist on re-writes. More often, they made minor changes and forwarded the article to typesetting—or, if the article was sensitive or likely to interest him, to the paper's longtime managing editor, Joshua Rumble.

CHAPTER 10, WEDNESDAY, JULY 26

PEACE COMES TO AUSTINBURG HOUSE ROW

Furniture Moved and Family Will Seek Another House
Police Stood Guard While Furniture Moved

Move Followed Conference With Mayor Knollman
Kentucky Times Star, August, 1939

Jack shouted an obscenity. He was late for work, and someone had shattered the windows and slashed the tires of his car. He looked around, but whoever vandalized his car was long gone. Jack went back to his room and called the newspaper.

An operator transferred his call to the assignment desk.

"This is Jack O'Brien," he told the Assignment Editor. "I'm going to be late."

"Just the tires?" the editor asked. "Or did they do the windows too?"

Jack hadn't mentioned why he would be late. "Both."

"Only the front windshield, or all the windows?"

"All of 'em," Jack said. "Do you bums have a pool going?"

"Yeah. I think Max won."

"Max?" Jack asked. "Max Seeger? The guy who covers state politics?"

"Yeah. He called a story in. We told him about the pool, and he wanted in."

"You could have told me what to expect," Jack complained.

"What fun would that be?"

"I'm not having fun." Jack took a deep breath and tried to focus. "Who should I call to fix what they did to my car?"

"The paper's got a contract with Covington Auto Glass," the editor said. "I'll get you the number. But, Jack, just so you know. The Mob guys aren't like the cops. They won't mess up your car a second time. If you provoke them again, they're liable to get a lot more personal."

***

When Jack made it to his desk in the newsroom, a veteran reporter approached and asked, "You're O'Brien, the new guy?"

"That's right, and you're?"

"Joe Dinklehaus." The older man put his thumbs under his suspenders. "I cover City Hall, which means I cover the trash collection contract."

"Yes?"

"I'm going to pretend you didn't know that," Dinklehaus said, "when you wrote your story about those flyers."

"I didn't. Besides, I didn't get the tip until after I left work Monday."

"Yeah, well, like I said, I'll let it go this time."

Jack gave the older man a long glance. "Thanks, but just so you know, I was working an angle about the trash collection contract before I started here."

"What angle?"

Lowering his voice, Jack said, "Mob influence over one of our Commissioners."

"That's applesauce."

"You've investigated that?"

"I don't have to," Dinklehaus said, shaking his head. "I've

been around long enough to know better." Before turning to walk away, Dinklehaus took a parting shot. "And long enough to know if you want to fit in, you need to stay in your lane."

***

After lunch, Jack found the courtroom of Kenton County Circuit Court Judge Ernst Chelone. He arrived just as proceedings were getting underway and positioned himself in the third row of the spectator seats, on the right-hand side, behind the prosecutor's table.

The Assistant Commonwealth Attorney, Leo Denton, was an experienced prosecutor, brusque and businesslike. "Good morning, Your Honor," he greeted Judge Chelone, as the balding jurist took his seat behind the bench. "We've got a little trial this morning, shouldn't take long."

Judge Chelone nodded.

"But before we get to that, I was hoping the Court would indulge me. Your Honor may recall seeing the story in the newspaper about a preacher apprehended running down the street naked after that fellow caught him in bed with his wife?"

Judge Chelone remained unexpressive.

"We've resolved that, I believe. And I was hoping Your Honor would take the plea. Should only take a couple minutes."

"Is he here?" Judge Chelone asked.

"Yes, sir," Reverend Jonah Breckinridge said, rising from the defense table. The usual gray-and-white striped jail uniform fit loosely over his frame. Bespoke creases and wrinkles gave it character.

Jack studied the preacher. Breckinridge hadn't shaven in days and probably hadn't slept much either.

"Call the case," Judge Chelone said to the clerk.

"Commonwealth of Kentucky versus Jonah Breckinridge,"

the clerk intoned, rattling off the case number.

"Reverend Breckinridge has agreed to plead guilty to public indecency, and the Commonwealth has agreed to drop the exposure count."

Judge Chelone looked up from the papers on his desk. When he did, Jack noticed the Judge's long, wrinkled neck and short, angled nose. Weekend work on his tobacco farm had tanned the jurist's face, but an unhealthy yellow mottled the tan and discolored his rheumy eyes. A hard shell of indifference protected him from the human misery that presented itself in his courtroom.

"Under the circumstances," Denton said, "the Commonwealth has agreed to recommend a sentence of seven days in the county jail, including time served, and the Reverend has agreed, upon completion of his sentence, to leave the county and not to return for at least five years. He has also agreed to have no further contact with Mrs. Fulton or other members of the choir."

Judge Chelone turned to the prisoner. "Reverend Breckinridge, did you follow what Mr. Denton just said?"

Breckinridge nodded. "Yes, sir."

"And is that what you agreed to?"

"Yes, sir."

"You understand that I'm not bound by what the prosecution recommends in terms of the sentence? I can impose a shorter or longer sentence?"

Reverend Breckinridge's eyes widened in alarm, but he said nothing.

"How do you plead to the charge of public indecency?"

"Guilty," Breckinridge said.

"Okay, then," Judge Chelone said. "I'm sentencing you to thirty days in the county jail, with all but seven days suspended. That's on the condition you leave town immediately after you complete your incarceration." Chelone looked at his notes. "You may not return to this county or have any more communication with that woman for five years." Looking up from his notes, Chelone added, "If you're smart, and that's an open question, you'll stay away longer than that."

"Your Honor, just to clarify," Denton said, "Reverend Breckinridge will get credit for the time he's served? In other words, he will only have two days more to serve."

"That's correct."

"Your Honor, can I say something?" Breckinridge asked.

"Make it quick. We've got a trial."

"I want to say how sorry I am. I've sinned and disgraced myself and brought shame to myself and others, and —"

"Get him out of here!" Judge Chelone snapped. "Clerk, call the next case."

***

At its regular Wednesday afternoon meeting, Mayor H. A. Knollman brought up the problem in the Austinburg neighborhood. He advised the other members of the City Commission that he and City Manager Theodore Kluemper had worked out a solution.

The black man and his wife agreed to move out, and the gentleman who sold them the house agreed to take it back. The City Housing Authority was working to find the couple a home in an *appropriate* neighborhood.

Mayor Knollman explained that he had used some of his office's discretionary funds to help pay for the extra moving expense and to smooth things over.

All of that had been in newspapers, so Harry Boyle and the other Commissioners already knew this, but like the others, Boyle listened as Knollman rambled on about his successful handling of the situation.

With an attempt at humor, Mayor Knollman concluded,

"Gentlemen, we have peace in our time."

Commissioner Frank Vaske spoke up. "I've been getting complaints that the guy who owns the Covington Waste Company was behind this whole thing. People are saying he put up the money for this Negro family to buy that house."

Boyle considered Vaske an ally.

"Same here," Commissioner Henry Meimann said. "There are flyers all over town. My phone has been ringing all day." Meimann was Boyle's other ally on the five-man Commission.

Mayor Knollman pursed his lips and hesitated before responding. "Did you see the article in the *Tribune* this morning?"

"I get the *Enquirer*," Vaske said. "What article?"

"I've got it here," Commissioner Carl Kiger said, handing the paper to Vaske. "It says the Syndicate is behind this. Goons operating out of Greta's rounded up some stiffs who needed money, gave them stacks of flyers, and then drove them all over town to distribute this nonsense. A reporter pretended to be out-of-work and got in line. The schmucks gave him a map and a stack of flyers."

Mayor Knollman cleared his throat. "The paper quotes Hamlin as denying what's in the flyers, and —"

"I wouldn't pay any attention to what's in that article," Boyle interrupted. "That reporter's new. When Covington Waste discovered its secret was out, it must have paid him to write this."

Mayor Knollman looked irritated. "What I was going to say is, Hamlin called me this morning, and he told me the same thing. He said he had nothing to do with that couple in Austinburg, and —"

"Of course, he denied it," Boyle said.

"It looks like I've got us off the agenda," Knollman said. "Shall we get started with —"

Boyle interrupted again. "May I make a suggestion? We're supposed to decide today on awarding the trash collection contract. If we award it to Covington Waste, we will have another riot on our hands. And more to the point, if we give the contract to Covington Waste, when the citizens of this fair city go to the polls, they will throw the lot of us out of office."

The Mayor looked pained. "Harry, we haven't reached that on the agenda yet."

"I think we should just face up to it," Boyle persisted. "We should decide right now that this disqualifies Covington Waste. We should award the contract to the other bidder. It's a bigger company. Maybe we'll see some improvement in service."

Kiger, Boyle's rival on the City Commission, saw his chance to make Boyle look bad. "Harry, this article says people will be able to tell who the Syndicate has under its thumb by how they vote on this contract. Do you suppose there's any truth to that?"

"The newspaper doesn't say that," Boyle shot back. "The newspaper quotes that young guy who wants my job as saying that. And he's just saying that to get his name in the paper."

Kiger snickered. "Touchy, aren't we, Harry?" Kiger was not just Boyle's rival. He was the most popular Commissioner with voters. The year before he had helped bring President Roosevelt to Covington. Roosevelt gave a speech in Latonia for Kentucky's Senator Barkley.

"Carl," Mayor Knollman said, "that was uncalled for and out of order. We need to get to the agenda."

Boyle slammed his fist down on the table. "Carl, do you have a basis for your accusation? Or are you just grandstanding again? If you have evidence that the Syndicate has bought my vote, let's hear it. Otherwise, you owe me an apology."

Kiger smirked. "I just asked if what your opponent is saying is true. I notice you haven't answered my question."

"Gentlemen, the agenda," the Mayor said.

"I suggest we table the contract award," Commissioner Meimann said, "and ask the City Solicitor to investigate whether

Mr. Hamlin and his company were behind that couple moving into Austinburg."

Boyle angered. Meimann, he realized, was having second thoughts about voting for the Cleveland company and having his vote thrown in his face by the newspapers, opposing candidates, and voters.

"So, moved," Commissioner Vaske said.

That meant Vaske was having second thoughts too. Boyle could feel his chest tighten and perspiration form on his forehead. He thought he could push the contract through, but the opportunity had just slipped away. He would have to explain what happened to Polizzi and wait for another day.

"Seconded," Meimann said.

"Any objections?" the Mayor asked.

There were none.

***

That evening, Jack entered the boarding house where he was staying. Just inside the front door, he stopped to check for mail before heading up the stairs to his second story room. He heard the door behind him open and turned to greet Mrs. Schickel, the woman who owned the building. Mrs. Schickel was a short, chubby woman with a hearing deficit and the disagreeable habit of interrupting, often before she understood what the other person was saying.

"Good evening, Mrs. –" Jack got out before Mrs. Schickel interrupted.

"Mr. Orion," Mrs. Schickel said. "I need to have a word with you." Even though it was after 6:00 p.m., she was still in her pajamas and housecoat. She had large pink rollers in her hair, and her plump cheeks were pink with emotion.

"It's O'Brien," Jack said.

Mrs. Schickel clutched in her hands two newspapers in mailing wrappers. The mailing slips had Jack's name and address on them. "Are these yours?"

"Yes, ma'am, thank you." Jack reached out his hand to accept the papers, but Mrs. Schickel jerked them away.

"They're German newspapers." Mrs. Scheckel's tone of voice made clear that this was not a statement of fact. It was an accusation.

"Yes, ma'am, that's right."

"I knew it! I knew it!" Mrs. Schickel said. The pink in her face deepened to something like the color of baked ham. "You're a German spy."

Jack grinned. "No ma'am. I'm a reporter."

"An exporter, huh?" Mrs. Schickel folded her arms but held tight to the newspapers. "Then tell me, Mr. Big Shot Exporter, what do you export?"

"I'm a newspaper reporter, ma'am," Jack said, his amusement with the situation waning. "I use those newspapers to keep up with —"

"Oh, so I ask what you export, and all of a sudden you work for a newspaper," Mrs. Schickel said. "How convenient." She nodded her head and stuck out her chin for emphasis.

Jack thought Mrs. Schickel should worry more about the moustache growing on her upper lip than his reading habits but reached into his pocket and pulled out his business cards. He peeled one off and offered it to Mrs. Schickel.

The woman unfolded her arms and reached out her right hand to take the card while clutching the German-language newspapers even more tightly under her left arm. She lifted the card close to her face and grunted. "This doesn't prove you work for the newspaper. Anybody can buy a business card."

Jack looked around for an idea. "Mrs. Schnitzel," he said, deliberating changing her name, but not speaking loud enough for her to tell, "do you get the *Tribune*?"

"The *Tribune*? Yes, but I don't believe a word it says. I only look at the advertisements. And the women's page."

"I want you to go inside and get this morning's *Tribune* for me. You can keep my German papers as evidence."

Mrs. Schickel narrowed her eyes and looked around. "How do I know you won't run away?"

Jack looked around, left and right, up the stairs and behind himself. He leaned forward and said, "Mrs. Schnitzel, if I were a German spy, I would have already knocked you on your head with my Luger."

Mrs. Schickel spun around and retreated into her room, slamming the door behind her.

Jack started to head upstairs to his room, but it occurred to him that if Mrs. Schickel were to return with the newspaper and he wasn't there, she would try to have him arrested for certain. He decided to wait.

A moment later, the door opened again, and Mrs. Schickel confronted him with her copy of that morning's *Tribune*.

Jack moved next to her and pointed to the front-page story about gangsters spreading flyers with false accusations about Silas Hamlin and Covington Waste. "I wrote that."

"You wrote that?"

"Yes, ma'am. That's why it has my byline."

"It has nothing to do with the bus line."

"Byline," Jack said, louder. "It has my name on it. I wrote it."

Mrs. Schickel squinted at the article, found Jack's name, and looked at Jack.

Jack smiled.

"That doesn't explain why you have German newspapers." Confident she had made an irrefutable point, Mrs. Schickel raised her chin again.

Jack was tired and debated with himself whether this conversation was worth having. "Mrs. Schickel, Germany seems determined to start another big war." Jack hesitated to be sure the woman was following. "If it does, I hope to get a job as a foreign correspondent or war correspondent. I'm trying to keep up with what's going on over there. I'm also working on my German in case that happens."

"Wait here," Mrs. Schickel said, handing Jack her cat and disappearing back into her apartment.

Jack's eyes watered. He sneezed. And then sneezed again.

Mrs. Schickel re-emerged and did a clumsy exchange of his German newspapers for the cat.

"What's your cat's name?" Jack asked.

"Eleanor, like Mrs. Roosevelt."

"Well, nice chatting with you," Jack said, turning toward the stairs. Over his shoulder, he said, *"Gute Nacht, Frau Schickel. Lassen Sie sich nicht die Wanzen beißen."* Good night, Mrs. Schickel, don't let the bed bugs bite.

CHAPTER 11, FRIDAY, JULY 28

**COVINGTON STATION WCKY
COMES INTO MATURITY
WITH 50,000 WATT POWER**
The Kentucky Post, July 28, 1939

The City of Covington and Kenton County conducted much of their business from offices in the imposing Courthouse building built at the end of the previous century. But the jail was in a smaller building, across a narrow alley from the Courthouse.

Jack delivered a bottle of Jack Daniels to the jail staff, and a jailor showed him to the small room reserved for meetings between jail inmates and their attorneys. Jack had tried to interview Reverend Breckinridge earlier in the day, but the staff told him to return during visiting hours.

After a lengthy negotiation and some coming and going, he'd gotten them to agree to allow him to use the small room set aside for attorney-client conferences and to allow him to conduct his interview outside of visiting hours. In exchange, he'd agreed to contribute the bottle of Jack Daniels.

While Jack settled in, the guard returned with Reverend Breckinridge. The preacher wore a dirty jailhouse uniform that reeked of sweat, body odor, and smells Jack didn't care to identify. He had apparently worn the same uniform and slept in it, to the extent he'd been able to sleep, since the day of his arrest. He looked despondent, surly, and sleep-deprived.

"Reverend Breckinridge, my name is Jack O'Brien. I'm a reporter—"

"I know who you are," Breckinridge said, jumping to his feet. "You're the spawn of Satan that had me arrested and wrote that story about me."

Jack flashed the preacher a big smile that masked the contempt he felt. "I was hoping you'd decided this was the Good Lord's doing, and I was just His humble instrument."

"I know who put you put you up to this, and it wasn't the Good Lord."

Jack's grin changed into a frown. "You *know* who put me up to exposing you?"

"Of course, I do. And so, do you. You're here to rub my nose in it."

"And who might that be?" Jack had no idea what the preacher was talking about, but sensed the preacher was aching to say something worth hearing.

Still glaring at Jack, the preacher ran his right hand through the thicket of his uncombed hair and then ran the back of the hand across the end of his nose but said nothing.

Jack sat down at the small table that took up much of the space in the cramped little room and gestured for the preacher to take the seat across from him. The table and benches were cheap metal affairs. Over the years, handcuffs and rough handling had scarred the table's surface.

"Here are the rules," Jack said. "I don't reveal my sources, and I'm not implicating myself in anything. You tell me what you think happened, and if you're square with me, I'll tell what you need to do to help yourself."

Breckinridge lowered himself onto the bench opposite Jack. "Cut the crap," he said. "It was Boyle. We both know that. I was spending time with his wife. After he saw your article, Boyle up and decided I was sleeping with her. He's decided to ruin me. Make sure I never preach again. And he sent you here to make sure I knew it was him."

Jack shook his head in amazement. "What made you think playing hide-the-sausage with Vice Mayor Harry Boyle's wife was a promising idea?"

"I didn't."

Jack thought the preacher's answer was rueful and maybe the only completely honest answer he'd get.

"You were paying her regular visits for what—two, three months?" Jack hoped the preacher wouldn't realize he was guessing.

Reverend Breckinridge stood again and paced. "Why are you here?" he asked. Then, just as abruptly, he stopped and faced Jack. "Did Boyle send you to let me know he's going to have me killed?"

Jack decided to try a different approach. "No. Now, sit down and hear me out."

Reverend Breckinridge studied Jack for a long moment but avoided eye contact. He sighed and sat back down.

Jack pointed to the duffel bag he'd brought with him into the room. "That bag has your clothes and belongings in it. I picked them up for you."

"I was naked, and ye clothed me," Breckinridge said, smirking. "I was in prison, and ye visited me. Matthew 25:36."

Jack exhaled slowly, cautioning himself not to lose patience. "Harry Boyle didn't send me. I got that story on my own, and it was a legitimate story." Jack tried to relax his face and smile. "But that doesn't mean I want you on my conscience."

The preacher studied Jack with the suspicion bred into the Appalachian poor, which is what, deep down, the preacher was. That suspicion was something, Jack thought, no amount of baptizing could wash out of a person.

"If Boyle didn't put you up to it," Reverend Breckinridge asked, "who did?"

"Nobody. I'm a reporter, and I smelled a story."

A flash of outrage spread across Breckinridge's face. "It was that nigger, wasn't it?"

Jack responded with a big grin that implied the minister had hit the jackpot. "I don't know what you're talking about."

"You know damn well what I'm talking about. You've been talking to that colored guy who works around the Boyle's yard—Two Penny, Two Penny something or other."

"I don't reveal my sources," Jack said, still grinning.

Breckinridge glared at Jack. His body tensed, the corners of his mouth turned down, and his chin stuck out like a loose brick. "That boy's in here now. Serves him right."

"You think this Two Penny fellow told me you were spending too much time with the Vice Mayor's wife," Jack said, "and that's why I did a story about you sleeping with the ladies in the choir?"

It took a moment for the preacher to process what Jack said. When the flaw in his logic sunk in, his shoulders slumped. Ignoring Jack's question, Breckinridge asked, "Then, why you are here?"

"I've been calling around the state," Jack said, "talking to some friends, calling in favors, and I've found you a position—as long as you don't mess up the interview."

"A position? As a minister?"

"Yeah."

"Where?"

"Out of town. But first things first. They will come to release you at four o'clock. If you're interested in the job I found for you, I've got a car, and I'll drive you. We'll meet up with a friend of mine. You'll stay at his place this weekend. That'll give you a chance to clean up and get some sleep. Looks like you could use it. Then, he'll take you for the interview Monday morning."

"How do I know I won't get killed somewhere along the way?"

"Because I'm a reporter, not a mobster. I'm looking for a story. To get the story I want, I need a source, and the best kind of source is one with a pulse."

"What kind of story?"

"I'm not sure, but I think you do. You seem to think Vice Mayor Harry Boyle had something to do with your arrest. Why don't we start with you telling me everything you know about Harry Boyle?"

Reverend Breckinridge shook his head. "No deal. I don't want to give him and the people he's involved with any more reason to kill me than I already have."

"Look –" Jack started.

"Besides," the preacher cut him off, "no newspaper will print a story based on what you claim I say his wife told me, about what she says he told her."

"You're smarter than you look," Jack said. "And you're right. But if you tell me what's going on, I'll at least know what I'm looking for. I'll find something, or someone, I can base a story on. That's how reporting works."

The preacher scratched the growth on his face. "I don't know you. I think I should put my trust in the Lord."

"Far be it from me to tell a preacher not to put his trust in the Lord," Jack said, standing. "And you're right. You don't know me. So, let me tell you a little about who I am."

Jack slid his notebook into his back pocket as if preparing to leave. "I'm a good reporter, and a good reporter learns things. For example, I've learned that your church has hired an accountant to go over its books. To make sure you weren't diddling with more than the choir ladies."

The preacher tensed. It wasn't obvious, and Jack might have missed it if he hadn't been watching for a response.

"This evening," Jack continued, "that accountant will meet with the church's supervising board and give them the unhappy news. He will tell them you've embezzled everything in the church's accounts, including the fund for church renovations and the fund for hungry children."

Reverend Breckinridge put his head in his hands.

"My story about that will be on the front-page tomorrow morning, and it will say you gambled the money away."

"Who told you that?"

"Like I said, I don't reveal my sources, but how 'bout I tell you a little more about myself. Two years ago, I was fresh out of college and working for a small paper down in the southeastern part of the state. I wrote a story about this Pentecostal preacher in Clay County, way down there near the Tennessee border. A Reverend Jedidiah Adair. Seems he was sleeping with the ladies of the choir, and when they ran him out of town, the church's money left with him."

Reverend Breckinridge folded his arms. "I know nothing about that."

"I checked," Jack said, "and there's a warrant out for that preacher, for embezzlement and some other things."

Breckinridge's eyes darted around the little room. "What makes you think that has anything to do with me?"

"Because I'm not stupid. He was your age, your physical description. He was good with the choir and good at quoting scripture. And the newspaper, the one I used to work for, still has a photograph of Reverend Adair, and whad'ya know? He looks just like you."

Reverend Breckinridge shook his finger at Jack. "Judge not, lest thou be judged."

"Mathew, chapter 7, verse 1," Jack said. "I'm not judging you. I'm just saying, you tell me what you know about Boyle and his friends, and then, when you walk out of here at four, I'll be waiting in my car. We should be long gone before the church supervisors find out about the missing church funds. And who knows, maybe the prosecutor never finds out about that problem in Clay County."

Reverend Breckinridge crossed his arms again and said nothing.

Jack forced a smile. "I'll drive you downstate. I won't ask, and you won't tell me what name you give your new employer."

The preacher unfolded his arms and studied his hands, but again said nothing.

"I'm asking you to help me expose what Boyle and his Syndicate buddies are up to. I'm giving you a chance to have something good come out of the mess you've made. But maybe you don't believe in the power of redemption."

Breckinridge snorted. "You don't get redemption from a newspaper."

"The Lord works in strange ways," Jack said, shrugging his shoulders. "But if that's how it's going to be, then when I leave here, I'm going to the prosecutor's office. I'll ask Mr. Denton for a comment on that accountant's report. And if the spirit moves me, I just might ask him if he's aware of that Clay County warrant. My guess is, you won't be getting out of here anytime soon. You might be living like this for a long time."

"That's blackmail."

Jack smiled. "I prefer to think of it as serving the public's right to be informed."

Breckinridge said nothing.

"Reverend, I'm Catholic," Jack said. "Catholics believe Christianity is all about forgiveness and redemption. Suppose we tell ourselves I'm doing the Christian thing and offering you a chance at redemption?"

The preacher began to protest, but Jack pointed to the clock on the wall. "Time's up. What's it going to be? Do you want to be a preacher or a prison inmate?"

Reverend Breckinridge followed Jack's glance at the wall clock and sighed. "What do you want to know?"

***

Jack drove the preacher from Covington down U.S. Route 42 toward Louisville. The highway wound its way through rolling hills, past large colonial-style homes, white horse-farm fences, and the occasional stacked stone fence. Along the way, small stores and filling stations marked intersections with east-west state roads.

After his stint in jail, Reverend Breckinridge enjoyed watching the scenery roll by, but he was a talker, and Jack found it easy to draw him out.

Before the jailer released Reverend Breckinridge, Jack had extracted what little the preacher knew or surmised about what Vice Mayor Harry Boyle was up to—all of which, while the stuff of a terrific scoop, had been vague. Jack suspected the preacher had more to reveal about Boyle, and he would get to that. But there were other things he was just curious about even if they didn't touch on what the Vice Mayor was up to. Those things seemed a safer place to start.

"This is none of my business," Jack said. "But how did you get involved with Boyle's wife?"

"I didn't set out to," Breckinridge said, slowly, as if trying to reconstruct in his own mind what happened. "I was raising money for the Hungry Children's Fund, and someone told me I should see her—that she could give me advice on how to run a charitable donations program up here.

"I was stupid and didn't think I needed anyone's advice. I was just hoping to get her to contribute. But asking her for advice seemed like the best way to approach her and get that conversation started." Breckinridge trailed off and seemed to get lost in watching the scenery.

"I heard she came from a well-off family," Jack said, "and has money of her own."

"Yeah, she and her sister inherited plenty. She kept her money separate from her husband's and invested it well. She told me she got through the Crash better than a lot of folks."

"How'd it go when you approached her?"

"She was generous with her time but frugal with her money. At first, she was just businesslike, telling me who to approach and what I needed to do. Then, one day, things took a strange turn."

"How so?"

"Her husband was coming home late, and on weekends, sometimes not at all. He was drinking a lot. Somehow, she found out he wasn't just hanging out with other politicians and Syndicate guys—drinking and playing poker. He was visiting a whorehouse. Agnes was mad as hell."

"Guess so." Jack tried not to react or do anything that would make the preacher more defensive than he already was.

"It went beyond being angry at his infidelity," Breckinridge said. "She was angry that he was throwing away what they could have had. I think she wanted to get back at him."

"So, you offered your services?"

"As God is my witness, no. Even I am not that stupid."

"What happened?"

"One morning she called me and said she had transferred funds to her account and was ready to make a donation. She said she also had something she wanted me to help her with if I could stop by.

"At the time, I knew nothing about her husband whoring or any of that. So, I stopped by, and it was obvious she'd been crying. There was a bottle of bourbon on the table and an empty glass."

Jack reduced his speed and eased his way through an "S" turn.

"I asked what the problem was. She wouldn't say."

"And then what?"

"Agnes showed me the check she'd written. It wasn't a lot—not what I'd expected. But to be honest, there wasn't much in the collection plate and the prospect of going hungry colors your thinking."

"For lots of folks," Jack said, remembering that the preacher was supposed to be collecting for hungry children. "So, what happened?"

"Agnes didn't give me the check. She laid it on the table and asked me if I would mind helping her with something in the bedroom. I thought she needed someone to a move a dresser or something. She pointed the way and followed me in. And then, she closed the door."

Breckinridge covered his face with his hands.

"Was it just that one time?"

"Yes."

"So, this was her way of getting revenge on her husband?"

Breckinridge nodded. "I think so."

Jack understood why the preacher thought Harry Boyle might hold a grudge. There was no point in asking Breckinridge where he thought his relationship with Mrs. Boyle would end. But while the preacher was getting things off his chest, there was something else Jack *was* curious about.

"The church money?" Jack asked, "You bet on the horses?"

"Wasn't like that," Breckinridge said. "I preach that gambling is a sin, and I believe that."

Jack said nothing, confident the preacher wanted to explain himself.

"Some of the men I pressed for contributions were with the Syndicate. Some tossed me a little money, but mainly they gave me the bum's rush. Then one day, this guy in an expensive, double-breasted suit shows up and says he needs to talk with me."

"Short, thin guy with a mustache? Black hair slicked back?" Jack asked, describing Sal Rizzi. "Dark dress shirt, white tie?"

"Yeah, that's right. Anyway, he says he knows I've been asking around for money to help the kids. He says he and his friends want to help, but—given their line of work—they can't exactly write me a check. I told him, I'd be happy to take cash."

"Watch out!" Jack shouted. He was rounding a bend when he saw a cow in the road. He swerved and missed the animal. When Jack glanced over at the preacher, the man acted as if he hadn't noticed how close they'd been to disaster.

"Long story short," Breckinridge said, "he said he couldn't do that either, but they had worked something out that was almost the same as cash."

"Like what?"

"He said the fix was in on a race at Latonia. They'd handle everything for me, and the kids would end up with plenty of money."

Jack shot another glance at the preacher.

Breckinridge shook his head at his own stupidity.

"So, you agreed?"

"Yeah, but I only put up a small amount—the money I'd gotten from Agnes."

"And you won?"

"Yeah. That's when he told me I was being stupid. He said he was trying to give me money for the kids, and I was betting chicken shit. He said he'd give me one more chance, but I had to come up with at least five hundred dollars, or he wouldn't risk placing bets for a preacher.

"I got to thinking about what it would mean if I could put in five hundred and get back triple that. I figured I'd give most of it to the fund for the kids and use the rest to get away before Boyle found out about his wife and me."

"Let me guess," Jack said, "your horse lost?"

Breckinridge nodded. "He told me the horse broke a leg coming out of the starting gate. Said it was just one of those things. He said they were sorry about what happened and wanted to make it up to me."

Jack shook his head. "He just happened to know about another race that was fixed? A sure thing?"

Breckinridge nodded. "By then, I was desperate. I needed to replace what I'd lost, and –"

"And what?"

"They frightened me. Now, there were two of them. The first guy and another man. It wasn't clear if they were asking me to bet the rest of the church's money or telling me to. They reminded me how bad it would be if I couldn't replace the money I'd lost. So, I gave them the money from the Hungry Children Fund and prayed things would work out."

Jack spotted a police cruiser coming up the highway in their direction. Neither he nor the preacher said anything until the cruiser passed. When the cop car kept heading up the highway away from them, both breathed easier.

"What are you going to tell the cops," Breckinridge asked, changing the subject, "when they figure things out and demand to know where I am?"

"Just like that song by The Ink Spots. 'Address unknown, not even a trace of you.'"

Breckinridge looked back to make sure the police cruiser had not circled back for them. When he didn't see any sign of the police car, he said, "I prefer Isaiah chapter 47, verse 11. 'Therefore, shall evil come upon thee; thou shalt not know from whence it riseth; and mischief shall fall upon thee; thou shalt not be able to fend it off; and desolation shall come upon thee suddenly, from where thou shalt not know.'"

"Is that for you or me?" Jack asked.

The preacher didn't answer. He just stared out the car window into the gathering dusk.

CHAPTER 12, MONDAY, JULY 31

**BRITAIN FAR MORE PREPARED
TO FIGHT THAN AT OUTBREAK
OF WORLD WAR 25 YEARS AGO**
The Cincinnati Enquirer, July 31, 1939

On Monday morning, as usual, Jack did the trip through the courthouse that was part of his job—checking the filing basket in the Clerk's office for new lawsuits and other new filings, chatting with the lawyers he saw in the halls, kibitzing with courthouse regulars, always looking for a story. This morning, he also stopped next door at the jail.

From the personnel in the jail, Jack learned that they did indeed have a colored inmate named Two Penny. His full name was Two Penny Smith, and they were holding him on charges of disturbing the peace and public indecency. Smith had been a guest of the City of Covington for a week, give or take. Jack insisted on the exact date and time Smith arrived at the jail. The jailer found the specifics for him.

Jack returned to the courthouse and tracked down the sparse court file in the Clerk of Court's office concerning the criminal charges against Two Penny Smith. He noted the trial date, then hurried back to the *Tribune* for a call he was expecting.

Jack took the call at his desk in the newspaper's bullpen—the open space crammed with hard oak desks and hard-bitten reporters. Fueled by coffee, the reporters worked the phones, bantered with each other, and pecked at typewriters—sometimes doing all three at the same time. Teletype machines rattled in the background, adding their clack-clack-clack noise to the overall cacophony.

"Jack," the caller said. "It's Ben."

"Ben! How'd things go with Reverend Breckinridge?"

"He wasn't singing halleluiahs when he found out where I was taking him."

Jack chuckled, imagining the scene in his mind. The plan was for Ben to take Reverend Breckinridge to the Army recruiter in Louisville.

"I had to take him across the street from the Army office to a little diner, buy him some coffee, and reason with him."

"Wish I could have been there," Jack said. "What did you tell him?"

"I told him that if he kept on his present course, he would end up in prison. Or dead. He was destroying other people's lives, and he needed to turn himself around. I said I had nothing against preachers, but nobody is better at turning someone around than the Army. Except maybe the Marines."

"What'd the Reverend say to that?"

"He prayed over it, and in the end, he decided I was right."

"The power of prayer, huh?"

"Could be, but I'm more inclined to think it was something else. While he was praying, the waitress came to our table to check on us."

"And?" Jack asked. Anticipating the answer, he grinned.

"And for a country girl, she was a knockout. Great smile, nice figure."

"I assume Reverend Breckinridge saw a soul in need of saving."

"Maybe," Ben said. "I reminded him he wouldn't be spending time with the ladies if he ended up in prison. But in the Army, there would be nurses and others who might need saving."

Jack shook his head.

"By the way," Ben said, "are you still seeing Maggie?"

"Yes, sir! In fact, I'm seeing her tonight."

"She's special. If you ever lose interest in her, let me know."

"Not going to happen, pal," Jack said. Laughing, he added, "Make your parents happy, and go find a nice Jewish girl."

CHAPTER 13, TUESDAY, AUGUST 1

KING SWOPE SPEAKS IN NEWPORT
Denounces Roosevelt and
Chandler Administrations
The Kentucky Post, August 1, 1939

From Reverend Breckinridge's revelations, Jack understood that Agnes Boyle had somehow learned her husband was frequenting Greta's and was spending time with gangsters. But Reverend Breckinridge didn't know how Mrs. Boyle learned of her husband's indiscretions. Breckinridge had also said a black man, Two Penny Smith, was frequently at the Boyle's, doing yard work and errands, but shortly after Jack's article about Reverend Breckinridge, the police arrested Two Penny.

Jack knew those things—Agnes Boyle's epiphany and Two Penny Smith's arrest—might well be coincidental. But his job involved sitting in on the occasional trial, looking for a story. Two Penny Smith worked for the Vice Mayor; that alone made sitting in on his trial worthwhile.

Jack positioned himself in his usual place, in the spectator seats on the right side, behind the prosecutor and three rows back. He watched as the bailiff led the defendant—Two Penny Smith — into the courtroom and directed him to sit at the table to the left of the prosecution table.

Smith was a thin man. Jack thought he looked to be in his late-forties, but the booking records would have his exact age. Smith's hair was short, crinkled, and greying. He wore the standard gray-and-white striped jail uniform, and handcuffs gripped his wrists. Smith looked frightened but maintained a reserve of quiet dignity.

"Stand when the judge comes in," the bailiff instructed Smith, "and don't try anything," The bailiff moved to his position at the edge of the courtroom and leaned against the wall, his posture as relaxed as the dull crease in his uniform slacks.

Jack looked around the courtroom. The Vice Mayor was not in evidence. In the last row, he saw a tiny colored woman. She wore what was almost certainly her Sunday-church dress. She was about the same age as the defendant and clutched a handkerchief in her right hand as if expecting to cry. Jack assumed she was Smith's wife.

On either side of her, looking angry and defiant, sat two young adults. Jack guessed they were her children. The older one, in his twenties, was a well-muscled fellow; the younger one, a beautiful young woman. The young man wore a long-sleeved cotton shirt and work pants. The young woman wore a simple frock dress.

The clerk read the name and the number of the case, *The Commonwealth of Kentucky vs. Two Penny Smith*, No. 39-M-119.

"Your Honor," Leo Denton, the prosecutor, greeted the judge. "The indictment charges Mr. Two Penny Smith,"—Denton gestured to the defendant— "with disturbing the peace and indecent behavior toward a white woman, a Miss April Bedwell, on July 25, 1939, at or about ten p.m., outside the Liberty Theater."

Denton looked up from his notes. "For the record, Your Honor, that's the movie theater at 608 Madison Avenue, here in Covington, Kentucky."

Judge Chelone leaned forward in his chair and fixed on Two Penny Smith the hate stare certain white people reserved for the colored man. Jack had seen that look in Covington and downstate. He'd also seen that same hate stare in Germany when he spent his junior year at the university in Stuttgart. But in Germany, patriots reserved the hate stare for Jews.

"As Miss Bedwell and a friend were leaving the theatre, and again this was last Tuesday, about ten o'clock in the evening." Denton hesitated, struggled to find a way to bring his sentence to a grammatical conclusion, and gave up.

"At that time and place, Your Honor," he said, charging ahead again, "the defendant approached Miss Bedwell and tried to engage her in conversation. When Miss Bedwell ignored him, the defendant asked her if she'd ever slept with a colored man. He then made, as the testimony will show, certain lewd statements. About then, Your Honor, the defendant became aggressive, and Miss Bedwell will testify she felt threatened. Her companion, a Miss May Goodnight, will corroborate her testimony."

As the prosecutor spoke, the defendant shook his head.

"Mr. Smith," Judge Chelone said in a voice that drifted higher in pitch as it rose in volume. "None of that shaking your head, you hear me?"

"Yes, sir," Smith said, confused and alarmed.

"Mr. Smith, you will stand when you address the court," Judge Chelone commanded.

Smith rose and mumbled, "Yes, sir, I'm sorry, sir, I didn't know. I ain't never been in court before, Your Honor."

"In court," Judge Chelone said, "even white folks stand when they address the judge, so I expect you to stand. We got that straight?"

"Yes, sir."

"Please continue," Judge Chelone prompted Denton.

"That's about it, Your Honor. I told Mr. Smith you'd go easier on him if he pled guilty, but he refuses."

"Mr. Smith, you're not going to insist on a jury trial, are you?" Judge Chelone asked.

Smith stood. "It wouldn't be right, Your Honor, for me to say I done something I didn't."

"Your neck," Judge Chelone said, shaking his head in disbelief. "Bailiff, bring in the panel."

The bailiff brought in the potential jurors. Judge Chelone administered the oath and delivered a perfunctory lecture on their duties.

Standing before the potential jurors, Denton introduced himself and the defendant and explained in summary fashion what the case was about. With those preliminaries completed, he asked if any jurors knew the defendant, or Ms. Bedwell, or her friend, May Goodnight. None did.

"Would any of you have a problem convicting a man, a Negro," Denton asked, "who made lewd and indecent statements to a white woman, if that's what the evidence shows?" None of the potential jurors admitted any reluctance to do their duty.

Denton surveyed the potential jurors, pausing and searching each person's face in turn. "Is there any reason," he asked, "that any of you could not render a fair and impartial verdict in this case?"

No one raised his hand.

"We're satisfied with jurors one through twelve," Denton announced.

That was the shortest *voir dire* Jack had ever seen. He suspected it may have been the shortest in the annals of Kentucky jurisprudence.

"Does the defendant have any objection to the panel?" Judge Chelone asked.

Smith stood but hesitated before he responded. "Them look like real fine folks, Your Honor." He turned and looked behind him, to a spot in the back of the courtroom. Turning back to face Judge Chelone, Smith said in a soft, tentative voice, "But it looks like somebody just shook the salt shaker and not the pepper."

"Speak up, boy," Judge Chelone snapped. "What are you talking about?"

Smith appeared rattled—as if a lightning bolt had just struck the ground in front of him. "Your Honor, I thought," he began, before hesitating and glancing at the back of the courtroom again. "All them folks are white, Your Honor. Can I have a jury with some colored folks, like me?"

Jack stared at Smith in amazement. There wasn't a colored person in Covington who didn't know the jury would be all white—if he was lucky enough to get a trial.

Jack turned and looked where Smith had glanced. In the back corner, a tall black man in a well-tailored tan suit adjusted his eyeglasses.

"Not the way it works," Judge Chelone said. "There are no colored people in my juries. And no monkeys either."

Eileen Bell, the court reporter, interrupted. "Do you want that in the record?"

"No, I guess not. Clean it up like usual."

"Thank you, Your Honor."

"Your Honor," Denton said, "as we've discussed before, the Supreme Court has held that a defendant has a right to a jury from which people are not eliminated based on race."

"Duly noted, Mr. Denton," Judge Chelone said. "And I'll say again, they don't give me a stipend to cover the cost of buying all those fancy books with the Supreme Court's nonsense, so you'll just have to settle with the law as I interpret it."

Judge Chelone turned his attention back to the defendant. "Mr. Smith, do you want to strike any of the jurors?"

"No, sir," Smith said, looking defensive. "I ain't never struck anybody in my life, 'less they hit me first."

Judge Chelone rolled his eyes, then dismissed all but the first twelve potential jurors.

Minutes later, the prosecution had its chief witness, April Bedwell, on the stand. In her twenties, Miss Bedwell was an attractive woman—tall, leggy, and blonde—although Jack suspected she was the drugstore-variety blonde. She wore bright red lipstick and a red satin dress that emphasized her bosom.

The combination struck Jack as an odd choice for the occasion. It reminded him of something he'd overheard in Harlan County. "A man shouldn't go to the market looking for satin," a sharp-tongued woman had complained to a friend, "when he's got silk at home."

The clerk administered the oath.

The prosecutor asked Miss Bedwell to state her name and address for the record.

Jack jotted down both.

"Are you employed, Ms. Bedwell?" Denton asked.

"Yes, sir."

"And where do you work?"

"At the brewery."

"At the Hanover Brewery?"

"Yes, sir."

Denton then led the witness through her testimony, much of which Jack thought sounded rehearsed.

When Denton concluded, Judge Chelone asked Smith if he had questions for the witness.

"Yes, sir, if it's okay," Smith said, rising.

"Go ahead."

Jack watched as Smith tried to compose himself. It was hard to tell because Smith held his hands against himself, but Jack thought Smith's hands were shaking.

"Miss April," Smith said, "why you sayin' them things when you know they ain't true?"

"Objection," Denton said. "Argumentative."

"Sustained," Judge Chelone ruled. "Mr. Smith, I will only allow you to question the witness if you handle yourself properly."

Smith looked rattled, but to Jack's surprise, and maybe to his own, he tried again. "Ms. April, is somebody making you say these things?"

Denton jumped to his feet again and objected.

Judge Chelone extended his neck and said, "Allowed, since it looks like we won't get done until he gets this out of his system."

Smith looked confused.

Turning to the witness, Judge Chelone asked, "Miss Bedwell, is anyone forcing you to testify to something's that's not true?"

"Oh, no, Your Honor." Miss Bedwell batted her eyes at the judge.

Focused less on the witness's demeanor than her cleavage, Judge Chelone asked, "And no one's paying you to testify a certain way?"

Ms. Bedwell leaned toward the judge, just enough to improve the view, and cooed, "No, sir."

"Do you know the defendant?" Chelone demanded. "Do you know why he calls you by your first name?"

"No, sir."

Chelone thanked and excused her.

Denton put on the corroborating witness, May Goodnight, and elicited much the same story from her. In fact, Jack thought, much of her story was almost word-for-word the same as the first witness's testimony. Denton also elicited that no one was forcing or paying her to testify.

The defendant, looking defeated, declined to ask any questions.

Denton put on the stand Patrolman Ricky Robinson, the policeman who arrested Smith. Patrolman Robinson testified that he arrested Smith in front of the Liberty Theatre and that the two women were still there when he made the arrest.

"Do you have questions for Patrolman Robinson?" Judge Chelone asked the defendant.

His motions slow and hesitant, like those of a student who wished the teacher hadn't called on him, Smith rose to his feet. "Yes, sir."

"Go ahead, but no speeches."

"Officer," Smith asked, "why you say that's where you arrested me when you know that ain't where −"

"Objection!" Denton said. The weary tone of his voice implied, *Do I even have to say this?*

"Sustained," Judge Chelone said, glaring at Smith.

"Isn't it a fact," Smith tried again, "that you didn't arrest me there in front of that movie house? That you arrested me at my home?"

"Objection," Denton said. "Argumentative. Compound."

"You're right, Mr. Denton," Judge Chelone said, "but let's get this over with. Officer, please answer."

Patrolman Robinson glanced at the police captain sitting in the first row of the public seating and squared himself. "I made the arrest right there at the scene. When someone's disturbing the peace and threatening decent people, you make the arrest then, not the next day."

Smith sunk into his chair.

"Patrolman, you're excused," Judge Chelone told the witness.

"The prosecution rests," Denton advised the judge.

"Mr. Smith," Judge Chelone said, "you can testify on your own behalf but you don't have to. And, I should warn you, it's generally a terrible idea for someone in your situation to testify, especially if they intend to perjure themselves."

"Can I just say I didn't do any of what they say I did?"

"If you want to testify, you have to come up here and take the oath, and then you can say what you want. But if you do that, Mr. Denton will cross-examine you, and I don't think you want that."

Smith's shoulders slumped. He sat down.

"Closing?" Judge Chelone asked the prosecutor.

"Yes, Your Honor," Denton said, standing. He took a position in front of the jury box and collected himself.

Speaking only a little longer than necessary, Denton explained what was necessary to prove the crimes of disturbing the peace and public indecency—which, in each case, he called the "elements of the crime." Denton summarized the testimony and explained how it proved each of the required elements.

If they agreed he had proven each element of the crime of disturbing the peace, he told the jury, it was their duty to convict. The same for public indecency. And if they agreed he had proven the elements of both crimes, it was their duty to return guilty verdicts for both violations. He concluded by asking the jury to recommend a jail sentence of ninety days.

"Does the defendant have a closing argument?" Judge Chelone asked.

"Just that I didn't do it, Your Honor, and that I don't know why they're saying them things because they ain't true and they know it."

"Thank you for that, Mr. Smith," Judge Chelone said.

For the next five minutes, Judge Chelone instructed the jury on its duties and the law and then sent the jury to deliberate.

***

Judge Chelone declared the court in recess and withdrew to his chambers. Jack made his way to the back of the courtroom and introduced himself to the tall, well-dressed colored man.

"Lincoln Cook," the man said, shaking Jack's outstretched hand. He pulled a business card from his jacket pocket and offered it to Jack.

Jack glanced at the card. It identified Cook as an attorney for the National Association for the Advancement of Colored People. "Mr. Smith could have used your services."

"I offered, but he turned me down," Cook said. "I even submitted an application *pro hac vice* in case he changed his mind at the last minute."

Jack held up his hands in surrender. "That's too much Latin for an underpaid newspaper reporter."

"I'm licensed to practice in Ohio and several other states, but not Kentucky. I asked permission to appear on behalf of Mr. Smith in this case."

"And Judge Chelone was okay with that?" That surprised Jack.

"No, he never ruled on my application. I think he knew if he denied my application, I would appeal and get him reversed. I expect I'll get his ruling in a day or two."

"Why didn't Mr. Smith want you to represent him?"

"He's afraid. More than that, I can't say unless he gives me permission."

"Is it all right if I talk with his family?"

Cook shrugged. "That's up to them."

Mrs. Smith and her daughter remained in their seats, but the young man was standing, looking impatient and angry.

Jack approached the young man. "I'm a reporter," he said, offering his hand. "My name is Jack O'Brien, and I'd like to talk with you and your mother about what this is all about. It's obvious they're railroading your father. Why?"

"Cause he ain't white," the young man said.

"Yeah, I got that, but how 'bout we start with your name?"

"Willis."

"Willis Smith?"

"Yeah."

The small woman stood and introduced herself as Mrs. Smith.

Jack extended his hand.

Mrs. Smith looked surprised that a white man would want to shake her hand, but she shook Jack's hand confidently.

"This is my daughter, Cora," Mrs. Smith said.

Jack shook hands with Cora Smith.

The bailiff and several courtroom hangers-on watched. Jack could see the hostility on their faces.

"I was hoping I could get a statement, Mrs. Smith. Find out what actually happened."

Mrs. Smith frowned and raised her eyebrows. "You for real?"

"Yes, ma'am."

From the front of the courtroom, the bailiff called out, "The jury's ready. Court resumes in five minutes."

"Let me think about it," she said. "Now, if you'll excuse me." With that, she hurried to the back corner of the courtroom and conferred with the NAACP attorney.

***

A few minutes later, the guard brought Two Penny Smith back into the courtroom. Judge Chelone emerged from chambers and ascended to the bench. When His Honor signaled he was ready, the bailiff brought the jury in.

The jury had been out less than ten minutes.

Judge Chelone went through the motions of inquiring whether the jury had reached a verdict, what the verdict was, and obtaining assurance that the verdict was unanimous. It was. The jury recommended a sentence of ninety days in jail.

"Mr. Smith," Judge Chelone said, "the jury has found you guilty of disturbing the peace and public indecency. Do you have anything to say before I impose sentence?"

"Only that I didn't do none of what they said I did. I don't know why Miss April and Miss May said that stuff. I always respected them, and they always treated me okay. And that policeman didn't arrest me at the Liberty because I weren't there. I was working. They arrested me the next day, at my home."

Judge Chelone was unimpressed. "Mr. Smith, the jury has found you guilty, so that's already been decided."

Smith hung his head.

"The jury recommends a sentence of ninety days. If it were up to me, I would sentence you to a lot more than that, but by law, that's the maximum sentence I can impose."

Mrs. Smith let out a cry.

Judge Chelone pounded his gavel. When the courtroom quieted, he ordered Smith to stand.

Smith was still standing and didn't know how to respond.

"Mr. Smith," Judge Chelone said, "I sentence you to ninety days in jail." To the Deputy Sheriff, he added, "Take him away."

"Nothing further here," Denton said.

"Then court's adjourned," Chelone said. He stood and, looking as perturbed as usual, stepped down from the bench and retreated to his chambers.

***

Jack sat in the small combination conference-room-and-library of the law firm of Solomon & Solomon, a marginally prosperous, two-attorney general practice firm that frequently represented, among others, colored people. The firm's father and son attorneys were white, but being Jewish, they were familiar with the bitter taste of discrimination. They quietly lent their conference room to the NAACP attorney whenever he came to town.

The length of the sentence infuriated Mrs. Smith. "You told me," she said to Lincoln Cook, the tall, slender, soft-spoken NAACP attorney, "that they'd only keep him for thirty days."

"That's what the prosecutor told me to expect," Cook said, "but that was before the case got re-assigned to Judge Chelone."

"Humph!" Mrs. Smith turned to Jack in a way that made Jack think of the long barrels of a battleship's guns turning and taking aim.

"So," she said, "you going to report that my husband got railroaded? That they locked him up for something they know damn well he didn't do?"

"I can report that's what you allege," Jack said. "But I can only report *as fact* things I can substantiate, not what you, or I, or somebody else believes."

"Humph!" Mrs. Smith retorted.

"What makes you so sure," Jack asked, "that your husband didn't do what they say he did?"

Mrs. Smith shot a glance at Cook.

Cook returned her glance but gave her no indication of what he thought she should do.

"First of all," Mrs. Smith began.

"Momma!" her daughter cut her off. "You know what Poppa said."

"And look what keeping his mouth shut and being a good nigger got him!"

"Let her talk," Willis, the older sibling said. "She's done made up her mind. She don't care what might happen to her or anybody else."

Mrs. Smith fastened her gaze on her son. "I'll take this up with you later," she said, menace in her voice. Turning back to Jack, she said, "I know my husband didn't do what they said he did because I know my husband. He never done nothing his whole life 'cept scrape and bow in front of white folks."

A secretary appeared and placed a pitcher of water and two Coca-Colas on the table. "Sorry, but I only got two Co-Colas," she said. "You'll have to fight over them."

"You be the one working here," Mrs. Smith told Jack, "so you help yourself. And you too, Mr. Cook."

The secretary laid a bottle opener on the table next to Jack. "There's the church key."

Jack opened one of the bottles. He pushed the other bottle and the opener toward Cook, who remained standing.

"You said that was the first thing," Jack said.

Mrs. Smith took a deep breath. "Why you care?"

Jack thought that was a good question. He flashed the smile he knew had a way of disarming people and considered his answer. "First of all," he said, mirroring Mrs. Smith, "because I'm a reporter. If they railroaded your husband, that's a heck of a story."

Jack took a sip of the soda, giving himself a chance to decide what he wanted to say next. "Second, if somebody framed your husband, they must have a reason. Maybe covering up something your husband saw. I'm guessing that's an even bigger story."

"You think," Mrs. Smith said, "one of them newspapers in this town would publish a story like that? You must not be from around here."

"Yes, ma'am, I do think they would publish it, provided I can back it up. And if I'm wrong about that, I'll take the story to the wire services, or to the newspapers in Cincinnati, Louisville, and Lexington."

"And why you gonna do that?"

"Because I'm a reporter. A real one, not some hack who just checks the police blotter and reports who got arrested for public drunkenness and who got arrested for spitting on the sidewalk."

"Humph," Mrs. Smith said. As usual, her head and body bobbed up and down as she fired off her retort.

Jack took another sip from the soft drink. It was her neck, and she had to decide for herself if she wanted to stick it out.

"So, if I tell you what's going on," Mrs. Smith said, circling back, "you're gonna put that in the paper?"

"Not right off the bat. Depending on what you tell me, I'll need to do some digging, to see if I can find evidence to back up what you say and to see where that leads me. If I write a story like this, I'll need more than just your say so."

"You serious about this?" Mrs. Smith demanded.

"I'm like a dog with a bone, ma'am. When I find a story, I'm not one to give it up."

Mrs. Smith cast another look toward the NAACP attorney.

He nodded. The gesture was almost imperceptible, but Mrs. Smith didn't miss it.

"Then," Mrs. Smith said, making up her mind, "you best be getting out your notebook."

***

After work, Jack crossed the street to Scrivener's. He was meeting Maggie there because she was reluctant to let her father know she was seeing him as often as she was. Jack settled into a booth and ordered a drink. He was a few minutes early.

When Maggie opened the door to the bar, she hesitated a moment to allow her eyes to adjust to the dark interior. When she paused, the light from outside shone on her like stage lighting. She wore a white linen blouse with a V-neck and a red pencil skirt that hugged her hips and draped down her long legs. Traveling in the opposite direction, a slit climbed partway up the side of the skirt. Her bright red lipstick matched her skirt and high heels.

Men called to her to join them. From near the back, a couple of Palookas whistled.

Maggie smiled, taking it all in like a Hollywood star on the red carpet. Jack stood, and she nodded to him. She waved at the others and got a good-natured, collective groan in reply. As she walked, the tight skirt accented the way her hips swayed. When she reached

Jack, she gave him a little peck on the cheek and sat down.

"Do you have any idea how many hearts you just broke?" Jack asked her.

"Oh, hush!"

That quick, the bartender was at their table. "What would the lady have?" he asked.

"Gin and tonic, please."

"Very good," the bartender said but didn't move.

"Hennessey, your tongue's hanging out," one the men at the bar called out to the bartender. Hennessy turned and hurried back to the bar.

"So, what's new and exciting in the reporting business?" Maggie asked.

"I watched a trial today. I'm almost certain the charges were bogus. After the trial, I spoke with the man's family. And with a NAACP attorney who was there to monitor the trial."

Maggie leaned in as if she were hanging on every word Jack said.

Jack suspected that was mainly feminine wile. Women knew there's little a man likes better than a woman listening to his stories as if they thrilled her. But knowing that didn't make it any less fun.

The bartender returned with Maggie's drink. She thanked him and turned her thousand-watt gaze back to Jack. "You were talking about a trial," she said. "There was a NAACP attorney there."

"Yeah, but that's all work," Jack said. "What's new with you?"

"Just the usual. Dad wants me to work in the office at the brewery or get a job as a secretary somewhere."

"I thought you majored in art and wanted to get a job in a museum or a gallery."

"I desperately want a job in a museum or a first-rate gallery," Maggie said, "and my mom and my aunt are pulling all kinds of strings for me. So are some of my college professors, but there aren't many jobs like that available. Lots of people would sleep with the devil to get one of the few positions that come open each year."

"I hope it doesn't come to that," Jack said, "but if an Irish devil will do, I'd be willing to help."

Maggie shook her head and rolled her eyes. "I'll let you know if I require your services. But for now, it's just this constant tug of war between my father wanting me to get a *sensible* job, and my mother and my aunt conspiring to help me."

"Your mother and aunt have connections with the art world?"

"Not really. A few, but mainly they've got money. These days, that's almost the same thing." Changing the subject, Maggie said, "You were telling me you saw a trial today. You think some poor man got convicted of something he didn't do?"

"Yeah, it's something that bothers me, but you don't want to hear about work."

"I do. It's so much more fascinating than sitting at home arguing with my parents."

"Are you interested, really?" Jack asked.

"Yes! I wish I'd studied to be a reporter. It sounds so much more exciting than anything I'll ever do."

"Much of the time, it's routine."

"Everybody says that about their own jobs," Maggie said. "I want to do something interesting before… before it's too late."

"I thought women wanted security and someone to keep them in money," Jack said, only half joking.

"They do, or at least a lot of women do, but I'd rather be like Amelia Earhart, flying off to the South Pacific or somewhere. Or like the nurses who were so close to the front lines in the war."

Jack eyed Maggie with amazement and concern. "Earhart disappeared two years ago. You've got to figure she's dead."

124

"Oh, I know, and I don't have a death wish. It's all so impractical. Besides, I'm sure if you spoke with Miss Earhart when she was flying around the world, she would have said a lot of what she did was boring. But can you imagine being able to fly off to somewhere exotic?"

"It sounds wonderful," Jack said, drinking Maggie in with his eyes.

"If I were a reporter, I could meet lots of fascinating people and see lots of interesting things."

"You make reporting sound thrilling."

"More thrilling than being a secretary and taking dictation and typing all day."

"Point taken," Jack said. He realized he was so in awe of Maggie that everything he could think to say sounded dull-witted.

"So, tell me about this case," Maggie said. "I want to hear all about it."

"The man's name is Two Penny Smith, and no I don't know how he got that name."

"See, that's why I should be a reporter. I would have found out."

Jack laughed. "Yes, I'm sure you would have."

"What did they arrest him for?"

"They said he talked to two white women coming out of the Liberty Theatre, said lewd things to them, and frightened them."

Maggie arched her eyebrows. "You don't think that's what happened?"

"His family says he was working then. And besides, they say he's very respectful of white folks, that he would never have done something like that."

"Where does he work?" Maggie took a sip of her drink.

"He works—or I guess, worked—at Greta's," Jack said. "It's

a… well, it's a bar and…"

"Oh, for God's sake," Maggie said, "I'm not a child. It's a brothel."

"Maggie, I think I'm in love with you."

"And you buried the lead."

"His family," Jack said, "claims the two women who testified against him work at Greta's too. The whole thing was a setup. Two Penny saw something or someone at Greta's he wasn't supposed to see."

"How do you investigate something like that?"

Jack shrugged his shoulders. "You find someone willing to talk."

Maggie removed first one earring then the other and rubbed her ear lobes. "Okay, I'll play along. How do you find someone willing to talk?"

"That's where shoe leather comes in."

Maggie took another sip from her drink and waited for Jack to elaborate.

"What's got under my skin about this is…" Jack hesitated and nodded at two reporters from the *Trib* as they passed by. "If some white guy said something rude to two women coming out of the movie, I can't imagine the police would have made an arrest."

Jack took a drink from his beer.

"And even if I'm wrong about that, there's no way a judge would sentence a white man to ninety days in jail for something like this—and complain he couldn't sentence him to more. It stinks."

Maggie thought for a moment. "Have you talked with the person who was in the ticket window the night the cops arrested him?"

"No, but that's a crackerjack idea," Jack said. "Let's get something to eat and then go the movies. We can talk to the person in the ticket window while we're there."

***

At the Liberty Theatre, Jack and Maggie waited while two other couples purchased tickets. Jack wanted to question the man in the ticket booth without a line behind him.

The feature film was *The Night Hawk* with Bob Livingston as a reporter. "Do you really want to see this movie?" Jack asked while they waited. "It's from last year, and it's –"

"Have you seen it?" Maggie asked. Her smile suggested she was teasing Jack. "You saw it with someone else, didn't you?"

"No, I haven't seen it, but it sounds silly, and it's from last year. I was thinking we could talk with the ticket guy, and then we could walk up the street to the L.B. Wilson."

"If you haven't seen it, why does it matter if it's from last year?"

"I guess it doesn't, but the Wilson has *Each Dawn I Die* with Cagney and George Raft."

"He's free," Maggie said, pointing to the man in the ticket booth.

Jack stepped up. The man in the booth was tall and blonde and had blue eyes under mounds of snowy white eyebrows. "I was wondering," Jack asked, "if you were working here last week?"

"You betcha. Every night—well, except Tuesday. That's my night off."

"I was hoping to talk to whoever was working the ticket booth last Tuesday."

"That'd be Carson. He covers for me when I'm off."

"He's not working tonight by any chance?"

"Not here."

"I see," Jack said. "Is Carson working somewhere else to-night?"

"Yah."

Jack could feel himself growing impatient.

Maggie stepped next to Jack. She turned her smile on the man. "You're from Minnesota, aren't you?"

"Yes, ma'am. The way I talk gives me away every time."

"There was a girl at my college from a small town in Minnesota. They said she was sweet as Minnesota spring corn."

"You want to know where Carson's working, don't you?"

Maggie beamed at the man.

"He's in the ticket booth right up the street, at the L.B. Wilson."

"And his name is Carson?"

"Kit Carson, like in all them dime novels."

"You've been very helpful," Maggie said. "Thank you so much."

"You don't want tickets?"

"I think we need to talk to Mr. Carson first," Maggie said. "Besides, I think I'd rather see the movie at the Wilson." She glanced at Jack. "He wanted to see this movie, but I don't know why."

Jack shook his head.

"I've seen 'em both, ma'am, and I'd have to agree with you. Course, I guess that's just a matter of taste."

Jack slid a quarter through the opening in the window. "Buy yourself some popcorn."

"That was fun," Maggie said as they hurried the two blocks up Madison Avenue to the J.B. Wilson.

"Do you want to question this Carson guy?" Jack asked.

"Is it all right if I do?"

"Go ahead –"

"Mr. Carson?" Maggie asked when they reached the Wilson's

ticket booth.

"Yes, ma'am."

"My name is Maggie Hanover, and this is Jack O'Brien. We're working on a story for the *Tribune*."

"Pleased to meet you," Carson said without taking his eyes off Maggie's chest.

"Your friend down the street at the Liberty told us you covered for him last week, Tuesday night, when he was off."

"Reckon that's right."

Maggie rewarded him with a small smile. "We're interested in something that happened just after the movie let out. Were you still in the booth then?"

"No, ma'am," Carson said. "The ticket booth shuts down about twenty minutes after the main feature starts."

Maggie was crestfallen. "So, you wouldn't have seen anything that happened outside, as people were leaving?"

"No, ma'am. But Sven might have. I wasn't feeling well, and he came to drive me home. He was outside waiting for me."

"Your friend's name is Sven?"

"Yes, ma'am, he's the fellow in the ticket booth at the Liberty. I reckon it was him that sent you up here."

Maggie thanked the man.

Jack was grinning ear-to-ear.

"Shall we talk to Sven?" Maggie asked.

"In for an öre, in for a Krona."

When she and Jack reached the Liberty again, Maggie asked the man in the ticket booth, "You're Sven?"

"You betcha. Change your mind about which movie you want to see?"

"Maybe. Mr. Carson says he wasn't feeling well last Tuesday

night, and you were waiting for him when the movie let out."

"Ya, you betcha."

"Did you see a colored man bothering two women as they were leaving the movie?"

Sven scratched his chin. "No, ma'am, sorry, can't say I did."

"Two policemen came and arrested the colored man," Maggie said.

"Gosh, no, didn't see anything like that."

"Were you standing where you would have been able to see something like that if it had happened?"

"No, ma'am. I wasn't standing anywhere. I was sitting in my car. But I parked right in front, so if there was a disturbance and the cops came, I would have seen it. But by golly, I saw nothing like that. Are you sure this was last Tuesday?"

Maggie looked at Jack.

"Sven, you've been a tremendous help," Jack said. "What time did Mr. Carson come out and you two leave?"

"Wasn't till almost eleven. Carson was supposed to be out sooner, but he was busy being sick. He was awful green around the gills when he came out."

Jack pulled out his notebook. "Sven, can I have your last name?"

"Swenson."

"Sven Swenson?"

"Yah."

Jack got Sven's address and phone number.

Sven glanced at the clock inside the booth. "I can sell you tickets," he said, "but the movie has already started. You'd be better off going back to the Wilson. The movie there hasn't started yet."

"Thanks again," Jack said.

"You betcha," Sven said. "Nice to meet you and the lady."

As they hurried back to the J.B. Wilson, Maggie asked, "Is this what you meant by shoe leather?"

"You betcha," Jack said.

"Be glad you don't have to do this in high heels."

CHAPTER 14, WEDNESDAY, AUGUST 2

CORRUPTION

And Graft Going

Judge Northcutt Avers
In Bromley Speech.
The Cincinnati Enquirer,
Kentucky Edition
August 2, 1939

After his morning courthouse rounds, Jack turned his attention to why someone had gone to the trouble of having Two Penny Smith arrested. The women who testified against Two Penny seemed as good a place to start as any. He found their names and addresses in his notes and checked the phone book. There were no listings for either woman.

Jack stood and walked to the large city map hung on the back wall of the newsroom. Using the map's index, he located the streets the women had given, but neither street had house numbers that ran as high as the numbers they gave.

Returning to his desk, Jack called the office of the County Property Assessor, the office that kept track of property values in the county and assessed taxes accordingly. The clerk checked and assured Jack there were no residential buildings—or any other buildings—at those addresses. There simply were no such street addresses.

Joshua Rumble, the long-time managing editor, bellowed Jack's name. Jack looked up and saw Rumble, an unlit cigar clutched between the forefinger and middle finger of his right hand, standing at the door to his office.

"Yes, sir!" Jack called out, but his mind lingered on the fictitious addresses the women had given.

"I don't have all day, Mr. O'Brien," Rumble said. "Get that lazy Irish ass of yours over here before I forget why I hired you."

Jack had heard Rumble summon pretty much every reporter in the newsroom with the same delicate approach. He hurried to his office.

Rumble asked, "You read German?"

"Yes, sir. Some." Jack put that on his resume but was surprised Rumble had read his resume, let alone remembered that detail.

"You took German in college?"

"Yes, sir, but I learned to speak German when I was a child. My father was the European sales manager for his company, and we lived in Zurich and later Berlin. My father insisted I learn to speak German."

"Then read that," Rumble said, handing Jack a letter a couple pages long.

Jack flashed a smile and said, "Yes, sir." He loved the old man's gruff style.

Rumble returned to the swivel chair behind his desk. He kept the unlit cigar between his fingers.

Jack scanned the letter briefly and read aloud in German. "*Sehr geehrter Redakteur: Ich schreibe, um die günstige Berichterstattung zu protestieren —*"

"Very funny," Rumble said. "Maybe I should take you off the news and put you in the funny pages."

Jack grinned. "Would you like me to translate?"

"If it's not too much trouble." Rumble leaned forward, his body language suggesting he had a mind to throttle Jack.

"Dear Editor," Jack translated, "I write to protest the favorable coverage your newspaper has been giving Chancellor Adolf Hitler and his brutal regime –"

"Propaganda!" Rumble interrupted, pointing his cigar at Jack. "Why are you wasting my time with that rubbish? You know I got a newspaper to run. Get out of here!"

With a big grin on his face, Jack stepped out of the editor's office, and then he hurried to get out of the newsroom before he drew a drudgery assignment.

***

Jack headed to the jail. On arriving, he presented himself to the guards at the front desk. He reminded them that he was a reporter for the *Trib*. The jailors remembered him. They wanted to know if he had any more Jim Beam.

"No, but if you're good, maybe at Christmas."

"And if we're bad?" a jailer who went by "Slim" asked.

"You'll be on the front page. I'll tell all our readers how you take advantage of rookie reporters."

"Have a seat, hot shot," the front desk man instructed Jack. "Slim will find your man and get you set up."

As directed, Jack took a seat. When summoned, he followed Slim to the prisoner interview room. Two Penny Smith was already there. He was in chains and looked confused and frightened.

"Mr. Smith, my name is Jack O'Brien. I'm a reporter with the *Tribune*." Jack sat down, pulled his notebook from his pocket, and laid it on the table. "How are you doing?"

"Tolable."

"I was in the courtroom for your trial."

Smith looked down and raised his shoulders almost as if he were trying to pull his head inside his torso.

"After the trial, I spoke with your wife and with Mr. Cook, the NAACP attorney. And your kids."

"Then, what you want to talk to me for?" Smith asked.

"I'm thinking about doing a story about your case, and—"

"Now why y'all want to go and do something like that?"

"I cover the courthouse, and it's my job to write about trials and things that go on in the courthouse."

"But why *my* trial? Nobody care if some colored gets locked up for something."

"I care," Jack said.

"Well, I care about my family, and I'm afraid if you stir things up and everything, something bad might happen to them."

"Has someone threatened you?"

Smith stood. "You fixin' to get somebody killed askin' questions like that."

Jack stood as well, reached his arm out, and put it on Smith's shoulder. "Mr. Smith, I'm sorry. I think we got off on the wrong foot. You're worried that if I write a story claiming somebody railroaded you, someone might take offense and do something to you or your family."

Smith hunched his shoulders and looked down, avoiding eye contact.

"I don't want that to happen to you or your wife, or your kids," Jack said. "And by the way, those are two fine kids you've got."

"Uh, huh," Smith said, not making eye contact.

"But I'll be writing my story one way or the other, so I'd appreciate it if you could answer a few questions and help me understand what you'd rather I not say, so I don't cause you or your family any undue concern."

Smith looked up, directly at Jack. "Don't be shining me on."

Jack sat back down. "Please, Mr. Smith, help me out. My editor's expecting a story, and frankly, if I don't write something about your case, I'm afraid your wife just might beat knots on my head."

Smith remained standing, untrusting.

"But that doesn't mean I need to write my story in a way that puts you in a bad place."

"Already in a bad place," Smith said.

"Yes, you are," Jack said. He picked up his notebook and turned to the first empty page. "Let's just talk about something safe, okay? Like where you're from?"

Smith sighed and sat down. "From Harlan County. My folks moved up here when I was about ten or eleven."

"I worked in Harlan County last year," Jack said. "My first job as a reporter was with the *Harlan Gazette*."

Smith folded his arms and said nothing.

"How far did you get in school?"

"Not very."

"Your son, Willis. Did he graduate from high school?"

"Yes, but please, Mr. O'Brien, just leave my kids out of this."

Jack studied the man. He looked beaten down and afraid. "Sure thing. I won't mention them in my article. You have my word on it."

"Then, why don't you call me 'Two Penny.' Everybody does."

"If you'll call me 'Jack'?"

Smith hesitated. "Yes, sir, Mr. Jack."

"Why don't we move on to something else? When and where did the police arrest you?"

"Don't suppose that'd do any harm," Two Penny said. "They came and got me at my home."

"When?"

"Middle of the afternoon."

"That was Wednesday, July 26?"

"I know it was a Wednesday," Two Penny said, "but don't remember the date and everything."

"They arrested you, took you to booking, and then they brought you here?"

"Yes, sir, they sure did."

Jack studied Two Penny. "What I'm getting at is— Did they take you straight to booking and then here?"

"That be about it."

"According to the records here, they showed up here at the jail at 3:05 p.m. Does that sound about right?"

For a moment, Two Penny closed his eyes, as if in concentration or embarrassment. "Yes, sir."

"You worked the night before?" Jack asked, careful not to mention *where*.

Two Penny considered the question before saying, "Yes, sir."

"Those women who testified against you, they said you bothered them about ten o'clock, while they were coming out of the movie show."

"That be what they said, but don't ask me why."

"Fair enough. Truth is, you were at work then, right?"

Two Penny nodded. "Yes, sir. And they were too."

Jack tapped his pen on the notebook. "At the trial, it sounded like you knew the women who testified against you." Jack wondered if Two Penny would answer.

"Of course, I do. Said so too."

"Yes, you did," Jack said. "That's a fact. No getting around facts."

Two Penny gave Jack a long, sad look, but said nothing.

It occurred to Jack that maybe the impossibility of getting around facts may not have been this man's experience. *Maybe if you were colored, you saw white folks getting around facts with some frequency.*

"You know Miss April and Miss May, cause you all work at the same place?"

"Uh huh, but you ain't going to put that in the paper, now are you?"

"Don't know yet," Jack said. "Before I could put something like that in the paper, I'd need corroboration. In other words, even if you wanted me to, and I know you don't, I couldn't put something like that in the paper based on what just one person says. I'd have to have a second person tell me that too. Or some other evidence."

Two Penny looked confused by the explanation but said nothing.

"Why do you think," Jack asked, "they testified that you pestered them in front of the movie place?

"Don't rightly know and wouldn't be saying nothin' about that if I did."

Jack decided to change the subject. "In addition to your regular job, you also do yard work and errands for Mr. Boyle and his wife?

"Yes, sir, I sure do."

"Does Mrs. Boyle treat you right?"

"Yes, sir, she treats me just fine."

"I want to call and talk to her, but I don't know her name," Jack said. "I mean her first name."

Two Penny folded his arms across his chest.

"Do you know her name?" Jack pressed.

"Mrs. Boyle."

"Do you know her first name?"

"Uh huh."

Jack smiled. "I can have the librarian at the newspaper look it up. I was just hoping you could save me the trouble."

"She be Agnes, but that ain't gonna help you none."

"If you mean she won't talk to me, you're probably right, but people surprise me all the time. I don't see any harm in my giving her a call or stopping by and seeing her. Do you?"

"Won't do you no good."

Jack raised his eyebrows. "Why do you say that?"

"Because she moved out and everything."

"She did?"

"Yes, sir, but you didn't hear that from me. Lordy! If you go telling people I told you that, I'd be up to my eyeballs in trouble and everything."

"When did she move out?" Jack asked.

"The weekend before they arrested me."

"Do you know why she moved out?"

"Ain't none of my business."

"Off the record, sir, just between us. Was Vice Mayor Harry Boyle a customer at Greta's?"

"If my wife told you that, she had no business saying that. Lordy, Lordy, she gonna get me in a bad way." Two Penny glanced around the tiny room.

"I understand. Again, not for publication, but just between you and me, so I understand what's what, okay? Was Mr. Boyle mad at you because he thinks you told his wife about him visiting Greta's?"

Two Penny leaned forward.

Jack leaned forward as well, so Two Penny could whisper his response.

"Just between you and me, and everything?" Two Penny said in a barely audible voice.

"Yes, sir. You have my word on it."

"Well then, just between you and me," Two Penny said, "what the Mayor thinks ain't none of your business."

Two Penny stood and called for the guard.

**

At police headquarters, Jack bantered with Sergeant Hayman, the usually cooperative policeman in charge of the police department's records.

Hayman got Jack the arrest report for Two Penny Smith. The report confirmed what Jack had heard in court. It documented that two Covington police officers arrested Two Penny Smith in front of the Liberty at 10:23 p.m. on Tuesday, July 25, 1939. It listed the two improbably named witnesses, April Bedwell and May Goodnight, the time of the arrest, the names of the police officers, and the gist of the complaint. Jack made careful notes.

When he finished with the arrest report, Jack requested to see the forms completed during the booking process. Sergeant Hayman balked. "I'm busy," he told Jack, "you're going to have to come back later for that."

Jack made a show of looking around the empty room. "How about you just show me the log, so I can see when the arresting officers turned him over?"

"I'm not sure where it is," Sergeant Hayman said.

"It's on that desk right behind you." Jack pointed at the logbook.

The policeman hesitated, then picked it up and tossed in on the counter in front of Jack. "*I* didn't let you see that."

Jack turned to the evening of Tuesday, July 25. It didn't show a booking for Two Penny Smith or anyone named Smith. Jack turned the page to the next day. At 2:37 p.m. on the afternoon of Wednesday, July 26, the entry for Two Penny Smith finally appeared.

Jack copied the information into his notebook. "Thanks, Sergeant, you're okay. I appreciate it."

The sergeant took the book back and returned it to the desk

behind him.

"Now," Jack said, "I'd like to see the booking papers."

"We sent them over to the Prosecutor's office," Hayman said, "and haven't got them back."

"Why didn't you just say so?" Jack gave the policeman an understanding look. "Guess I'm done here then." Jack returned his notebook to his jacket pocket and his pen to his shirt pocket. He turned to leave, but after a couple steps toward the door, he stopped and turned back. "Sergeant, may I borrow your phone for a second?"

The policeman buzzed Jack through a gate in the counter and gestured toward the phone.

Jack dialed the Commonwealth Attorney's office and asked for Leo Denton.

"Mr. Denton," Jack said when the prosecutor picked up, "Jack O'Brien from the *Tribune*. I was wondering if you still had the police files on a Mr. Two Penny Smith."

"Sent them back right after the trial," Denton said. "What do you want with them? That was a nothing case."

"I'm new with the *Tribune*, and my managing editor wanted me to check on them and some other files. He thinks you fellows run a loose ship and can't keep track of the paperwork. He thinks a lot of it gets lost."

"Rumble thinks that?"

"I don't know. It may just be hazing, you know, like in the fraternities. But he said not to come back until I saw them and some other files with my own eyes."

"Like I said, I sent them back right after the trial. Talk to Sergeant Hayman in the Police Department's records room."

"I'm calling from there," Jack said, smiling at the sergeant. "The problem is, Sergeant Hayman says you didn't send them back. He didn't come right out and say it, but he implied you'd lose your private parts if they weren't attached."

The police sergeant's face turned an angry red.

"Put him on," Denton said.

Smiling, Jack handed the phone to the police sergeant. "He wants to have a word with you."

The police sergeant took the phone. "Sergeant Hayman here, and I never –."

Hayman listened to whatever the prosecutor said, before responding, "I never said any—"

The prosecutor must have interrupted because Hayman stopped talking.

"Yes, sir, but I was told not to let anybody see—"

Hayman paused again, and said, "But Captain Frazier said–"

The police sergeant held the phone away from his face and asked Jack, "Can you wait until tomorrow?"

"If you don't turn them over now," Jack said, keeping his voice amicable, "I'm going to call the newsroom from that pay booth downstairs and arrange for more reporters and a photographer to join me. Your picture will be on the front page of the *Tribune* tomorrow morning, along with the prosecutor's."

"Did you hear that?" the sergeant said into the phone.

Jack hoped Denton didn't decide to call his bluff.

"Yes, sir," the police sergeant said into the phone, followed in short order by another, "Yes, sir."

Sergeant Hayman hung up the phone and glared at Jack. "He says I should take another look for the files."

"Thank you, Sergeant, I appreciate the extra effort."

Minutes later, Jack was poring through the booking records. Several of the documents confirmed the booking time, but aside from that, he saw nothing of interest. He made a note of the date and time of the booking and Two Penny's age, then returned the papers to the sergeant and thanked him again.

***

Jack asked for an appointment to speak with Police Chief Al Schild, but Schild's office re-routed him to Deputy Police Chief David Rasche. A large man with short hair and a crisp uniform, Rasche appeared to be in his fifties. His office was small but neat. Framed photos showing him with various dignitaries decorated the walls.

"I'm really sorry to bother you with this," Jack said, "but I'm the new guy, and you know how it goes, the new guy always gets stuck with the –"

"With what?" Deputy Police Chief Rasche demanded.

"We got a complaint from some citizens about a couple of your officers," Jack said. "But if I can, Chief, so I can salvage something from this, can you tell me something about yourself? Even if I don't have a story today, like I said, I'm new, and I don't often get a chance to meet people like you, the people that actually run things in this town."

"What do you want to know?" Rasche asked. If Jack's attempt at flattery moved him, he didn't show it.

"You know the drill. How long have you been with the police force, what commendations have you won… the highlights?"

Deputy Police Chief Rasche gave Jack the basics, and Jack pressed for more. He asked the cop, "Anybody ever shoot at you?"

"Couple times, but as you can see, they missed," Rasche said, revealing less than Jack had learned from the *Tribune*'s clippings room.

"Amazing!" Jack gushed. "Have you ever shot anybody?"

"Twice," Deputy Police Chief Rasche said. "Shootouts that didn't end well for the bad guys. Look, I'm sure your paper has articles about all that. What's this all about?"

Jack realized that his effort to flatter the no-nonsense cop

143

wasn't working. "Some church ladies say two policemen hassled some poor guy who was trying to sleep in front of the Salvation Army Store on Madison Avenue."

A look of frustration and impatience spread across the Deputy Police Chief's face. "We can't have hobos sleeping all over the place. If those cops hadn't roosted him, somebody would be complaining about that too."

"Good point, good point," Jack said. "but —"

"And so, would your newspaper."

"See," Jack said, "that's why I wanted to get your perspective. But these ladies say that your men kicked the tar out of this old man—"

Jack could see the police officer's expression change.

"And then," Jack said, "they urinated on him."

"You sure about this?" Rasche said.

"I wasn't there," Jack said, shrugging his shoulders. "But these ladies say their minister had just been telling them about Jesus and the Sermon on the Mount, and how we should feed the hungry—"

"When was this?" Deputy Police Chief Rasche interrupted.

"Couple nights ago," Jack said, flipping through his notes. "Here it is," he said stopping at the page on which he'd written the information from the report of Two Penny's arrest. "It was Tuesday night, July 25, about 10:25 p.m."

"They didn't get the officers' names, did they?"

"Yes, sir," Jack said. "They're talking about having their church hold a prayer vigil there or something."

"Give me the names," Rasche demanded.

"Let's see," Jack said, turning the pages in his notebook forward and then backward. "Here it is. Patrolman Robinson and Patrolman Vance."

"Wait here," Rasche said, rising from his chair.

Jack remained seated.

Ten minutes later Rasche returned. "I just checked," he said. "Robinson and Vance patrol that area, but they work the day shift. They weren't even working that night."

"You're sure?" Jack asked, certain his question would irritate the cop.

"I just told you," Rasche said. "I checked. Are you sure you've got your story straight?"

"I've only got what these women told another reporter," Jack admitted. "Maybe they're confused, or maybe the other reporter got the details wrong."

"I'm going to investigate," Rasche said. "Maybe they got the night wrong, or the names of the patrolmen wrong, or something. And for the record, we take complaints like this seriously. But I want you to hold off on your story until I do some checking."

"Well," Jack equivocated.

"I just don't want you putting something in the paper about two officers who weren't involved—weren't even working then for Chrissake."

"Can I tell these ladies the Police Department is checking into their complaint?"

"Yes, of course, that's what I just said."

"Then, if I turn in a story, I will say those officers weren't even working then," Jack said. He stood and gave Rasche his business card. "Look, it's been terrific meeting you, and I'm really sorry to take up your time with this."

"All part of the job, kid," Deputy Police Chief Rasche said.

***

"Officer Robinson!" Jack called out. He had been hoping to catch patrolmen Ricky Robinson and Dennis Vance at the little Greek chili parlor not far from the Liberty Theatre that was a cop favorite. But as Jack approached, he spotted Robinson leaving and heading away. He called the cop's name again.

The cop pivoted. "Yeah?" Robinson was about forty, with a double chin, a beer belly, and a pugnacious attitude.

"I'm Jack O'Brien, with the *Tribune*." Jack pulled out his notebook. "You're Patrolman Ricky Robinson?"

"Yeah."

"I need to ask you something. It'll only take a moment."

"About what?"

"I covered the trial of a Mr. Two Penny Smith and saw you testify," Jack said. "I wanted to ask you –"

"I said everything I've got to say in court. Now, if you'll excuse me."

"I just wanted to clarify when you made the arrest. Was it Tuesday night, there in front of the movie house?"

"Like I said in court, I arrested that coon right there in front of the Liberty. I thought you said you heard me testify."

"Yes, sir, I did, but the booking report says you arrested him the next day."

"I got nothing to say, and if you're smart, you'll go write about something else."

"Why? Was the arrest a frame up?"

Robinson stepped closer and got in Jack's face. "Listen, kid, you don't know what you're messing with."

"So, tell me," Jack said, refusing to back down. "What am I messing with?"

Robinson gave Jack a little shove—just enough to let Jack know who was in charge. "For someone so stupid, you've got a smart mouth."

"Did Captain Frazier tell you why he wanted Mr. Smith framed?"

"I'm thinking," Robinson said, putting his hand on his baton but not removing it from his belt, "I just might have to arrest you for disturbing the peace and assaulting a police officer."

"If you do, the headline in tomorrow morning's paper will read, 'Cop Arrests Reporter Who Threatened to Reveal Frame Up.'"

Robinson gave Jack a hard shove, sending him sprawling. Robinson laughed, turned, and got in his cruiser.

***

Jack returned to the Police Station and asked the police sergeant at the front desk if he could see Captain Frazier. The sergeant hardly looked up. "Halfway back, on the right."

Jack found Captain Frazier's office and knocked on the door. A voice from inside shouted, "Come in."

Jack opened the office door. "Captain Frazier?"

"Yeah."

"I'm Jack O'Brien. I'm a reporter with the *Tribune*."

"I don't talk to reporters," the police captain said. He was a well-built man in his forties with a dark complexion and a thick mustache.

"I'm writing a story about the arrest of a Mr. Two Penny Smith. I noticed you were in the courtroom during his trial." Jack pulled out his notebook and opened it.

"It's part of my job to monitor how my men handle themselves in court. Beyond that, I've got nothing to say." Frazier leaned back in his chair and folded his hands behind his head.

"When you were in the courtroom monitoring Patrolman Robinson's testimony, were you aware that he was not on duty the night he claims he arrested Two Penny Smith?"

"I don't know what you're talking about."

"Then, let me break it down for you. Robinson and Vance worked the day shift. They weren't on duty when they claim to have arrested Two Penny. My question is: Did you know that?"

Frazier's face colored. He unfolded his hands and leaned forward. "No comment. Now, get out of my office."

"The story I'm writing." Jack bluffed, "is going to say you had patrolmen Robinson and Vance arrest Mr. Smith on trumped-up charges. I thought you would want to comment."

"That's bullshit," Frazier said. "The jury convicted him, so he's guilty, and that's that."

"Did Vice Mayor Boyle want you to arrest this man?"

Frazier clenched his hands into fists. "I've never talked with Boyle in my life, and like I said, I don't talk with reporters. Now, if you'll excuse me, I've got work to do."

"I apologize for the interruption," Jack said. "But if I could, I'd like to ask you one more question."

Frazier glared at Jack.

"Mr. Smith and the women who testified against him all work at Greta's. Did someone from Greta's want Mr. Smith arrested?"

Captain Frazier stood. "If you don't get the hell out of my office, I'm going to have you arrested."

"I'm done," Jack said. "Again, I apologize for the interruption."

"I want you out of my office—"

"I'm leaving, I'm leaving," Jack said. "But would it be alright if I sent the paper's photographer over later this afternoon to get a photo for my story? It won't take but a minute or two, and his photo would look much better than the headshot your press officer will give me."

"I had nothing to do with that arrest," Frazier said. "And God help you if you say I did."

"Everybody in town knows Greta's is a house of prostitution. Why haven't the police arrested anyone there?"

Frazier came around his desk and shoved Jack out of his office. "I need a patrolman," he called out, "to come over here and arrest this man."

"Not necessary," Jack said. "I'm leaving."

***

Jack dug through his desk drawer and found the business card he got from Lincoln Cook, the NAACP attorney from Cleveland. He placed a long-distance call to the attorney.

"Mr. Cook, this is Jack O'Brien from the *Tribune* in Covington. We met with Two Penny Smith's family."

"Yeah, Jack, I remember you. You got something new on his situation?"

"Plenty. The most important thing is, the Deputy Chief of Police just confirmed that the cops who arrested Two Penny work the day shift. They weren't on duty when the say they arrested him. Plus, the department's records confirm that they showed up with him at booking on Wednesday afternoon."

"That's consistent with what Mrs. Smith told us."

"I'm not done investigating, but can I switch gears and ask you about something different."

"What's that?"

"Mr. Cook, do you know anything about a trash collection company in Cleveland called Mayfield Disposal Company?"

"Call me Lincoln or Link."

"Sure."

"Off the record?"

"Yeah, of course. I'm just sniffing around, trying to find a story."

"Then you've got good instincts," Cook said. "Are you familiar with the Mayfield Road Mob?"

"Can't say that I am," Jack said.

"It's the group that runs things in Cleveland for the Syndicate. Frank Milano ran it until he skipped the country to avoid the feds. Alfred 'Owl' Polizzi took over and runs it now."

Jack jotted that in his notebook and made a note to check to see if the paper's librarian could dig up anything on the Mayfield Road Gang or Polizzi.

"On paper, Polizzi's cousin, Shorty Polizzi, owns The Mayfield Disposal Company," Cook said, "but everybody assumes Owl Polizzi actually owns it."

"The City of Covington," Jack said, "has used the same company for trash collection for years. It's a local company, cheap, and gets the job done. The city has to put the contract out for bid every few years, and this year, the local company is the low bidder, but the City Commission is acting like it's looking for an excuse to give the contract to the Cleveland company."

"I know."

Cook's response surprised Jack. "You do?"

"Yeah," Cook said. "Covington Waste employs a lot of my people. They're afraid if Mayfield gets the contract, they'll be out of work."

"Won't the new company have to hire local people to do the work?"

"Yes, but Mayfield won't hire colored people."

"What else do I need to know?" Jack asked, tossing out the wrap-up question every experienced interviewer ends with.

"Mayfield plays dirty. It's doing a lot of expansion, and everywhere it goes, there are rumors of bribes, strong-arm tactics, what have you. No one's proven anything yet, but they leave a stink everywhere they go. I'll send you the news clippings I've got."

"Thanks!"

"Listen," Cook said, "do you remember meeting Two Penny's

daughter, Cora?"

"Sure, nice girl."

"I've got some business in Cincinnati in a couple weeks, and I'm coming to town the weekend before. Cora is going to be singing at Blackstone there in Covington on Saturday night. Not this weekend, but next weekend."

"I know where it is," Jack said. It was a colored joint that had a reputation as a hot place for jazz musicians. "I didn't know Cora sang."

"So far, she's only sung in church and school. This is her debut. I was wondering if you would be interested in joining me there?"

"Sure." Jack didn't know if he'd be welcome in a colored joint but figured the best way to find out was to show up and see what happened. He worked out the logistical details with the NAACP attorney.

"Jack," Cook said, "about Mayfield. I hope you poke around and see what you can find out, but if you do, watch your back. These people are dangerous."

***

After dinner, Jack walked the half-dozen blocks from the boardinghouse where he was staying to the 11th Street neighborhood where Mrs. Smith and her family lived. It was early evening, but it was still warm and humid, and he could feel his shirt cling to his skin. When he reached the building, he had no trouble finding Mrs. Smith. She was sitting on the front step talking with a neighbor.

"Mrs. Smith, do you remember me? I'm –"

"I remember you," Mrs. Smith interrupted, "but I ain't seen nothing in the newspaper 'bout what they did to my husband."

"That's why I'm here, ma'am," Jack said. "I wanted to let you know that I'm still working on it. And I'm trying to do it in a way where the consequences will be on the newspaper and on me, and not on you or your husband."

"Humph!" Mrs. Smith said. She crossed her arms over her chest.

Jack smiled. When St. Peter announced her fate at the Pearly Gates, Jack was sure Mrs. Smith would give the same suspicious reply.

The neighbor lady had not moved away.

"Excuse my manners," Jack said to the woman. "My name is Jack O'Brien. I'm a reporter for the *Tribune,* and I'm working on a story about Mr. Smith's arrest. I need to speak with Mrs. Smith."

"And I'm Mabel," the neighbor woman said. "I live right next door."

The woman hadn't taken the hint and left, but Mrs. Smith didn't seem bothered by her presence. Jack took a deep breath and turned his attention back to Mrs. Smith. "I need to confirm something. When was your husband arrested? The timing is important."

"It was in the afternoon, but I weren't here. I was working."

"Wednesday afternoon?" Jack clarified.

"Mabel," Mrs. Smith asked, "did you see when the police came and got Two Penny?"

"I sure did," Mabel said. "The whole neighborhood did."

"What time was that, if you recall?" Jack asked.

"It was after lunch sometime, can't say for certain."

"Around one-thirty?"

"That be about right," Mabel said, but her attention was elsewhere. "Ebba," she called to a heavyset woman sitting on the front step of the next building. "Come here. You got to help us."

The neighbor lady stood but took her time moving her heavy body.

"She walks so slow," Mabel complained to Jack, "they have to set stakes to see if she's movin'."

152

"What you need?" Ebba asked when she'd closed half the distance.

"This here's the reporter that's fixin' to write about Two Penny. He wants to know what time it was when they came and arrested him."

"It was after lunch, say 'bout 1:30, I guess, but Velma would know, 'cause she got that watch she's always showing off."

Mabel reached out and snared a youngster who happened to be running past. Jack immediately thought of a shortstop grabbing a ground ball.

"I need you to go get your Momma," she told the kid.

"I'm —"

"Don't be giving me that," Mabel said firmly, twisting the kid's ear. "Now, go get your Momma for us. This here's a newspaper reporter, and he ain't got no time for your foolishness."

"Yes, ma'am." The kid sounded put upon, like a chained dog unable to chase a squirrel.

Mabel let the youngster go, but warned him, "No dilly dallying, you hear?"

The kid was running and chose not to answer.

"You wait right here," Mabel commanded Jack. "I be right back." With that, she charged across the narrow street, coming to a stop at the front step of the apartment building opposite the one in which Mrs. Smith lived.

"Itty!" Mabel shouted in the direction of the second-floor window, "Itty, get your itty-bitty ass down here."

A small woman popped her head out of an open window.

"Mabel, that you? What you hollerin' about?"

"We need you down here," Mabel shouted back. "It's important."

Jack smiled. He'd found the neighborhood busybody. In short

order, a dozen people huddled around him.

"So, to confirm," Jack said to the group, "two policemen came and arrested Two Penny about one-thirty or so on Wednesday?"

The crowd agreed, but one member of the group, an older man with gray hair, had a question for Jack. "What difference does it make when dey arrested him? Dey got him in jail, and now he can't work or support his family. Dat's what's important if you ask me."

"The police say they arrested him the night before, outside the Liberty."

"Bull puckey!" the man said. "Why dey say something stupid like dat?"

"They claim he was disturbing the peace," Jack said, "pestering some white women coming out of the movie."

"If he be pestering white women, dey would'a arrested his sorry ass on the spot," the man said, winning a round of head nods and amens from the group.

"Besides," Ebba interjected, "he works nights. He wouldn't have no occasion to be over there bothering white women."

"That's helpful," Jack said. "Where does he work?"

"Greta's," several people responded, giving Jack a source other than Mrs. Smith for that important fact.

"Greta's?" Jack asked.

"It's that whorehouse over there at Sixth and Philadelphia," the man said. Several people voiced or at least nodded agreement.

"What does he do there?" Jack asked.

"He be the janitor," Mabel said. "Now, what you think," she said, "they be having a colored man do in a place like that? He cleans the toilets and mops the floors and whatnot."

Two Penny's son Willis approached, concern etched in his facial features. As he got close enough to get the gist of the conversation, he pushed himself into the middle. "This here's nobody's business," he said, "except my family's. This reporter wants to do a story that's gonna get Pop killed."

"Ain't your Pop's fault if this reporter does a story about him," Mabel said.

"The men that run Greta's won't like seeing their business in the newspaper," Willis said, his voice strong and firm, a natural leader's voice. "And you know who they gonna blame."

Mabel put her hands on her hips. "But –"

"This is about our family, and we got to decide for ourselves if we want to have this reporter get us killed."

When nobody moved, Willis repeated himself. "Now, everybody, if you'll excuse me. I've got to speak with Mr. O'Brien in private."

Like churchgoers after the free coffee and donuts run out, the neighbors drifted away.

"That means you too, Miss Mabel," Willis said. "I'm sure Mr. O'Brien appreciates your help, but I've got to speak with him in private."

"I knew you when you were knee-high to a grasshopper," Mabel complained. "You used to treat me like I was part of your family. You called me 'Aunt Mabel.' Now, you gonna treat me like I'm some red-haired orphan?"

Willis smiled but refused to yield.

Mabel exhaled noisily and retreated, shaking her head and muttering to herself.

When no one remained but Willis, his mother and Jack, Willis moved to within inches of Jack. "You're going to get someone killed," he said, his voice and posture full of threat. "My Pop, or my mother, or me. Why can't you just leave us alone?"

"I'm trying to figure out why they did this to your father," Jack said, refusing to back down. "And I'm trying to find a way to write this story without making it sound like your father or your mother were my sources."

Willis remained in Jack's face.

"Thanks to this little neighborhood gathering," Jack said, "I can now attribute some things to your neighbors. And just so you know, I've found other people to corroborate some of what your mother told me – including the Deputy Chief of Police."

Willis stared at Jack, then relented. "Sorry, but I ain't never dealt with a situation like this," he said. "This is just another story to you, but it's my family."

"I'd feel the same way," Jack said. "But just so you know, this isn't just another story for me. I think this is the most important story I've ever worked on."

"Baloney! They arrest coloreds all the time for crazy shit they didn't do. What makes this story so important?"

Jack turned the question over in his mind. He needed to decide the answer to that question for himself. He also wanted to give Willis a chance to calm down.

"Reporters should cover every time someone gets railroaded," Jack said, "*especially* if the one getting railroaded isn't white."

Jack searched Willis's face for a reaction but saw only skepticism. Willis, he thought, was his mother's son.

"But your father's story is particularly important to me," Jack said, "because I think I can get it published. And if I do, who knows? Maybe other reporters will realize they don't have to walk away from stories like this."

Willis remained impassive.

"There's another reason," Jack said, "but it's personal."

"I take you getting my Pop killed personal."

"All I can say," Jack said, "is I'm trying to do this in a way so that won't happen."

Willis spit on the sidewalk.

Jack decided to take a different approach. "Can I buy you a beer?"

"They don't let my kind in your bars."

"There's a place on the corner," Jack said, pointing to a neighborhood saloon.

"That place is for coloreds."

"Can I buy you and me a beer there," Jack asked, "without creating trouble for you?"

Willis shrugged his shoulders. "Probably. It's mainly white folks get upset about coloreds and whites mixing."

Jack absorbed what Willis said. "Listen, can I ask you something?"

Willis allowed a smile to show. "From what I've seen so far, I doubt I could stop you even if I wanted to."

Jack smiled back. "Let's go see if I can buy us some beer, and then I'll ask my question."

**

The bar was small and dark, with only a few tables. Cigarette smoke, sweat, and stale beer smells filled the air, but two overhead fans stirred the air and made it marginally cooler than outside. Two men sat at the bar. Jack moved toward one of the tables where the presence of a white man would be less intrusive.

"Tell me what you want to drink," Willis said, "and I'll get it."

"Whatever they have on draft and get yourself whatever you want." Jack pulled a couple bills out of his wallet and handed them to Willis. "And some pretzels. On me."

Willis took the money and returned shortly with two beers and a bowl of pretzels.

"You said you wanted to ask me something," Willis said. "Go ahead, as long as it doesn't have anything to do with my father's situation."

"Thanks," Jack said. "I was talking this afternoon with Mr. Cook, the NAACP attorney."

Willis squinted at Jack. "About my Pop?"

"About something else."

Willis hadn't touched his beer. He folded his arms and leaned back in his chair.

"When we were wrapping up, he told me that your sister is a singer. He said she's going to be making her first professional appearance next weekend at Blackstone."

Willis grinned. "That's right." His face beamed with pride.

"He wants me to go with him to see her sing."

"Uh, huh."

"Here's my question," Jack said. "If I go, am I going to be welcome? I don't want to do anything that will take away from your sister's big moment."

"You want to know if you're going to get yourself killed going into a colored joint?"

"I want to know if I'd be going where I'm not welcome," Jack said. "I don't want to show up where I'm not welcome and ruin things for your sister."

"If they know you're a reporter doing a story about Cora," Willis said, "you should be fine."

"Good," Jack said.

"Of course, *you* just might find a way to get yourself killed," Willis said, smiling.

Jack laughed. "I'm sure this is big deal for Cora, and I'm happy for her, but –" Jack hesitated and chose his words with care. "But she's young. Late nights and bars can be hard on the soul. Wouldn't it have been better to wait till she's at least out of school?"

"With Pop in jail, Mom needs the money. The landlord was threatening to put her and Cora out on the curb. Ma told Cora she'd have to get a job. Cora would rather sing, which is what she's always wanted to do, than get a job somewhere as a maid or waitress."

"What's your story?" Jack asked. "You sing? Play music?"

"Nah, my sister got all the talent."

"So, what do you do?" Jack asked. "You have a job?"

"I work for the Covington Waste Company. I'm a garbage collector."

Jack sensed that Willis was watching his reaction, expecting a snide remark or worse, something patronizing. "Are you worried," Jack asked, "about the contract with the City going out to bid?"

"I worry about a lot of things," Willis said, "but not much I can do about something like that. If you're colored and you pick up other people's garbage for a living, nobody cares what your opinion is."

Jack sipped his beer.

Willis ate one of the pretzels and washed it down with a beer chaser. "Do you think there's gonna be another big war?"

"I hope I'm wrong, but yes, I'm afraid so. From everything I've read, including the German press, Hitler's itching for a war."

"As big as the last one?"

Jack shrugged his shoulders. "If I had to guess, I'd say at least as big. What do you think?"

"I don't know about all that, but things sure sound bad from what they say on the radio."

"I'm not saying I want a war," Jack said, "but if there's going to be one, that's a story I want to cover."

"You think we'll get involved like we did the last time?" Willis asked. "Roosevelt don't seem like he wants to get involved."

"Yeah, we'll get involved, but I think it'll be like last time – not right away. In the Great War, President Wilson didn't want to get involved, but eventually, he didn't have much choice."

Willis leaned forward. "If we do get involved, do you think they're gonna want coloreds to fight?"

"My crystal ball is as cloudy as the next person's," Jack said. "But if there's another big war, yeah, I think Uncle Sam is going to want everybody."

Willis shook his head in disgust. "If you white folks want to shoot each other and blow each other up, why can't you just leave coloreds out of it? You don't want nothing to do with us any other time."

Jack smiled and raised his beer as if to toast. "I think you're on to something. If there is a war, I hope this time, your leaders make it clear your people aren't going to go unless there are some major changes in this country."

"If we don't go, they'll just throw our asses in jail."

"Wish I could say you're wrong," Jack said. "But at some point, they'd have to reconsider."

"Humph," Willis said, sounding like his mother.

"But if there is a war and you do end up serving, remember, there *is* a difference this time. It's not just Jews that Mr. Hitler doesn't like. He thinks Aryans—Germans—are a superior race, and everybody else is inferior. If he has his way, it's gonna be real hard on your people. So, if there is a war, you don't want him to win."

"White people are messed up," Willis said. "You know that?"

"Yep," Jack said. "Most days that's what the headline in the newspaper should say: 'White People Still Messed Up'."

For several long moments, both men stared into their beers without saying anything, only occasionally drinking.

"I talked with Cook about this out-of-town company that's bidding for the garbage collection contract," Jack said. "He tells me that it's mobbed up. He says there are rumors it uses bribes and other shenanigans to get contracts."

"Don't know nothing about that," Willis said.

"If the Mob wanted to get to someone who could make sure they won the trash contract, I can't think of anyone better to get to than Harry Boyle."

"They're all crooked, ain't they?" Willis said, finishing his beer.

Jack finished his own beer and pushed more cash toward Willis. "You want another round?"

"Just one," Willis said. "I got to get up too damn early to be up late drinking."

When Willis returned with the beers, Jack spoke in a lower voice. "No, not all politicians are crooked. Covington's not like Newport, least not yet."

Willis shrugged. "I figure even if that other company wins the new contract, they'll still need someone to do the work."

"That's the thing," Jack said. "Cook says this Cleveland company refuses to hire colored people."

"Man, you ain't nothing but rotten news."

"Hear me out," Jack said. "Greta's, that place where your Dad works, it's mobbed up, isn't it?"

"Pop don't talk about it much, but I've heard him say that there's always some of those men there in their fancy suits strutting around. He just tries to mind his own business."

"If Harry Boyle's hanging around Greta's, then the Mob has already got to him, and you and the other colored people who work for Covington Waste are screwed."

"Shit, man," Willis said. "Remind me never to drink with you again. You're downright depressing."

"Sorry, I guess it comes with what I do. Most news these days seems to be depressing."

"I hope you're wrong about the mob getting to Boyle," Willis said. "He and his Missus always treated my father okay. But if they've got to him, there ain't nothing I can do about it."

"Maybe not, but I can—if I can get evidence that Boyle's a customer there. If I can get –"

"Un-unh," Willis said, leaning back in his chair.

"What?" Jack asked, then realized with chagrin he'd just given the impression he wanted Willis or his father to provide that information.

"If I tell you something," Willis said, "will you promise not to put it in your story?"

"You can tell me something off the record, sure, but if I can get the same thing from someone else, I'll print it."

Willis thought that over. "Okay," he said. "After they arrested Pop, one of the Syndicate men visited Pop and told him to keep his mouth shut about where he works and anything he's seen there. This guy told Pop if he did that, he'd have a job when he got out. Maybe not at Greta's, maybe at some other joint, but they'd see that he landed on his feet."

Jack nodded to show he was following what Willis was saying.

"But they told Pop that if he starts talking about where he works or about anything he's seen or heard there, it would go bad for him. And they made a point of telling him they know where his family lives."

Jack nodded. "Did they tell him why they were setting him up?"

"No, just that he had pissed off someone, and now he had to take his medicine."

"I figured it was something like that. But I wasn't thinking of asking your father to put his neck out. What I was going to say is that I need to figure out a way to find out when Boyle is at Greta's and then get a photo of him leaving. Pulling up his zipper so to speak."

"Can't help you with that," Willis said. "But even if somehow you figured out a way to do that, they wouldn't let you and your photographer take a bow and walk away with that photo."

"There's got to be a way," Jack said, as much to himself as to Willis.

"You seem like good people," Willis said. "But you're gonna get somebody killed. Probably yourself."

Jack laughed. "You're not the first person to tell me that."

CHAPTER 15, THURSDAY, AUGUST 3

CLEW TO PARTY FATE IS SEEN
IN KENTUCKY PRIMARY VOTE

Conservative, New Deal Eyes Scan Outcome
The Kentucky Post, August 3, 1939

Jack arrived at the newsroom early, picked up a copy of that morning's *Tribune*, and spread it across his desk. He read the international and national news first, but finished disappointed, as he did every morning. He wished the *Tribune* and the other local papers devoted more coverage to the events unfolding in Europe, China, and Japan.

On the local scene, the *Tribune* reported that the Covington City Commission delayed awarding the city's trash collection contract to resolve complaints about the low bidder, Covington Waste Company.

Joe Dinklehaus covered the City Commission meeting. He reported that the Commissioners expressed concern about rumors that Silas Hamlin, the owner of Covington Waste, had put up the money for the black couple to purchase a house in the Austinburg neighborhood. Commissioners debated rumors that Hamlin was encouraging his workers, many of them colored, to buy into other white neighborhoods.

More specifically, Dinklehaus reported, the Commissioners worried about a voter backlash if they awarded the contract to the company and put off a decision to allow the City Manager and City Solicitor to investigate.

In his article, Dinklehaus explained that a larger company from Cleveland also submitted a bid, but the local company's bid was significantly lower. Everything else being equal, the local company would hang onto the contract. Some Commissioners had privately expressed concerns about renewing its contract.

Jack got a cup of coffee and on his way back to his own desk, stopped at his colleague's desk.

Joe Dinklehaus was middle-aged and medium height and build, but otherwise unremarkable. From what Jack had seen, Dinklehaus had two suits, one gray and the other brown. Neither suit was new, but neither was so old as to draw comment. He had one pair of leather shoes, which he shined himself.

"Joe, nice piece this morning on the trash collection contract," Jack said.

"Thanks," Dinklehaus responded. "We can't all chase naked preachers."

"What do you know about that Cleveland company?"

"Just what's in my piece," Dinklehaus said. "Why, hotshot? You bored with the courthouse already? You want to horn in on my beat some more?"

"Joe, how long have you been reporting on City Hall?"

"When I got this beat," Dinklehaus said, "the girls in your grade-school class were making fun of you." Dinklehaus put the little finger of his right hand into his ear and moved it around. He pulled it out and looked at it as if inspecting it for wax. Jack didn't think the guy was even aware of the gesture.

"Given that," Jack said, "what are the chances a rookie reporter like me could scoop you on something going on in City Hall?"

"Slim and none," Dinklehaus said, "and Slim just left town."

"Then, I guess you don't have anything to worry about, do you?"

"Who said I was worried?"

"You said Slim left town," Jack said, wondering what made Dinklehaus think that shopworn line could still be funny. "Did your wife go with him?"

"No such luck. Now beat it, kid. I've got work to do."

The exchange hadn't gone the way Jack had hoped. He made a mental note to try harder to get on the good side of the hack… *if he could find his good side.*

***

Scrivener's Bar and Grill was an old-fashioned place. Large circular fans hung from the ceiling and framed photographs of celebrities, many local, decorated the walls. Years of wear, dirt, and spilled beer had stained the hardwood floors black. The air was thick with cigarette smoke, rumors, and laughter.

It was a favorite hangout for reporters from the local newspapers and the local radio station, WCKY. Jack didn't want to be a regular, but he liked to go there often enough to make friends and contacts and soak up the prevailing wisdom from the older hands.

Today, Jack had arranged to have lunch with Max Seeger, the veteran reporter who covered politics statewide. Max was gregarious and fun. He was also a superb journalist. Two months earlier, Max had snagged a statewide award for his investigative reports on WPA leaders downstate using workers to support the Democratic ticket during the previous year's Congressional and Senate campaigns.

Max spent much of his time in Frankfort. Even so, Jack believed Max was someone he should get to know. If he was going to get serious about his career, he needed to learn from someone like Max.

As he and Max waited for their lunches to arrive, other reporters and local pols made a point of stopping by to say "hi." Each wanted to get Max's insight on the gubernatorial race. The Democratic primary pitted the sitting Lieutenant Governor, Keen Johnson, against former Congressman John Young Brown. The primary was on Saturday. Kentucky was solidly Democratic, so whoever won the party's nomination would be the almost-certain winner in November.

Max bantered easily with all comers but was noncommittal on who he thought would win. Governor A. B. "Happy" Chandler was backing his Lt. Governor in the primary, but that had less to do with loyalty to Keen Johnson than animosity toward Johnson's opponent.

John Y. Brown was a well-known Lexington trial lawyer. Elected to an odd statewide slot, Brown had served one term in Congress. Brown backed Chandler for Governor and expected Chandler in turn to support his run for re-election to Congress in 1935. Chandler backed his primary opponent instead, leaving Brown out of office and bitter.

But the differences between the two sides went deeper than Brown's feeling of betrayal. Brown and his supporters were New Dealers and open to civil rights measures. Keen Johnson was from the traditional Southern wing of the Democratic Party—fiscally conservative and opposed to any softening on race issues.

L.B. Wilson was one of those to stop by to say "hi" to Max. "L.B." was the well-known local businessman who was co-owner and Executive Vice President of the People's Liberty Bank & Trust Co. He was also the owner of the WCKY radio station and several movie theaters, including the L.B. Wilson and the Liberty.

"Who's going to win," L.B. asked, "Keen or John Y.?"

"Too early to say," Max said.

"Christ Almighty, Max," L.B. said, "you sound like a politician. When will you be able to say? A businessman needs to know who to bet on."

"As soon as they count votes," Max said.

L.B. laughed and continued to make his rounds, meeting and greeting familiar faces as if *he* were a politician.

"You're in town for King Swope's speech?" Jack asked. Swope was the sure-thing candidate for the Republican nomination for Governor, but unlikely to win in November.

"Yeah, I get to hear that gas bag give his stump speech again."

"Say," Jack said, "you've known Rumble a while, right?"

"Yeah, of course."

"What's his thing with the cigars? I almost never see him light up."

Max smiled. "He used to smoke so much, we called him The Little Dragon. Then, he had a bout of double pneumonia that nearly killed him. After that, his doctor and his wife ganged up on him. The doctor told Rumble if he didn't cut back on his smoking, he wouldn't live long enough to retire. His wife put her foot down and said she was going to leave him if he didn't stop. He made her a deal. He promised not to light up until after 4:00 p.m."

"But what's with the unlit cigars?"

"I think he found it easier to cut back on smoking if he still had a cigar handy. It was a crutch. And then it got to be a habit. But I'll tell you this. I was damn glad to be in Frankfort when he first cut back. Think he's cranky now? You should have seen him then."

The waiter delivered their lunches.

"I saw your piece on that preacher you caught with his pants down," Max said. "Outstanding job with that."

"Thanks. That was a hoot."

"So, what are you working on now?"

"Rumble has me assigned to cover the local courts, but it's a bit frustrating. He told me if anything really good comes along, like a murder trial, he'll assign that to the crime reporter."

"Yeah, yeah, that's what Rumble has you covering," Max said. "But you strike me as smart and ambitious. What are you *working* on?"

"I'm following up on something the preacher told me. He was spending time with the wife of our Vice Mayor, Harry Boyle. She was helping him with a fund drive for hungry children here in Covington."

"Uh, huh?"

"He told me that the last time he saw Mrs. Boyle, she was upset that Harry was spending too much time hanging out with mobsters, cooking up God-knows-what. That, and spending too much time at a whorehouse called Greta's."

"Rumor has it," Max said, "if Keen Johnson wins, he'll appoint Boyle to something important in his administration."

"Good to know, thanks," Jack said.

"Sounds like a splendid story. Can you prove any of that?"

"Not yet, but I've learned something strange. The cops arrested the colored guy who takes care of Boyle's yard and does errands for Mrs. Boyle. This guy also works at Greta's as a janitor. That was a week ago, a few days after my article on the preacher. Not sure if that's related, but the timing is interesting."

"Are you looking for my suggestions?"

"Sure."

Max took a bite of his sandwich and grunted approval. Max had ordered a goetta-and-fried egg sandwich.

Jack figured Max was thinking about his response. He used the pause to take a bite of his own sandwich.

"Two things," Max said. "First, I'm not going to steal your story, but you need to be careful who you talk to about this. When you know for sure you've got something, let Rumble know what you're working on. Otherwise, watch who you talk to."

Jack nodded.

"Boyle's running for re-election, isn't he?" Max asked.

"Yeah, but people think he's a lock."

"Has he got an opponent in the primary?"

"A young attorney named Vic Morgan is going after him hard. But Vic's not well known."

"Get to know Vic or his campaign manager, or someone who's close to him. If Boyle is frequenting whorehouses or playing footsie with the Mob, they may be chasing that too."

"I've already talked to Vic. He doesn't know anything, but he thinks the Mob is working with Boyle to throw the city's trash collection contract to a Mob-controlled company. My problem is, Rumble has Joe Dinklehaus assigned to cover City Hall. I don't want to step on his toes."

"So, don't," Max said. "Dance around him. But watch yourself. Joe will raise holy hell if he thinks you're getting onto his turf. And when you're not looking, he'll stab you in the back."

"Thanks, I guess. What do you know about Dinklehaus?"

"He's just your average joe. He's not much of a writer, but what-the-heck, he gives the bums in copyediting a reason to believe their jobs are necessary. His real talent is, he keeps his head down and doesn't give the Big Cheeses heartburn."

Jack re-arranged the napkin holder and salt and pepper shakers. "I'm having trouble making a connection with Joe. You know anything about him personally?"

"Let's see," Max said, turning the question over. "He smokes, about a pack a day, but he's fastidious when it comes to alcohol. Joe only drinks on special occasions or when someone else is buying."

Jack laughed.

"I believe Dinklehaus is registered to vote, but without party affiliation. He thinks that's important to maintain the appearance of journalistic objectivity. He's Protestant, but he's not unfairly biased toward any particular denomination."

Max took a bite of his sandwich and took his time chewing it.

He seemed to be searching his memory for more detail.

"I heard Joe brag once that he attends church regularly, but I think that means every Easter and Christmas. He used to talk about joining the Rotary or the Elks, but never got around to it."

Jack mulled that over. "Nothing obvious there I can use to try to build a relationship with the guy, but thanks."

"Don't mention it," Max said, chuckling. "I'll let you know if I hear anything about Boyle. Meanwhile, keep in touch with that guy you said is running against him."

Max took another bite of his sandwich and another sip of coffee.

Jack started to say something, but Max held up a finger. "If you're not getting anything from his opponent, who else has it in for Boyle?"

"I'll give that some thought," Jack said. His first thought was Silas Hamlin at Covington Waste Company but kept that thought to himself.

"It takes a while to build up your contacts," Max said. "Over time, you'll find people who want to help you or who want to use you to embarrass someone—which can be just as good. They didn't build Rome in a day and all that crap."

Young and in a hurry, Jack bristled at the reminder that success takes time. "So, really," he asked, "who's going to win? Keen Johnson or John Y. Brown?"

"I think it'll be close," Max said, "but if neither makes a mistake, I'd put my money on Keen. People in this state like Roosevelt and his programs, but not if it means giving colored people an even shake. That's why they don't trust John Y."

"I've seen plenty of evidence of that," Jack said, "both downstate and since my return to Covington."

"Too damn many people in this state," Max said, "would rather burn in hell than give up the notion that no matter how lazy or stupid they are, they're still better than colored folk."

Another visitor stopped by to greet Max and ask his opinion on the Governor's race. Jack concentrated on his sandwich and fries while Max bantered with the visitor.

"What about that Hitler fellow?" the visitor asked. "What do you think he's got up his sleeve?"

"He's not on the ballot in Kentucky," Max said, "so I wouldn't know. But you read the papers. What do you think?"

"I'd say it looks like there's going to be a shooting war," the visitor said. "I just hope we stay out of it this time."

Max had his mouth full but nodded.

"Well, you take care now," the visitor said and moved on.

"Who was that?" Jack asked.

"Damned if I know," Max said.

Both men laughed.

***

Jack had serious reservations about discussing what he knew, or could guess, about the arrest of Two Penny Smith with Leo Denton, the Commonwealth Attorney who had prosecuted Two Penny and convinced the jury to convict him. If Denton was crooked, or just incorrigibly racist, doing so would simply be giving him time to hide his tracks.

But he had no choice. He was writing a story that implied Denton had—knowingly or unknowingly—obtained the conviction of a man based on false testimony. He couldn't get an article like that published without giving Denton a chance to comment. If he tried, Rumble—or any editor—would call him on it. Worse still, Rumble would wonder if he knew what he was doing.

When Jack arrived, Denton's secretary was away from her desk, but Denton's door was open. Jack stuck his head in Denton's office and asked if he still had time to see him.

"Sure, come on in and sit down," Denton said. His tone was amicable.

After the usual greetings and banter, Denton asked Jack what prompted his visit.

"I've been digging into the Two Penny Smith matter," Jack said, "and the information I've dug up doesn't seem to square with what I heard in the courtroom."

Denton looked at Jack searchingly. "I remember you calling me about the records on that, but I still don't know why you're interested in that case. There have to be a bunch of cases around here that newspaper readers would rather read about."

"You're probably right," Jack said. "I'm new, and I may be making some rookie mistakes, so I appreciate your letting me ask you about what I found."

"Sure."

Jack didn't see any obvious signs of defensiveness on the part of the prosecutor. That could mean Denton had no reason to believe there was anything amiss with the prosecution. Or, it could mean Denton felt confident he could explain away whatever Jack might have found. Jack wouldn't know for sure until he showed his cards—and maybe not even then.

"I talked with Mr. Smith's family and his neighbors, and they don't believe Mr. Smith did what he was charged with."

"Of course not," Denton said.

"I agree that's not surprising," Jack conceded. "But part of the reason they don't think he did it is that he was working when this incident supposedly occurred."

"Where does he work?" Denton asked, still showing no obvious signs of defensiveness.

"He works as a janitor at Greta's, over at Sixth and Philadelphia."

"I know it," Denton said. "It's a high-class whorehouse, but for some reason, the cops can't find their way to busting the place."

"Right. Smith works there most evenings."

Denton said nothing. He had apparently decided to see where Jack was going with this.

"The police report," Jack said, "indicates that the patrolmen arrested Smith outside the Liberty Theatre about 10:30, just after the evening show let out."

"That's right," Denton said. "So, he couldn't have been at that whorehouse when this took place."

"I talked with Smith's family and neighbors," Jack said. "Neighbors mainly. They say the police actually arrested Smith at his home the next afternoon, about 1:30."

"A bunch of coloreds who didn't testify told you that?" Denton asked. "They could have come into court, taken the oath, and testified if that was true."

Jack ignored Denton's comment. They both knew why that wouldn't happen even if the neighbors had known the police were claiming to have arrested Smith the evening before.

"I checked to see when the arresting officers booked Mr. Smith," Jack said, "and it wasn't the night this incident supposedly occurred. They delivered him to booking the next afternoon, shortly after the neighbors say they arrested Mr. Smith at his home."

Denton had been twirling a pen between his fingers and stopped.

"I checked the jail records," Jack continued, "he arrived at the jail about an hour after the patrolmen brought him to booking."

"That's interesting," Denton said.

Jack took that to mean, *interesting, but not important. Maybe the cops messed up and hadn't arrested Smith at the scene. Maybe someone had chewed them out, and they made the arrest the next day. So, what?*

"So, I talked with Deputy Police Chief Rasche, and he checked and told me that Patrolmen Robinson and Vance weren't on duty the night of the arrest. They work the day shift."

Denton put the pen down. "Robinson was the officer who testified?"

"That's right," Jack said. "I also checked on the two women who testified."

"And?"

"And the home addresses they gave don't exist. They testified they work at the brewery, but Mr. Smith says they actually work at Greta's. I don't have an independent source for that yet."

"You've put some effort into this," Denton said. He picked his pen up again and made some notes on a legal pad. "Anything else?"

"After the cops arrested Two Penny, one of the Syndicate guys from Greta's told him that he'd pissed off someone. He told Two Penny if he kept his mouth shut, they'd have a job waiting for him when he got out, but if he talked, it would go bad for him and for his family. So, Two Penny didn't want to go there."

Denton shook his head. "You don't happen to know who he pissed off, do you?"

"No, but I've got a theory."

"Why am I not surprised? Let's hear it."

Jack pursed his lips. "First, I need to know where you stand in this. Did you know this was a setup?"

"No, Jack, I didn't. I swear."

Jack didn't say anything. He let the accusation hang in the air.

"I try a hundred cases each year," Denton said. "Maybe more. On these small cases, I get the file the day before the trial, maybe two days before if I'm lucky. I can't go out and investigate everything that lands on my desk. I have to trust the cops."

"Mr. Smith is sitting in jail," Jack said, "and his wife doesn't know how she's going to pay the rent. His kids are angry and disillusioned."

"I'm going to investigate this, Jack," Denton said, his face reddening. "I didn't go to law school and work my ass off to get where I am to frame people."

Denton got out of his chair, moved around his desk, and seated himself on the front edge of his desk. "Jack, if you just blew into town, here's something maybe you don't know. Last year, I got a grand jury to indict the Lookout House on forty-five counts, mainly gambling. I also got an injunction against the place."

Jack watched Denton carefully.

Denton spoke in a calm, non-threatening voice. "The only reason the Lookout House is still open is that it's not in Covington. It's in Lookout Heights, and the police there won't serve the papers or enforce the injunction, and the State Police don't have jurisdiction. Well, that and somebody beat the crap out of my witnesses, and they got cold feet."

Jack wondered if Denton had just given him a scoop. "Has that —"

"It's all been in the papers," Denton said, anticipating Jack's question, "including the witness tampering."

Jack decided to trust Denton. He hoped he wouldn't regret it. "I don't know who wanted Smith framed or why, but here's what I do know. Smith worked at Greta's *and* on the side, he did odd jobs for Harry Boyle and his wife."

"Harry Boyle, as in Vice Mayor Harry Boyle?" Denton asked.

"Yes."

"Oh, shit."

Jack flashed Denton a big grin. "Can I use that as your official comment in my story?"

"I'll give you a quote," Denton said. "When are you publishing?"

Jack could see worry lines form on Denton's face. "I haven't written this up, and my editor hasn't seen it, but I'm hoping to get my story in tomorrow morning's paper, Saturday morning's latest."

Denton stood and returned to the chair behind his desk. "Can you wait until I've had a chance to look into this? If you run your story before I can get to the bottom of it, it'll make it that much harder to sort out."

"I don't have everything in place, but as soon as I do, I need to get to get this story out."

"Christ, Jack, it's going to look like I was part of this."

Jack thought a moment. "Here's what I can do," he said. "I can say that you are investigating allegations that the testimony was false. And if you do something concrete that you can share with me before I turn my story in, I'll include that too."

"That helps," Denton said, "but I'm still going to look like the bad guy." Denton hesitated. "There's a grand jury in session. Who, in your judgment, should I drag in front of the grand jury to get the ball rolling?"

The question surprised Jack. "Can you bring in the arresting officers?"

"They'll take the Fifth and refuse to testify." Denton picked up his pen and began twirling it between his fingers again. "I guess I could just follow your footsteps and get the arrest report, booking records, the records from the jail, and bring in the Deputy Chief."

Jack leaned forward. "When I pressed Sergeant Hayman about the booking records, he said something he probably didn't mean to. He said that Captain Frazier told him not to release them."

"That's right," Denton said after a long pause. "Have you talked with Frazier?"

"Yeah, he threatened to have me arrested. Wasn't that Frazier in the courtroom during the trial—sitting in the front row?"

"I know Frazier," Denton said. "That was him."

Jack made a note. "I asked Frazier if he knew, when he heard Robinson testify, that Robinson and Vance weren't working the night shift the night this incident supposedly occurred."

"What did he say?" Denton asked.

Jack smiled. "Like I said, he threatened to arrest me."

"How about the arresting officers?" Denton asked. "Did you talk to them?"

"I talked to Robinson. He knocked me on my ass and told me I didn't know what I was dealing with." Jack smiled. "He threatened to arrest me too."

Denton shook his head. "Maybe you need to work on your people skills."

"Yeah, my people skills—that's the problem."

"If your editor gives your story a green light," Denton asked, "can you give me a heads up?"

"I'll give you a call. But if you come up with something that I can use in the article to show that you're on top of this, let me know."

Denton nodded. "I'll do that, but I can't tell you anything about the grand jury," he said. "At least not on the record."

Jack stood to leave.

"Jack," Denton said, then stopped.

"What?" Jack asked.

"From now on," Denton said, "you don't get to come in here with that baloney about how you're a wet-behind-the-ears rookie reporter looking for help. You've used up that ticket."

"Then, it's true what they say?" Jack said, grinning. "You're only young once?"

CHAPTER 16, FRIDAY, AUGUST 4

LOCAL PRIMARIES FEATURE CLOSE RACES
Two Kenton Races Spark Most Interest
Brown Predicts Sweeping Victory
The Kentucky Post, August 4, 1939

In a light rain, Jack hustled to the Bridge Café and took his usual seat at the table where George Hanover was reading the morning paper. Woody was already there.

Hanover greeted Jack and launched into a lawyer joke. He spoke louder than necessary to make himself heard over the noises of the diner.

Jack suspected Hanover meant the joke for the lawyers sitting at the table to his left but laughed anyway. "That reminds me," he told Hanover, "the brewery came up in a trial I covered this week —"

Dressed as usual in a dark, double-breasted suit, a dark shirt, and white tie, Sal Rizzi slid into the chair next to George and exchanged greetings with Jack and Woody.

Rizzi waved at Emma. He asked Jack, "What's new?"

"I was just telling George," Jack said, "I'm covering the courts for the *Tribune* now, and I was in the Circuit Court earlier this week, covering a routine matter—a Negro man arrested for pestering some white women leaving the Liberty."

Jack hesitated. He wasn't sure that George, who was leafing through the newspaper again, was paying attention.

"Anyway," Jack said, "first one of these women, then the other one, says she works for George."

George Hanover lowered the newspaper. "For me?" His tone conveyed a challenge.

"For Hanover Brewery," Jack corrected himself.

"So, what?"

Emma arrived, handed Sal a cup of coffee and refilled the others' cups. "Whadda ya have, hon?" she asked Sal.

"Same as usual, Emma, scrambled eggs, bacon, and a biscuit."

"One Trifecta. Anything else?"

"Just this coffee."

"How about you?" Emma asked Jack.

Jack ordered the same thing.

"I'll put a rush on it," Emma said and hurried off.

"Speaking of trifectas," Sal said, reaching into his pocket. He pulled out a bulging envelope. He placed it on the table in front of George.

George placed his newspaper over the envelope and ran his finger across the edges of the bills inside it. "Gentlemen," he said, "breakfast is on me this morning."

"Thank you, George," Jack said.

"Tank stew," Woody chimed in.

George slid the envelope into the inside pocket of his suit coat.

"Like I was saying," Jack said, "these women both said they worked at Hanover Brewery, but something seemed, I don't know, not right about their stories. I checked, and they don't live where they said they did—"

"You sure?" George interrupted. "They could live with someone —"

"See, George, like I keep telling you, you would have made a swell newspaper reporter if you weren't so unreasonably opposed to being poor."

George scoffed.

"Thing is, George, the addresses they gave don't exist."

George looked at Jack, his curiosity engaged.

"So, naturally," Jack said, "I was wondering if maybe they didn't work for you."

"What kind of story are you working on?" George asked.

"I don't know if I have a story or not, but these women looked like ladies whose virtue might not be beyond reproach, if you follow my drift, and —"

"Cold beers!" Woody said, smiling as if he'd just made a clever joke.

Jack cautioned himself not to allow the interruptions to get to him. He didn't want to do anything that revealed how important this was to him.

Emma arrived with Jack and Sal's meals.

"Emma," George said, "I'm picking up all four tabs today."

"Sure thing, dear."

Emma bustled off, and Jack tried to pick up the thread again. "If I do find a story," he said, "and other reporters call the brewery, asking what these women do for you –"

A businessman on his way to a nearby table waved and said, "Morning, George."

"Morning, Bill," George said, nodding at the businessman.

"Anyway," Jack said, "I thought maybe you could check and see if these women work for you. That way, if the police or reporters start asking questions, you won't get caught off guard."

George took a drink of his coffee, temporizing.

Jack wrote the names of the two women on a blank page in his notebook, tore the page out, and slid it across the table to George.

Emma returned and asked if anyone wanted anything else. When no one did, she laid the four breakfast tickets on the edge of the table. The total for the four tabs appeared in a bold scrawl on the top ticket. "Y'all take care now," she said and dashed off to her next table. As she did, she brushed the tickets, and they fell on the floor.

Woody bent over and scooped them up. He glanced at each of the tickets and the total. He handed the tickets to George and said, "Automatic hair."

George looked at Woody, then at Jack.

Jack shrugged his shoulders, signaling he too had no idea what Woody was trying to say.

Woody pantomimed writing with a pencil.

Jack slid his pen and notebook in front of Woody.

Woody wrote "$5.97" on a blank page and then put a line through it. Beneath that he wrote, "$4.37."

George looked at the tickets. Emma had written "$5.97" as the total of the four tickets. He turned the ticket over and jotted down the totals from each of the four tabs. He added the four figures and came up with $4.37. He double checked his addition and got the same result.

"Two Dagos," Woody explained.

"Apologies to Sal," Jack said, "but I think he means she added Sal's tab twice."

George checked. Woody was right. "I'll be damned," he said. He rose and went to show Emma the mistake.

"You did that in your head, that fast?" Sal asked.

Woody shrugged.

"You said he was a college professor," Sal said to Jack.

"That's right."

"What kind of professor? What did he teach?"

Even though Sal had asked Jack, Woody tried to answer. "Wombat socialists."

"He taught math and statistics," Jack said.

"Wombat socialists," Woody repeated, nodding in agreement with Jack.

"You still looking for work?" Sal asked Woody.

Woody nodded yes. "Looting forward."

"We could use somebody like you at the store," Sal said.

Jack understood that "store" was a euphemism for the handbook operation where Sal worked.

"But I need to know," Sal said, "that if I vouch for you, you're not going to tell anybody anything about what you see or hear."

Woody nodded, his face solemn.

"Not even Jack."

"Donut hole him," Woody said, struggling and failing to get out the words he wanted to say.

Sal smiled and looked at Jack. "I think he said he don't know you."

"Suits me fine," Jack said smiling. "He can buy his own damn breakfast."

Sal looked back at Woody. "I'm dead serious now. You can't tell nobody nothing."

Woody nodded again. "William Tell," he said. "No bottle, nut hen."

Sal shook his head and laughed.

"I don't think," Jack said, "you need to worry about Woody talking out of school."

"Nobody would understand him if he did," Sal said. Standing up, he said to Woody, "Come with me, and we'll see what the boss says."

George arrived back at the table just as Sal and Woody were leaving.

"Don't ask," Jack said. "You don't want to know."

"Probably not," George agreed. "Listen, I'll have my personnel manager check on those women and call you."

***

The sign outside the bar at 12th and Greenup Streets read "Pug's Stag Bar." The bar was too small to be profitable and had no business being open at that hour in the morning. Woody followed Rizzi in.

Behind the bar stood a short, stout man with a short, wide nose. A white apron wrapped around his beer belly, and a cigarette hung from his lips.

Rizzi nodded at the man. "Morning, Pug."

Pug pushed a button under the counter.

Woody followed Rizzi through a door and a dozen feet down a narrow hallway to another door. Rizzi knocked on the door and stepped back.

Someone behind the door opened a speakeasy window and said, "Who's that with you?"

"Someone I want the boss to meet."

The man said, "Just a minute," and unlocked the door.

Rizzi stepped through the door.

Woody followed.

After another ten feet, they came to another locked door and repeated the process.

When Woody stepped through that door, he could hardly believe his eyes. He was in a very large room. The far wall was almost two stories high and a hundred feet long. Blackboards covered the wall from floor to ceiling. Tall ladders ran on tracks in front of the wall, close enough to allow workers to make chalk entries on the blackboards. The entries showed the odds and results for horse races and baseball games around the country. In the bottom right-hand corner, someone had chalked in the odds for war in Europe and for Roosevelt running for a third term.

Closer to Woody stood tables, each spaced a few feet from the next. At the tables, a dozen men, some wearing green eyeshades, answered phones, and made entries in ledgers. Taken together, Woody guessed the tables held more phones than City Hall.

"Ever been in the backroom of a handbook?" Rizzi asked.

Woody shook his head.

"Whad'ya think?" Sal asked.

"Cat shit and cucumbers!" Woody said, wide-eyed and grinning.

Rizzi chuckled and said, "Follow me."

Woody followed Rizzi to the right, to a door at the far end of the room.

Rizzi said something to the large man guarding the door. The man opened the door and stepped aside. Rizzi signaled for Woody to follow him in.

Woody found himself in a small waiting room outside the boss's office. The décor was early modern shabby and consisted of a small couch or love seat, a lamp table with a cheap lamp, a worse-for-wear cocktail table, and a couple chairs. In short, but for the large mirror on the opposite wall, the room looked like the waiting room outside many a small office.

"Have a seat," Rizzi said.

Woody sat on one of the chairs. There were none of the usual magazines, but there were copies of days-old issues of *Racing News* and a ragged, months-old girlie magazine.

Woody ignored the reading material and watched as Rizzi knocked on the door to the inner office.

A gruff male voice on the other side shouted, "Come in."

Rizzi went in.

Woody looked at the large mirror. It was too large for the small room. He figured it was a one-way mirror. Odds were, the man inside the interior office was sizing him up.

Five minutes later, Rizzi came back out. "The boss wants me to introduce you to Louie. He'll show you what to do." Woody stood and followed Rizzi out of the office and back into the large room.

Woody was familiar with chalk and blackboards. Mathematicians and math professors, after all, frequently worked out their equations on black boards. But working in a bookie would be an entirely new equation.

***

Jack headed to Vice Mayor Harry Boyle's office. He didn't have an appointment, but Boyle agreed to see him.

"I'm a rookie reporter with the *Tribune*," Jack said. "I cover the courts. I appreciate your allowing me to ask you a few questions."

"Happy to do it," Boyle said, "but you're barking up the wrong tree. I have nothing to do with running the courts. That's the county and a whole different branch of government."

"Yes, sir, but you see, I covered the trial of a Mr. Two Penny Smith, and I understand that you may know in him."

"Two Penny?" Boyle said. "Yeah, he's done work for me—yard work, that kind of thing."

"Were you surprised to hear the cops arrested him?"

"Yes, I suppose so, but with his kind..." Boyle left the thought trail off.

"By 'his kind' you mean colored?"

"Yes, I do," Boyle said, not backing down. "What's your point?"

"No point, sir," Jack said. "It's just you're an important man, and I'm still new and… well, I'm just trying to make sure I get everything right."

Boyle looked skeptical, but he was a politician and waited for the young reporter's next question.

"Is it true," Jack asked, "that Mr. Smith also worked at a brothel, a place called Greta's?"

"I wouldn't know anything about that," Boyle said, standing. "I hope you're not intending to smear me because some colored I hired to cut my grass may have done something I know nothing about."

"You didn't know he worked at Greta's?"

"Of course not," Boyle said, letting his exasperation show. "If you think that colored engages in criminal activity, you should talk with the prosecutor. I have nothing to do with that. Now, if you'll excuse me—"

Jack didn't stand. "Have you been to Greta's? Did Mr. Smith see you there?"

"Did that colored tell you that?"

"Mr. Smith?" Jack asked. "No, sir. When I tried to talk to him about you, he flat refused to talk to me and got his back up. Just like you're doing."

Boyle looked at Jack with disgust. "If you've got a question about me, you ask me. Don't go talking to my yard boy."

"Yes, sir," Jack said, "I'll do that."

"Are you done?" Boyle asked in a tone that suggested *he* was done and he expected Jack to be as well.

"Just one or two more questions, Mr. Mayor, if I may. Was Mr. Smith arrested," Jack asked, "to keep him from revealing that you've visited Greta's?"

"This is ridiculous," Boyle said, his eyes fixed on Jack's. "I told you. I've never been to Greta's. Period. Full stop. End of story."

Jack jotted down what Boyle said.

Boyle glared at Jack. "If you say I've been to that whorehouse," he said, "I swear to God you'll regret it. I'll sue, and I'll own your ass. And the newspaper too."

Jack nodded and did his best to look intimidated. "If I can switch topics," he said, "I've got a question about the trash collection contract."

Boyle sat back down. "What about it?"

"There are rumors that the Mob controls the company from Cleveland, Mayfield Disposal. Do you know anything about that?"

"I haven't heard that," Boyle said. "It's up to the City Manager to investigate the bidders and make sure everything's kosher."

"Has the Syndicate tried to influence you to vote to award the contract to Mayfield?"

"No, and if they had, I would have reported that to the prosecutor," Boyle said. "Look, I think you're confused about how this works. When the city puts a contract like this out to bid, the contract goes to the low bidder—unless there's something irregular about the low bidder. Votes on contracts are practically formalities."

"So, you've not had any communication with anyone associated with the Syndicate about the trash contract?"

"No, goddam it, I just told you that." Boyle rubbed the bottom of his nose with his forefinger. "You or that young lawyer who wants my job are just making up this crap."

Jack stood to leave. When he did, he noticed a half empty bottle of Woodford Reserve and a glass on Boyle's credenza and wondered if Boyle had been drinking. "Mr. Mayor," he said, "thank you for your time and for letting me interview you. I'm sorry if I offended you, but I needed to give you a chance to deny this stuff."

"If you even think about putting any of that crap in the paper, I'll have your job. And that won't be the worst of it. You'll wish to

God getting fired was the end of your problems."

"Are you threatening me," Jack asked, "with physical harm?"

"Get the hell out of my office, or I'll have the police remove you."

Three minutes later, Jack stepped out of the city building and headed back to the newsroom. As he walked down Madison Avenue, in a voice that was little more than a hum, he sang he sang the refrain from a popular song. "I'm just wild about Harry, and Harry's just wild about me."

***

When Jack reached the newsroom ten minutes later, the first person he saw told him, "Rumble wants to see you." So, did the next person. And so did each of the other reporters he passed on the way to the managing editor's office. Even a reporter from the far side of the bullpen called out to him. "Hey, Jack, Rumble wants to see you."

Jack knew it was his colleagues' way of letting him know the irascible managing editor had a larger head of steam than usual. Jack also believed, or wanted to, that the teasing was a backhanded show of support.

The last reporter Jack passed was the exception. Slick Sullivan, whose desk was closest to Rumble's office, shook his head and said, "Hey, kid, it's been nice knowing you."

The door to the managing editor's office was open. Jack knocked on the door jamb and stepped inside. Rumble took the unlit cigar from his mouth and pointed it in the general direction of the chairs on the other side of his desk.

"Sit down, Jack," Rumble said, "and tell me why I've got the Vice Mayor AND his attorney calling me to complain about you. They're demanding that I fire you."

"He called you already?" Jack said, trying to a get a read of the situation.

"Me, and the Editor-in-Chief. So, tell me why I need this heartburn."

"I was at the courthouse the other day and saw some Negro guy get convicted of a crime that never happened. The whole thing was a setup job, and –."

"I assign you to cover the courthouse," Rumble interrupted, "and right away, you know more about who's guilty and who's innocent than the prosecutor and the judge?"

"Yesterday," Jack said, refusing to let Rumble rattle him, "I reviewed what I found with the prosecutor who tried the case. He agreed to re-open the case. That's my lead — 'Responding to a *Tribune* investigation, the prosecutor who won a conviction three days ago is now exploring whether the police officer and witnesses who testified in the case perjured themselves.'"

"He's investigating the police officer?" Rumble asked. Like a headline spanning the screen during the newsies before a movie, a new attitude spread across the editor's face.

"The cop who testified said he and his partner arrested this guy outside the Liberty Theater, where he supposedly pestered two white women. But the cop and his partner didn't arrest this guy outside the Liberty. They weren't even working that evening. They were working the day shift and arrested him at his home the next afternoon."

"What's that got to do with the Vice Mayor?"

"Maybe nothing, maybe everything," Jack said and sat down in a chair on the visitor's side of Rumble's desk. "This colored guy works—worked—for a brothel, Greta's over there at Sixth and Philadelphia. He was the janitor. The women who testified against him work at Greta's too. Plus, this guy also does yard work and errands for Boyle."

"That doesn't make Boyle responsible for whatever happened between this man and those women." Rumble gave every sign he was losing patience again.

"A source told me that Mrs. Boyle has left him—moved out. I've called her quite a few times and get no answer. I've even stopped by their house during the day, and no one answers.

"I suspect," Jack continued, "Mrs. Boyle found out her husband was frequenting Greta's and left him. And I'm thinking, maybe her husband, the Vice Mayor, thinks this guy told his wife about his activities at Greta's. I think the Vice Mayor had him arrested to punish him. Or to keep him out of the way until after the election."

Rumble looked at Jack, expecting more.

"Boss, I know I can't prove that. And I won't put that in a story until I can."

Rumble took a deep breath. "Boyle was screaming, 'Nigger this,' and 'Nigger that.' Did you accuse him of having this colored man arrested?"

"The colored man –" Jack hesitated. "The colored man's name is Two Penny Smith. He's got a wife and kids."

"I don't give a goddam," Rumble said. "Everybody has a family. Did you accuse the Vice Mayor of arranging this guy's arrest?"

"I asked Boyle about it to see what reaction I'd get. I figured if he blew a gasket, I'd know I was on to something and needed to keep digging."

Rumble put his elbows on his desk and buried his face in his hands.

Jack squirmed in his chair. He looked at his watch. He squirmed more.

Rumble looked up. "Go write your story, and I'll arrange for legal review."

***

Jack grabbed some coffee and settled in at his desk. He pulled out his notebook, reviewed his notes, and outlined in his mind the story about the arrest and conviction of Two Penny Smith.

Breaking Jack's attention, the phone rang. It was Preston Pell, the personnel manager at Hanover Brewery. He had no record of either April Bedwell or May Goodnight having ever worked at the brewery. Jack made a note in his notebook, then turned back to the blank paper in his typewriter. *Who? What? Where? When? Why?* Jack reminded himself. He typed:

Investigation Calls Arrest, Conviction into Question
by Jack O'Brien

Earlier this week, Assistant Commonwealth Attorney Leo Denton tried public indecency and disturbing the peace charges against Two Penny Smith, a Negro, age 45, and got a conviction. Now, responding to questions raised by a *Tribune* investigation, Denton has asked a Kenton County grand jury to determine if the police framed Mr. Smith.

According to Officer Ricky Robinson's arrest report and trial testimony, he and Patrolman Dennis Vance arrested Mr. Smith in front of the Liberty Theatre on Madison Avenue, Covington. They charged Smith with making lewd statements to two white women, April Bedwell and May Goodnight. The arrest, Patrolman Robinson testified, occurred at 10:23 p.m., July 25, in front of the theater.

After a brief trial on Tuesday, August 2, a jury found Mr. Smith guilty of public indecency and disturbing the peace. Kenton County Circuit Judge Ernst Chelone sentenced Mr. Smith to ninety days in jail.

The *Tribune* has uncovered discrepancies in the witnesses' testimony that call the arrest and conviction into question.

Max Seeger stopped by Jack's desk. "Sounds like you ruffled some feathers."

"Seems that way," Jack said.

Max laughed. "You never find the snake in the henhouse without ruffling feathers," Max said. "Anything I can do?"

"Yeah," Jack said, pulling out his wallet and offering Max some money. "I've got a short deadline. If you're headed out to lunch, can you bring me back a ham-and-Swiss sandwich?"

Max turned down the money and said, "On me, kid. Hang in there."

The older reporter left, and Jack picked up typing where he'd left off.

> Although the arrest report indicates Patrolmen Robinson and Vance arrested Mr. Smith on Tuesday at 10:23 p.m., Deputy Police Chief David Rasche told the *Tribune* that the two patrolmen work the day shift and were not on duty the evening of the alleged incident and arrest.
>
> Sven Svenson, who was waiting in front of the Liberty for a friend when the disturbance allegedly occurred, said he saw no disturbance and was not aware of any arrest.
>
> Neighbors say the officers arrested Mr. Smith at his home about 1:30 p.m. the following day. Police Department records confirm that the patrolmen delivered Mr. Smith for booking after 2:00 p.m. on Wednesday, over fifteen hours after the claimed arrest.
>
> When questioned about the discrepancy, Patrolman Robinson warned, "You don't know what you're messing with." He threatened to arrest this reporter if the *Tribune* reported on Smith's arrest and conviction.

Police Captain Douglas Frazier monitored the trial of Mr. Smith. He also instructed the police records department not to allow the press to see the booking records that show when the patrolmen made the arrest. When questioned, Captain Frazier declined to comment. He also threatened to have this reporter arrested.

At trial, Miss Bedwell testified that she lives at 1154 Garner Street, and Ms. Goodnight stated that she lives at 951 Seiler Street. Both women testified that they work at Hanover Brewery Company.

Neither street, however, has house numbers that run as high as those given by the women, and Hanover Brewery says neither woman has ever worked for it.

Apparently fearing for his life, Mr. Smith refused to answer questions for this article, but his neighbors and others say Mr. Smith works as a janitor at Greta's Place, at Sixth and Philadelphia in Covington.

The *Tribune* has not been able to confirm reports that Miss Bedwell and Miss Goodnight also work at Greta's or that Mr. Smith's arrest was related to something he witnessed at Greta's.

The *Tribune* has confirmed that, in addition to his full-time work at Greta's, Mr. Smith did yard work for Vice Mayor Harry Boyle. The Vice Mayor denies knowing Mr. Smith worked at Greta's Place. He also denies having ever been to Greta's Place or having any connection to Smith's arrest. "I've never been to Greta's," Mr. Boyle said. "Period. Full stop. End of story."

The *Tribune* has no evidence tying

```
Mr. Boyle to Greta's Place or to Mr.
Smith's arrest.
```

Jack pulled the last page of the article out of his typewriter just as Max returned with a sandwich.

"So, how's it going?" Max asked.

"Here's my first stab at it. Can I get you to look at it for me?"

"Sure," Max said. He took the copy back to his own desk.

***

At 2:30 p.m., Assistant Commonwealth Attorney Leo Denton stepped out of the courtroom where the grand jury was meeting and walked past the two Deputy Sheriffs guarding the courtroom door. Roscoe "Fats" Mascelli and a Mob lawyer, Charles Lester, were waiting for him in the hallway.

Mascelli wore a dark, double-breasted suit, dark shirt, and a canary-yellow tie and held a fedora in his hand. Lester wore a brown suit, white shirt, and a tie that attracted less attention than his badly-in-need-of-a-shine wingtips.

Neither the gangster nor his attorney was happy. Lester stepped in front of his client and swaggered toward Denton. He stopped just inches from the prosecutor's face.

"You don't subpoena somebody to testify before a grand jury," Lester growled, "on the day you want them to testify."

"Get out of my face, before I have those officers remove you," Denton said, pointing to the Deputy Sheriffs on either side of the courtroom door.

Lester glared at Denton but took a step back. He signaled for his client to step forward. "Leo, this is my client, Roscoe Mascelli."

Denton did not offer to shake hands with Mascelli, and Mascelli made no attempt to shake hands with him.

"Leo," Lester said, "what the hell is this about? Is Mr. Mascelli the subject of the grand jury's investigation?"

Denton shook his head. "Not at this time. I'm investigating the circumstances surrounding the arrest of a colored guy who works at Greta's. He has an odd name, Two Penny Smith. I believe he was a janitor there."

"What about him?"

"He got into an altercation with two white women," Denton said, "and got himself arrested."

"It's my understanding," Lester said, "you already tried and convicted him."

"That's right," Denton said. "But there have been some new allegations."

"What kind of allegations?"

"A young newspaper reporter claims the testimony was false," Denton said. "He may be talking with a NAACP attorney, who would like to make something out of this. The primary's tomorrow, and my boss doesn't need him writing a story saying I railroaded this guy."

"Mr. Mascelli knows nothing about the incident involving Two Penny and those women."

Denton looked down for a long moment as if studying his shoes, or maybe Lester's. Looking back up and locking eyes with Lester, he said, "Charles, I can see this going in a couple of different directions."

Denton put his hands in his pockets. "For example, I can see Mr. Mascelli testifying that Mr. Smith and the two women work for Greta's, and in fact were working at Greta's, performing their assigned duties, at the time of this alleged altercation."

"Their assigned duties?" Lester asked.

"I won't ask, and he doesn't have to say what the two women do," Denton said. "He only needs to say they were working at Greta's and, therefore, could not have been coming out of the movies and having an altercation with Mr. Smith when this supposedly occurred."

"Why would my client do that?" Lester asked.

"Because then I can go to Judge Chelone and say Mr. Smith's conviction depended on testimony I now have reason to believe was not reliable and get the conviction set aside. Mr. Smith gets out of jail, and this thing blows over."

"I don't buy that," Lester said.

"Like I said," Denton said, "there's more than one way this thing can go. If Mr. Mascelli doesn't want to cooperate, when I get him in front of the grand jury, I can ask what these women do at Greta's, who their customers are, and what Mr. Smith saw that made someone decide to have him arrested on trumped up charges."

"Greta's is a legit joint," Lester said. "You got nothing, and if you insist on dragging my client in front of the grand jury, he will not testify to anything. He will take the Fifth."

Denton looked at Roscoe "Fats" Mascelli. "Mr. Mascelli," Denton said, "you might want to confer with your counsel. If we do things my way, Mr. Smith gets out of jail, you get your janitor back, and with any luck this thing blows over.

"Or, we can do things the way Mr. Lester proposes, and I launch a full-scale investigation into what's going on in your joint, why someone wanted your janitor locked up, and who's involved. And Mr. Lester racks up substantial legal fees at your expense."

Fats Mascelli's face reddened, but he said nothing.

"And if I know your attorney," Denton said, "when you end up spending time in the Big House, he'll offer to take Greta's off your hands cheap."

"I ain't never heard of them broads," Fats Mascelli said.

Denton thought that over. "That contradicts what this reporter thinks. If you tell the grand jury that, I can tell this reporter his facts don't check out."

Fats Mascelli looked at his attorney.

"He's bluffing," Lester said. "He's got nothing. Just take the Fifth."

"And if he's not bluffing, you going to represent me for free?"

"Free legal advice is worth what you pay for it," Lester said. "You don't do anything for free, and neither do I."

Mascelli looked at Denton. "I'll testify that I don't know them broads, but you better not be messing with me."

***

Jack stood and stretched. He cast another glance at the wall clock. Time was ticking down. He saw Max by the coffeepot with what he assumed was his draft in his hand. Jack headed to Max.

Max handed the draft to Jack. "Great story, but the lawyers will rip you to shreds. You need proof that those women work at Greta's, or you need proof that Boyle has been sampling what Greta has on offer. Without one or the other, the lawyers will eat you alive."

Jack had gotten down only half of the ham-and-Swiss sandwich Max had gotten for him, but it felt like he'd swallowed a brick.

"Without that, they will make you take out that stuff at the end—the stuff about the girls and the stuff about Boyle."

"Should I go ahead and take those paragraphs out?"

"Nah," Seeger said. "The rest of your piece is solid. You have to leave them something to take out, or the lawyers will make you take out something important."

Jack tried to smile.

"Listen, Jack. This story was too big for you to land by yourself. You should have gotten backup, but you did good. It's a heck of a story."

"Rumble will be back any minute, and he wants me to meet with the paper's lawyers. Any suggestions?"

"Yeah. See if you can drag it out with the lawyers. Don't piss anyone off, but don't give up."

"What's the point of dragging things out?"

Max grinned. "Time for the cavalry to arrive." He looked around the room and spotted one of the paper's runners. He summoned the kid, who didn't look older than about sixteen. The runners were boys, usually in their teens, the paper retained to pick up and deliver documents and run similar errands.

The kid hustled over to where Jack and Max were standing.

"What's your name?" Max asked the runner.

"Nicky," the kid said.

"That's right," Max said. "Nicky."

"Rumble will be back any minute now," Jack said. "If you're asking me to buy time, it'd help if I knew what for."

"It's Nocky's birthday today," Max said. "He just turned eighteen —"

"Nicky," the kid corrected. "I'll be seventeen in November."

"Nicky-Nocky here's never been with a girl. Hell, he hasn't even kissed a girl —"

"I've kissed plenty of girls," Nicky said, unconvincingly.

"—and it's his birthday," Max said. "We're going to get him laid."

Nicky's eyes widened. "You are?"

"Sure thing," Max said, "it being your eighteenth birthday and all."

Max looked around the newsroom. "Flash!" Max called out to Dick Watson. "We need a photographer pronto."

"What's up?" Watson asked.

"This is Nicky," Max said, putting his arm around the kid's shoulders. "It's his eighteenth birthday, and he's still a virgin. We're taking him to Greta's to get him laid."

Watson said, "They won't let me walk in there with a camera."

"Get the hat box!" Max commanded.

Watson hurried to the closet in the back of the room. On the top shelf sat a large, round, gift-wrapped hat box with a bow on the lid. Designed for a woman's wide-brimmed hat, the box was just large enough to hold his camera.

Max cast his glance around the newsroom and called out the names of several more reporters. "You're coming too," he shouted. "Get your butts in gear."

A reporter entering into the newsroom called out, "Rumble is on his way up."

"Let's go, boys," Max shouted. "If Rumble asks," he said, "tell him we're chasing the big story and keep moving."

Jack watched Max and his crew rush out of the newsroom. Jack's grin was almost as big as the grin on Nicky's face.

***

Roscoe "Fats" Mascelli took the witness oath and moved his considerable girth into the chair in the witness stand. He surveyed the grand jurors and nodded to those bold enough to look directly at him.

Leo Denton had Mascelli recite his name and address for the record and then went to the matters he wanted to cover.

"Mr. Mascelli, am I correct that you own and operate an establishment here in Covington known as Greta's Place."

"I run it," Mascelli said. "I'm the main owner, but there are other investors."

Denton wanted to ask who those other investors were, but that would have to wait for another day. "Mr. Mascelli, does Greta's employ a man by the name of Two Penny Smith?"

"Not anymore," Mascelli said with a smirk. "Not since he went and got himself arrested."

"Did Greta's employ Two Penny Smith before his arrest on or about Tuesday, July 26, of this year?"

"Yeah, he worked for me."

"The police arrested Mr. Two Penny Smith," Denton continued, "based on certain statements he allegedly made to two women outside the Liberty Theatre on the evening of Tuesday, July 25. This was as the movie was letting out, a little after ten in the evening."

Mascelli looked around at the grand jurors again. He had a smug grin on his face as if he were privy to a funny secret.

"At that time, Mr. Mascelli," Denton asked, "was Mr. Two Penny Smith an employee of Greta's?"

"Yeah," Mascelli said, still smirking. "He was the janitor."

"And at that time, did Greta's employ a young woman by the name of April Bedwell?"

"Never heard of her," Mascelli said.

"Are you certain of that, Mr. Mascelli?"

"Yeah, I'm certain. We don't hire any girls to work upstairs unless I meet them first."

"At the time of Mr. Smith's arrest, did Greta's employ a young woman who calls herself May Goodnight?"

"Never heard of her either," Mascelli said. He favored the jurors with another smirk.

"You're quite certain of that?" Denton prodded.

"Yeah, I'm sure," Mascelli said. "Are we done?"

"Just a few more questions," Denton said. "Are you certain that neither woman worked for you, perhaps under their real names?"

"Like I already told you, I don't know them broads. They never worked for me, not then or ever."

"Has Vice Mayor Harry Boyle been a customer at Greta's?"

The question went beyond what Mascelli thought he'd agreed to, and Denton could see Mascelli's demeanor change. Denton assumed Mascelli would invoke the Fifth Amendment but hoped the big grease ball would want to show he didn't need a lawyer.

"Ever?" Mascelli asked.

"Let's say in the last year," Denton said, dangling the bait in front of Mascelli. "To the best of your knowledge, has Vice Mayor Harry Boyle been a customer at Greta's in the last year?"

"Not that I know of," Mascelli said. "Maybe he was there to have a drink or something when I wasn't out front, but I ain't never seen him there."

"You've never met with or spoken to Mr. Boyle there?"

"I ain't never met him anywhere," Mascelli said. "We don't exactly move in the same social circles."

The comment generated a chuckle among jurors.

Mascelli grinned broadly. He was having fun showing off.

"Did you have anything to do with Mr. Two Penny Smith's arrest?" Denton asked.

"They ain't deputized me yet," Mascelli said, hamming it up for the jurors. "So, no, I had nothing to do with that."

"Did Mr. Boyle ask or suggest that you arrange for Mr. Two Penny Smith to be arrested?"

"No," Mascelli said. "Like I said, I ain't never spoken with Mr. Boyle in my life. Besides, he's the Vice Mayor. If he wants somebody arrested, all he has to do is tell the police."

Denton stared at Mascelli a moment longer, collecting his thoughts and deciding what to do next.

Playing to the jurors again, Mascelli volunteered, "Me and the police, we ain't on such good terms. I'd be the last person the mayor would talk to if he needed the police to do something."

Denton nodded. "Did you ask Captain Frazier to have Mr.

Smith arrested?"

In an instant, Mascelli's face reddened, his eyes narrowed, and his chin went up. He looked as if he wanted to rip Denton's head off but said nothing.

"Mr. Mascelli, did you ask Captain Frazier," Denton repeated, "to have Mr. Two Penny Smith arrested?"

"I'm pleading the Fifth. I'm not answering that."

"If Captain Frazier testified that you asked him to have Mr. Smith arrested, would he be telling the truth?" Denton had not called the police captain to testify and doubted he could have wrung a confession from Frazier. But Mascelli would have no way of knowing that.

"If Frazier said that," Mascelli said, "he's a damn liar. And I ain't answering anything more about that. I'm pleading the Fifth."

"Mr. Mascelli, you can't testify *and* invoke the Fifth Amendment. You can only do one or the other, and you've now testified that you did not ask Captain Frazier to have Mr. Smith arrested, so you can't invoke the Fifth Amendment."

"Watch and see," Mascelli said. He stared at Denton.

"I have nothing further," Denton said.

Mascelli stood up.

"Mr. Mascelli, the grand jurors have the right to ask questions, so please be seated."

Mascelli hesitated, then sat back down. He glared at the jurors, daring them to question him.

One of the jurors, a prim, gray-haired fifty-something woman, who wore a dress that buttoned up to her neck, stood. "Is Greta's a brothel?" she asked. "I mean, do you have prostitutes on the upper floors like everybody says?"

"I'm invoking my right not to testify," Mascelli said.

"Mr. Denton asked you about Vice Mayor Boyle," the woman persisted. "In the last year, have any other members of the City

Commission been customers at Greta's?"

"I don't have to put up with this," Mascelli said. "I'm done." He stood and stepped down from the witness stand. He stopped and glared at Denton.

"Mr. Mascelli," Denton said, "the grand jury has more questions. We're not done."

"Yeah, well, I am." Mascelli put on the fedora he'd been carrying and adjusted it.

"If you leave now, you will be in contempt of court."

"Talk to my lawyer about it," Mascelli said. "And hope I don't take this up with you personally."

"What do you mean by that?" Denton shot back. "If you're going to threaten me, have the guts to say so."

"I warned you not to mess with me," Mascelli said. He turned and walked out of the courtroom.

As he watched "Fats" Mascelli waddle splay-footed out of the courtroom, it was Denton's turn to smirk. If it weren't for his fat neck, Denton thought, Mascelli would look like an angry, oversized duck in a fedora.

***

The *Tribune* team charged merrily into Greta's with the astonished messenger boy in tow. Max Seeger commandeered a round table in the center of the room. Watson, the photographer, put the large round box with its wrapping paper and bow under the table. Only Dirk "Dirt" Driscoll, the crime reporter, had not come in with the rest. He waited outside by the door.

Two Syndicate men sat at the bar chatting with the bartender. Otherwise, the ground-floor room, with its polished brass and French-boudoir-elegance, was empty. The piano player and the after-work drink crowd wouldn't arrive for several hours, and the men looking for more than a drink and music wouldn't show up until much later.

When the bartender approached the group, Max did a drum roll on the table with his hands and announced, "Barkeep, beers all around!"

The bartender raised an eyebrow. "Including the kid?"

"This is Nicky," Max said. "It's his eighteenth birthday, but tragically, Nicky has never been laid. Never even kissed a girl. And we're here to remedy that."

"You want me to get Greta?" the bartender said, grinning.

"Pronto, my good man," Max said. "Eighteen years is a long time to go without getting laid, and we don't think Nicky should put it off a moment longer than necessary."

The bartender returned to the bar and said something to one of the Syndicate men, who left to find Greta. The bartender busied himself with serving the beers.

Five minutes later, Greta arrived. She was a short, wiry woman of a certain age, who had been wound too tight, wore too much make up, and smiled only when the occasion required it. "Gentleman," she greeted the group, "I understand you've got a lad here for his birthday, and you want one of my girls to make a man of him."

"Nicky, stand up and take a bow!" Max commanded. The other men pounded the table and cheered.

Nicky stood and nodded in Greta's direction.

Max pulled a scrap of paper from his pocket. "Greta," he said, "I have it on good authority that your two best girls are Miss April and Miss May. Any chance either of those young ladies might be available to help Nicky here get over his condition?"

"His condition?" Greta asked, not finding this to be one of those occasions when it was necessary to smile. "Has he got something contagious?"

Nicky sat back down, looking sheepish and confused.

"Not to embarrass the young man," Max said, "but it seems

he's still a virgin, and we're hoping to find him a cure."

Greta looked at the lad.

"Nicky," Max said, "stand up and pull your zipper down, so Greta can see what we're talking about."

Nicky's face reddened.

"That won't be necessary," Greta said. "We don't expect business this early in the day, but I'll go see who's available."

"April Showers," Max said, "May Deflowers."

Several minutes later, Greta returned with two buxom and attractive women, both in their mid-twenties, both bottle blondes.

Greta introduced one of the young women as "April" and the other as "May." April winked and said, "Hi, Nicky." May blew Nicky a kiss.

"Who do you want?" Greta asked.

"Stand up, Nicky," Max roared. The other men joined in demanding that he stand.

Nicky stood, gangly and awkward, and had trouble making eye contact with either woman.

"We're not waiting until you turn twenty-one," Greta said. "Who do you want?"

"Wait! Wait!" Max said, standing. "We've got a present for Nicky."

Dick Watson picked up the brightly wrapped box from the floor and put it on the table.

"While you're fooling around," Greta said, "who's going to pay?"

"How much is it?" Max asked.

Greta named a price.

"Too much!" Max said. "It's his first time. It'll be over in two minutes. Besides, it's his birthday."

"I should charge extra," Greta countered.

"Okay, okay," Max said, tossing the money on the table.

Watson popped the lid off the box, reached in and pulled his camera out.

Greta said, "No photos."

Max shouted over her, "Girls! Big smiles."

The women flashed smiles, and Watson got the shot.

Even before the light from the flash disappeared, the Syndicate heavies at the bar were on their feet, heading toward Dick Watson and his camera.

Watson bolted for the front door.

Max grabbed his money and shouted, "Run! Run!"

Driscoll had been waiting by the front door for the camera flash. As soon as he saw it, he burst in, shouting, "Fire! Fire! The building is on fire!" With the money Driscoll had given them burning holes in their pockets, two neighborhood kids came running in behind Driscoll shouting, "Fire! Fire!"

For just a second that froze the two Syndicate men.

"The whole back of the building is on fire!" Driscoll yelled.

"Check it out," the larger of the two gangsters said to his companion. "I've got this."

"On it," the other tough said, turned, and headed in the opposite direction.

The big guy started forward again.

Nicky, crestfallen, was the last to move. When he did, he collided with the Syndicate man and went sprawling. The larger man lost his balance and went down as well.

Nicky was up before the big guy and sprinted for the door. Caught up in the excitement, one of the neighborhood kids jumped on the big guy's back, slowing him down.

By the time Nicky reached the street, Driscoll was behind the wheel of his Packard, and the rest of the reporters were inside the car or climbing in.

Nicky turned and saw the Syndicate man was at the door and closing fast. He jumped onto the Packard's slim running board and pounded on the roof. "Go! Go!" he shouted. "Now!"

The Packard roared off.

***

Jack rode the elevator with Rumble to the top floor of the *Tribune* building, where the Editor-in-Chief, Publisher, and other luminaries had their offices. He followed Rumble into a small conference room and took the seat Rumble pointed to. They were there to review his draft article with the newspaper's lawyers, but Jack couldn't shake the feeling he was going to the principal's office for a scolding.

Jack laid his draft on the table and began to re-read it when he heard the elevator open and saw the lawyers arrive. The older attorney looked to be about sixty. He was tall, thin, bald, and as ramrod straight and stern as an Army boot camp instructor. He wore a tailored suit, a silk pocket handkerchief, and a gold fob watch. His black, calfskin wingtips had a fresh shine, and his burnished leather briefcase exhibited just the right amount of wear. His younger associate, who appeared to be in his mid-twenties, wore a department-store suit and the unhappy look of complete subservience.

The attorneys greeted Miriam Happelmeyer, the newspaper's pleasant, long-serving executive secretary. The younger attorney gave the woman a friendly smile and a polite nod but deferred to the senior attorney the business of exchanging pleasantries. Taking charge, the older attorney chatted with Mrs. Happelmeyer for what Jack guessed was precisely sixty seconds. When the attorneys had thus fulfilled their social obligations, they pivoted and marched in tight formation into the conference room.

"Mr. Bearbeiter," Rumble said, rising and extending his hand, "good to see you again. This is Jack O'Brien, the young reporter who seems to have gotten under Vice Mayor Boyle's skin."

"Good afternoon, Mr. Rumble," the attorney said, nodding his head slightly. He gave Jack an appraising look. "Mr. O'Brien, my name is August Bearbeiter, and this young fellow is my colleague, Cecil Mauser."

Jack noticed that the attorney kept the German pronunciation, "Bay-AR–by–ter." Jack liked that. He thought too many families had Americanized their German names. But he didn't warm to the man who bore the name. He couldn't help but think of Bearbeiter as an updated version of the Grim Reaper, armed with a briefcase instead of a scythe, but nonetheless there to rob the soul from his article.

Jack shook hands first with Bearbeiter, then with Mauser.

Bearbeiter seated himself, and the others took that as their cue to do the same.

Rumble slid a copy of Jack's article across the table to the older attorney and a second copy to his colleague.

Bearbeiter ignored the article and looked at Jack. "You are the author of this?"

"Yes." Jack ignored the man's accusatory tone. But he couldn't escape the unsettling the impression that, unlike the rest of the older man's tautly controlled presence, Bearbeiter's thick eyebrows were unruly and somehow angry.

Bearbeiter pulled a pair of horn-rimmed glasses from his inside jacket pocket, put them on, and looked down at the article.

"Would you like me to provide some background?" Jack asked.

Bearbeiter looked up from the article, removed his eyeglasses, and frowned at Jack. "Will you be at the breakfast tables of the newspaper's subscribers to provide *them* with *background?*"

"No," Jack said, "only what's in the article."

"Then, I think it best we read your copy without the benefit of *background."*

Fair enough, Jack thought. Still, the man's eyebrows mesmerized him. They seemed to claw the air, trying to reach him.

Bearbeiter repositioned his glasses and focused his attention on the typewritten pages.

Jack watched the attorneys read and re-read the article.

After a third perusal, Bearbeiter looked up from the copy, removed his glasses again, and rubbed the bridge of his nose. Without checking with his young associate to see if *he* had any thoughts, Bearbeiter asked Rumble, "Do you know Deputy Police Chief Rasche?"

"I can't say I know him," Rumble said, "but I've met him several times at civic functions."

"It would be useful," Bearbeiter said, "if you were to call him and confirm that these officers were indeed not working when they claim to have made this arrest. That *does* seem to be the crux of the matter."

"Sure," Rumble said. He stood, picked up the receiver from the phone on a credenza next to the wall, and dialed his secretary. "Helen, I need the phone number for Deputy Police Chief Rasche."

Jack hadn't told Rumble that he had misled Rasche. Uncertain what to do, he looked for and found the page in his notebook of his conversation with the Deputy Chief.

Rumble repeated the phone number as his secretary gave it to him, and Jack jotted it down.

Rumble hung up on his secretary and dialed the Deputy Police Chief's number.

Jack's mind was racing. "Before you talk with Rasche," he said, "there's something you should know."

Rumble hung up the phone.

Bearbeiter stared at Jack.

Mauser looked up from his legal pad.

"Spill it," Rumble ordered.

"I didn't know if Deputy Chief Rasche was in on framing Two Penny, so I told him a story about how some church ladies saw two cops rousting and beating up a vagrant across the street from the Liberty. I gave him the names of the cops who arrested Mr. Smith. He checked and said they weren't working that night."

Bearbeiter shook his head. "You made a false report of a crime to the Deputy Chief of Police?" Bearbeiter's voice was stern and unforgiving. His eyebrows, perhaps sensing opportunity, twitched.

"I used artifice to secure the truth," Jack said with more bravado than he felt.

"Call him right now," Rumble commanded, "and get this straightened out before I kick your artifice."

Jack jumped to his feet and placed the call. A secretary put him through.

"Chief Rasche," Jack said, "I'm Jack O'Brien from the *Tribune*. I'm here with my managing editor, Joshua Rumble. I think you know him."

Jack listened as Rasche responded.

"This is about my interview with you. We're going to run a story tomorrow on the arrest of a Negro man by the name of Two Penny Smith."

Interrupted by Rasche, Jack listened, then responded, "No, sir, this isn't about the incident we talked about. You see, sir, I made up that incident. The officers whose names I gave you claim to have arrested Mr. Smith outside the Liberty Theater, at the time I gave you. That's what their arrest report says, and that's what one of them testified to in court. But like you told me, they weren't working that night. They actually arrested this fellow the next afternoon, and —"

Jack listened again. "Yes, sir, you're right, and I apologize. That's why I'm calling. Two minutes ago, when I told Mr. Rumble what I'd done, he insisted I call you, set the record straight, and apologize."

Jack listened and glanced at Rumble. "Yes, sir, you're absolutely right, and I apologize. But if I may, I want to be sure you understand the story we're working on. It will say those officers claimed to have arrested this Negro man outside the Liberty movie theater. They charged him with disturbing the peace and making lewd comments to two white women as they left the movie."

Jack listened again.

"Yes, sir, but it turns out those women lied about where they live and where they work. The home addresses they gave don't exist. They claimed they work at the Hanover Brewery, but the brewery never heard of them. We believe they work at Greta's, which is also where this Negro man worked, and –"

Rasche had a question.

"Yes, sir, I believe this arrest was a complete frame up," Jack said. "I've informed Leo Denton, the prosecutor who tried the case, and he's investigating."

Jack went silent again, concentrating not just on what Rasche was saying, but his tone as well.

Thirty seconds later, Jack responded, "Captain Frazier was at the trial. He told Sargent Hayman not to let anyone see the booking records for Mr. Smith, which show when the patrolmen made the arrest. When I tried to interview him, he threatened to have me arrested. So, you might start with him."

Again, Jack listened. "Yes, sir, Mr. Rumble is right here. I'll put him on."

Rumble took the phone and exchanged greetings with the Deputy Police Chief.

"That's right," Rumble said, "I'm going to kick his ass so hard his brains will rattle."

It was Rumble's turn to listen.

After a minute, Rumble turned to Jack and asked, "This Negro also works for Vice Mayor Boyle, right?"

"He does yard work, minor repairs, errands –"

Rumble repeated what Jack said to the Deputy Chief.

After taking in what the Deputy Chief said in return, Rumble gave the phone number for the conference room he was calling from and his own office phone.

"Thanks, and sorry about this," Rumble said. He hung up.

The lawyers looked at Rumble.

"He confirms those patrolmen weren't working that night," Rumble said. "He will call me back if he learns more."

Bearbeiter's associate, Mauser, wrote a long note on his yellow legal pad.

Bearbeiter himself had moved on. "The draft says this Two Penny Smith fellow works at Greta's. Do you have sources for that?"

"Yes," Jack said. "He was a janitor or clean up guy there. He told me that himself, and so did his wife, his son, and half his neighborhood."

"*I see*," Bearbeiter said. "And what about these women? How do we know they work at Greta's?"

"Mr. Smith confirmed that when I interviewed him."

Bearbeiter drummed his fingers on the table. "Do you have a source for that other than the accused?"

Jack thought for a moment. "No, sir."

"*I see*," Bearbeiter said, tapping his fingers on the table again. "*I see*." His wiry eyebrows made menacing twitches.

The associate, Mauser, frowned and made a note.

Rumble scowled at Jack.

"You say here," Bearbeiter said, "that this Negro also does yard work for Vice Mayor Boyle."

"Yes, sir, he does," Jack said. "He told me that, and Mr. Boyle confirmed it."

Mauser scribbled a note on his legal pad.

"You quote Mr. Boyle as denying that he has ever visited Greta's. You also say he denied knowing this Negro man worked at Greta's."

"Yes, sir," Jack replied. "Mr. Boyle was emphatic on both points."

"Yes, I imagine he was," Bearbeiter said. "Do you have sources who say Mr. Boyle *has* frequented this place?"

"No, I don't. That's why I don't accuse him of that."

"*I see.*" Bearbeiter drummed his fingers on the table again. "*I see.*" His eyebrows twitched angrily.

"Do you have a source who says Mr. Boyle knew his yard man worked at Greta's?"

"Only Mrs. Smith, and that's second hand. Two Penny won't talk about it."

Bearbeiter's fingertips drummed the table.

Young Mr. Mauser jotted a note on his legal pad, then turned and watched the older attorney, as if waiting for the Lord High Chancellor to announce his decision.

"You cannot place these women at Greta's," Bearbeiter said. "That has to go."

The young associate nodded approvingly and made another note on his legal pad.

"And, unless you have sources that place him there, you cannot say Mr. Boyle denied frequenting this whorehouse. Otherwise, you might ask *anyone* to deny *anything*. 'Mr. Boyle today denied that he is a Bolshevik.' 'In response to close questioning, *Tribune* Managing Editor Joshua Rumble today denied sleeping with Eleanor Roosevelt.'"

Mauser nodded in firm agreement. He memorialized Bearbeiter's dictum in his legal pad.

Bearbeiter removed his glasses and returned them to his inside jacket pocket, signaling he had rendered judgment in full.

Rumble stood. "Jack, you should know better, and I should have caught that. Go downstairs and do another draft. Bring it up here when you're done."

"Yes, sir," Jack said, standing.

"And don't take all goddam day about it."

But before Jack could move, the conference room door swung open, and Max Seeger entered, a big grin on his face. "Pardon me, gents," he said. "And you too, Bear Biter."

"I don't remember inviting you," Rumble growled.

"That's all right, no hard feelings," Seeger said. "I've got confirmation those tarts in Jack's story work at Greta's. They're members of the oldest profession."

"And just *how* did you confirm that?" Rumble asked.

"Several of us took one of the messenger boys to Greta's. We told Greta it was the kid's birthday, and we wanted to get him laid. We asked Greta if April was there. Or May. Whad'ya know? Those fine ladies came down and greeted us. Greta said Nicky could have his choice."

"Tell me," Rumble said, standing and clenching his fists, "that you didn't pay for one of our messengers to get laid at that whorehouse."

"No, but Flash got a picture of the women. He's in the darkroom developing it now. When he's done, Jack can confirm they're the same women who testified at the trial."

Rumble reached into his jacket pocket and pulled out a cigar. He stripped off the wrapper, dropped the wrapper in a wastebasket, found a match, and lit the cigar. "Max," he said, after finishing the ritual, "why aren't you downstairs writing this up? I don't pay you to gloat."

"You don't pay me what I'm worth either," Seeger said. "Bear Biter, pleasure talking with you again."

Bearbeiter ignored Seeger.

Mauser made sure not to smile.

"Jack," Rumble said, "get me a re-write. The women can stay, but you still can't imply the Vice Mayor had anything to do with framing this colored guy. You aren't there yet."

CHAPTER 17, SATURDAY, AUGUST 5

HEAVY LOCAL BALLOTING IS SEEN
600,000 TO VOTE IN PRIMARY
Fair Weather Boosts
Turnout in Rural Areas
The Kentucky Post, August 5, 1939

Harry Boyle did not need to remind himself that today was the primary. The big race was the Democratic primary that pitted Lt. Governor Keen Johnson against Lexington attorney and former Congressman John Y. Brown. Old hands expected it to be a tight race, but Johnson did better during the campaign than Brown. Boyle had campaigned for Johnson, and Johnson had promised him a high-level position in his administration.

Boyle himself wasn't on the ballot. Covington stuck stubbornly to its practice of holding the primary for its officeholders later, closer to the actual election. It was stupid and expensive for the city, but it kept the election campaign for City Commission short. That made it difficult for a challenger. So, all was good.

But that damn newspaper.

Sipping coffee and eating toast at his kitchen table, Boyle read and re-read the two articles—Jack O'Brien's article about Two Penny Smith's trial *and* Max Seeger's piece tying the women who testified against Two Penny to Greta's. O'Brien's article made it clear the arrest was a frame-up but didn't point the finger at anyone, except a Captain Frazier. The article didn't even mention that Two Penny had done yard work for him.

Boyle lit a cigarette. The article said nothing to suggest a tie between him and the arrest. Still, it was worrisome that Leo Denton, the Assistant Commonwealth Attorney, was investigating. *If he was investigating—and wasn't just blowing smoke up the young reporter's skirt.* Boyle thought about calling Denton on Monday. He could say he'd always liked Two Penny and ask if there was anything he could do to help the poor guy. That might give him a chance to get a read on where Denton was on this. But Denton was smart and might read too much into a call. Boyle put off a decision on that.

Max Seeger's article was fun—or would have been under other circumstances. Seeger was a damn fine writer, and it showed. But his article was more worrisome than O'Brien's. It drew attention to Greta's in a way that might make it impossible for the police to continue to ignore the place. Fats would be livid.

But bottom line, nothing in either article connected him to the arrest or put his re-election in jeopardy. He stood and put on the tie he had selected. It was time for him to go to his precinct and vote. He slid on a sport coat and checked himself in the mirror.

The doorbell rang, followed by a fierce pounding on his front door. Boyle cursed, went to the door, and opened it.

Two of Fats' thugs were on his front porch. "Fats wants to have a chat with you," one of them said. He was a large, intimidating man, with a chiseled face, broad shoulders, and a bulge under his jacket that suggested a gun in a shoulder holster. His voice was deep and guttural, and his manner self-assured.

The man did not identify himself, but Boyle remembered his name. Gus Panzer. Boyle had seen the other thug at Greta's as well but didn't know his name.

"The primary's today," Boyle said. "I've got to go to the precinct and vote. Joe Dinklehaus from the *Tribune* and a photographer will be there. I'll stop by and see Fats when I'm done."

"When God gave out patience," Panzer said, "Fats figured he wouldn't be a doctor. He said he didn't need any."

Boyle forced a laugh. "I understand. As soon as I vote and give a quote to the reporter, I'll head right over to see him. It won't take long."

"Fats wants to see you now. Follow me. We'll take you there."

"Oh, for Chrissake," Boyle fumed, not budging.

"If Fats has to wait, he gets upset," the big man said. "It's bad luck to make Fats upset."

"It is, huh?"

"Yeah. People who make Fats upset—sometimes, they have accidents. Sometimes, they fall and break an arm. Or, they get hit by a car."

"Okay, okay," Boyle said. "I'm coming. He stepped onto the porch, locked the front door, and followed the big man.

Sitting in the backseat of the mobsters' car, he watched as Panzer took a round-about route to Greta's, stopping twice to make sure no one was tailing them. Neither Panzer nor his companion said anything to the other or to him. Boyle said nothing to them.

When they reached Greta's, Fats was in his office, eating a fried egg sandwich and washing it down with a Coke. Using the back of his hand, Fats wiped egg yolk and crumbs from his mouth and chin. He gestured for Boyle to sit and asked, "Your guy going to win?"

Boyle assumed Fats meant Keen Johnson. "Yeah, I think so. I don't think it will even be close."

"Harry, I'm trying to be happy for you, but it ain't easy." Fats pushed aside the paper wrapper his sandwich came in. "See, I get up this morning, and the newspaper says somebody framed Two Penny. Something like that gives me heartburn, you know what I mean?" Fats' hands clenched into fists. "And then, I see this other story, and it says Two Penny and those girls work here. They've even got a photo of the broads."

"It's that young reporter, Jack O'Brien." Boyle leaned in and grasped the front edge of Fats' desk with his hands. "I don't know how he figured out as much as he did, but he hasn't got anything on either of us."

Fats stood. "Don't tell me, 'he ain't got nothing.' He's got that prosecutor investigating who framed Two Penny."

Boyle removed his hands from the desk and leaned back. "The primary is today. Denton just said that, so he wouldn't look bad in this morning's paper. Wait and see. Denton won't do anything. At most, he'll go through the motions until this reporter is off on some other toot and forgets all about this."

"That's so, huh?"

"Fats, don't get worked up over this. You'll see. Denton won't do anything." Boyle said this with more conviction than he felt, but when he heard himself say it, it sounded right.

"You know where I was yesterday," Fats asked, "when those pricks from the newspaper were here?"

"Not a clue, Fats. Where were you?"

"Denton had me in front of a grand jury, asking questions about whether them girls work for me."

Boyle felt like someone had grabbed his intestines and twisted them. "You took the Fifth, didn't you?"

"I testified that I knew nothing about them girls. Never heard of 'em."

Boyle tried to keep his face neutral. He couldn't believe how stupid this guy was, but the last thing he needed was to do or say something that would give Fats an excuse to lose his temper.

"When I finished with the grand jury and got back here," Fats said, "I found out them reporters had just left. And then I found out they got a photo of those broads I swore didn't work for me."

"I had nothing to do with any of that, Fats. I swear." *Denton was using a grand jury to investigate even before O'Brien got his story published? What the hell was going on?*

"You're the one who wanted me to have Two Penny arrested. So, now, I don't have a janitor. And yesterday, that prosecutor had his hand down my pants, feeling around for my balls, wanting to squeeze 'em. And this morning, this story about my place is on the front page of the goddam newspaper."

Not sure what he could say that wouldn't make things worse, Boyle said nothing.

"Now, I got to send them broads to Cleveland, or Detroit, or somewhere, and get them out of town. And Owl, he's wondering if you will come through for him."

"The contract's up for approval Wednesday," Boyle said. "If he does what we agreed to, he'll get the contract, and he'll get it on his terms."

"Yeah, well, Owl wants to make sure. He's coming down here, and we're gonna have a meeting, and you're gonna tell him that to his face. I ain't vouching for you."

"That's fine," Boyle said, trying to sound confident. "Lookout House? Same as last time?"

"Yeah."

"I'll be there," Boyle said. "No problem."

Fats grabbed a bottle of Coca-Cola from the credenza behind his desk and sat back down. He picked up a bottle opener and pried the cap from the bottle. The bottle cap fell into his lap.

Fats picked up the cap, bent it between his fingers, and threw it the length of the room at a poster of James Cagney. The cap bounced off the poster and landed among several Louisville Slugger baseball bats stacked on the floor.

"Go vote," Fats said. "I wouldn't want your guy to lose because you forgot to vote for him."

***

Jack and Maggie decided to see a movie at the Kentucky, the newest movie house in the city. It was about three dozen blocks south of the Ohio River, in Latonia, the Covington neighborhood that lent its name to the Latonia race track.

But first, he and Maggie had dinner. It was only hamburgers, French fries, and Cokes at a diner not far from the movie house, but Maggie was talkative and fun.

"Great article about that that trial in this morning's paper," Maggie enthused.

"Thank you—and thank you for suggesting we talk to that fellow at the Liberty."

"You betcha!" Maggie said and grinned.

Jack got more serious. "I think that story was the best reporting I've ever done."

Maggie coaxed some ketchup from the bottle the waitress left on the table. "Your story on that preacher got the attention of more readers."

"If it did," Jack said, dipping one of his fries into the ketchup on Maggie's plate, "it's because of the photo Flash got. But I'm hoping my story on Two Penny makes a difference. Someone set him up to take the fall for a crime that never happened."

"Have you figured out why?" Maggie took a bite of her sandwich.

"No," Jack said, shaking his head. "I still think he saw something at Greta's he wasn't supposed to see. Or he saw someone there he wasn't supposed to see, and whoever it was wasn't happy about it."

Maggie leaned in and batted her eyes. "My star reporter."

Jack rolled his eyes.

Maggie used her finger to separate the fries from her sandwich and pushed the pickle slices off to the edge of her plate. "Are you any closer to getting a position as a foreign correspondent?"

"No." Jack sensed a mood change in Maggie. "What's new in your life?"

"My aunt has found a project she wants me to get involved in," Maggie said, then hesitated. "My mother thinks I should get involved in it too."

Jack studied Maggie's face. Tiny worry lines formed around her eyes, and her smile disappeared. "What project?"

"The idea is to convince European art collectors to loan their paintings and other artwork to museums here and in Canada, to protect them in case there's a war."

"Who's behind this?" Jack took a bite of food.

"It started with some people concerned about the aerial bombing of civilians in Spain—Guernica and the rest. They persuaded some museums and universities to organize the effort. I'm just learning about this, but as I understand it, the people running it are working with the Red Cross, Jewish groups, others."

"What would you do?"

"I'm not sure. Aunt Agnes says with my major in art, I might help track down who has valuable artwork. I took French and spent a year in France, so she thinks I could help write letters to art collectors there." Maggie shrugged her shoulders. "At this point, I don't know, but they've invited me to come to New York to talk with them, to give me a chance to learn more."

"When?"

"I'm going up next weekend and meet with them on Monday. I'll take the overnight train after I meet with them and be back sometime Tuesday."

"Something about it bothers you," Jack said.

"Aunt Agnes and Mom say it would help me make contacts with museums and collectors." Maggie looked around the room. "That's true, but it makes you think about how horrible war is. And not just war. I mean, look what they're doing to Jews in Germany, making them wear stars, not allowing them to work or go to school." Maggie shuddered.

"That's why this project is important. But why you?" Jack smiled. "I'm sorry. I think you'd be wonderful at this, but aren't most of the people who own these paintings old people—family patriarchs, dowagers? Aren't there people who are museum offi-cials or curators, who are closer to their age, who would be in a better position to persuade that sort of person to part with a pre-cious family heirloom?"

Maggie smiled. "The same thought crossed my mind."

Jack took another bite of food. He noticed Maggie had eaten little.

"My aunt, God bless her," Maggie said, "says she told them all about my junior year in France."

Jack wondered if Maggie was getting closer to what bothered her. "Just that you spent a student year in France, or something special about your time there?"

Maggie had just taken a bite and chewed instead of answering.

"Don't tell me," Jack said. "You lived on a farm in the south of France, ate fresh produce and cheese, and drank wine at lunch and dinner. You went to the sea on weekends and had long walks on the beach with dashing young Frenchmen."

"Sounds lovely, but no. I lived in Paris and attended all my classes. But the thing is, the family I lived with–" Maggie stopped and took of a sip of her Coke.

Jack took another bite of his own food.

"Monsieur St. Pierre was the curator and acquisitions director of a small museum," Maggie said. "Very small. But he seemed to know anyone and everyone in Paris—and maybe the whole coun-try—who owned an artwork of any significance, especially Impres-sionists."

Jack studied Maggie's expression, but waited for her to explain what was on her mind.

"I'm afraid," she said, "that the people in this project want to exploit my connection with him to get him to help them."

Jack tilted his head sideways and raised his eyebrows. "Would that be so bad?"

"I don't want to take advantage of Monsieur St. Pierre's willingness to take me into his household for a school year—if that's why they're interested in me."

"Maggie, I imagine they are as enchanted with you as I am. Their interest may have nothing to do with some old Frenchman who takes in pretty female students, so everyone will know how cosmopolitan he is."

Maggie frowned.

"But let's say you're right," Jack said. "I don't think you would be taking advantage of this St. Pierre guy. He's French. He won't help if he doesn't want to help."

Maggie gave Jack a wry look that fell somewhere between an eye roll at his stereotyping the French and reluctant agreement with his conclusion.

"And who knows?" Jack said. "If he's as savvy as he sounds, he may agree with the people behind this project. He may be happy if you were to reach out to him."

Maggie sucked the ketchup from a fry before chewing and swallowing it. "After they meet me, they'll probably decide to use me as a part-time volunteer writing letters to old French matrons who wouldn't give up their one valuable painting if the Boche were a block away."

"You'll charm them, just like you charmed me."

"Your story on that Negro man," Maggie said, evidently wanting to change the subject, "what happens to the poor man now?"

"That depends on Judge Chelone, and he's a dyed-in-the-wool racist. So, I'm not sure." Jack shrugged.

"That's a shame." Maggie pulled a compact from her purse and checked her lipstick.

"I did learn something interesting. Two Penny's daughter will be making her first appearance as a singer Saturday night. Lincoln Cook, the NAACP lawyer, wants me to come and see her sing."

"What kind of singer?"

"Jazz."

"You've got to take me!"

"Maggie, it's at Blackstone's. A Negro jazz joint."

"So, what?"

"I'm a little nervous about going myself. I'll probably be the only white person in the whole joint. I'm just hoping they'll think it's okay for me to be there because I'm a reporter."

"If you take me," Maggie said, "you won't have to worry about being the only white person there."

"Your father would kill me."

"So, don't tell him. I'm a big girl. Jack, I love jazz, and it wouldn't be the first time I've been to a Negro jazz joint."

Jack shook his head. It also wasn't the first time that Maggie had surprised him. "Around here?"

"No, at school. Sometimes we'd go to a local place, not far from Barnard, and sometimes a bunch of us would go to Harlem."

"I'm so out of my league with you."

Maggie smiled and put her hand on his. "You've got your charms."

"If you're dead set on this, I'll pick you up at your parent's house at eight Saturday night."

"Make that nine," Maggie said, "and even then, we'll still be the first ones there."

"Then, how about we get dinner somewhere first and then go —"

"You're a dear," Maggie said looking at the clock on the wall, above the milkshake machine. "But if we're not careful, we will miss the movie."

The Kentucky was a block or so from Ritte's corner, the center of Latonia. The movie house's newspaper ad bragged that it was "scientifically air-conditioned."

The Saturday night feature was *A Girl with Ideas*, a goofy comedy from two years earlier, starring Wendy Barrie and Walter Pidgeon. The trailer touted, "Beauty on a deadline!" and "Newshawks on the run!"

If pressed, Jack would have admitted he was more interested in the air conditioning and the newsreel. And, of course, the girl with ideas who was his date.

CHAPTER 18, TUESDAY, AUGUST 8

**NAZI PRESS STARTS
ATTACKS ON POLAND,
CHARGING THREATS**
*The Cincinnati Times-Star,
August 8, 1939*

**JOHNSON LEAD CONTINUES
TO GROW IN STATE**
Keen Johnson Holds 30,000 Vote Margin
The Kentucky Post, August 8, 1939

On Tuesday morning, Jack was shaving when his phone rang. The caller was Silas Hamlin, the owner of Covington Waste Company.

"Mr. O'Brien, I want you to know my people aren't responsible. We had nothing to do with it."

"I'm glad to hear that, Mr. Hamlin, but can you back up and tell me what it is your people didn't do?" Jack wiped the remaining shaving cream from his face.

"You haven't heard?"

"I just got up. I'm shaving."

"In the middle of the night last night, somebody dumped garbage over a bunch of yards there in Austinburg, where that trouble was."

Jack sat down at the little desk in his room, grabbed his notebook and pen, and tried to get down what Hamlin was telling him.

"Everybody will think," Hamlin said, "my people did it to get back at the idiots who threw bricks at that house. You know, the one that the colored couple tried to buy."

"You're sure none of your people were involved?"

"I'm certain, because we lock our trucks in at night," Hamlin said.

"Look, I'll do what I can, but I imagine my editor has already assigned someone to cover this. Joe Dinklehaus, most likely. You should call him."

"I called Dinklehaus, but he won't return my calls."

"He may still be at the scene," Jack said, "trying to interview people."

"I was hoping you would listen to my side of the story," Hamlin said. "I don't trust Dinklehaus. It seems like he's bending over backward to help that Cleveland outfit."

Jack thought better of saying anything about his colleague.

"Will you help me, Mr. O'Brien?"

Jack wasn't sure how to respond, but his instincts as a reporter were taking over. "Mr. Hamlin," he asked, "what do you plan to do—how do you plan to respond?"

"I've got my men picking up as much of that garbage as they can. And, I've got my supervisors down there going door-to-door trying to assure people we didn't do this."

"How's that going?"

"Not well," Hamlin said, sighing. "Nobody believes us."

"It sounds like you're doing all the right things."

"It won't matter what we do," Hamlin said, "unless the newspapers clear up who did this. Otherwise, this will kill us tomorrow when the Commission votes on the contract."

A thought occurred to Jack. "Mr. Hamlin, I imagine you know more about trash than I ever will, but let's say someone from Cleveland sent those trucks down here to make you look bad."

"We both know damn well that's what happened."

"If that's the case, wouldn't there be envelopes with Cleveland addresses on them, Cleveland newspapers, other stuff that would show where that trash came from?"

"Sure," Hamlin said. "I should have thought of that."

"Can you have your men collect some of that for me?"

"How much you need?"

"Just whatever they can find quickly. Can you have them get it to me by, oh, let's say 11:00?"

"I'll have my men get right on it," Hamlin said. "Tell me where you are."

Jack thought Hamlin sounded relieved just to have something to do to fight back. "Bring them to the *Tribune* building. Have the guard or receptionist call me, and if I don't answer, have them bring your guy up to the newsroom."

"I'll do that."

"And Mr. Hamlin…"

"Yes?"

"I'm a reporter. It's not my job to tell you what to do but be sure your men collect material for you too. You should take it, or have your attorneys take it, to the City Commission meeting to-morrow."

***

At the newsroom, Jack went straight to Managing Editor Rumble's office. "Who's covering the trashing of those yards in Austinburg?"

"Dinklehaus," Rumble said. "Why?"

"I was shaving this morning, and Silas Hamlin, the owner of Covington Waste, calls me. He says his company had nothing to do with trashing those neighborhoods in Austinburg."

"Why didn't he call Dinklehaus?" Rumble asked. "He's met him."

"He said Joe won't return his calls." Jack took a seat across from the editor. "I was hoping I could get a piece of that story."

Rumble picked up an unlit cigar and pointed it in Jack's general direction. "Why don't you humor me and act like I'm the managing editor, and you're the new reporter?"

"Yes, sir," Jack said. "Which is what I was about to say."

Rumble gave Jack a look that gave full expression to his skepticism. "If you have nothing better to do than annoy me, why don't you go get me some coffee?"

"Happy to," Jack said, without stirring. "Like I was saying, with all your experience, I'm sure it occurred to you that Boyle and his Cleveland mobster friends were behind those trucks dumping that garbage in Austinburg."

"Dinklehaus has already been over there and written it up," Rumble said. "He says it was that Covington company. The men who did this were Negroes, and that Cleveland company doesn't hire Negroes."

"Did Joe get a statement from the Covington company?"

"Jack, you're beginning to irritate me. I told you, Dinklehaus has that story." Rumble picked up his coffee cup and looked in it. "I thought I sent you to get coffee."

"Going," Jack said, taking the cup from Rumble.

Jack went to his own desk and grabbed his own coffee mug. At the coffee stand, he filled both cups, then hurried back to Rumble's office. He sat Rumble's cup on his desk, turned, and closed his boss's door.

"When you close that door," Rumble said, "you're supposed to be on the other side."

"Can I see Joe's piece on the trash story?"

"You're like a damn dog with a bone, aren't you?" Rumble rifled through the stack of stories he expected to run in the next morning's newspaper.

"I think the mob is behind this," Jack said. "Just like they were behind the flyers. But even if I'm wrong about that, we should include a statement from the local company denying involvement."

Rumble glanced through the article. "Go talk to Joe about it."

"I've got a friend who works for the biggest bookie in Covington," Jack said. "Joe owes them a lot. He can't afford to give this local company a break."

"Dinklehaus has worked here a long time," Rumble said. "Now get the hell out of my office."

Jack realized he'd overstepped some boundary, maybe more than one. "I won't repeat that," he said. "I'll tell Joe the company called me and gave me a statement. I'll just say I promised to pass it on to him."

"You do that," Rumble said, picking up his phone to make a call—a sure sign the conversation was over.

***

Jack went back to his desk and typed up the statement Silas Hamlin had given him. He pulled the page from his typewriter, proofread it, and carried it to Joe Dinklehaus' desk.

He waited for Dinklehaus to finish typing before speaking.

"Joe," he said. "Silas Hamlin from the Covington Waste Company called me at home this morning and gave me a statement. He says his company had nothing to do with that incident last night. Rumble says you've got that story, so I wanted to pass this along." Jack dropped the page into Dinklehaus' in box.

"Why'd he call you?" Dinklehaus asked.

"He said he couldn't reach you."

Dinklehaus looked more than skeptical. "You could have told him to call me."

"I did. He said you wouldn't call him back. I told him you were out getting interviews with the neighbors."

Dinklehaus picked up the page Jack put in his in-box and read it. "This is baloney."

"We always print denials when we can get them. Most of them are baloney."

Dinklehaus threw the page in his wastebasket and stood, putting himself inches from Jack. Pressing his finger against Jack's chest, he said, "If those coloreds that work for Covington Waste didn't do it, then tell me, wise guy, who did?"

Jack willed himself not to take the bait and get into a scuffle. "Hamlin believes that Cleveland trash company is behind this."

"Horse feathers!" Dinklehaus poked his finger into Jack's chest again. Dinklehaus' face was flushed.

Jack took a step back, pulled out his wallet, and tossed a five-dollar bill on Dinklehaus' desk. "Five dollars says that trash came from Cleveland."

Dinklehaus looked uncertain. Five dollars was a lot. He crossed his arms and grunted.

"You're willing to destroy this company and put a bunch people out of work," Jack taunted the older man, "but you're not sure enough of your story to bet five dollars?"

Dinklehaus pulled five singles from his wallet and tossed them on his desk. "I'll be glad to take your money."

The security guard from the ground floor entered the newsroom, followed by an immense, ebony-colored man with bulging biceps and a bald head. "Mr. O'Brien," the guard said, "this man is here for you."

Jack walked to the door and introduced himself.

"Mr. Hamlin said to give these to you," the man said. He held up two large bags.

"This is some of what they dumped in those yards in Austinburg last night?" Jack asked in a voice louder than necessary.

"Yes, sir."

"Follow me," Jack said and returned to Joe Dinklehaus' desk. "Sit them right here next to this desk."

Dinklehaus jumped up. "I don't want that crap."

Jack looked at the large man holding the bags of trash. "Joe, here," Jack said, pointing at Dinklehaus, "says there's no way the trash those men dumped last night came from Cleveland. He wants to publish a story in tomorrow morning's paper that blames the company you work for. It will put your employer out of business and cost you your job. Maybe you should show him what you found."

The large man grinned and sat a bag next to Dinklehaus' desk. He opened the other bag and dumped its contents on Dinklehaus' desk. The papers spewed across the desk and onto the floor. They carried with them the pungent aroma of decay.

"Goddamn it!" Dinklehaus shouted. Looking at Jack, he said, "You S.O.B."

"I'll be getting back to work," the big man said. "Y'all have a blessed day now."

"Take this crap with you," Dinklehaus called out.

The large black man continued walking away, ignoring Dinklehaus.

Jack picked up an envelope from the pile. "Hmm, this has a Cleveland address and a Cleveland return address." He noticed Rumble standing at the door to his office, watching.

"That doesn't prove anything," Dinklehaus said.

"Here's a page from the *Cleveland Plain Dealer*," Jack said, picking up the page. "And look, here's another envelope with a Cleveland address. And these are coupons for a Cleveland grocery store."

Dinklehaus stared at Jack. "You're a backstabbing bastard."

Jack reached into the stack and pulled out a dozen more papers. He announced what each paper was, stressing its connection to Cleveland, and then tossing each into Dinklehaus' in-box.

"Jack," Rumble interrupted in a booming voice. "You've made your point."

Jack stepped away from Dinklehaus' desk.

"Joe," Rumble said, "you owe Jack five dollars, and you owe me a re-write." His voice was all gravel and no nonsense.

Dinklehaus ran his hand through his hair and then rubbed the back of his neck. He took a deep breath, exhaled, and nodded his acquiescence.

"And Jack," Rumble said, "get your ass in my office. Now."

***

Rumble slammed the door to his office after Jack entered. "You've got a bug up your ass about this, Jack, and I need to know why."

"The Mob is trying to steal the trash collection contract from this local company. I think Harry Boyle is working with the Mob, helping them pull this off. People will lose their jobs, and –"

"Headquarters is looking for reporters to send to Europe in case war breaks out," Rumble interrupted. "They especially want reporters who speak German. I've put your name in, but I need to know I can trust your judgment. Have you got anything tying Boyle to the Mob and this contract?"

"Not yet," Jack said, "but I'm so close I can almost taste it." The revelation that Rumble had put his name for an overseas position shifted Jack's focus. "Headquarters, sir?"

"Overseas Wire Service, actually." Overseas was the company's foreign news service. Rumble waved his hand. "Don't change the subject. If you've got something on Boyle, let me hear it. But if this is just a hunch, I want you to give yourself a chance to be sure you're being objective. Otherwise, you're just pissing people off and putting your career in jeopardy."

A secretary knocked on Rumble's door. Jack stood and opened the door. "Jack," the woman said, "Leo Denton from the Commonwealth Attorney's office called. He wants you to call him back as soon as possible."

Rumble picked up an unlit cigar from the ashtray on his desk. "Go call him. We're done."

***

Jack sat in the small waiting space outside Leo Denton's office, chatting with Denton's secretary.

On the phone, Denton had been cryptic. He had reminded Jack that he could not divulge what a grand jury was up to. But added that if Jack could be at his office about four o'clock, he thought he'd have a scoop for him.

It wasn't hard to guess what that meant: Denton expected the grand jury to return an indictment or indictments. That Denton had called *him* meant the indictment would have to do with the phony charges against Two Penny Smith. But that left open an important question: Who would the grand jury indict?

At quarter after four, Denton bounded into the anteroom. He handed Jack several pieces of paper and asked his secretary, "Any emergencies?"

"No emergencies, but your wife called. She said she's having dinner with your mother."

Jack ignored the chatter and focused on the indictments. The first charged Roscoe Mascelli with perjury. The second charged patrolman Ricky Robinson with filing a false report, perjury, and false arrest. The third indictment charged Captain Frazier, Patrolman Robinson, and other persons, "known and unknown to the grand jury," with obstruction of justice and conspiracy to obstruct justice.

"Aces!" Jack said. He flipped through the papers again. "No indictment against the other cop, Vance?"

"Let's do this in my office, so Dorothy can do her work."

Jack followed the exultant Denton into his office.

"Close the door," Denton said.

Jack complied.

"Jack, I have to be careful what I say," Denton said. "Speaking generally now, not about this case, okay?"

Jack indicated he was following.

"When you see someone like Vance not get indicted, it's a fair guess that the prosecutor has turned him, and he's agreed to testify for the prosecution."

Jack nodded. He wrote nothing in his notebook.

"Frazier is as high as it goes?"

Denton shrugged his shoulders. "Unless I can get Frazier to talk, I'll never know how high it goes."

"What about Two Penny?"

"I've got a motion ready to file, asking Judge Chelone to set his conviction aside." Denton rooted through the papers on his desk and found the folder he was looking for. He pulled out several pages, stapled together. "That's your copy," Denton said, handing the motion papers to Jack. "I'll file it first thing in the morning."

"Thanks, but I meant, did you get Two Penny to testify?"

Denton shook his head. "No, he's too scared they'll do something to him or his family."

Jack glanced at his watch. "Thanks again for the story, I appreciate it. But if I want to make deadline, I've got to run."

"Go write your story," Denton said, pulling a cigarette from a pack of Lucky Strikes. "You can buy me a scotch later."

***

As Harry Boyle pulled his car into the driveway leading to the Lookout House, he felt confident. All day at the office, his phone had been ringing. Many of the calls came from Austinburg residents angry that Covington Waste had dumped garbage in their yards. Other calls came from elsewhere in the city, from citizens who had heard about the trashing and were upset.

Other Commissioners told Boyle they were getting calls as well. Boyle had secured promises from two—Meimann and Vaske – to award the trash collection contract to the Cleveland company. With his vote that would be a majority.

When Boyle reached the Lookout House entrance, he pulled his car to a stop, got out, and tossed his keys to the waiting parking attendant. He told the young man he expected to be about two hours. Once inside, Boyle informed the receptionist he was meeting some men in a private room. "Brink made the arrangements."

Jimmy Brink was the well-known and well-connected owner of the Lookout House. During Prohibition, Brink worked for Cincinnati's notorious bootlegger, George Remus. In 1933, with Prohibition ending, Brink purchased the Lookout House and remodeled the sprawling facility. The big attraction—and the source of most of its revenues—was the large casino.

Boyle took in the dining room's Louis XVI Palace on-the-cheap décor and watched the waiters and busboys—some carrying trays loaded with plates and bowls—bustle between tables. Boyle wondered if the better restaurants only hired thin waiters, or if the waiters kept thin from all the walking and standing they did.

Brink arrived, introduced himself, and gave Boyle a tour, lingering in the casino with its view of Covington and downtown Cincinnati. After the tour, Brink delivered Boyle to a small party room on the second floor.

A waiter took Boyle's drink order and left three menus on the table. Boyle glanced through a menu but put it down when the door opened. Brink ushered in Owl Polizzi and Fats Mascelli. Two additional men came with Polizzi, but remained outside the door. Polizzi was about forty, medium build, with curly hair and a pugnacious attitude. He wore a suit, white shirt, and tie. Except for the bodyguards, he could have passed for the owner or manager of any prosperous business.

Boyle exchanged greetings with the mobsters. Polizzi insisted they order drinks and supper before talking business. Boyle guessed he didn't want a waiter or busboy to overhear their business. He sensed Polizzi and Mascelli were tense and unhappy, but he figured that was not unusual in their business. Besides, they were here to lean on him, to make sure he would deliver the waste contract.

Like the other men, Boyle ordered a steak. Owl Polizzi ordered a bottle of wine for the group. After the waiter served the meals and left, and the men began to eat, Owl broached the subject that brought him to town. "So, Harry, are we going to get this contract tomorrow?"

Harry smiled. "People are hopping mad about what happened to those yards in Austinburg. My phone wouldn't quit ringing today, and from what I gather, that's true for the other Commissioners as well. They wouldn't dare give the contract to Covington Waste. Barring something unexpected, gentlemen, I don't think we have anything to worry about."

Polizzi looked to Fats. "Tell him."

Fats swallowed and wiped his mouth with the white cloth napkin. "We got a guy inside the *Trib*." Fats paused to use his fingernail to pry something loose from between his teeth. He looked at his finger to see what he'd dislodged, then wiped his finger on the tablecloth. "Tomorrow morning, the paper will run a story saying Owl had those yards trashed."

Boyle had learned a long time ago not to panic, but he could feel his chest constrict and his mouth go dry. He took a sip of wine. "Yeah, well," he said, "the newspaper doesn't have a vote on the City Commission, and I know my fellow Commissioners. If they've got to place a bet, and their only choices are, 'I don't want coloreds moving into my neighborhood' and 'Voters believe what they read in the newspaper,' they won't bet on literacy."

Polizzi stared at Boyle. His look was the hard, bitter look of disgust.

"Who wrote this story?" Boyle asked. "Do you know?"

"It's coming out over Joe Dinklehaus's byline," Fats said. "But remember that young guy, the one who wrote that piece blaming me when you had us distribute the flyers? He went to the editor and got the story changed around."

"There you go," Boyle said. "His name's O'Brien. Covington Waste has him in its pocket. I can sell that."

"Harry, you said you would get us this contract," Polizzi said, sounding irritated. "Then, you said we needed to spread those flyers. That blew up in our faces. And then, you said we needed to trash those yards. And now the newspapers are going to trash us—again." Polizzi picked up his fork. "Every time you tell us things are rosy, we end up in the papers, and--"

"Look, I told you this wouldn't be easy," Boyle said, interrupting Polizzi He immediately regretted interrupting the Syndicate boss, but there was no undoing his blunder.

"You told me, you could get this done," Polizzi said, his voice hard and cold.

Boyle said nothing.

"I want this contract, Harry."

Boyle nodded.

"What's the name of my company?" Polizzi demanded.

"Mayfield Disposal," Boyle answered. He hated being forced to answer as if he were reciting his homework for a third-grade teacher.

"That's right," Polizzi said. "You know why we named it that?"

Boyle gave the obligatory shrug.

"'Cause you can dispose of a lot of bodies under all that garbage."

Boyle felt cold.

"One more body wouldn't make much difference."

Boyle heard little of what Polizzi said after that. Thirty minutes later, the meeting over, he walked out—feeling like he was in a bad dream.

CHAPTER 19, WEDNESDAY, AUGUST 9

ALL GERMANS

To Be Registered

**For National Defense
Plan, 15 to 70**

Army Officers To Instruct
Hitler Youth Group – Oil
Stations To Ration Gas

--

*The Cincinnati Enquirer,
August 9, 1939*

The next morning, Harry Boyle's day began badly and promised to get worse. He nicked himself shaving and had to use a styptic pencil to stop the bleeding. When he retrieved the morning papers, it was raining, turning his shirt into a soggy mess.

It was frustrating to have to deal with things like that before the coffee had even finished brewing, but he also knew those things were the least of his concerns. If what Fats said at the Lookout House last night was true, the *Tribune* would have an article about the trash collection contract and the trashing of the yards in Austinburg.

Boyle forced himself to fix toast and pour coffee before he read the paper. To his surprise, the big headline in the local news section of the *Tribune* was not about the trash dumped in yards in Austinburg. It was worse.

The headline read: "Grand Jury Indicts Three for Framing Negro, Prosecutor Wants Verdict Set Aside." Boyle took a deep breath and let it out.

The grand jury indicted Patrolman Ricky Robinson for filing a false report, perjury, and false arrest. It charged both Robinson and his superior, Captain Douglas Frazier, with obstruction of justice and conspiracy to obstruct justice. The grand jury also indicted Roscoe "Fats" Mascelli for perjuring himself during its investigation.

Boyle felt relief he was not the object of the indictments. Still, even if Fats had brought this on himself by testifying before the grand jury, Fats might well blame him for the whole mess.

A little further down, the article quoted the prosecutor, Leo Denton, as saying he had not yet determined why someone wanted to have Two Penny Smith framed. But it also quoted Denton as suggesting that Smith, who worked at Greta's Place, may have seen someone or something there he wasn't supposed to see.

Boyle didn't care what Fats did about the indictment itself. Fats might force Denton to take the case to trial, hoping Denton wouldn't be able to prove his case. Fats might even help things along by trying to intimidate a witness or bribing jurors. Or, Fats might plead guilty to avoid further attention.

What he cared about was whether Fats would blame him—not in court or in the court of public opinion, but where it counted. He was the one who insisted on having Smith arrested. Boyle cursed himself for being so stupid. All of this because he'd wanted to punish Two Penny. *Truth was, you couldn't expect more loyalty from a damn dog.*

Boyle took a bite of his toast and a sip of coffee. He turned to the second story. The article reported that the trash spread around the yards in Austinburg, near where that colored couple wanted to live, was from Cleveland—as was the second bidder on the Covington trash-collection contract.

Alfred "Owl" Polizzi and the Mayfield Road Gang controlled the Cleveland company, the article reported, citing widespread rumors. The company had a reputation for using bribes and dirty tactics to win municipal contracts. The article also quoted Denton—this time saying he was still investigating the full extent of Mob efforts to win the contract for the Cleveland company.

Boyle could feel his chest tighten, and for a moment, he found it difficult to breathe. He forced himself to get up and go to the sink where he filled a glass with tap water and downed it.

One thing was clear. If he couldn't convince the City Commission to give the damn contract to Polizzi's company, he was in trouble. He considered leaving town, maybe leaving the country. But without being able to tap into Agnes' money, that was out of the question. He wouldn't have enough money to live on.

Boyle steeled himself to the fact he had few options. He had to figure out a way to make sure Polizzi got the contract. But if the City Commission voted on the contract today, as scheduled, it would have to vote to give the contract to the local company. The scandal would only get worse if the Commission gave the contract to Polizzi's company while people were still talking about it trashing Austinburg to stir up race issues. He had to get today's meeting, or at least today's consideration of the contract, postponed.

Halfway through his second cup of coffee, Boyle made a decision. He would talk with Leo Denton about his investigation of Mob influence over the Cleveland trash company and the trashing of the yards in Austinburg. No matter what Denton said, he would then tell his colleagues they should postpone the contract award a couple weeks, to allow Denton time to complete his investigation.

He found Denton's number in the phone book and called. Denton wasn't in yet. He'd check again when he got to work. He would get the decision on the contract postponed. And then he'd think of something. He always did.

***

That evening, Jimmy Durante was about to perform in Covington's Devou Park, and the crowd was enormous. Jack was glad he and Maggie had arrived early and got good seats.

Nestled in the hills that overlooked Covington on the west, the park had once been the 500-acre farm of the Devou family. The family's heirs donated the land to Covington for use as a park. Earlier in the year, the Works Progress Administration constructed an amphitheater at the base of a bowl formed by converging hills. The City of Covington put up $25,000 toward the $125,000 project.

Mayor Knollman walked to the center of the amphitheater, tapped on the large microphone to be sure it was on, and welcomed the crowd.

"Oh, Christ, look who it is!" a man to Jack's left said. "A lousy, back-stabbing, snake-in-the-grass hack."

Jack looked toward the voice. It was Vice Mayor Harry Boyle, trying to make his way down the aisle. He was holding tight to a pint bottle in a brown paper bag.

"Your career's over, you know that?" Boyle said, slurring his words. "I will see to that personally." Boyle tried to take a step forward, but nearly lost his balance and apparently thought better of it.

On stage, Mayor Knollman continued his introductory remarks.

"Mr. Boyle, you've had too much to drink," Jack said, standing. "Why don't you head home before you embarrass yourself?"

"You don't mind embarrassing me, you son-of –"

"Mr. Boyle, I'm with a lady. She doesn't need to hear –"

Maggie stood.

Boyle sneered. "Well, well. Little Maggie's home from school and all grown up. What are you doing with this bum?"

"Uncle Harry, Jack's right. You're embarrassing yourself. Let us take you home."

"Not on your life, sweetheart. Besides, I'm fine." Boyle put the bottle between his knees and pulled a pack of cigarettes from his pocket.

"Now, ladies and gentlemen," Knollman bellowed over the loudspeaker, "without further ado, the one and only Jimmy Durante!"

While the band played "Inka Dinka Doo," Boyle fumbled a cigarette from the pack, found his matches, and lit the cigarette. He took a deep drag.

"Maggie's right," Jack said. "You're in no condition to drive. Let us –"

Boyle retrieved the bottle from between his knees and pointed it toward Jack. "If you keep sticking your nose where it doesn't belong, you're going to get yourself killed, that's what you're going to do."

Maggie moved closer to Boyle and in a lower voice said, "Come on, Uncle Harry, you're making a scene."

"STOP da music, everybody!" Durante shouted, interrupting the song with his trademark line.

Boyle removed the cigarette from his mouth. "I'm fine. It's your boyfriend –"

"Mister," someone behind Boyle called out, "Sit down and shut up, or leave."

Boyle turned toward the scold and said, "Piss off!" He turned back to Maggie. "You're a good kid, sweetheart. Make sure you're not with this bum when the Mob catches up with him. You don't want them to do to you what they'll do to him."

Boyle returned the cigarette to his lips, turned around, and staggered off, stumbling over people and drawing complaints as he did.

Maggie plopped down in her seat and put her face in her hands.

***

Durante ended his show, and the stage lights went off except for a spotlight that followed Durante as he headed off stage. Halfway, Durante stopped, turned back to the audience, and said, "Good night, Mrs. Calabash, wherever you are."

The crowd gave a rousing round of applause. Some whistled.

And with that, mindful it was a weekday night, people began to gather their belongings, stand, and leave.

Jack put his hand on Maggie's forearm.

Maggie looked at Jack, her face tense. "How much danger are you in?"

"Maggie, I'm a reporter. If they went after me, all the newspapers in town would raise a stink."

Jack could tell his evasion didn't satisfy Maggie. "Look, I haven't had any direct confrontations with the Mob," he said. "At this point, I don't think I represent more than a minor nuisance to them. So, unless I get closer to exposing them than I am now, I don't think I'm in any danger."

"At this point?" Maggie said. "For now?"

"Your uncle is worried about himself. The city's trash collection contract is up for bid. There are two bidders—the local company that's been doing this for years, and a Cleveland company the Syndicate controls. I can't prove it, but I think the Syndicate is leaning on your uncle to make sure the Syndicate company gets the contract."

Maggie's eyes widened. She put her hand to her mouth.

"Your uncle is trying to convince himself that I'm the one they will blame if they don't get the contract. Given the shape he was in, it doesn't look like he's having much success with that."

"Jack," Maggie said, "can I tell my aunt what you just told me?"

"Sure," Jack said. "But I think she knows, and that's why she left. Well, that and the fact that Harry was spending too much time at Greta's."

Maggie looked around to be sure no one was close. "She knew about him spending too much time at Greta's. She also knew he was spending too much time with Syndicate men, but she didn't know what they were up to."

"Where is your aunt? Can I talk with her?"

"She doesn't want anybody to know where she is."

"What's the big secret?"

"She's afraid."

"Of Uncle Harry?"

"Him and his Mob friends, but you can't use that. You can't use any of what I've just told you."

Jack stared at Maggie. He knew she was in a difficult position. "Can you get me an interview with your aunt—so you're not in the middle?"

Maggie pulled away and folded her arms.

"Just ask her. Let her decide."

Maggie stared at Jack. Around them, the stands were emptying. Maggie sighed, "I'll talk to her, Jack, but I don't think she'll agree."

"I understand, Maggie, but you've got to talk to her for me."

"I will. But please, don't get your hopes up. Uncle Harry is the one who loved the limelight, not Aunt Agnes. And now, she's afraid—and she's not someone who scares easily."

Jack stood and helped Maggie up. He glanced back at the stage where Durante had been. "Good night, Mrs. Boyle," he said, "wherever you are."

CHAPTER 20, FRIDAY, AUGUST 11

DANCING RAPPED BY BAPTIST GROUP

"Maysville, Ky. The Bracken Association of Baptists ...
adopted a resolution condemning
dancing in public high schools."
The Kentucky Post, August 11, 1939

On Friday morning, when Jack and Woody arrived at their usual table in the Bridge Café, George Hanover was already there and visibly perturbed. The heat of his conviction reddened his face and had even prompted him to remove his jacket.

Jack took in the place's sounds and smells. Always busy at this hour, the breakfast-and-lunch joint was humming with conversations, punctuated from time-to-time with laughter or shouts. Waitresses hustled between tables, alternately flirting with customers and prodding them to hurry up and decide. Every minute or so, Sam, the cook, rang a bell to signal he had placed an order on the service window. The noise didn't crowd out the smells of bacon grease and cigarette smoke.

"Top of the day, George," Jack said.

"Tax Day, Porridge," Woody chimed in, echoing Jack's tone, if not his words.

Hanover folded his newspaper and tossed it on the table in disgust. "They're talking about that socialist Roosevelt running for a third term. They ought to impeach the man, not —"

Emma interrupted. "Coffee, gents?"

"Yes, ma'am," Jack said.

Woody nodded enthusiastically.

"George, hon, you ready to order?"

"Yeah, ham and eggs, hash browns."

"How 'bout you fellows?"

Jack placed orders for himself and Woody.

"I'll put your orders in and bring your coffees," Emma promised and hurried away.

"I swear," Hanover said, "I just don't understand this palaver about that cripple running for a third term. He's a damn socialist, and he's going to ruin this country."

Woody pulled out his wallet, fished out his Social Security card, and holding it up for Hanover to see, said, "Yam vocalist."

"Yeah," Hanover groused, "Professor Spuds-for-Brains, you probably *are* a damn socialist."

"Bean up," Woody said, standing. He headed to the restroom to clean up.

"Jack, before Sal gets here," Hanover said, in a quieter voice, "I need to have a word with you."

"Yes, sir."

"You're doing a crackerjack job at that newspaper, but what if the Syndicate decides you're a problem?"

"It comes with the territory," Jack said. "Coppers, soldiers, others have jobs that involve risks. Doctors catch things from their patients and die. I think what I'm doing is important." Jack shrugged his shoulders. "I'll take my chances."

"Well, I can't take a chance with my daughter. I—."

"Maggie told you about our run-in with the Vice Mayor?"

"She certainly did and let me tell you—"

"He was drunk—"

"I'm sure he was, but he was right about the risk you're exposing Maggie to, and I won't stand for it. I don't want you seeing Maggie anymore."

Emma returned with coffees for Jack and Woody.

"With all due respect, sir, that's up to Maggie."

"Well, I won't stand for it."

Sal Rizzi arrived. "Won't stand for what?"

"George was telling me," Jack said, "that he won't stand for Roosevelt running for a third term. He says we don't need a cripple running the country. He thinks we need a strong leader, someone like Chancellor Hitler."

"That so?" Sal asked Hanover, grinning.

"You think that's funny," Hanover said, "but maybe that's exactly what this country needs—someone with a strong hand, who can take charge. I mean, look at what Hitler's done to their economy. He's rebuilt their military, and—"

"Oh, come on, George, you can't be serious." Jack shook his head.

"Now listen here, Jack, I'm dead serious. If someone like him were president, we wouldn't have a bunch of Jews running the government, telling business how to run its affairs, letting bums freeload off the rest of us—"

"Your buddy, Hitler," Jack said, "may be about to start another war."

Sal waved at Emma.

"Bull puckey!" Hanover's face reddened. "Chamberlain will back down again. People in England and France remember what they went through during the Great War, and they won't put up with that again. Mark my words! They won't lift a finger over this dispute between the Germans and the Poles."

Emma arrived with coffee for Sal. "Same as usual?" she asked.

Sal cast a glance at Hanover and Jack. "Yeah, Emma, same as usual."

***

Jack and Woody lingered in the diner after Hanover and Rizzi left. "Do you have to be anywhere?" Jack asked.

Woody shook his head "no."

Jack looked around to be sure no one was sitting too close. "I've got a shot at an assignment overseas. Headquarters in New York is looking for reporters who speak German, and my editor has forwarded my name to them along with the stories I've broken. He thinks I've got a shot at it."

Woody made a "thumbs up" gesture. Speaking slowly and with great concentration, he added, "Con–rat–you–lotions."

"Thanks, but I haven't got anything yet. Lots of reporters are begging for gigs as foreign correspondents, and I just started."

"Mule bit it."

"I don't know. I may be a longshot. But if I do get it, they'll want me to leave right away." Jack reached into his pocket and retrieved a key. He placed the key on the table and pushed it across to Woody. "This is for my room. If I get the gig, I think I can work out a deal with Mrs. Schickel, so you can have the room."

Woody shook his head and pushed the key back.

"I want you to keep it," Jack insisted. "I'm not done digging into what Vice Mayor Boyle and his buddies are up to, and if I hit pay dirt, they may decide to play rough."

"Pluck 'em!"

Jack shook his head. "Hear me out. They know if they go after me, they'll get a boatload of bad press and attention from lawmen. But if they beat the crap out of you, or worse, they stand a better chance of getting away with it."

Woody ran his hand over the stubble on his face. "Pluck 'em!"

"If something happens to me, I want you to have the room. It'll be safer than your shanty."

Woody made a writing gesture.

Jack handed him his notebook.

"Stop with Boyle," Woody wrote. "Not worth it."

With his finger, Jack drew a small circle on the table top before responding. "Look, it's a dangerous world. I can't go through life acting like I'm still a college boy. What I do is important, I'm good at it, and I'm not going to stop. It wouldn't be right."

"U could end up dead," Woody wrote. "Or like me."

"I'll be okay, but I'm worried about you."

"Don't!" Woody scribbled.

"Then, I want you to come with me. I'll show you the room."

Woody wrote, "Your room's not safe."

"If I hit pay dirt and you're still working for that bookie, the Syndicate's liable to take out its frustrations on you."

"Let me know if you do," Woody wrote.

"Maybe you should take your shanty to Louisville. I'll ask Ben if he can help get you situated."

Woody stared at Jack, grimly, and scribbled in the notebook. "Can he find me a job?"

"If he can, will you promise me you'll go to Louisville before the Mob kills you?"

Woody stared at Jack, noncommittal.

"This is important. If I can prove the Syndicate has its hooks in Boyle, and Ben can find a job for you, will you promise me you'll go to Louisville?"

Woody sucked in his lips, and all the muscles in his face tightened. Giving vent to his frustration at the lack of good choices, he banged his fist on the table and said, "Horseradish!"

Jack let a smile show. "Promise me."

Woody threw up his hands. "Aisle dough."

CHAPTER 21, SATURDAY, AUGUST 12

**CIANO SEES HITLER
AFTER LAST-MINUTE
CALL TO MUSSOLINI**
*Kentucky Times-Star,
August 12, 1939*

**NEARLY 2,000 JEWS EMBARK
IN GREEK SHIPS IN BLACK SEA
FOR SMUGGLING TO PALESTINE**
The Cincinnati Enquirer, August 12, 1939

"Maggie, you look gorgeous," Jack said. "And this place is nice." They were eating dinner at Chez Nora, a popular restaurant on Main Street, before going to Blackstone to hear Cora Smith sing. Maggie wore a little black dress with the wasp waist that was very much in style. The dress showed off her figure.

"You wouldn't say that," Maggie said, "if you'd seen me this afternoon. I was at the Baker-Hunt Foundation, trying to teach some kids how to paint. I was in an old smock and had my hair tied up."

Jack knew Maggie had been volunteering at the local art school but had not seen her in her painting garb. For just a second, he tried to picture her in an artist's smock with her hair pulled up, and a smudge of paint on her cheek. He imagined her in a room with sunlight streaming through tall windows, the air fragrant with the smells of charcoal, chalk, linseed oil, and turpentine. In his mind's eye, he saw earnest, adoring children gathered around her, vying for her attention. He smiled.

Maggie showed Jack her palms. "I've still got paint on my

hands," she said. "And my arms. I couldn't get all of it off."

"Maggie, you're pretty as a picture. I don't know another woman who wouldn't give her eye teeth to look as beautiful as you do."

A waiter took their orders and brought their drinks and salads. The menu was more extensive than Jack expected and the surroundings interesting. While he and Maggie sat in the ground floor dining room, which was not full, some customers opted to dine on the third-floor open-air dining space, where a jazz band would perform later.

A gentleman who had been dining on the far side of the room settled with the waiter, and on his way out, stopped and greeted Jack.

"Mr. O'Brien, I'm not sure you remember me. I'm Ben Solomon, of Solomon & Solomon."

Jack stood. "After Two Penny's trial, Lincoln Cook invited me to use your conference room to interview the Smith family."

Benjamin Solomon was sixty or more, with a slight paunch, baggy eyelids, and long, boney hands. He glanced at Maggie.

"I'm sorry, Mr. Solomon," Jack said. "Pardon my manners. This is Maggie Hanover. You may know her father, George Hanover."

"My pleasure, Miss Hanover," Solomon said. His voice was deep and had a haunting sadness in it. "This young man you're having dinner with," he said, "is helping to undo an injustice done to one of the many unfortunates among us. He has—and I didn't think it was possible these days—persuaded a prosecutor to ask the court to set aside a conviction he himself obtained. Truly remarkable."

Maggie flashed a smile at the older man. "It's very kind of you to say so, Mr. Solomon."

"Yes, well, this young man has been a breath of fresh air." Solomon pulled a handkerchief from his pocket. "I've taken up enough of your time. If you'll excuse me."

"Mr. Solomon," Jack said, as the older man turned and walked toward the door. "Thank you. I'm honored."

Without looking back, Solomon waived a peremptory goodbye with his left hand, while continuing in halting, arthritic steps toward the door.

Maggie looked around the little restaurant and leaned in toward Jack. "He's right, you know. It really is something that you got the prosecutor to ask the judge to let Two Penny out of jail. If you hadn't dug into this that wouldn't have happened."

The waiter arrived, carrying a tray. They exchanged the usual bromides with the waiter as he served their meals—pork loin and sweet potato for Jack and a pasta dish for Maggie. The waiter asked if they needed anything else and hurried off, taking the tray with him.

"The whole thing about Two Penny is a puzzle with a lot of pieces missing."

"Like what?"

"Two Penny saw something, or someone, he wasn't supposed to see at Greta's, but I can't establish what, or who. Two Penny won't discuss it. I'm stuck." Jack thought for a moment. "I'm hoping your aunt can explain what happened or at least point me in the right direction. What can you tell me about her?"

Maggie spoke for several minutes about her aunt, with whom both she and her mother were close. She talked about going on special outings with her aunt to the art museum, the Krohn conservatory and elsewhere.

Jack asked about her uncle.

"He was okay. We were just never close. He and my father would go to the study and drink and talk—argue mostly—and chase me away if I got near. I wasn't supposed to bother my Mom and aunt either, but they never chased me away, and as soon as I was old enough, they would ask me questions and encourage me to chat with them."

"Any chance of my getting to talk to her?"

"I told her you want to talk with her. She's thinking about it."

"Thank you, thank you." Jack took a sip of his wine. "Why don't I talk so you can eat?"

"Is that why guys talk so much on dates?" Maggie asked, grinning. "So their dates can eat?"

Jack gave a fake smile.

"And here I thought," Maggie said, "it was because they liked to hear themselves talk."

***

Jack and Maggie arrived at Blackstone about nine thirty. The place was dark and warm and smoky. A long mahogany bar ran the length of one wall. Some waitresses loitered with regular customers; others scurried around their tables. One or two stood at the bar, waiting for the bartender to complete their orders.

When Jack's eyes adjusted, he spotted Lincoln Cook and led Maggie to his table. As they got closer, he made out Mrs. Smith and Willis Smith seated at the table. On stage, the musicians were warming up and doing riffs, settling the crowd.

Jack introduced Maggie and ordered drinks for the two of them. Before the drinks came, the lights dimmed, and Bacchus Blackstone came to the microphone. A spotlight shined down on the stage and focused on him. He was a big man, over six feet, with broad shoulders, long arms, and big hands. The ivories in his broad smile were white as piano keys. At the sight of his imposing figure, the crowd quieted.

"Ladies and Gentlemen," he said. The sound system amplified his voice, reverberating around the room. He moved back from the microphone and repeated, "Ladies and gentlemen." The sound was loud, as intended, but without the unintended feedback.

"We have a special treat for you tonight. We are introducing, for the first time, our own, the very lovely and talented, Miss Cora Smith."

Jack and Maggie and everyone around their table yelled and clapped. Regulars in the crowd joined in.

"Cora grew up right here in Covington, but I believe she will be a big star, and when you hear this little lady sing, I'm sure you will agree. Let's hear a big round of applause for Cora Smith."

As Blackstone took his exit, the lights darkened, and Cora walked onto the stage. When she reached the center, the spotlight shined on her. Cora wore a long, shimmering, gold dress that clung to her figure.

The crowd applauded and cheered.

For a second, Cora looked awed by the crowd and the noise, but when the band played, and the noise died down, she regained her poise. She waited until the right moment and began singing "Strange Fruit," the poem written about the Southern tradition of lynching black men. Billie Holiday had made it a hit song earlier in the year among people of color.

The song—and Cora's rendition of it—mesmerized the audience. The song was something of a national anthem for people of color. But it was more than that. It stirred up fears and resentments and melancholy; it gave voice to hope and resistance and to feelings of futility.

When Cora finished, she got an emotional round of applause. Jack and Maggie and people around the joint stood and applauded or yelled or whistled. Mrs. Smith remained seated. A tear ran down her face.

Maggie moved her chair closer to Mrs. Smith and asked. "Are you okay?"

Mrs. Smith shook her head. "That's what they did to my pa," she said, wiping away tears with her fingers. "They strung him up and made us kids watch. I don't know what I feel more—angry at what them men done or happy for my baby girl."

One of the band members joined Cora, and they sang two of the Ink Spots' current hits, "If I Didn't Care" and "Address Unknown."

Cora took her bow, and the hometown crowd cheered and called for more.

Bacchus Blackstone re-took the stage. "Ladies and Gentlemen, as we sit here tonight, storm clouds are gathering over Europe. That man Hitler is spouting his racial theories, and millions are saluting him. The police are rounding up Jews. It wouldn't surprise me none if they were arresting people like us too."

The room was quiet. Waitresses stood still, listening, wondering what Blackstone would say. Patrons watched the big man and sat mute.

"I'm just a jazz musician and the owner of this place."

Blackstone looked around.

"I don't know if there's a going to be another big war, but I'm old enough to remember the last time things were like this, and how President Wilson promised to keep us out, and how we ended up getting involved anyway.

"You young people, sitting here tonight with your favorite guy or girl on your arm, are too young to remember all that. But lots of young men, including some of us coloreds, had to tell sweethearts good-by, saying we'd be back when it was over and making other foolish promises.

"Some of us lived to keep those promises, and some didn't. And some that lived, came back changed and couldn't keep the promises they'd made. Or they found that girl they'd promised to return to had grown up some herself and had moved on.

"So, I'm not saying that there will be another war, and I'm certainly not saying there won't be one. I'm just saying, all this talk got me to remembering a song we heard a lot during the Great War.

"Cora wasn't even born then, but I asked her to learn that song and to sing it for us tonight. For you youngsters, it's called 'Till We Meet Again.'

"Cora, come on out and take us all back to that time." Blackstone took a place with the band and picked up his saxophone.

Cora returned to the stage to another round of applause. She composed herself, and the band began playing. After the song's long introductory music, she sang the lines:

> Smile the while you kiss me sad adieu
>
> When the clouds roll by I'll come to you
>
> Then the skies will seem more blue...

For the older folks, the ones who could remember the Great War and what it had been like, the song evoked feelings long put aside. For the younger folks, whose memories did not go back so far, it elicited thoughts of whether a similar experience awaited them—and whether they would measure up.

Cora dug deep and purred out the refrain.

> Every tear will be a memory,
>
> So wait and pray each night for me,
>
> Till we meet again.

She was a huge hit with the crowd.

Jack looked at Willis. "I wish your father could be here."

"Me too, but I'm hoping he'll be out soon." Willis tipped his beer glass to Jack in an understated toast.

It was late when Jack and Maggie left. Both were subdued.

CHAPTER 22, SUNDAY, AUGUST 13

President Sails On Vacation;
May Go To Newfoundland
The Cincinnati Enquirer,
August 13, 1939

On Sunday morning, Jack went to Mass at the imposing St. Mary's Cathedral of the Assumption on Madison Avenue. Inspired by the Notre Dame Cathedral in Paris, the church was Covington's preeminent landmark.

Jack disagreed with nothing the priest said in his homily, but he wondered why he had never—not once—heard a priest use his Sunday sermon to condemn Jim Crow and segregation or racial bigotry. Or why he had never heard a priest tell his congregation that placing bets with bookies supported the Syndicate and made the bettor party to the Syndicate's criminal activities.

And not once had he heard a priest condemn Fascism and Nazism. In fact, the Catholic Church tolerated Father Coughlin, who preached antisemitism and pro-Nazi views on his weekly radio broadcast that reached millions.

After Mass Jack took a few minutes to study the murals that decorated the arm of the church to the right of the altar. Covington artist Frank Duveneck painted the murals. Jack smiled when he remembered what Maggie had said about the murals when they had toured the Cathedral together. *Yes, Duveneck painted them. But not on his best day.*

Jack wished he were spending the day, his day off, with Maggie, but she had left for New York to talk with the people who ran the Art Rescue Consortium.

He couldn't tell if Maggie's parents were encouraging her to explore that to put some distance between Maggie and himself. He wanted to believe they found the prospect of Maggie moving back to New York almost as alarming as her dating him. But he suspected the Hanovers thought Manhattan was an ideal place for a young woman with brains and breeding to find a husband "with prospects."

Jack returned to his room in the boardinghouse. As he stepped into the room, the phone rang. It was the *Tribune*'s Assignment Editor. "Assistant Commonwealth Attorney Leo Denton is trying to reach you," he told Jack. "He says it's urgent and for you to call him." The editor gave Jack the phone number.

"Denton," the prosecutor answered when Jack dialed the number.

"Leo, it's Jack."

"Remember Patrolman Robinson's partner, Denny Vance? I got him to agree to testify against Robinson and Frazier in exchange for immunity."

"I remember." Jack sat down at the little table in his room. With an introduction like that, what followed would be ugly.

"He's dead. He was at the American Legion Hall in Latonia last night, drinking. When he left, they got him. Someone beat him to death with a baseball bat." Latonia was the largely residential Covington neighborhood that gave its name to the race track.

Jack swallowed and tried to get out of his head the image of someone beating the cop to death with a baseball bat. "Who killed him? The Mob or the cops?"

"Good question. I don't know, but my money is on the Mob. Fats Mascelli warned me not to mess with him."

"When?"

"In front of the grand jury." Denton hesitated. "Sorry. You

can't say it was in front of the grand jury. Can you just say in front of witnesses?"

"Sure." Jack rubbed his forehead and tried to think. "Did the police find the baseball bat? Are they sure it was a baseball bat and not a police baton?"

"Yeah, whoever did this wiped his prints off, but left the bat at the scene, next to the body."

"Leo, are you in danger? Are they going to come after you next?"

Denton paused before answering. "I don't think so. I don't think they would want the uproar they'd get if they killed a prosecutor. But just in case, I sent my wife and kids out of town. And I'm taking other precautions. Which reminds me, don't share this phone number with anyone."

"Who's running the police investigation?"

"Deputy Chief Rasche assumed responsibility, which gave me some hope we'd at least get an honest investigation, but Chief Schild stepped in and assigned the case to Internal Affairs. He said it was important the Department follow established procedures, so no one can criticize the investigation."

"And?"

"And, I've got a hunch that's the last we'll hear of it."

"Vance. Did he have a family?" Jack asked.

"Wife and two kids."

"What is your office going to do? Are you going to convene a grand jury to investigate?"

"I haven't talked to my boss yet. He's… It's Sunday, who knows." Denton hesitated. "Jack, for the record, this was the brutal murder of a police officer. The Commonwealth Attorney's office will pursue this aggressively." Denton paused again. "Off the record, I don't know what we can do. If Frazier or Robinson or someone else in the police force did this, the Department will close ranks. And if it was Fats Mascelli or his men who did this…"

Jack understood what Denton was trying to say. If it was a Mob hit, they would likely never solve the case. He shared Denton's frustration, but he also needed to know if this was his story. "Leo, were you at the scene?"

"Yeah, Deputy Chief Rasche called me at home last night. It was…" Denton's voice caught. "Vance's head looked like a watermelon that fell off the back of a truck. They cracked his skull open. You could see the guy's brain."

Jack hesitated a moment to allow Denton to collect himself.

"Was anyone from the *Tribune* there?"

"There were no reporters there. Vance was one of the cops' own. The police kept it off the radio."

"You okay?" Jack asked.

"No. I need a couple stiff drinks, but I've got to keep my head screwed on straight in case my boss calls or the cops turn up something."

Jack wrapped up his call with Denton and called the Assignment Editor back. He told him what he was working on. Jack wanted his byline on the story in Monday morning's paper.

"Driscoll's off today," the editor said. "It's yours."

***

At the Police Department, Jack got a prepared statement from the police officer assigned to press relations. The statement recited that Patrolman Dennis Vance died at the hands of an unknown assailant or assailants, where, and when. It also provided details concerning Vance's length of service, his wife's name, and the ages of his two children, but little about the murder and nothing about why someone had murdered him.

"Can I speak with Police Chief Schild?" Jack asked.

"You're O'Brien, right?" The cop was pugnacious and had an

attitude larger than the beer belly that overhung his thick police belt.

"Yes, sir. With the *Tribune*." Jack tried to smile, hoping to charm the cop.

"Chief Schild's not available."

"Then, can I speak with Deputy Police Chief Rasche?" Jack raised his eyebrows.

"He's not available." The cop smirked but maintained eye contact with Jack.

Jack refused to look away. "How about the officer in charge of the investigation?"

"He's busy." The cop folded his arms across his chest.

"Can you give me the names of the officers who were the first on the scene?" Jack asked, knowing what the answer would be, but forcing the cop to be explicit with his noncooperation.

The cop stared at Jack for a long moment. "No."

"Were there any witnesses to the murder?" Jack asked.

"We can't reveal that." The smug expression on the cop's face remained.

"Can I have your name for my story?" Jack smiled when he asked that.

"We're done here," the cop said. "If you'll excuse me."

"Thank you," Jack said. "I feared the Department would try to cover up what happened. Our readers will be glad to know you're being so forthcoming."

The officer put his hand on his nightstick. "O'Brien, you've got a bad attitude, you know that?"

Jack asked, "Did a cop kill Patrolman Vance?"

"The problem with a bad attitude," the officer said, ignoring Jack's question, "is it's like a flat tire. When you got one, you're not going to get anywhere."

Jack wasn't sure, but he thought the cop was giving him more than a metaphor about life. He figured there was a good chance the cops would slash his tires. He could feel his anger rising but forced a smile. "I thought it was the other way around," he said. "A flat tire gives a fellow a bad attitude. Makes him want to find out who did it."

The cop shook his head in disgust and left.

Convinced he would get nothing from the police, at least not on a Sunday, Jack decided to go to the newspaper's office to check in. But by the time he stepped out of the building, he had a different idea. He drove to the house on Front Street where Vice Mayor Boyle lived.

Harry Boyle answered the door.

"Mr. Vice Mayor," Jack asked, "could I get your reaction to Patrolman Dennis Vance's murder?"

Boyle looked surprised. "This is the first I've heard about it." Boyle stood in the doorway, but didn't invite Jack in. "When did it happen?"

"Last night, after eleven."

Boyle frowned and shook his head. "They usually notify me when something like this happens. Was he on duty?"

"No, he had just left the American Legion Hall in Latonia."

"I'm sorry, but I know nothing about it."

"Do you want to give me a comment?"

Boyle collected himself. "This is a terrible situation. I want to express my deepest sympathy for Patrolman—ah — Blancher's family." Boyle paused while Jack got that in his notes. "An attack on a police officer is an attack on all of us. The City will use all its resources to track down who did this."

Jack realized the patrolman's name meant nothing to Boyle. "Sir, do you know who Patrolman Vance is?" Jack corrected himself. "Was."

"I don't recall meeting him, but I may have and am just drawing a blank. Like I said, this is the first I heard of this, and it's... well, tragic."

"He and his partner, Ricky Robinson, arrested Two Penny. Vance agreed to testify that Captain Frazier arranged it. That's why the grand jury didn't indict Vance along with Frazier and Robinson. Presumably, it's also why someone—the Mob or a fellow police officer—killed him."

Boyle put the palm of his hand on the back of his neck and sighed. "So, that's why you're here. You still think I had something to do with Two Penny's arrest. I didn't. I swear to God, I had nothing to do with that. You've got to get that into your head."

Jack had nothing to tie Boyle to Two Penny's arrest, and therefore nothing to tie him to Vance's murder. "Mr. Vice Mayor," Jack said, "I caught you off guard. I wonder if you want to add anything to your statement?"

"Give me a chance to check with the Police Chief. You going to be in your office?"

"Yes." Jack put his notebook in his pocket. "Actually, I'll be in and out, following up on the story."

"I'll call you, and if you're not in, I'll leave a statement with somebody."

Jack excused himself and headed to Latonia. Beside the race track and a golf course, the neighborhood included churches, a couple movie theatres, the Green Lantern restaurant, and the American Legion Hall.

At the Legion Hall, Jack tried to find someone who had seen anything—the murder, the dead body, the police who investigated the murder. But the folks who held forth in the Legion bar on Saturday night were home nursing their hangovers – or listening to baseball on the radio. The Sunday afternoon bingo crowd was a separate set of folks, women mainly, who had not been around the evening before. No one knew anything.

Jack struck out with the neighbors too. He was about to leave when he saw a kid of about ten or eleven leaning against his car. The kid was holding his bike and was waiting for Jack.

"You want to know about that cop they killed last night?" the kid asked.

"That's right."

"You with the newspaper?"

"Sure am," Jack said. "Why, do you know something?"

"Uh-huh, but I don't want to be in the newspaper. I'm afraid they'll get me."

Jack pulled his notebook out. "In the newspaper business, sometimes people don't want their names in the newspaper in situations like this. When that happens, we keep their name confidential, no matter what."

"You do?"

"Yeah," Jack said. "Where do you go to school?"

"Holy Cross."

Holy Cross was the parochial school a few blocks from the American Legion. "You're Catholic?" Jack asked.

"Yes, sir."

"With reporters, it's like when you go to confession, and the priest can't tell anyone what you said. What's your name?"

"Mikey."

"Mikey what?"

"You want to know what I saw?"

"Absolutely."

"It's gonna cost you a dollar."

Jack pulled a dollar from his wallet but held it where the kid couldn't grab it and run off. "I'll pay you if you saw something, but if you're conning me, I'm not paying up."

The kid bit his lip.

"I need your last name."

The kid looked around. "Chlanda."

Jack opened his notebook.

The kid volunteered the spelling of his name.

"What did you see?"

The kid kicked at the dirt.

Jack stuck the dollar bill in his pocket.

"Aw, come on, Mister."

"Tell me what you saw, and no tricks. If I put something in the paper, it better be the God's honest truth."

The kid kicked the dirt again. "I didn't see anything, but my parents did. After the police came, they went across the street to see what happened. All the neighbors did. Except for old man Kline. He never comes out."

Jack sucked in his lower lip and squeezed it between his teeth. Those were the neighbors who had just told him they had seen nothing, not even the police. "Where do you live?"

"You going to tell my parents?"

"No, I just need it for my notes. I can look it up in the phone book. You'll just save me time."

Mikey Chlanda gave Jack his home address.

"The dead man was a cop. His name was Vance. Dennis Vance. Do you know where he lived?"

"Yeah. His kids go to my school."

"Where do they live?" Jack asked.

"On Southern, about three blocks from Church Street."

Jack gave the kid a quarter and drove to Southern Avenue. He went down Southern Avenue several blocks and doubled back. On his return pass, he spotted two ladies taking food to a frame house near the end of the block. Jack parked and crossed the street.

When he arrived on the porch, the ladies were handing their food offerings to the widow. As custom and common sense demanded, they also turned down the obligatory invitation to come inside.

When the neighbor ladies turned to leave, Jack introduced himself to the widow. "Mrs. Vance, my name is Jack O'Brien. I'm a reporter with the *Tribune*. I hate to intrude, but I was wondering if I can get a statement?"

"They told me not to talk to the press."

"The men who killed your husband told you that?"

"No, the officers who were here last night. Look, I don't want to talk right now."

"I understand, but in my story, I need to mention something about the officer's family. The police press officer says your name is Alice. Is that correct?"

Mrs. Vance glanced up and down the street, before answering. "Yes."

"How old was your husband?"

"Thirty-seven."

"You have two kids?"

"Yes. Ages nine and twelve. Now if you'll excuse me."

"Where will the visitation be?"

"Connley Brothers, but I don't know when." Conley Brothers was new. It occupied a large, white building closer to Church Street.

"Someone killed your husband because he agreed to testify against his partner, Ricky Robinson. And Captain Frazier. Was he worried that would happen?"

"I can't talk. Please let me alone." She clenched her hands together against her chest. Her eyes kept darting around the street.

She refused to make eye contact.

"Did someone on the force do this?" Jack tried to ask this as a close friend might.

Mrs. Vance looked offended. "No. I don't even know why you would say something like that. It was the Mob. They warned him."

Jack tried hard not to react. "Who did?"

"I don't know. The prosecutor told Denny if he didn't agree to testify, they would put him in prison. The Mob told him he'd better get amnesia. Either that or make sure he kept his life insurance paid up. Denny didn't know what to do."

"Do you think someone on the police force told the Mob where they'd find your husband?"

"I can't do this. Excuse me." Mrs. Vance closed the door. Jack could hear a deadbolt slide into place.

Jack returned to his car and finished his notes. He had one more stop to make, but first, he wanted to check in at the newspaper. He wanted to remind the Assignment Editor he was working on the story and to check for messages. And he wanted to find a photographer.

***

Forty-five minutes later, "Flash" Watson followed Jack to his Ford Cabriolet. "I like this car," Watson said. "Can I have it when they kill you?"

Jack shot Watson a glance. "That doesn't help."

His jaw clenched, Jack drove the short trip to Greta's without saying another word. A wide sidewalk stretched from the building's front doors to Philadelphia Street. Jack parked on a side street and hurried across the lawn to the building's front door. Shorter and carrying a large camera, Watson had to hustle to keep up with him.

The place was empty except for the bartender, a paunchy, pasty-faced, balding man.

"I need to speak with Mr. Mascelli," Jack said.

"He ain't here," pasty-face said. "And tell your friend to get lost. We don't allow cameras in here."

"What's your name?"

"I forget. Now, get lost. Both of you."

Jack turned to Watson. "Get a picture of this guy. His mug will look good tomorrow morning on the front page."

The bartender pushed a button to alert the back office there was a problem and turned his back to Watson.

Watson raised his camera but didn't take a photo of the bartender. Instead, he focused on the rear door and waited for the cavalry to arrive.

Moments later, Fats Mascelli himself burst through the door, a .38 revolver in his hand. Flash focused and got the picture.

"Get the hell out of here," Mascelli said heading straight for Jack and Flash, "before I shoot both of you."

"I'm unarmed," Jack said. "I'm a reporter, and I'm reaching for my notebook." Moving as if in slow motion, Jack pulled his notebook out of his jacket pocket and opened it.

"I don't talk to reporters," Mascelli said.

"I'm here to get a comment about the murder of Patrolman Vance. With him dead, do you think the prosecutor will drop the case against you?"

Mascelli's face contorted. "I don't know what you're talking about."

"Mr. Mascelli," Jack said, "Patrolman Vance was going to testify against his partner, Ricky Robinson. Did the cops kill Vance?"

"I told you. I don't know what you're talking about." Mascelli moved to within three feet of Jack and kept the revolver pointed at his chest.

Flash retreated, got Mascelli holding the gun on Jack in focus, and snapped the picture.

Mascelli fired a shot into the floor in front of Flash. "Drop the camera and get the hell out of here. Next time, I'll aim higher."

"Did you kill that cop last night," Jack asked, "or did your men do it for you?"

Mascelli took another step forward and put the gun against Jack's jaw. "I told you. I don't talk with reporters. I'm not telling you again."

Jack smiled. "I appreciate your patience. Just one more question. Not about the cop. About you. I need a little something interesting about you for my story. So, my readers will know something about you."

Mascelli pulled the gun back a few inches "Tell 'em I think you're a lousy reporter. Now, get outta here."

Jack shut his notebook and returned it to his pocket. "You're holding that gun in your left hand. Do you bat lefty too?"

Mascelli slashed at Jack's head with the butt of the gun.

Jack pulled back in time.

"Mr. Mascelli says he knows nothing," Watson cautioned Jack. "We should go."

Jack turned his back to Mascelli and walked toward the door. Flash followed Jack, but walked backward most of the way, keeping an eye on Mascelli.

"If I ever see you in here again," Mascelli shouted after Jack, "I'll kill you."

Jack spun around and stopped. He slowly opened his jacket and pulled his notebook out again. "That will be on the front page of tomorrow morning's paper," he said. "I want to be sure I get it right."

Mascelli raised his gun and fired.

The bullet slammed into the wall above Jack's head. It was another warning shot. Jack doubted a third shot would be a warning. He turned and walked out the front door, followed by Watson.

Jack hurried across the lawn to his car. Once again, Watson struggled to keep up with the taller and younger O'Brien.

When they folded themselves inside Jack's car, Watson sat his camera on the floor and fumbled for his cigarettes. "Jack, you're going to get yourself killed."

"A smart reporter doesn't bury the lead," Jack said, turning the key in the ignition. "And a smart mobster doesn't bury a reporter."

"I wouldn't count on that," Watson said. His hand trembled as he tried to light the cigarette. "Besides, I don't think that guy is smart."

Jack stepped on the accelerator. The tires on his car squealed as he pulled away from the curb.

***

That evening, about 7:30 p.m., Jack lay on top of the sheets on the bed in his room. He'd filed his story on the murder of the cop and a second story on his encounter with Mascelli. Now, he was trying to collect his thoughts.

The window in the room was open, but there was no breeze. The air was hot and humid. Down the street, kids were shouting and laughing.

The phone rang. Jack got up, crossed over to the little desk, and answered the call.

"Mr. O'Brien?" a man asked.

"Speaking."

"You don't know me," the caller said. "My name is Sydney Krumpleman. Victor Morgan—he's running for City Commission—gave me your number and told me to call you."

"About what?" Jack lowered himself onto the desk chair, picked up his pen, and jotted down the man's name.

"Last Tuesday night was my daughter's birthday. She turned eighteen, and my wife and I wanted to take her someplace nice to celebrate. So, we took her to the Lookout House."

"Yes, sir," Jack said.

"We ordered our meal, and next thing you know, Harry Boyle, the Vice Mayor of Covington, comes in. Jimmy Brink greets him like he's a celebrity and shows him upstairs."

Jack had asked Morgan to let him know if any of his supporters saw Boyle in a Mob joint. Jack asked, "Did you see anything else?"

"You're darn right we did," Krumpleman said. "A few minutes later, we see a couple gangsters come in. Two big men—they looked like thugs out of some lousy gangster movie—followed them. You know what I mean, big guys in dark suits, dark shirts, flashy ties."

"Did you recognize the men?" Jack asked.

"No, of course not," the caller said, sounding offended. "But Jimmy Brink did. He's the fellow who owns the Lookout House. They say he has ties to the Mob."

"What happened?" Jack didn't want the caller to lose his train of thought.

"Brink comes up and greets these men. He tells them he's got a room set up for them, and off they go, walking right by our table."

"Bit of excitement for your daughter's birthday?"

"Mr. O'Brien, I don't think that's the sort of thing a family should be exposed to," the caller said. "I know the Mob runs Newport, and the politicians over there are all corrupt, but if we can't get rid of that filth altogether, I'd like to think our leaders would try to keep it limited to Newport."

"You're right. I agree with you." Jack wondered why, if that's how he felt, this guy took his family to the Lookout House with its large casino and rumored Mob ties. He reminded himself the news business depended on people doing unexpected and illogical things.

"There must be a lot of rooms in the Lookout House," Jack said. "Are you sure Brink took Boyle to the same room as the Syndicate men?"

"I just saw them go upstairs," Krumpleman admitted.

Jack wanted to throw the phone against the wall. This guy's story was so damn close, but he couldn't identify the men who looked like mobsters, and he couldn't place Boyle in the same room with them. Jack couldn't do anything with what the man told him.

"My wife and daughter had never been to the Lookout House before," Krumpleman continued. "After we had our meal, they wanted to explore the place. So, we walked around, taking everything in. Upstairs, the two men I thought looked like bodyguards were standing outside one of those side rooms. I mean, it was just like in the movies."

"Uh-huh." Jack tapped his pen on the desk.

"You see, they have a cocktail lounge upstairs. Just as we were about to walk past the bodyguards to go see the cocktail lounge, the doors to this little side room open, and Harry Boyle comes walking out with the men we saw downstairs."

"You saw them walk out together?" Jack asked, scribbling down what Krumpleman had just said.

"Yes, sir."

"What time was this?"

"A few minutes after nine."

"I think I asked you this, but you don't know who the other men were?" Jack asked. "The ones Boyle was with?"

"No, sir," Krumpleman said. "But my wife is from Cleveland. She grew up near Little Italy. She says one of the men was Alfred Polizzi. She didn't know the other man."

Jack wrote that down. "Mr. Krumpleman, do you know what it means in my business when someone says, 'you buried the lead?'"

"I was taught," Krumpleman said, sounding miffed, "that when you tell a story, you should start at the beginning and continue until you reach the end, and then stop."

"Sounds like a good rule," Jack said. He doubted this gentleman knew he was reciting the rule laid down by the daft King in Lewis Carroll's *Alice in Wonderland*. "Have you reached the end?"

"Yes, I think so," Krumpleman said.

"Did these men recognize your wife?"

"No, I don't think so," Krumpleman said. "Delores," he said to his wife, who was apparently sitting next to him, listening to what he said. "Those men didn't recognize you, did they?"

Jack waited.

"Mr. O'Brien," Krumpleman said, "my wife says they wouldn't know who she was, but she wants to speak to you if that's okay."

"Of course."

"Mr. O'Brien, my name is Delores."

"Please call me Jack."

"There is one more thing. I don't know if it's important, but I think it might be."

"Yes, ma'am."

"Just before Owl Polizzi left, I saw him and Mr. Brink talking with the Vice Mayor. I was nosey and dragged my daughter over to where they were. I told Mr. Brink that we'd never been to his place before, that we enjoyed it, and thanked him."

"Yes, ma'am," Jack said.

"As we were approaching, I heard Mr. Brink ask, 'See you next week?'"

"What did Boyle say?"

"I don't think he said anything, he wasn't looking good. But Owl Polizzi said, 'Maybe. We'll let you know.'"

Jack made a note.

"Anything else?"

"No, I don't think so," Mrs. Krumpleman said.

"The man you didn't recognize. What did he look like?"

"He was short and fat." Mrs. Krumpleman stopped to think. "He was wearing a fedora and looked impatient like he was running late for something. That's all I remember. But can I ask you a question?"

"Yes, of course."

"Are you the reporter who did the story on the naked preacher?"

"Yes, ma'am."

"I'm glad you caught him, and I hope he never gets another church to run."

"Thank you, ma'am. I appreciate your saying that. Can I get your address and phone number?"

Mrs. Krumpleman gave the phone back to her husband to handle that.

Mr. Krumpleman gave Jack his contact information and responded at length to Jack's questions about where, in the Lookout House, he and his family had their dinner. Krumpleman was still upset, it seemed, that the maître d' sat them so near the entrance.

Jack wanted to ask Krumpleman if he tipped the maître d', but he was sure he could guess.

By the time he hung up, Jack had the beginnings of a plan in mind. He found his cap and left the boarding house, headed for Woody's shanty boat.

CHAPTER 23, MONDAY, AUGUST 14

COMPROMISE

ON DANZIG URGED

Tokyo Weighs Axis Alliance
Against Soviets –
Nazi Envoy Quits Paris

--

The Cincinnati Enquirer
August 14, 1939

It was almost 3:00 a.m. when Kost Kozlowski rose from his bed and used the bathroom. This was not unusual. Most nights he woke at least twice, and recently, it was often three or four times. And then, he had trouble getting back to sleep. The doctor said he should go back to bed anyway. *But what did that young quack know about what it was like to be old?*

This night, like most nights, Kozlowski did the one thing the doctor told him *not* to do: He went to the kitchen and brewed a pot of coffee. He filled his cup, turned off the kitchen light, and took his coffee to the chair by the window of his second-floor apartment. He sat the cup on the little lamp table. He did not, as he sometimes did, complain to himself about the slight tremor in his old hand.

Kozlowski parted the curtain just a little. His wife Zofia would have scolded him and made him go back to bed, but she was dead now three years. What did it matter if he drank coffee and watched the goings on in his neighborhood? He was old, his heart was weak, and he would die soon anyway.

Of course, at this hour, there were seldom any goings on, but... *Co to kurwa jest?* What is that?

A black sedan with its headlights off pulled up behind that nice little Ford Cabriolet. A young man, who did not even live on the street, parked it there sometimes. Kozlowski did not know the young man's name.

Two men got out of the black sedan and approached the Ford. The men wore fedoras pulled down over their foreheads and had their backs to him. Even so, Kozlowski felt certain he did not know them.

Kozlowski could feel his pulse quicken.

One man popped open the hood, bent over the engine, and did something. The other man took off his hat, laid on his back on the street, and reached under the car. Kozlowski pulled the curtain back an inch or two more, widening the space through which he looked, and squinted to see better. The tremor in his hand was worse. This time, he cursed it.

Kilka minut. To wystarczyło. A few minutes. That's all it took.

The men hurried back to their sedan, looked around one more time to be sure no one was watching, got in, and drove off.

Kozlowski knew exactly what the men had been up to. He knew from the crime novels he used to read before the cataracts. He'd even seen it in the talkies. *Yes, that's what he would say, if anyone were to ask how he knew what the men had done. And it would be true.* But his knowledge was not entirely secondhand. He would not tell the authorities how he had first learned about such things. Not even his beloved Zofia, *may God have mercy on her soul*, knew that.

He went back to the kitchen, taking his coffee with him, and turned on the light. He looked around until he found paper and a pen. He sat them on the table. Still standing, he picked up his coffee cup and blew on it, thinking about what he would write.

After a moment, he sat down and picked up the pen. In bold letters at the top of the page, he wrote:

BOMB!
PLEASE READ!!!

Kozlowski laid the pen down and read what he'd written. He thought more about what he needed to say and how to say it. He took a sip of coffee.

"Two men placed a bomb under your car," he wrote. "They wired it to go off when you turn the key in the ignition. Do NOT turn your key in the ignition."

That was enough.

Kozlowski took another sip of coffee and re-read what he'd written.

He did not question whether he should get involved. He had known from the first moment he must warn that young man. *Maybe then God will have mercy on my soul.*

Kozlowski stood. His knees were stiff and sore from arthritis. He swore at the pain and hobbled to his bedroom. He changed from his pajamas to the pants and shirt he had worn the day before. He found his shoes and the socks he'd left on the floor. He sat in the armchair next to his bed and put the socks on, but even that little exertion—and his chronic shortness of breath—left him winded.

He curled up on the bed and closed his eyes. He needed to rest for a moment, just long enough to catch his breath.

When he opened his eyes again, three hours had gone by. He cursed, but it was only going on six in the morning. He could still get to the car in time.

Kozlowski stood and allowed the stiffness and pain in his knees to subside before he tried to move. There was no sense cursing the pain now. It would be worse when he made his way down the stairs to the street. And it would be worse still after he climbed the stairs back to his apartment. He would curse it then.

After he used the bathroom, he put on his shoes. He went to the kitchen and found the note he had written. Clutching it in his hand, he went to the front room. He stopped at the window and checked to be sure the car was still there.

It was but... *Co ten pierdolić?* What the...?

Kozlowski turned and headed to the front door, but his arm was numb, and he felt dizzy. He stopped and coughed.

Old age was a terrible thing.

He realized he had a headache. A terrible headache. *Maybe the worst headache he had ever had. Yes, the worst.*

His arm became weak, and he could no longer control his steps.

Dizziness overwhelmed him. And then, everything went dark.

***

The *Tribune's* Monday morning editorial demanded that the police get to the bottom of who killed Covington Patrolman Dennis Vance—and why.

Ignoring its own demand that the police determine *why* someone had killed the cop, the editorial asserted that the answer was obvious: Someone had killed Patrolman Vance to keep him from testifying about who framed Two Penny Smith. And to make sure Vance didn't reveal anything else he might know. The Police Department needed to get to the bottom of that too.

It was also high time, the editorialists thundered, for Circuit Court Judge Ernst Chelone to rule on the prosecutor's motion to set aside Smith's conviction.

The other morning paper, the Northern Kentucky edition of *The Cincinnati Enquirer*, ran an editorial to much the same effect. Its editorial also questioned whether Covington was becoming as corrupt its next-door neighbor, Newport.

Sitting at his kitchen table, his toast eaten and his second cup of coffee half empty, Harry Boyle was sure that the evening papers, the *Times-Star* and the *Kentucky Post* would beat the same drum. He used his handkerchief to wipe away the beads of sweat that were forming on his forehead. He looked at his watch. It was 7:30.

Boyle tried to focus on what his response should be. But he had trouble concentrating on that. In his head, he kept replaying the same scene: *Fats Mascelli pops the cap off a bottle of Coca Cola, crushes the cap between his thumb and finger, and then throws it across the room. The cap bounces off a Jimmy Cagney poster and lands in a pile of baseball bats.*

Boyle had no doubt who killed the cop. Or why.

What he couldn't understand was how anyone could be as stupid as that fat bastard. Or why he'd let himself get involved with someone like that.

He thought he'd agreed to deliver a contract to a bidder willing to pay for his help. Yes, he'd known he was dealing with the Syndicate, but that only meant the company would get the contract anyway, even if he declined to help. Others would have stepped up.

He had not realized—or had not let himself admit—that he was selling more than his help, his vote, on a contract. He had sold control over his life. He had mortgaged his future. And maybe his soul.

He needed to find a way to make sure the Syndicate got the trash collection contract, and then he needed to find a way out. If Johnson won the race for Governor, he'd accept whatever position the new administration offered him in Frankfort. He'd distance himself from the Syndicate and patch things up with Agnes. He would explore investing in real estate or find a business that would do well if war broke out in Europe. He would get out of politics altogether.

But how was he supposed to get the City Commission to give the contract to the Cleveland company?

Boyle finished the rest of his coffee and stood. He picked up the empty cup to take it to the sink. He had never been so angry, so frustrated, so... *what?*

So not in control of what happened in his own life.

He looked at the cup in his trembling hand. He shouted an obscenity and threw the cup.

It crashed against the wall and shattered.

***

Just before 8:30 a.m., Jack walked the three-and-a-half blocks from the boarding house to the nearby street where—in the hope the cops wouldn't find it—he'd parked his car.

Yesterday, the temperature had hit 88°, and the forecasters expected today to be just as hot. In fact, it was already warm, and the humidity made it worse. His shirt had surrendered its fresh-from-the-laundry crispness. Something in the air burned his eyes and made it hard to breathe.

It was trash collection day, and garbage cans lined the curb. Some already exuded pungent odors, and the smells would become worse as the sun cooked them. Eventually, Jack knew, strong men would heft the cans from the curbs where they stood and dump their contents into the back of a garbage truck. He was glad he did not have to make his living that way.

When he was close enough to see his car, Jack stopped and swore. Someone—probably the police—had smashed the windows. He hurried to the car. The cops had found his car during the night and set to work on the windows with their nightsticks. For once, they had spared the tires. He saw no cop car.

Jack swore once more, this time more in frustration than anger. He turned and headed back to the boarding house. He would call the newspaper to let the Assignment Editor know he'd be late and the auto glass shop to have his car towed.

***

Surrounded by row houses and other shops, Covington Auto Glass was on Russell Street, on Covington's westside. No bigger than a gas station, the building sat two car lengths back from the street. It featured a small office and two garage doors a little to the right of the office. The lifts were of no use in replacing auto windows. The owner had converted the bays behind the garage doors into storage space for auto glass and the equipment needed to install it.

Ogden Haggerty, the shop's only employee, unlocked the door to the shop. He wore dark-colored work clothes that were already damp and discolored with sweat. His shoes had thick soles, and a pair of work gloves stuck out of the back pocket of his pants. He hadn't shaven, and his hair was uncombed.

Haggerty had drunk too much the night before and felt terrible. When he'd gotten home, his wife wouldn't stop complaining that he was spending the rent money on booze, and he'd had to slap her around. And now, in the morning, his head ached. He was nauseous and in a foul mood.

In truth, he'd been miserable for two weeks, ever since his boss had gone into the hospital with bleeding ulcers. *He's home now "resting up," but he expects me to run the shop and do the work of two.*

The mutt that hung around outside the shop arrived, wagging its tail. Haggerty found the water bowl he kept for the dog, took it into the restroom, rinsed it out, and re-filled it. He sat the bowl just outside the office door. He took a piece of the jerky he kept in a desk drawer and put it out for the dog.

The phone rang. Haggerty answered, but only because the ringing hurt his head and he wanted it to stop. It was that young reporter, the one that kept aggravating the police.

Haggerty promised the reporter he would come right away. But first he tended to his morning constitutional. He took his time, reading the newspaper. Next, he put money in the soft drink machine and got himself a Coca Cola. He gulped it down and belched. Only then did he search for and find the keys to the tow truck. He summoned the fair-haired dog to go with him. The hound stood and jumped into the truck

The reporter's car was a late model Ford Cabriolet. The car's windows had cracked under police interrogation. The tires, like lawyers informed in the night of clients' misfortunes, had managed to greet the day undeflated.

Haggerty had O'Brien sign for the work and then hooked the car to the tow truck.

The young reporter, full of piss and vinegar, paced back and forth and looked at his watch every two seconds. The headline chaser announced he would walk to work.

Haggerty didn't care how O'Brien got to work. Or if he got to work. As far as he was concerned, O'Brien could take the day off. It was all the same to him.

"My car—can you deliver it to the *Tribune* when you're done?" O'Brien asked, handing his car key to the mechanic.

"No way," Haggerty said. "I'm the only one working today. I can't leave the shop. You'll have to come get it." Truth was, he had to deliver the paperwork to the bean counters at the newspaper and could have delivered it. He just wasn't in the mood.

O'Brien looked at his watch. "When will it be ready?"

"Twelve-thirty earliest, maybe a little later."

"Okay, thanks," O'Brien said, frowning. "See you then."

Haggerty towed the Cabriolet back to the glass shop and lowered it in front of the garage.

***

At the newsroom, Jack grabbed a copy of the morning newspaper and some coffee. He settled in at his desk to enjoy seeing his stories about the murdered cop and his run-in with Fats Mascelli in print. Almost immediately, his phone rang. Jack muttered at the interruption and answered.

"Jack, this is Leo Denton. Judge Chelone set aside Mr. Smith's conviction."

"That's wonderful news. Thanks for letting me know."

"It'll take a little while for the paperwork to get over there. I thought you might want to see him before they let him go."

"I'll do that."

"By the way," Denton said, "that was a heck of a story in the paper this morning about your run-in with Fats Mascelli. Are you okay?"

"Thanks. I'm okay, but someone smashed the windows on my car. And I don't think it was Mascelli. He had already made it clear he doesn't like my reporting."

"I should know better than to ask," Denton said, "but then who did it?"

"I'm pretty sure the credit goes to our local constabulary. They didn't appreciate my interest in who killed Vance."

"Jack, you can get new windows for your car. But I'm worried about you. You embarrassed Fats Mascelli on the front page of the newspaper. I'm afraid he's going to come after you."

Jack sat up straight. "Are you saying you think he might try to kill me?"

"Yeah." Denton paused. "I don't know. Maybe you'll be lucky, and his goons will just beat the tar out of you and put you in the hospital. But I wouldn't count on it."

"Any suggestions?"

"Can you leave town, at least for a while?"

"Leo, thanks for the warning, but you got a grand jury to indict Fats. You know what happened to Patrolman Vance. Are *you* leaving town?"

***

Mrs. Retta Goldbach, a short, plump widow in her sixties, checked her watch. It was after nine a.m., well past time for her daily foray into the world. She needed to run errands and pick up some things from the grocery.

God knows, she had wasted too much time watching that stupid tow truck remove the car from across the street. And watching that young man, who owned the car, pace up and down. She'd heard he was a reporter, but he was so young. *What did a pisher like him know that was so important it had to be in the newspaper? He only began to shave yesterday. He knew nothing.*

Mrs. Goldbach put her shopping list in her purse, stepped out the door to her second-floor unit, and locked it behind her. She turned around and knocked on the door to Mr. Kozlowski's apartment. He didn't answer.

That was unusual. *Maybe he had fallen asleep sitting up at the front window again.*

She banged on the door harder and shouted, "Mr. Kozlowski, do you need anything from the store?"

No answer.

Mrs. Goldbach glanced at her watch. She waited for what she would say later was thirty seconds before knocking on the door again. "Mr. Kozlowski, it's me. Are you okay?"

No answer.

Mrs. Goldbach re-opened the door to her own apartment and went to the kitchen. She rooted through the drawer where she kept the spare key Kozlowski had given her in case she should ever need it.

She unlocked the door to the old man's apartment and called out his name.

No answer.

She pushed open the door. And saw his body on the floor. Mrs. Goldbach put her hand to her mouth and muttered a prayer.

She called Kozlowski's name again. When he did not answer, she bent over, something she did not do easily, and gave him a nudge, and then another.

Mr. Kozlowski did not respond.

She retreated to her apartment and called an ambulance. Her

phone was a party line. Within minutes, she was sure, the whole neighborhood would know about poor Mr. Kozlowski.

Returning to his apartment, she studied the old man. He had had heart problems for years. And now, his body did not move, and he did not seem to be breathing. She did not like the look of the man's skin. She *knew* he was dead.

I told him, she said to herself. *If you keep eating Kielbasa with gravy and cabbage with butter, you will die of a stroke.*

Mrs. Goldbach noticed a paper in the poor man's hand. She could only see the back side of the paper. She wasn't a *yenta*, a busybody. *But what if the note was important?*

She bent down and lifted the corner of the paper and was able to make out the heading. "BOMB! — PLEASE READ!!!"

Mrs. Goldbach gasped. She thought her heart would stop.

It took a moment, but she composed herself. She pulled the paper loose from Mr. Kozlowski's hand and read it. "Two men placed a bomb under your car. They wired it to go off when you turn the key in the ignition. Do NOT turn your key in the ignition."

Mrs. Goldbach shook her head in frustration. *Crazy old fool! You know I don't own a car. You must have gone soft in the head.*

And then a thought occurred to her. *The old man liked to sit by his window and watch the street. Did he see someone plant a bomb in one of the cars parked along the street?* She told herself that she must have been too flustered to have thought of that at once. She pushed herself up and carried the note back to her apartment to call the police.

On the way, another thought occurred to her: *Was that why they towed the car?*

Then, an even more terrible thought occurred to her. *What if, God forbid, they towed that car not knowing about the bomb?*

Or, what if it wasn't that car that was about to explode, but another of the cars still parked along the street?

She called the police. And then she called the neighbors to warn them.

***

A jailer brought Two Penny into the visitation room.

Jack stood. "I hope you remember me. I'm Jack O'Brien, with the *Tribune*."

Two Penny nodded and rubbed his eyes. He looked like he had just woken.

"After the paper published my article about your arrest, the prosecutor asked Judge Chelone to set aside your conviction. You know that, right?"

Two Penny blinked and raised his hands a few inches.

Jack wasn't sure what that meant. "This morning, Judge Chelone agreed to set aside your conviction. They're processing the paperwork now, and they will release you shortly."

"Say what?"

"The judge agreed they should never have arrested you. As soon as they process the papers, you'll be a free man."

"Thank God! Thank God!"

Jack understood the sentiment but was hoping to get at least some of the credit. "You understand why they're letting you go?"

Two Penny nodded. "Course I do. My wife told me."

"About my articles?"

Two Penny shook his head. Still standing, he looked at his handcuffs or his feet, Jack couldn't tell which.

"What did your wife tell you?"

"That the preacher said God would make things right."

Jack waited to see if Two Penny would elaborate. When he didn't, Jack asked, "Did the preacher say why he was so sure they would release you?"

Two Penny nodded.

"And why's that?"

"God don't like ugly."

Jack had heard the expression before, from blacks he'd interviewed. It meant, *God didn't like injustice.* Personally, Jack wasn't so sure. *Right now, there was a lot of ugly in the world, and there were no obvious signs God was all that exercised about it.*

A jailor stuck his head in the visitor room. "Sorry," he said to Jack, "but we've got the paperwork, and I need him, so I can process him out."

Jack held up his hand, forefinger raised. "One minute."

Jack stepped closer to Two Penny. "Listen, I don't think it would be smart for you to go back to Greta's."

"They always treated me okay and everything."

"They're the ones who had you arrested."

"They did?" Two Penny's eyes widened.

"Yeah, I'll tell you about it after you get out of here."

Two Penny looked at Jack, but his face revealed nothing.

"I know the man who owns Hanover Brewery, and I think I can get you on at the brewery as a janitor. I haven't spoken to him about this, but would you be willing to go with me to the brewery and see what we can work out?"

Two Penny looked at his feet again.

The guard coughed and rattled his keys.

"What's the problem?" Jack asked Two Penny.

"Mr. Jack, why you be doing this?"

Jack shrugged his shoulders. "Because I think you got a raw deal. Because I want to help. Because I can."

Two Penny frowned. "You want me to tell you if I saw the Vice Mayor at Greta's."

"And get you on the wrong side of Fats and his people? No, sir. I've written about how someone framed you, and today, I'm going to write a story about the court setting aside your conviction. Then, I'll need a new story."

"You don't want me to tell you what happened?" Two Penny asked.

"Sure, I do. I've got a feeling that would be a heck of a story. But I know why you can't do that."

"You shinin' me on?"

"No, sir, I'm not. Look, I just think you got a raw deal and want to help. And to be honest, I'd also like to get you away from Greta's. You and your family will never be safe as long as you work there."

Two Penny shifted his weight and searched Jack's face.

"I'm sure if you asked that preacher," Jack said, "he'd tell you God doesn't like whorehouses."

Two Penny snorted. "He liked Mary Magdalene well 'nuff."

Jack smiled, but the guard was losing patience. "It's time for you to go with that man and get out of here." Jack put his hands in his pockets. "Your decision. If you want to go with me, I'll wait for you. Otherwise, I need a statement from you about how it feels to have the court set aside your conviction."

Two Penny smiled. "'Course I'll go with you and everything."

***

Forty-five minutes later, Jack escorted Two Penny into the main entrance to Hanover Brewery. The lobby was large, more than two stories tall, and impressive with its Art Deco design.

A mosaic comprised of small amber or ale-colored tiles covered much of the wall above and behind the receptionist's desk. Across the top of the walls and the ceiling, white tiles glistened. The white presumably represented the color of beer foam. Bold, curved lengths of stainless steel crisscrossed in front of the amber and white background. On either side, huge beer caps, at least a yard in diameter, decorated the walls.

"I'm Jack O'Brien," he announced to the receptionist. "I was hoping to see George Hanover." The receptionist's desk, modern in its glass and metal design, sat on a raised dais.

"Is Mr. Hanover expecting you?" The receptionist eyed Two Penny with suspicion.

"No, but I'm a friend. And I'm dating his daughter."

"I'll see if he's available."

Jack stepped away from the receptionist's desk. Two Penny looked tense and wary. "You okay?" Jack asked.

Two Penny cleared his throat. "Mr. Jack, you don't suppose they want me here?"

Jack grinned at Two Penny and winked. "I may have to persuade 'em a little."

"Mr. O'Brien?" the receptionist called to Jack.

Jack returned to the receptionist's desk.

"Mr. Hanover is in a Board meeting. I'm sorry, but I can't disturb him."

"The truth is," Jack said, putting a thick coat of varnish on the truth, "he told me to see his personnel manager." The unvarnished truth was, Hanover had said no such thing.

"I'll ring Mr. Pell."

Several minutes later, Preston Pell entered the reception area. Pell was a short, paunchy man of some indeterminate age over forty, who wore a gray suit, also of an indeterminate age. His facial expression held an uncertain middle ground between insincere interest in Mr. O'Brien and sincere annoyance at the interruption.

"Mr. O'Brien?"

Jack stepped forward and introduced himself. He gave Pell his business card and a smile that exuded confidence.

Pell studied the card, then Jack. "How may I help you?"

"This is Two Penny Smith," Jack said, putting his hand on Two Penny's shoulder. You may have seen my articles in the *Tribune* about him, about the police framing him."

Pell looked at Jack, then at Two Penny, and sniffed. "I get the *Enquirer*."

Jack ignored Pell's response. "My articles struck a chord with Mr. Hanover. He told me to bring Two Penny here when the court released him. Mr. Hanover promised he'd find him a position as a janitor. This morning, the court overturned Two Penny's conviction, and he's a free man, completely exonerated. Knowing Mr. Hanover's feelings on the subject, I brought Two Penny here straight away."

Pell removed his glasses and squinted at Jack. "Mr. Hanover didn't say anything about this."

"There was no way to know when the court would do the right thing and let Two Penny out."

Pell returned his glasses to his face and straightened his tie. "Why don't you leave Mr. Penny's name and phone number with the receptionist. I'll be in touch after I've had a chance to speak with Mr. Hanover."

Jack turned to Two Penny and said, "Why don't you have a seat over there, while I talk to Mr. Pell?"

Two Penny walked ten feet away but remained standing.

Jack moved closer to Pell and spoke as if sharing a confidence. "Here's the thing. I need to write a story for tomorrow morning's paper about the court exonerating this man. I wanted to work into my story what a standup guy George is. And what a standup company the brewery is. I mean, hiring Two Penny after all he's been through, that's a first-rate thing. But I've got a deadline to meet, and—well, you can see the problem."

Pell adjusted his tie again as if to loosen its grip on his neck by some small amount. "Do you know Mr. Hanover?"

"I have breakfast with him every Friday. And more importantly, I'm dating his daughter."

"Mr. Hanover didn't say anything about this," Pell repeated, fidgeting.

"Let's do this," Jack said, still speaking as if sharing confidences between colleagues. "Let's take Mr. Smith upstairs and get him signed up, figure out when he starts, how much his pay will be, and all that. You can hold the paperwork until George gets out of his meeting."

Pell's expression was that of someone whose disposition might benefit from the addition of prunes to his diet.

"Is there a problem?" Jack asked. "If I didn't know better, I'd think you were looking for an excuse to rob George of his good deed—and the publicity." Jack tilted his head and arched his eyebrows. "Say, you're not one of those fellows who's always trying to undermine the boss behind his back, are you?"

Pell glanced at Jack's business card. "Mr. O'Brien," he said in a whisper, "we don't hire coloreds."

Jack nodded. "Yes, I know. That's why George said he could only take Two Penny on as a janitor."

"You're dating Mr. Hanover's daughter?"

"Yes, sir. We're practically engaged."

Pell adjusted his glasses, pulled at his tie, and glanced down at his shoes.

Jack looked at his watch. "Like I said, I need to file a nice little story about the court exonerating Two Penny. I'm hoping it will be on the front page of tomorrow morning's paper. I'd like to work in something nice about George and the brewery. And then, I'm having lunch with Maggie and Mrs. Hanover. I don't want to be late."

Pell made a decision. "Well, like you say, we can take care of the paperwork and get Mr. Hanover's approval later. If you'll follow me."

Jack signaled for Two Penny to join them, then turned and patted Pell on the shoulder. "You're a good man, Pell. I don't care what George says about you."

***

No other new business had come to the glass shop, and by noon, Haggerty had the Cabriolet done. He called the business office at the *Tribune* and gave the shop's contact there the final figure on the work. The man said he would need the paperwork. Haggerty called O'Brien, but he was out, and no one seemed to know where he was.

The Cabriolet was a nice little car. Haggerty decided to take it for a spin and deliver it to the *Trib*. He told himself he wanted to make sure the windows didn't leak, but even he knew that was just an excuse. By the time he got to the *Trib*, maybe O'Brien would be there. If he was, he would have O'Brien drive him back to the glass shop. And if O'Brien wasn't there, so much the better. There was a little bar close to the *Trib* where he could get a sandwich and a beer. Or two. And place a bet.

Haggerty picked up the paperwork and the key to the Cabriolet. A cigarette hung from its accustomed place between his lips.

The phone rang. Haggerty put the paperwork and car keys on the desk, removed the cigarette from his mouth, and answered the phone. "Covington Auto Glass."

"Can you fix stained glass?" the caller wanted to know.

"What kind of car," Haggerty asked, "has stained glass windows?"

"You only do automobiles?"

"Yeah. That's why the name is Auto Glass."

"You can't fix stained glass windows?"

"You a preacher?" Haggerty took a drag on his cigarette and exhaled the smoke.

"Yes, I'm Reverend Arch. I'm the new pastor of the Church

of the Sacred Word. We're at Sixth and Garrard. One of our windows has a crack in it."

"Listen, Reverend, we only do automobiles. And trucks. Why don't you go perform a miracle or something?" Haggerty tapped ash from the end of the cigarette into an overflowing ashtray.

"You don't have to be rude," the minister complained.

"And you don't have to be stupid. Did you get that way from thumping your Bible or from humping choir ladies?"

His voice tinged with aggravation, the minister said, "You need to pray and find peace…"

Haggerty slammed down the phone. *Stained glass windows! It was unbelievable how stupid some people were.* He put the cigarette between his lips, picked up the keys to the Cabriolet, and stepped out of the shop. *Stained glass windows!*

He locked the office door.

Christ Almighty, it's hot. And sticky.

Haggerty crossed the lot, opened the door of the Cabriolet, and slid into the driver's seat. He put the key in the ignition.

And let loose a string of obscenities. He'd left the damn paperwork in the shop. He got out of the car, took the cigarette from his mouth, tossed it on the ground, and crushed it out with his foot. He hustled back to the office.

But even before he had unlocked the front door, he could hear the phone ringing again.

***

Jack was working on an article and deep in thought when Watson startled him. "Jack, I need the newsroom car. The assignment desk says you've got it. Are you done? Can I use it?"

"I'm done," Jack said, "but I promised it to Driscoll." Dirk Driscoll was the paper's crime reporter.

"Then I'm screwed."

297

Jack wished he'd just returned the keys to the Assignment Editor and let him decide who got to use it next. "Sorry."

Watson's eyes brightened with a new idea. "Say, where's your car?"

"The cops, or somebody, broke the windows again. It's in the shop." Jack looked at his watch. "It should be done. Let me call and find out."

"Covington Auto Glass?" Watson asked.

Jack pulled the shop's business card from his pocket. "Yeah."

Driscoll showed up at Jack's desk, and Jack tossed him the keys to the "pool" car.

"Wait up a second," Watson said to Driscoll. "I may need to have you drop me off."

Jack dialed the number for the shop.

"Auto Glass."

The voice was the raspy voice of someone who smoked too many cigarettes. Jack recognized it as belonging to the mechanic who towed his car.

"This is Jack O'Brien. You've got my car. You towed it this morning."

"It's done."

Jack put his hand over the receiver and told Watson, "It's ready."

Watson turned to Driscoll. "Can you give me a lift to Auto Glass? It's on Russell at —"

"I know where it is," Driscoll said. "Did the cops do a number on Jack's car again?"

"Yeah, I told him things could get ugly," Watson said as he followed Driscoll out of the newsroom. "He won't listen."

***

Haggerty dug the pack of Camels he'd started that morning

out of his shirt pocket. There were only three cigarettes left. "What's your friend's name, so I know I'm not giving your car to a thief?"

"Watson. Dick Watson. He's the paper's photographer, and he's got an assignment."

"I was about to bring the car to you," Haggerty complained.

"Thanks, but he's already on his way."

"I still need to drop off the paperwork with your bookkeepers," Haggerty said, "so we can get paid."

"Give the paperwork to Watson. Tell him to drop it off for you when he gets back here. The bean counters won't pay you until the first of the month. You know how they are."

Haggerty didn't know. The owner took care of schmoozing with clients and bill collection. "Okay, whatever."

Haggerty lit a cigarette, waved the match till it went out, and tossed the used match into the ashtray on the desk. He took a long drag and exhaled slowly. He still felt lousy. He decided a hair from the dog that bit him might help. He stood and faced the shelving behind the desk. Reaching around behind some catalogues and manuals, he found his gin bottle.

He didn't think the gin tasted good or bad. He had stopped thinking about such things long ago. He just waited for the clear liquid to restore his sense of wellbeing.

***

Things had not gone well for Dick Shortwood. After his attempt to hold up the Bridge Café, he'd been unable to pay the rent, and his landlord evicted him. Since then, he'd slept wherever he could—in flophouses when they had room, and when they were full, in parks or behind houses.

He got most of his meals, when he was lucky enough to get a meal, from soup kitchens. When he wasn't waiting in line for a meal or a place to sleep, he spent his time looking for work. He had nothing to show for his efforts. He'd tried to get on with the W.P.A, but they were laying people off. He'd tried to enlist in the Army but couldn't pass the physical.

He got by mainly on shoplifting and petty theft, which he hated—and wasn't good at. He went to the Cathedral every Saturday and confessed his thefts and prayed for absolution and work. But if he couldn't find work, he wanted to go back to the Bridge Café, where they had humiliated him, and empty the cash register. And then get the hell out of town. Maybe he'd have better luck somewhere else.

Not that he had anywhere in mind or any way to get there.

Preoccupied and hungry, Shortwood was walking down Russell Street. Covington Auto Glass was just ahead. The garage his uncle used to own was on the other side of the street. Neither place would hire him—he'd asked often enough.

Shortwood saw Ogden Haggerty, the jerk who worked at the glass shop, get into a nice little Cabriolet and then get out again. Haggerty went back into the office.

When Shortwood reached the glass shop, he took a little detour into the lot. Out of habit, he looked to see if the keys were in the car. They were in the ignition.

Shortwood pulled his baseball cap down and glanced around. Haggerty was still in the office.

A dingy straw-colored dog stood and growled. The hair on its neck stood.

Shortwood made a rash decision.

***

Haggerty answered the phone, "Auto Glass."

"You picked up a Ford this morning, with its windows broken?" The voice was a deep bass voice, like it came from deep inside a kettle drum.

"What if I did?" Haggerty said.

"Don't start it," the voice said. "Don't turn over the ignition."

Haggerty rubbed out his cigarette in the ashtray. "And why not?"

There was a pause. Haggerty heard the dog bark.

The caller said, "Kaboom!" And hung up.

Haggerty looked at the phone. And then he looked for the keys to the Cabriolet, but they weren't on the desk.

The dog barked again.

Haggerty jumped out of his chair like an electric shock had jolted him.

***

Driscoll dropped Watson off across the street from Covington Auto Glass.

Even before he got out of the car, Watson spotted Jack's Cabriolet and noticed the young man loitering around it. At first, Watson thought nothing of the young man's presence. He thanked Driscoll, and carrying his camera, started across the street.

The young man took a quick, furtive glance toward the office. He pulled his cap down over his face and looked around again, but in an unfocused way.

Instinctively, Watson looked around as well, to see what the young man was looking for. He saw a police cruiser turn the corner into the street, but the cruiser was not yet in the young man's line of sight.

A dog barked.

Watson stepped onto the lot. The young guy opened the door to Jack's car and slid into the driver's seat.

The dog barked again.

Watson slowed as his hands turned his camera on and made an adjustment. He stopped, raised his camera, and focused on the young man. None of that was something he decided to do. It was purely professional instinct.

The police cruiser pulled to a stop behind Watson.

The fellow who worked at the place came running out of the office.

The young man in Jack's car looked up, directly at Watson.

Watson snapped a picture.

The police cruiser's light and siren went on.

The Auto Glass mechanic shouted something in the direction of the car.

It took a second for the sound of the mechanic's shouting to register in Watson's brain. The mechanic was shouting, "Stop, don't –!"

The young man in the car froze.

The dog barked again.

Watson snapped another photo, this one capturing the glass shop mechanic closing in on the car.

Behind Watson, the cops were out of their vehicle, shouting at the kid. "Don't…"

Shortwood panicked and turned the key.

The explosion was loud. It lifted the little Ford several feet off the ground and dug a crater in the ground beneath it. The blast blew Haggerty off his feet and threw him backward. Ten feet further away, it knocked Watson down.

Glass and metal shards flew in every direction, ripping pockmarks in the building and cracking a window in the police cruiser. One shard pierced the gas tank of the Cabriolet and set off a second explosion. Flames and acrid black smoke poured from what remained of the vehicle.

The dog rose slowly from its prone position on the pavement and went to the unconscious body of Ogden Haggerty. It licked blood from his face and barked once, unconvincingly, before becoming interested in a nearby piece of debris that not long before had been one of Shortwood's fingers.

One of the officers radioed the police dispatcher. "We've got an explosion and car fire. One dead, one in bad shape. And a third guy, I don't know yet," he said. "We need some ambulances and the fire department."

CHAPTER 24, MONDAY, AUGUST 14

Afternoon – Evening

LIVESTOCK
FEATURED AT FAIR

WOMAN'S PLEA
FOR DIVORCE GRANTED.

The Cincinnati Enquirer,
August 14, 1939

Jack's phone rang, and he picked it up. It was the Assignment Editor.

"O'Brien, I've got a reporter on the line. He's from the radio station. He wants to know if you're dead. What should I tell him?"

"Let me talk to him. What's his name?"

"Bill Trimble."

A moment later, Jack had Trimble on the line.

"Mr. O'Brien, this is Bill Trimble from the WCKY news desk. The police radio says a Ford Cabriolet blew up, killing someone. We heard it was your car, and—you know, given the stories you've been writing—we thought maybe the Mob put a hit on you."

It took Jack a moment to process what the reporter was saying. "Are you at the scene?"

"No, I'm at the radio station. From what I gather, someone rigged it, so your car would explode when you turned the ignition."

Jack ran his thumb and forefinger across his eyelids and then squeezed the bridge of his nose. He tried to concentrate.

"Do you have a comment?" Trimble asked.

"Someone bashed in the windows on my car this morning. I guess they did me a favor because I didn't try to start my car. I had it towed."

"Do you think Fats…"

Jack stood and looked around the newsroom. He was no longer processing what Trimble was saying.

"Dick Watson, our photographer," Jack said, interrupting Trimble, "was on his way to the glass shop to borrow my car. Have you heard anything about him? Is he okay?"

"The police are saying one dead, two injured."

Jack cringed. "Thanks for the call. I've got to run." He hung up the phone and headed for the door.

"O'Brien!"

It was Rumble's voice. Jack turned.

"Where the hell do you think you're going?"

Jack watched as Rumble closed the distance between them.

"Driscoll has the newsroom's car. I told Watson he could borrow mine. I need to find out if he's okay." Jack was shaking.

"Watson just called me," Rumble said. "He's okay. It knocked him out for a minute, and he's got some cuts and scratches. They're patching him at the hospital now. He'll be here shortly."

Jack exhaled. He made a slow, noisy sound as he did. And then he said, "Thank God."

"You are not covering this story. Understood?" Rumble put his hand on Jack's shoulder. "You're too close to it."

Jack nodded.

"Go find Driscoll. Tell him he wants to interview you."

***

Dirk "Dirt" Driscoll, Max Seeger, and a copyeditor interviewed Jack for the story the newspaper would run in the morning paper. Driscoll would write the story. Seeger wanted to be sure Jack was okay. He would look for his own angle on the story.

"The cop handling press inquiries yesterday didn't seem happy that I was covering the story about Patrolman Vance's murder. He told me a bad attitude was like a flat tire. Just in case the police were thinking about going after the tires on my car again, I parked it a couple blocks away from the boarding house where I'm staying."

"Where exactly?" the copy editor asked. "What street?"

Jack gave the street name.

"This morning, when I got to the car, someone had bashed in the windows. I didn't even get in. I went back to my room and called that glass shop."

The copy editor pressed for details.

"I'll tell you everything I can," Jack said. "But first, what the hell happened?"

"We're still trying to piece that together," Driscoll said, "but it looks like some stiff was trying to steal your car. He died in the explosion. The guy who works at the shop caught a bunch of flying glass and debris. He died at the hospital. Still working on his name."

"The cops showed up seconds before the explosion. They yelled for the kid not to turn the key, but the kid panicked."

"You look white as a sheet," Seeger said. "You okay?"

Jack nodded. "Were the cops hurt?"

"No, they weren't close enough."

Jack described his call to the Glass Shop to let Haggerty know Flash would pick up the car.

A secretary interrupted. "Jack, Leo Denton wants to talk to you. He says it's important."

Jack excused himself and took the call.

Denton asked Jack if he was okay. Jack assured him he was. "Can I call you back?"

"Sure, I just wanted to make sure you're okay, but before you go, I've got something you might find interesting."

Jack glanced at his watch. "What's that?"

"In your article about your confrontation with Mascelli, you said he was holding his gun in his left hand. Well, the coroner says whoever hit Vance was a lefty."

"Can I use that?"

"Yeah, sure, just don't use my name."

Before returning to the interview, Jack gave the secretary some money and asked her to get him a carton of soft drinks.

"Tell me about yesterday," Max said when Jack returned. "About your visit with that meatball at Greta's."

Jack described his encounter with Fats Mascelli.

"Why did you go there in the first place?"

"I was angry."

"Next time," Max said, "be smart. You'll live longer."

"Some old guy saw two men plant the bomb," Driscoll said, pulling the interview back to the attempt on Jack's life. "He wrote a note and was going to put it on your windshield, but the old coot had a stroke and didn't make it."

"Second floor apartment, always watching things from his window?"

Driscoll shrugged his shoulders. "A neighbor, a Jewish woman, found him, saw the note, and called the police."

Jack looked at the crime reporter. "When?"

"That's the thing. She says she called a little after nine this morning."

Jack could feel himself anger.

"She says a couple detectives came about fifteen minutes later and took her statement. And the note. She says she told them all about the tow truck."

"That would have been, what, about 9:30 or so?" Jack asked.

"Right."

Jack stood. "And the cops didn't show up at the glass shop until…"

"About 12:30." Driscoll said.

Jack clenched his fists. His face reddened.

"You've got a right to be angry," Max said. "But remember. It's better to be smart."

The secretary arrived with a carton of cold Coca Colas and told Jack he had another call. Jack took one of the Cokes and invited Driscoll and Seeger to help themselves.

The call was from Deputy Police Chief Rasche. He had the same question as Denton. "Are you okay?"

"I'm fine, sir," Jack said, "but two men are dead, and our photographer got knocked down. His face is cut up."

"Our men are on it, Jack. I've told them to make this a priority."

Rasche sounded sincere, but Jack had no misconceptions about what would happen when Rasche's order made its way down the ranks. "A woman called the Covington Police Department this morning about nine," Jack said. "She told your detectives two men had planted a bomb on my car. Your detectives interviewed her and left her place about 9:30. She told them about the glass shop towing my car."

"A glass shop towed your car?"

"Yes, sir, a couple of your finest smashed in the windows on my car again—you know, the usual."

In his official voice, Deputy Commissioner Rasche said, "I don't know anything about that."

"For the record," Jack said, "why did it take three hours for your men to warn Auto Glass? Were they reluctant to interfere with a Mob hit?"

"Jack, this is the first I've heard about the delay. I'll look into it. We'll get to the bottom of what happened."

Smart is better than angry. Smart is better than angry.

"Chief Rasche, sorry," Jack said. "I guess I'm more shaken up than I realize."

"Understandable. No offense taken."

Jack found a bottle opener in his desk and pried the cap off the soft drink. "Did you see my article in this morning's paper about my encounter with Fats Mascelli—the Mob guy that runs Greta's Place?" Jack pulled his pen from his pocket. "You know, that fancy whorehouse at Sixth and Philadelphia?"

"I saw it." Rasche's tone was defensive.

Smart is better than angry. Smart is better than angry.

Jack tapped his pen on his notebook.

Screw smart.

"Not one of your men has questioned me about that incident." While he waited for the Deputy Chief's response, Jack tossed his pen aside and took a sip from the Coke.

"Did you file a complaint?" Rasche asked.

"Yes, sir," Jack said. "I filed it with the editors at the copydesk, and they put it on the front page of this morning's paper so your detectives couldn't miss it."

There was a pause on the Deputy Chief's end.

Jack could almost feel Rasche struggling not to react.

"I'm sure," Rasche said, "our detectives will follow up, just give them time."

"Why is it, sir, that every politician in this city seems to know exactly where Greta's Place is, but no one on the Covington Police force can find it?"

"Jack, it's not a matter of finding it." There was condescension in Rasche's voice. "To bring charges, we need to have proof they're doing something illegal. We've tried. We just haven't been able to build a case."

"You've got my number," Jack said. "Call me when you find out why it took three hours for the Covington Police Department to do something after they learned someone rigged my car to explode."

"Jack, that's going to take time," Rasche said.

"Then tomorrow morning's paper will say the Covington Police Department is unable to explain why it took three hours to act after it learned a *Tribune* reporter's car was rigged to explode. The delay cost two men their lives."

"Jack," Rasche protested. "Be reasonable."

Jack slammed down the phone.

Someone put a hand on Jack's shoulder.

Jack turned around. It was Rumble.

"The Editor wants to see you. He's in the conference room upstairs with the editorial writers. You know—the smart guys who tell the rest of us what to think."

Jack nodded. "Now?"

"Yes, but I'm going to buy you a few minutes. Before you go upstairs, I want you to go throw some water on your face or something. You need to calm down."

Jack nodded.

Rumble smiled at Jack. "I wouldn't want you to take a swing at one of them."

***

310

After visiting with the editorial deities on Mt. Olympus, Jack called Maggie. He wanted her to know he was okay. He regretted not calling her sooner.

Mrs. Hanover answered. She told Jack that Maggie wasn't available and asked Jack if he was okay. "I heard on the radio..."

"I'm fine. That's why I'm calling. To let Maggie know I'm okay. Will she be back later?" No sooner had Jack said that then he remembered she'd gone to New York.

"She went out of town for a couple days. She didn't tell you?"

"Yes, ma'am. In all the excitement, I forgot."

"Well, she gets back tomorrow. I'll be sure to tell her to call you."

"Thanks."

"Jack, be careful."

Fifteen minutes later, George Hanover called. "Jack, I heard about what happened. Are you okay?"

"Yes, sir, thanks for calling."

"I—Lillian and I—want you to come over tonight for dinner."

"I thought Maggie was out of town," Jack said. *George is concerned about Maggie's safety, and he wants to pressure me to break up with her.*

"Lillian and I want to make sure you're okay. We're concerned about you."

Jack asked what time.

George told him to come from work and named a time.

Jack decided to make the best of the situation. "I was hoping to talk to you anyway. You remember my articles about Two Penny Smith, the fellow someone framed."

Pause. "I remember," George said.

"The court freed him this morning, and I brought him over to your shop and introduced him to Mr. Pell."

Pause. "I heard all about it," George said.

Jack knew the well-off have a way of expressing disapproval by what they don't say—by a short pause, followed by a deflecting comment. Just such a silence had preceded each of George's responses.

"I was hoping," Jack pressed ahead, "that you could see your way to giving him a position as a janitor."

Pause. "We can talk about that tonight at dinner."

Jack hesitated for a second. "Then, I'll see you in a bit."

In quick succession, Jack got several more calls from people asking if he was okay. One was from the well-connected Lincoln Cook, the NAACP attorney, whose contacts in the area had alerted him to the day's developments.

"I was going to call you about Two Penny's release," Cook said, "but first how are you doing? They say someone tried to kill you."

"The Mob planted a bomb under my car and wired it to go off when I turned the ignition," Jack said. "But I wasn't around when it blew up. Two other men died." Saying that made him uneasy.

"Jesus, man, be careful," Cook said. "Those Syndicate guys are a bunch of cold-blooded killers."

"So I hear." Jack pulled the paper out of his typewriter, wadded it into a ball, and tossed it in his wastepaper basket "The good news is, Judge Chelone finally set aside Two Penny's conviction. He's a free man."

"Jack, I think you deserve all the credit for that. Thanks."

Jack brushed crumbs and dust off his desktop. "I took him to Hanover Brewery this morning and tried to get him a job as a janitor, but that may have been a mistake."

"Jack, Hanover Brewery doesn't hire coloreds. They should— God knows we drink enough of their beer—but I'm sure they're a no-go for the Negro."

"I know the owner, George Hanover. I thought I could persuade him. Remember meeting Maggie? She's his daughter."

"You're working all the angles," Cook said, laughing.

"No, this time, it's all going to come down on me. Maggie is out of town, and George just invited me to his home to have dinner with him and his wife. He worried about Maggie dating me before today, and now, he will put his foot down." Jack glanced at the big clock on the newsroom wall.

Cook chuckled. "This hasn't been your day."

"It gets worse. I've got a hunch he will tell me he'll hire Two Penny if I agree to break up with Maggie."

Cook hesitated a second before saying anything. "Jack, I wasn't just joking when I said my people drink a lot of Hanover beer. I've got an idea."

Jack could almost see Cook's broad smile as he laid out his scheme. Jack didn't think Cook's scheme would work, but all the same, he left for the Hanovers' with a lighter step than if he'd had no plan at all.

***

The Hanovers lived in a magnificent home on Second Street. The house was a three-story Federalist townhome with tall white Corinthian pillars. It sat high off the street to minimize damage from those times when the Ohio River rises above flood level—but even that had not been high enough to protect the house from the '37 flood.

Beneath the flat Federal roof, elaborate cornices protruded. Intricately shaped brackets fastened beneath the cornices. A window with a rounded top centered the third floor. Smaller rectangle windows hid within the cornices themselves. On the second floor, rectangular windows stood in a row, and on the first floor, more rectangular windows stood on either side of the handsome front entrance. Windows with half-round tops stood in pairs on either side of the main facade. Additional extensions, set back from the main face of the building, completed the picture. Tall trees and well cared for shrubbery spread around the house's exterior.

Inside, the house was just as magnificent. Beneath recessed ceilings, elaborate white woodwork and cornices vied for attention. The white woodwork contrasted with wine-red walls. Large landscape paintings decorated the walls, and oriental rugs lay on hardwood floors. None of that eased Jack's trepidations.

George was already home and nursing a drink. Lillian came from the kitchen. She wore a pink crepe dress with the same silhouette as the dresses Maggie preferred—puff sleeves that stopped just above the elbow and a belted waist—but her dress had a collar and a bow at the neck.

Jack offered his greetings. His mouth was dry, his palms damp.

George ushered Jack into a well-appointed study lined with built-in bookcases, dark Duveneck-style oil paintings, and its own small liquor cabinet and bar. "Tell us about what happened to your car," George said, "and what that was all about."

"George," Lillian said, "you didn't offer Jack a drink." Turning to Jack, she asked, "What can I get you?"

"I'm fine, ma'am, but thanks."

"Well, maybe at dinner then."

"Sunday afternoon, I was working on a story about the murder of that cop, Patrolman Vance," Jack said. He tried to sound both sober about the event and nonchalant. "The police wouldn't give me the time of day, so I paid a visit to the mobster that runs Greta's Place. He's the prime suspect in Vance's murder. I wanted to see if he would give me a statement to use in my story."

Lillian Hanover put her hand to her mouth. "Wasn't that dangerous?"

Jack smiled. "I didn't think so at the time. I wasn't even sure he would be there, and I didn't think he would talk to me if he was."

Jack wished he had mentioned none of this. "Besides," he said, "I figured if Fats was there and willing to talk to me, he'd just deny everything."

Jack was still feeling for solid ground.

"Really, it sounds more dangerous than it is," he said. "There's a ritual to this." He gestured with his hands as if interviewing a witness and scribbling answers in his notebook. "You ask a few questions, you get some smug denials, and you put the denials in your article."

George rattled the ice in his cocktail glass. "Is that what happened?"

Jack shook his head and flashed a puckish grin. "Not exactly. Turns out this guy isn't too smart. He comes out waving a gun. He tells my photographer and me to scram."

"Oh, dear," Lillian said. "That must have been terrifying."

George looked at Jack. "What are you leaving out?"

"Well, I'm sure you've both read the story in the paper. I don't want to –"

"What are you leaving out?" George demanded.

Jack frowned and rubbed his hands together. "This guy beat that cop's head in with a baseball bat." Jack looked at Lillian Hanover. "Sorry, ma'am. I didn't mean to be so plainspoken."

"Are you sure you don't want a drink?" Lillian asked.

Jack shook his head. "I had just come from talking with the dead cop's wife. She has two kids. What's she supposed to live on? What are her kids supposed to do for a father?"

"Did you say something stupid?" George asked.

Lillian watched Jack's face and body language.

"I asked him my questions, and he denied everything. I asked him to tell me something about himself that I could share with readers, and he said I could quote him as saying he thinks I'm a lousy reporter." Jack smiled. "I thought we were getting along famously."

George frowned at Jack but said nothing.

Jack hesitated, then continued. "Whoever killed Patrolman Vance was left-handed. I noticed this goombah was holding his gun in his left hand. I asked if he batted lefty."

"Fats Mascelli was holding a gun on you," George said, "and you asked him that?"

Jack shrugged and grinned. He took the question to be rhetorical.

"We heard the police vandalized your car, and that's what saved you." Lillian stated this as fact, but Jack understood it was a question.

"Somebody did," Jack said. "The police weren't happy that I was investigating Vance's murder, and that's how the cops express themselves when they're not happy with someone they can't arrest. So, yes, ma'am, everyone assumes it was them."

A small black woman, perhaps fifty years old, came to the door of the study. "Dinner's ready. I's 'bout ready to serve it, 'less you want me to hold it up."

"Thank you, Henrietta," Lillian said. "We'll be right in."

Lillian led the way to the dining room and let Jack know where he should sit. She went to the kitchen to speak with Henrietta

Over dinner, George held his thoughts to himself. Lillian questioned Jack about his family and expressed the appropriate condolences when she learned Jack's parents had only recently died. She asked what Jack's father did for a living, where the family lived, and if he had any siblings.

Jack spoke about his experiences growing up in Covington, in Connecticut, in Geneva, and in Berlin. He regretted not having any siblings.

Henrietta picked up the plates and asked if she should bring out the dessert. "It's rum cake. It's so soggy you need to eat it with a spoon."

Lillian said that would be fine, but to bring coffee first. After dessert, they would be talking with their guest.

Henrietta excused herself.

"About Two Penny," Jack said.

George shook his head. "The brewery has never hired a Negro."

Henrietta re-entered the room with coffee and began by filling Jack's cup. "I be bringing the rum cake next."

Neither George nor Lillian said anything.

"Henrietta," Jack said. "I don't want to put you on the spot but tell the truth. Do you like Hanover Beer?"

"Why course I do." Henrietta poured coffee into Lillian's cup.

"But isn't it true that in general colored people just don't like Hanover Beer?"

"Jack," Lillian said, "I think you're putting Henrietta—"

"Oh, Lordy, no," Henrietta said. She moved to George's place at the head of the table and filled his coffee cup. "We like Hanover Beer just fine. We probably drink more of it than anybody."

Henrietta said, "Now, if y'all excuse me, I'll go git that rum cake."

"Jack," George said, "like I was saying about –"

"Is Henrietta right, George?" Jack asked. "You must know something about this."

"We sell a lot more beer than you'd think to coloreds. In fact, our sales manager thinks we should put out a brand aimed at the colored market, but we've already got so many of them drinking our product, I don't see what good that would do."

"A NAACP lawyer called me this afternoon," Jack said. "He called me about Two Penny getting out of jail."

"NAACP!" George nearly spilled his coffee. "They're a bunch

of trouble makers. Why would you talk to them?"

"Same reason I talk to preachers, policemen, politicians, and other public enemies. It's my job."

"Speaking of which," George said, seizing his opportunity to broach the subject on his mind. "Your job—"

"Don't tell Maggie I said so," Jack said, interrupting again. He lowered his voice to a confidential tone. "But, George, you're absolutely right about the NAACP being a bunch of trouble makers."

"Jack, I'm concerned about—"

"You're absolutely right to be," Jack said.

Henrietta returned with three small dishes of rum cake and served them. Except to thank her, no one said anything until she left the room.

Jack spoke first. "I made the mistake of mentioning to this NAACP lawyer that I took Two Penney to the brewery, looking to see if I could get him a job."

George flushed. "Jack, if I hire one colored, those rabble rousers will push for me to hire more. And then where will I be?"

"George, someday, I'm sure that's true, but for now, I got the impression they're just concerned about Two Penny. They're upset at the way he got railroaded and, according to this fellow, they would see it as a special favor if you were to find a way to hire him."

"They would, huh?" George shook his head and made a tsk sound.

Jack's father had often made the same sound when disgusted. Jack had learned the hard way that when his father made that sound, it was not an auspicious time to press his luck.

"Remember, I'm just the messenger here," Jack said, "but I got the distinct impression they'd also take it as a special affront if you were to refuse to hire him, after all he's been through."

George took a sip of coffee. "Jack, you're a con artist. You're making this crap up, but I'll tell you what. You promise not to see Maggie anymore, and I'll hire this colored guy."

That was the demand Jack feared George would make.

"George, with all due respect, I care very much about Maggie, and —"

Henrietta stuck her head in the room, and Jack hesitated.

"But it's up to Maggie to decide if she wants to continue seeing me."

"Yes, Henrietta?" Lillian asked, sounding annoyed at the interruption.

"There's a phone call for Mr. Hanover. I think it's important."

Jack snuck a glance at his watch.

"Excuse me," George said. He stood and threw the cloth napkin that had been on his lap onto the chair. "I will be right back."

Jack smiled at Lillian Hanover and said, "ma'am, you have a beautiful house, and it was a lovely dinner."

"George—well, we're both—worried about the risks your job exposes you to. And Maggie. Besides, reporters don't make very much, do they?"

"Ma'am, I've fallen hard for Maggie. I—" Jack hesitated. "But I'm also looking beyond Covington. If there's war in Europe, I'm going to find a way to cover it."

Jack took a sip of coffee and decided he needed to refocus what he was saying. "The important thing is," he said, "I think Maggie wants her own adventure."

Jack hesitated again and looked at Lillian Hanover. "I hope I'm wrong, but I'm not sure you have as much to worry about—as far as Maggie and me—as you think."

Lillian Hanover took a strategic sip of her own coffee. The corners of her eyes crinkled, but she said nothing.

"But Maggie may be a little headstrong," Jack said, "like—"

"Like her father," Lillian completed the thought.

"I love Maggie, but I don't want her giving up her dream of an adventure and holding on to me to spite her father."

Lillian gave Jack an appraising look.

"Pushing the issue about me might be the worst thing you could do."

Lillian smiled. "You're smarter than George gives you credit for."

Jack gave Lillian a sly smile.

George stormed back into the room but did not take his seat.

Jack looked at the older man.

"That was an NAACP lawyer." George looked at the note he'd written. "Lincoln Cook." George's face had more than the usual amount of color. "The son-of-bitch had the nerve to call me at home."

Jack said nothing.

Lilian looked at Jack for a second before becoming preoccupied with her coffee. But in that second, Jack thought he saw a twinkle in her eyes.

George tossed the note on the table and sat down. "Jack was right," he said to Lillian. "He threatened to have his people boycott our beer if I don't hire this Two Penny character."

"George, what did you say? Please tell me you didn't lose your temper."

"I told him I'd sue their black asses and get an injunction."

Jack thought George said that more ruefully than in anger.

"Oh, George!" Lillian brought her hands to her mouth. "What did he say?"

George turned to Jack and gave him an accusatory look. "The S.O.B. chuckled and said that would be wonderful. He said the newspapers would have a field day with that, and the NAACP could use the publicity to make sure word got around about their boycott."

Jack studied the rum cake.

George turned back to Lillian. "I remembered what Jack told me. We talked about whether, if I hired this fellow, they would turn around and press me to hire more…" George picked up his coffee cup but continued talking. "Like Jack said, this guy claims they see this fellow as a special case."

George took a sip of his coffee. "Then he began going on about how if there's war, and we get involved, the brewery might need to hire coloreds to fill the places of the men the military takes." He shook his head at the man's ignorance. "Can you believe it? He thinks there's going to be another war, and we're going to be stupid enough to get involved."

"Where did you leave it with him?" Lillian asked. "Maggie is going to be upset if—"

"I told him Two Penny can start tomorrow or as soon as he's ready."

"Sir, Mrs. Hanover," Jack said, "it's been wonderful, but—as you can imagine—this has been a very difficult day for me."

George looked at Jack. "I'm calling the NAACP tomorrow and make sure this guy is for real—that's he not someone you put up to this."

"George, he called me to thank me for my stories about Two Penny. I didn't call him. But if you're going to call to check up on him, remember, he's with their Cleveland office."

George frowned and pushed out a skeptical lower lip. "Jack, someone nearly killed you today."

"I appreciate your concern, I really do. But I…"

George glared at Jack. "I don't want you seeing my daughter. I don't want you getting Maggie killed. What if she'd gotten into that car with you?"

Jack frowned. "It was first thing in the morning, sir. Are you suggesting Maggie is the kind of girl who would—"

"No, no, I'm just saying –"

"Sir, your daughter is a proper lady," Jack objected.

"Now look here," George said, "I never meant to imply otherwise."

There was a knock at the front door.

"George," Lillian said, "what on earth did you mean to imply?"

Jack was grateful for the assistance.

"You know good-and-well," George said, "what I meant."

"Well," Jack said, "I'll let you explain that to Maggie…" Jack turned and saw Henrietta answer the door.

"Taxi for Mr. O'Brien," Henrietta announced.

"Be sure to tell Maggie about your decision to hire Two Penny," Jack said. "She'll be very proud of you."

"Jack," Lillian said, standing, "thanks for coming on such short notice."

"It was my pleasure, ma'am." Jack nodded to George. "Now if you'll excuse me."

George stood and walked to where Jack was standing. "Jack," he said, "I need a minute with you." George looked at Henrietta. "Tell the taxi driver Jack will be a minute."

Jack shifted uneasily on his feet. He suddenly felt drained.

"Jack, you're a bright young man. I could use a new advertising manager. What do you say, you give up this newspaper nonsense and come to work for me? I'll pay you more than that newspaper does, and you won't have to worry about people trying to kill you."

Jack wasn't sure how to respond. All he knew was he was bone tired.

George dug a business card out of his pocket. On the back, he'd written a dollar figure. "That would be the starting salary. In a few years, someone as bright as you could move up in the company. And besides, like I said, you'll live longer."

Jack forced a smile and took the card. "I'll think about it, sir. I will. I'm just too wiped out tonight to know what to say."

"You've been through a lot today," George said, patting Jack on the back. "Think it over."

"Yes, sir."

"But until you decide, you're not to see Maggie again. Understood?"

"George," Lillian said, approaching, "let him go before he passes out on us."

"I just want his word–"

"It was a lovely dinner," Jack said and headed out the door.

CHAPTER 25, TUESDAY, AUGUST 15

**NAZIS TAKE OVER SLOVAKIA
POUND AT POLES' BACK DOOR**
Associated Press,
August 19, 1939

GERMANS
*PUT IN COMMAND
OF SLOVAK ARMY UNDER*
MILITARY TREATY
The Cincinnati Enquirer
August 19, 1939

Outside the Courthouse, a newspaper boy hawked copies of the *Enquirer*, the morning paper that competed with the *Tribune*. "Extra, extra," the kid yelled on Jack's approach. "Mob tries to kill reporter. Read all about it!"

Jack wasn't sure what he was supposed to feel. Anger at the attempt on his life, at the destruction of his father's car? Regret that two men had died? Or relief, that the explosion had not killed him or Flash? Was he supposed to be upset that the police had vandalized his car? Or thankful that the cops had—inadvertently—saved his life?

"Hey, Mister," the newsboy pleaded as Jack drew near, "don't you want to know the truth about what happened? Three cents."

Jack dug into his pocket. The smallest coin he had was a dime. Jack recalled a line in an E. M. Forster novel — "the coin that buys the exact truth has not yet been minted." Jack gave the dime to the kid and told him to keep the change.

"Hey, thanks, Mister," the kid said as he handed Jack the newspaper.

Jack smiled. "Glad to be able to do it."

***

After his courthouse run, Jack returned to the newsroom and pored over the morning newspapers. Both papers covered the attempt on his life, but the *Trib* had the better coverage, thanks to the dramatic photographs recovered from Flash's camera. Jack felt Flash deserved an award of some sort, maybe even a Pulitzer.

The *Trib* story hit harder on the Covington Police Department's unexplained delay in notifying Auto Glass and Jack of the tip that someone had rigged his car to explode, leading to the deaths of two men. The *Enquirer* had more details on Kost Kozlowski and lengthier quotes from Mrs. Retta Goldbach.

And for the second morning in a row, both the *Tribune* and *Enquirer* editorialists took umbrage at how the Covington Police Department and City Hall were responding to events in which Jack had played a role. The editorialists demanded to know why the Police Department had not acted sooner on the tip about the bomb in Jack's car. Both papers also cheered a statement by the Commonwealth Attorney that his office was opening its own investigations into the murder of Patrolman Vance and the attempted murder of newspaper reporter Jack O'Brien.

Jack turned to the national and international news. An item in the national section of the *Tribune* caught Jack's eye. Jules Bache, a famous New York financier whose brokerage house was second only to Merrill Lynch, had just returned from three months in Europe.

The article quoted Bache as saying he had been resting and "watching the world worry about a war which is not going to happen." Hitler, Bache said, "is a highly intelligent man, although he is a bit crazy, as we all are." The Reichsführer, he asserted, "has 80,000,000 Germans in his pocket and doesn't want to lose them to gain another 300,000," referring to the German-speaking population of Danzig.

Jack wondered if Bache was right. If so, maybe he should put aside the idea of being a foreign correspondent and look for a job with a bigger newspaper in a larger city. Or take George up on his offer of a job at the brewery and propose to Maggie.

***

Harry Boyle's office was on the same floor of the Courthouse that housed other City of Covington functions. Boyle stepped out of his office and headed down the long hallway to the restroom.

"Harry!" Mayor Henry Knollman called out. Knollman was coming from the opposite direction and seemed intent on talking.

Boyle forced a smile. "Good morning, Mr. Mayor."

"Harry, I was hoping we could get that blasted trash contract resolved this week." The Mayor looked at Harry. "Are you okay? No offense, but you don't look well."

Boyle rubbed his nose. He couldn't tell if Knollman was inquiring about his health or asking if he'd been drinking. "It's too hot. I haven't been sleeping well."

"Sweltering," Knollman said. "Well, about that contract. Have you heard anything from Leo Denton? We need to get that wrapped up."

"I'll call him, but with all the hullabaloo over someone killing that patrolman and then that car explosion yesterday…" Boyle lost his train of thought.

The Mayor pursed his lips and looked impatient.

"With all that," Boyle said, "I don't see how Denton could have made any progress sorting out who trashed those yards, let alone whether the Syndicate had anything to do with it. That's fiddle-faddle compared with the murder of a policeman and the attempt, if that's what it was, on that reporter."

Knollman moved closer to Boyle. "You don't know anything about the situation with that reporter, do you?" He spoke quietly but looked directly at Boyle.

Boyle looked Knollman in the eye. "Only what I've read in the papers, and I'm not sure how much of that is true. I've met O'Brien, and he's a pain in the ass."

A passerby waved at Knollman, and he nodded at the man.

"But speaking of the dead cop," Boyle said. "His funeral is tomorrow morning. We're all going to want to go to that. The Police Department will be out in force. I was thinking we should just cancel tomorrow's City Commission meeting."

Knollman frowned. "The funeral mass and parade are in the morning. We should have plenty of time –"

"It's a matter of respect, Henry. Besides, after all that, no one will want to think about the crap on this week's agenda."

"Harry, we've already circulated the agenda, and…"

Boyle rolled his eyes. "For Chrissake's, Henry. It's the middle of August, and it's hot as hell. We should all be on vacation."

Knollman took a step back and glanced at his watch. "I'll talk to the others. But Harry, if we cancel tomorrow's meeting, then we'll have to deal with the trash contract next week."

Boyle shifted his weight from foot-to-foot and ran his hand through his hair. *Knollman is an insufferable windbag.*

"The current contract expires at the end of the month," Knollman said, speaking in a voice that was noticeably more formal. "No one wants to have to explain to the voters why no one is picking up their trash."

Boyle realized he'd run out of rope. "That's fine. I'll let Denton know we have no choice."

***

Jack was working on instinct. When Mr. and Mrs. Krumpleman called him, they told him about seeing Vice Mayor Boyle with Owl Polizzi at the Lookout House. They focused on the fact that the Vice Mayor met with a mobster. That was the important thing. But that meeting occurred the night before a City Commission meeting in which the Commissioners were supposed to award the trash collection contract.

The Commission hadn't awarded the contract then, and Dinklehaus confirmed it was on tomorrow's agenda. Although by no means a sure thing, that raised the possibility Polizzi might meet with Vice Mayor Boyle at the Lookout House again this evening.

Jack was reviewing his plan to catch Boyle with Polizzi when Rumble's voice startled him. He grabbed his notebook and pen and headed to Rumble's office.

"Jack, how are you doing? I imagine you had a difficult night last night when you realized how close you came to getting yourself killed."

Jack nodded. The newspaper had put him up in a hotel in Cincinnati overnight, but even so, he'd found it difficult to get to sleep and had woken several times.

Rumple took a sip of coffee. "I'm not sure this will help you sleep any better, but headquarters wants you to come to New York to interview with the wire service folks for a position as an overseas correspondent."

Jack broke into a big grin. "Aces! When?"

"You need to take the train to New York on Thursday. Your interview is Friday morning." Rumple reached across his desk and handed Jack a piece of paper with the details.

Jack stood and took the paper. "Thank you, sir."

"Don't thank me yet." Rumble motioned for Jack to sit back down. "It's just an interview. I don't know if you paid any attention to the story in this morning's paper, but the President is leaving for vacation. He wouldn't be doing that if he thought war was about to break out in Europe."

Jack nodded again.

"What I'm trying to say is, those penny pinchers in New York won't increase our coverage over there unless it's a sure bet there will be a war."

"Understood." Jack sucked in his lips.

"I'm just saying, don't get your hopes up too much. I don't know how many folks they're thinking about adding, and I don't know how many people they're interviewing for those spots."

Jack nodded.

"And that Hitler fellow might disappoint you and decide not to start a war."

"I understand what you're saying, sir. But –"

"Jack, Jack, Jack," Rumble said. "Don't give me a lecture about Hitler." Rumble gave Jack a fierce look, then broke into a chuckle. "Don't tell anybody, but I agree with you about him."

Jack smiled.

"Couple more things," Rumble said. "New York wanted you to take the overnight to New York Thursday night, and I told them absolutely not. You wouldn't be worth crap by the time you got there."

Jack rolled his eyes. "Thank you, sir."

Rumble stood and came around his desk and put his hand on Jack's shoulder. "Don't tell anyone about this. Just say you're taking a couple days off."

"Yes, sir."

Rumple shook Jack's hand. "And good luck."

***

When Jack returned to his desk, a message slip told him Maggie had called and left a phone number. Jack didn't recognize the number.

The number turned out to belong to Baker-Hunt, the art academy in Covington where Maggie volunteered part time. Someone else answered the phone and summoned Maggie.

"Jack?" Maggie asked.

"Yours truly."

"I don't know where to begin," Maggie said. "Mom told me what happened. She said you're okay. Are you?"

"Yeah, Mags, I'm fine."

"About last night, about my Father," she said. "Jack, I can't do this here, over the phone. Can I see you? Can you get free?"

Jack was anxious to see Maggie. "Sure. Where?"

"Can you come here? We can talk in the garden."

Half an hour later, Jack arrived at the art school with ice cream sundaes he'd bought on the way.

The Baker-Hunt Foundation—like most people, Jack thought of it as an art school—occupied a charming old home in a neighborhood of three-story residences. The neighboring homes bristled with spires and dormers, mansards and gables, and other architectural details whose names Jack had never mastered.

The Baker-Hunt building itself sat up from the street. Tall trees shaded a pleasant lawn, which the Baker-Hunt Foundation embellished with bushes and flowers. The art school called the lawn a "garden," but Jack thought that overstated the case. Still, the landscaping created a small space of calm and natural surroundings alongside what had become a busy street.

When he arrived, Maggie was working in the "round room." Its tall windows let in the natural light that painters love. Maggie hurried him into the garden, and the moment they were alone, she threw her arms around his neck and kissed him. Surprised, Jack struggled to respond with the appropriate romantic enthusiasm without spilling the sundaes. When Maggie released him, he smiled and said, "I'm happy to see you too."

Maggie moved to a distant corner of the lawn where there were chairs and a small table. Jack followed her lead and offered Maggie her choice of the sundaes.

Maggie took the strawberry sundae and put it on the table. She searched Jack's face. "Level with me. How much danger are you in?"

"I don't know," Jack said. He swatted away a tiny insect. "I don't think they will try anything while they're getting all this attention." Jack shrugged his shoulders. "But then I didn't think they would try something in the first place."

"They?" Maggie's voice was full of frustration. "Who did this?"

"The police are still investigating, but I believe it was Fats Mascelli, the Syndicate guy who runs Greta's Place. He wasn't happy about me digging into who framed Two Penny. He was even less happy about me asking him questions about the cop someone killed."

"Is he going to keep trying to kill you?"

Jack shrugged again. "Rumble—my managing editor—assigned the investigation into who killed Vance to Dirt Driscoll, the crime reporter. Driscoll's also got the investigation into who bombed my car. So, I don't think there's any reason for Fats to come after me again. He's made his point."

Maggie picked up the sundae and took a taste. She raised her eyebrows to show she liked it. "I didn't get home from the train station this morning until after Father left for work," she said. "Was he horrid to you?"

Jack took a bite of his own, butterscotch sundae. "He's just worried about you."

Maggie took another bite of her sundae, making sure this time she had plenty of strawberry syrup with the ice cream. "It'll be my turn when he gets home tonight. He will forbid me to see you."

Jack feared that too, but he didn't know what to tell Maggie. He wasn't going to tell her to ignore her father, and he certainly wasn't ready to end things with her. "How was your trip?" he asked, watching Maggie's face.

Maggie sat her sundae down and pushed a strand of hair from her eyes. "I expected to talk with them to learn more about what they're doing and what they wanted me to do. But when I got there, it turned out they invited me up for what amounted to a job interview."

Jack tried not to show any reaction. "How did that go?"

"I thought I could do much of the research they needed here, at the Cincinnati Public Library and the Cincinnati Art Museum. They're both wonderful. And I figured I could write letters from anywhere." Maggie gestured with her hands as she spoke.

Jack's eyes searched Maggie's face for clues about what she wasn't telling him. "But?"

"They're looking to hire someone to work out of their office in Manhattan." Maggie hesitated. "And to go to France and the Low Countries and convince collectors they need to do something *now*, before war breaks out and it's too late."

"Is that something you want to do?" Jack asked, his eyes fixed on hers.

Maggie broke eye contact and looked at her fingernails for several seconds before answering. "I wouldn't be honest if I said I didn't want to." Her eyes searched Jack's face for a reaction. "I'd be doing something important and exciting. I'd get to use my education." Maggie sighed. "I'd get to use my head for something other than a place to put a hat."

Jack responded to her last remark with a forced smile.

Maggie pushed the strand of hair from her face again. "But they haven't decided anything. At least, they didn't offer me a position. And I didn't commit to anything."

"Everybody's watching," Jack said, shaking his head, "to see what Hitler does."

"It's all everyone in New York talked about. And argued about. Or pretended not to think about."

As she spoke about New Yorkers' attempts to deal with the crisis in Europe, her hands and body joined the conversation. When she mentioned people in New York talking, she gestured with her shoulders and hips. At the mention of arguments, she turned and stuck up her head up as if in anger. She ended by putting her hands over eyes.

Jack's heart fluttered. He loved being with Maggie. She was so alive she made him feel more alive. Everything seemed more exciting when he was with her. He wanted never to lose her.

Maggie threw up her hands in frustration. "There are gangsters here, killing people," she said. "And gangsters over there, threatening war. Why can't decent people run things!"

"What will you do if they offer you a position?" Jack pressed. "If they ask you to come to New York to work? If they ask you to travel to France and wherever?"

Maggie looked into Jack's eyes. "If someone offers you a foreign correspondent position in Europe, what will you do?"

Jack exhaled. "If you were in France, or God forbid, the Low Countries," Jack said, avoiding Maggie's question, "and the Germans attacked like they did in the last war, you could be in danger."

Maggie shook her head. "I don't think these people would let anyone they hire stay if it looks like that might happen." Maggie forced a smile. "Besides, I could be *in danger* getting into a car with a certain reporter I know."

"Would your folks let you go?"

"Father doesn't think there will be a war. Besides, I haven't told him that the position might involve travel to Europe. He's more worried about me being with you than my taking a job in Manhattan."

Jack looked down at the ground. He watched an ant disappear under a leaf. "Maggie," he said, looking up. "An hour ago, my boss called me into his office. That's where I was when you called."

Jack brushed his slacks, rubbing his hand along the crease. "He says headquarters—actually, our overseas wire service—wants to interview me for a position in London. Me and several of other reporters."

Maggie hid her reaction. She leaned forward and looked Jack in the eyes. "When?"

"I take the train up Thursday and interview Friday morning."

Maggie became interested in her sundae again. She took a bite and swallowed. "When will you be back?"

"Rumble says I should spend the weekend in New York, see the sights, let things here simmer down."

Maggie shook her head in frustration. "Our timing is terrible. If it was last weekend, I could have shown you around the city."

"I would have loved that." Jack looked at his hands. "It's not much fun sightseeing by yourself. I was planning on coming back as soon as I could get away, so I could see you."

Maggie shook her head. "I'd rather you were safe. And I think it would be better on the home front if we didn't see each this weekend. Give my folks a chance to calm down."

"Maggie," Jack said, "I don't want to lose you."

"I feel like the world is trying to pull us apart."

Jack took Maggie's hands in his own. "I'm madly in love with you."

Maggie sucked in her lips for a long moment. "Jack, I love you too, but if they offer you the job in Europe, promise me you'll take the position."

"Only if you promise me that if these museum people offer you a position, you'll take it."

"I love you for saying that, but, Jack, being a foreign correspondent is something you've always wanted to do."

Jack squeezed Maggie's hands. "Promise me."

"If you go off to be a foreign correspondent, and I go to New

York to be a do-gooder, will we ever see each other again?"

"Your father offered me a job as the advertising director for the brewery. Do you want me to talk to him about –"

Maggie shook her head and pulled her hands from Jack's. "The world is on the brink of, of… God knows what. If there's a war, would you be happy being the advertising guy for my father's beer company?"

Jack looked down. He rubbed the back of his hand across the bottom of his chin.

"Jack, it's okay." Maggie put her fingers under Jack's chin and pushed it up. "Do you really think I want to spend my time hosting teas and playing bridge when I could be…"

"Doing something exciting and important?" Jack asked. "Doing something you'd be proud of the rest of your life?"

Maggie looked at Jack. Her eyes were moistening.

Jack gently rubbed the tears from her eyes with his fingers.

Maggie gave Jack a long, tender kiss.

***

Late that afternoon, Jack did the courthouse runs again, stopping at both the federal courthouse and the local courthouse. On his morning visit, the clerk's office personnel, lawyers, and other courthouse regulars peppered him with questions and expressions of concern. But by late afternoon, he was old news. The courthouse regulars had salted away their concerns for the next time when he would almost certainly not be so lucky. Jack knew what they would say. *You could see how this was going to end a mile away.*

On his return to the newsroom, he banged out his stories on the days' new lawsuits of interest, indictments issued, pleas entered, and jail sentences handed down. He checked the clock frequently.

Dinklehaus stopped by. "Thought you'd want to know, hotshot, the City Commission cancelled tomorrow's meeting."

Before Jack could respond, his phone rang, and Dinklehaus

left. Jack picked up the phone. "O'Brien here."

"Grandpa elephant, -phant…"

It was Woody's voice. Jack tried to ignore all the newsroom sounds and focus his attention on what Woody was saying. Or rather, on what he was trying to say.

Woody started over. "Grandpa taint combing winner."

"Grandpa can't come for dinner?" Jack repeated what he thought Woody was trying to say.

"Next beak."

"Grandpa will come for dinner next week instead?"

"Yeah." A pause. "Lotta snow." The line went dead.

Jack nodded. *Owl Polizzi wasn't coming to town this week. He put it off until next week. Gotta go.*

CHAPTER 26, FRIDAY, AUGUST 18

**WAR PACT
IS BEING REACHED**

BY GERMANY, HUNGARY,
BERLIN INDICATION
The Cincinnati Enquirer,
August 18, 1939

Jack had taken the train to New York to interview with Overseas News Service. The interview team consisted of four men. Jack guessed each man was in his mid- or late-thirties, although one might have been forty.

The men asked Jack about the recent attempt on his life and joked about whether they might need him in Covington to cover the war there. Jack took it as a good sign that they were familiar with his recent scoops—and that he might well be in danger if they left him in Covington.

But he also worried about the general drift of other questions—his age, relative inexperience, the fact that he'd never worked in New York or another large market.

Without knocking, a tall man with bushy eyebrows and a thick mustache, broad shoulders and an air of authority entered the room. The man reminded Jack of pictures he'd seen of the 19th century Prussian chancellor, Otto von Bismarck.

Like soldiers jumping to attention when a general enters their presence, the other men sprung to their feet. Jack stood and tried to suppress a smile as the men seemed to trip each other to be the first to say, "Good morning, sir."

One of the interviewers introduced the man. "Jack, this is Heinrich Vogel, he's our—"

"As you were, Gentlemen," Vogel said.

The others sat down.

Jack remained standing.

"Du bist O'Brien?"

"Jawohl," Jack said. *"Freut mich, Sie kennen zu lernen, Herr Vogel."* Pleased to meet you, Mr. Vogel.

Vogel proceeded to grill Jack, in German.

Jack kept his answers short and crisp.

"Sie lebten auf dem Kontinent?" Did you live on the Continent?

"Als Kind. Wir lebten in der Schweiz und dann in Deutschland." As a child. We lived in Switzerland, and then in Germany.

"Wie lang?" How long?

"Insgesamt vier Jahre, eine in der Schweiz, drei in Berlin." Four years altogether, one in Switzerland, three in Berlin.

Universität?

Jack was glad for the reminder. *"Juniorjahr, an der Universität Stuttgart."* Junior year, at the University of Stuttgart.

"Wie hast du das gemacht?" How did you do?

Jack smiled. *"Ich habe es gut gemacht. Ich reiste, verbrachte viel Zeit in Kneipen, las, praktizierte mein Deutsch, jagte ein paar Mädchen."* I did well. I traveled, spent time in pubs, read, practiced my German, chased some girls.

Vogel frowned. *"Hast du es schon mal zu deinem Unterricht gemacht?"* Did you ever make it to your classes?

"Jawohl. Regelmäßig." Yes, sir. Regularly. Jack smiled. *"Aber nicht so oft, um meine Ausbildung zu stören."* But not so often as to interfere with my education.

Vogel laughed. *"Sind unsere europäischen Freunde gehen, um sich einen anderen Krieg?"* Are our European friends going to have themselves another war?

"Ja!" Jack said. Yes.

"Was halten Sie von Bundeskanzler Hitler?" Vogel asked. What do you think of Chancellor Hitler? Vogel's face was fierce but gave no more clue to his own thoughts on the matter than a piece of granite reveals about its political views. Even so, his fierceness, his bearing, his attitude suggested Herr Vogel might well be pro-Nazi.

Jack was certain of just one thing: If he hesitated before he answered or if he equivocated, he would not get the job.

Jack looked the stony-faced older man in the eye and said, *"Kanzler Hitler ist ein böser Bastard."* Chancellor Hitler is an evil bastard.

The older man let a hint of a smile show. He glanced at the interview team and at Jack again. *"Haben dich diese Wischtücher gefragt, warum du nicht in eine Ivy-League-Schule gegangen bist und warum du nicht in Manhattan lebst?"* Did these ass wipes ask you why you didn't go to an Ivy League school and why you don't live in Manhattan?

Jack smiled. *"Ich denke, diese Herren waren auch dabei."* I think these gentlemen were about too.

Vogel glared at the interview team again, turned back to Jack, and said, *"Versuche nicht, mit diesen Arschlöchern über deinen eigenen Schwanz zu stolpern."* Try not to trip over yourself with these ass-holes.

Jack smiled at the advice but said nothing.

As abruptly as he'd entered, Vogel turned and fast marched out of the room, letting the door slam behind him.

"Do you know Vogel"? one of the men asked Jack.

Jack shook his head.

"What did he tell you?"

"Nothing. He just asked a few questions. I think he wanted to find out if I can speak German."

"What did he say about us?" another of the men asked.

Whatever his rank, Jack took that fellow to be the smartest one in the group and the likely leader in the discussion that would take place after the interview. Jack flashed a big grin. "My German is a little rusty, but I think he said you were gentlemen and scholars."

The men laughed.

At the end of the interview, Jack felt optimistic, but understood the wire service would make no decision until the interview team met two more candidates. He left with no commitments, no idea how many positions were open, how many candidates were vying for those spots, or when Overseas would make a decision. The only definite thing was, if they selected him, they would likely need him to leave for London on short notice.

"So, I should get my affairs in order?" Jack pressed, hoping for some hint how he'd done.

Shoulder shrugs.

Everything depends on what happens over there.

***

After the interview, Jack went to the large Manhattan bank that managed his parents' estate and the funds they left for him. He went to the floor where the bank's safety deposits were and found Mrs. Kohl, the woman in charge.

Mrs. Kohl was a prim, older woman, whose movements were careful and economical. In the bank's unflattering lighting, Jack thought her complexion resembled the color of boiled cabbage.

"What number?" Mrs. Kohl asked.

Jack identified the box number and produced the safety deposit key.

Mrs. Kohl studied Jack and the key, before checking her records. While she did, Jack studied her. He took in the bun in which she wore her hair, the tight expression on her face, and the chain that kept her eyeglasses, when they were not on her face, from escaping.

"If you will follow me," Mrs. Kohl said, standing.

Jack followed the woman into the vault and went through the rituals of unlocking the deposit box. When Mrs. Kohl left, Jack sorted through the contents until he found his mother's engagement ring and removed it. He tried not to think about any of the other items in the box and their associations with his parents.

Jack studied the ring for a moment and then slid it into the ring box he had purchased for the purpose. He slid the box into his pocket and retreated from the vault, letting Mrs. Kohl know he was leaving.

Jack returned to the Algonquin Hotel where he'd stayed the night before. He thought about having a drink in its Blue Bar or checking out the famous Round Table where the "Algonquin Round Table" of writers and critiques had once held court.

But without company, without Maggie, none of that seemed interesting. He gathered his belongings and checked out. From the hotel, he headed to Grand Central Station and bought a ticket for the overnight train to Cincinnati. He picked up a copy of Evelyn Waugh's book *The Scoop* but couldn't interest himself in it.

His thoughts focused on the week to come. He believed the next several days would be crucial if he was going to write the story he so badly wanted to write… and if he was going to get the "exclusive" his heart craved.

CHAPTER 27, SUNDAY, AUGUST 20

REICH ARMY

Has 100,000 Men

--

On Polish-Slovak Line,
As Tension Mounts

--

The Cincinnati Enquirer,
August 20, 1939

Founded in the 19th Century, the Cincinnati Art Museum sat atop Mt. Adams, the hill that overlooked downtown Cincinnati. The museum and the nearby Eden Park were jewels in the Queen City's crown.

But it wasn't art or the surrounding park that drew Jack to the museum on his day off. He came to see Maggie. She had come to the museum on the pretense of visiting it with two girlfriends. Jack enjoyed lunch with Maggie and her friends in the Terrace Café, the museum's small eatery. After lunch, Maggie's friends excused themselves to allow Maggie and Jack time together.

"Have you heard from the wire service?" Maggie asked. "Did you get the job?"

"I haven't heard anything. I've contacted the other wire services, but they can have anyone they want."

Maggie put her hand on Jack's. "The Art Rescue Consortium telegrammed me. They want to hire me."

"Congratulations!" Whatever his misgivings, Jack meant it. "See, I'm not the only one who recognizes how special you are."

"That's sweet, but I think it helped that Mom and my aunt offered to donate to the project." Maggie laughed. "They're probably covering my salary for the next six months."

"Have you accepted?"

"Not yet. My parents insisted I think about it over the weekend."

"And?"

For a moment, Maggie said nothing. She sat still, her elbows close to her body and her hands folded, while her eyes searched Jack's face. "Would you be terribly disappointed if I accepted?"

"Maggie, I'd be thrilled for you."

"Honestly?"

"Yes, absolutely. When would you leave?"

"Wednesday morning."

Jack's jaw dropped. "So soon?"

"You've been following what's happening in Europe."

Jack nodded.

"Before I forget," Maggie said, "I spoke with Aunt Agnes again. I told her about the attempt on your life."

Jack bit his lower lip anticipating more disappointment. He knew Mrs. Boyle was worried about her own safety. "And?"

Maggie smiled. "Aunt Agnes agreed to talk with you."

Jack's eyebrows shot up and his mouth opened. "You talked her into giving me an interview?"

"You can't talk Aunt Agnes into something she doesn't want to do. I told her we were seeing each other, and that Father was apoplectic about that. I told her about the stories you've written. She said she wanted to meet you."

"Maggie, thanks. I don't know what to say."

"That would be a first," Maggie said, breaking into a smile.

"Aunt Agnes will be in town Monday to meet with her attorney and to take care of some business, but you can't tell anybody that until she's out of town again and safe."

"Of course. How do I contact her?"

"She wants you to meet her at her attorney's office." Maggie looked in her purse and pulled out the attorney's business card. "Can you call him first thing Monday morning and schedule something?"

Jack grinned. "You betcha."

Maggie stood. "Let's walk. There's so much to see here, and who knows when we'll get a chance to see it again."

As they walked, Maggie put her arm through Jack's arm or held his hand, but each time only briefly. She would see a painting and begin talking about it or about its history or about the painter, and when she spoke, she moved her hands—to point, to gesture, or just to accompany what she was saying.

Maggie captivated Jack, but that didn't keep him from volunteering his own thoughts about what was happening in Europe and what might happen next. He also talked about doing something special with Maggie on Tuesday night before she left. He spelled out his plan. Maggie agreed, contingent on her parents not blowing a gasket over her going out with him the night before she left town.

Maggie saw another painting she said she admired. She talked about how wonderful it would be if she could convince someone to lend a piece like that to a museum in this country for safekeeping.

For his part, Jack wondered what it would be like to be the advertising director for a prosperous beer company and married to Maggie.

***

Later, after Maggie and her friends left, Jack returned to Covington. He stopped at a bar, the only one he could think of within walking distance of his rooming house, aside from Scrivener's, that didn't offer slots or betting, and thus had no obvious ties to the Syndicate.

The bar featured a sausage, sauerkraut, and boiled potato plate it called a hearty meal for "the wurst times." Jack ordered it and a beer and let his thoughts wander. He thought about his conversation with Maggie and his interview in the morning with Agnes Boyle. He thought about how his investigation into Vice Mayor Boyle might be about to come to a head.

Jack also thought about events in Europe. He had a sense that things there might come to a head too, but in truth, aside from the new pact between Hitler and Stalin, nothing much had changed. All summer, Hitler had threatened and bullied, and the democracies had dithered and protested, but each time had done nothing.

Would Hitler move on Danzig and the German Corridor? Would Poland resist? Or would it fold like Austria, Czecho-Slovakia, Hungary, and Romania had? If it did resist, would France and Great Britain come to its aid?

Would Overseas offer him a position? And if it did, should he accept it? In Germany, the Nazis and secret police would apply pressure to make him report only what they wanted. By all accounts, they could be far more muscular in their efforts than their counterparts in the Covington Police Department.

The waiter brought his meal and the beer. Jack cut into the sausage and wrapped a piece in sauerkraut and took a bite. While he chewed, he picked up the beer and studied the label. He wondered if it would be so terrible to be the advertising director for a brewery with deep roots in the community and the surrounding area.

If things in Europe fizzled out, he'd be set. And if war came and the United States got involved, he could enlist. Or the government might conscript him. Either way, he would get his big adventure.

He thought about his affair with Maggie. Was it just a summer fling? Would it survive a separation? Or would it merely be a pleasant memory, a might-have-been, as ephemeral as last summer's news?

Jack poured the beer and waited for the foam to come to a head.

CHAPTER 28, MONDAY, AUGUST 21

QUARTER-MILLION GERMANS ON LINE

TROOPS MASS

--

AT FOUR PASSES
INTO POLAND OVER TATRA
MOUNTAIN BORDER

Roads Choked As Full War
Equipment Is Moved Into
Region 250 Miles Long

The Cincinnati Enquirer,
August 21, 1939

The law firm of Dunlevy & Shaw occupied an upper floor of the Carew Tower, the department store and office building that loomed over downtown Cincinnati. The firm's reception area was impressive, with enormous oil paintings of bucolic landscapes on the walls and a quiet elegance that whispered money.

Jack announced himself to the receptionist, and after only a brief wait, a prim secretary materialized. She introduced herself as Mrs. Jamison and said, in a quiet, almost confidential tone, "Mr. Harrington will see you now. If you will follow me."

Jack shadowed the woman through carpeted halls decorated with oil paintings and old maps. Office doors, mostly closed, guarded the privacy of the attorneys within, but the occasional open door revealed glimpses of heavy furniture, oriental carpets, and shelves crowded with legal tomes.

Arriving at an interior conference room, Mrs. Jamison stopped and gestured for Jack to enter. Inside, an oriental rug covered the polished hardwood floor. A dark cherry conference table centered the room, and a small stack of yellow legal pads and pencils, perfectly aligned, lay at the precise center of the table. On the walls, large oil paintings depicted sailing ships battling high seas under dark, threatening skies.

Jack wondered how anyone not born into wealth could enter this temple of money and power without being thoroughly intimidated.

A trim, fifty-something man, dressed in a dark pin-stripe suit, crisp white shirt, and a regimental tie, rose and strode around the conference room table to greet Jack. The man was in excellent shape and had impeccable posture, suggesting someone who may have been a military officer earlier in life.

"Mr. O'Brien," the man said, extending his hand. "I'm Duncan Harrington. So good of you to come."

Jack shook the older man's hand. Harrington then turned to the equally well-dressed woman seated at the conference table. "Let me introduce you to my client and dear friend, Agnes Boyle."

"Pleased to meet you," Jack said. Dressed in a Mary Pickford-style suit, Mrs. Boyle was an animated woman of considerable presence, whose petite body showed none of the usual signs of middle-age thickening. Her eyes, and the little crinkles around them, suggested a woman of keen intelligence and quick humor. The only discordant note was a cast that extended from under her jacket and wrapped around her left wrist and hand.

"Mr. O'Brien," Harrington said, "please have a seat."

As Jack pulled back a chair from the conference table and sat, the attorney asked if he would like coffee.

"Please," Jack said, "if it's no problem."

Harrington glanced at Mrs. Jamison, who had remained standing at the entrance to the conference room. "How do you take your coffee?" she asked.

"Black."

Mrs. Jamison left, and Harrington took charge. "Just to recap our conversation on the phone," he said in a lawyerly tone, "you have agreed that under no circumstances will you reveal how you found Mrs. Boyle or where she lives."

Jack nodded. In fact, he did not know where she was living. He suspected she had taken up residence in Manhattan, probably in the Upper Eastside, and that Maggie had stayed with her during her recent trip to the City. But that was purely a guess.

"Mrs. Boyle fears for her life if her whereabouts were to become known," Harrington continued. "She has, if I may say so, placed a great deal of trust in you by agreeing to this interview. I hope you will not betray her trust."

"Understood," Jack said. "Completely."

"Very well," Harrington said. "Mrs. Boyle, do you have any questions before we begin?"

"May I call you Jack?" Agnes Boyle asked.

"Yes, ma'am, please."

"You know Maggie thinks very highly of you."

"And I think the world of her," Jack said. "I understand you helped Maggie find a position."

"Oh, dear, yes, we've been quite preoccupied with that. I believe we have found something suitable."

Mrs. Jamison returned, placed a cup of coffee on a thick wood-and-cork coaster next to where Jack was sitting, and left. The aroma of the coffee was reassuring.

"I can't tell you how happy I am," Jack said, "that Maggie arranged for me to have this chance to speak with you."

Mrs. Boyle tipped her head down and peered at Jack over the top of her eyeglasses. "Are you under the impression I decided to talk to you because you're dating my niece behind her father's back?"

Jack wasn't sure how to answer. After a moment's hesitation, he said, "Maggie didn't put it that way, but I assumed—"

Mrs. Boyle flashed a big smile. "I suppose that would be reason enough, but that's not why I agreed to talk to you."

Jack took his notebook from his jacket pocket and placed it on the table. "Then, why?"

"When I moved out, I thought I could keep all this quiet. But after that attempt on your life, I realized I had to speak up."

Jack admired the woman's spunk and determination.

"Plus," she said, smiling, "there was that article you did on poor Reverend Breckinridge."

Her response confused Jack. "You liked my article?"

"I most certainly did not!" Mrs. Boyle said, flashing another big smile. "That poor man."

Jack felt even more confused.

"Reverend Breckinridge wanted to raise money for hungry children, but his congregation was too small and too poor, and he wasn't from around here. He didn't know what he was doing."

Jack jotted down as much of what she was telling him as he thought would be helpful.

"Someone told him to see me for advice."

"And so," Jack asked, "you made suggestions?"

"Yes, although I think he really just wanted me to donate money and leave him alone. But over time, I believe Reverend Breckinridge decided it was to his advantage to follow my suggestions."

"I guess my article was a surprise?"

Mrs. Boyle gave Jack another glance over the top of her glasses. "Maybe not as much as you might think."

Jack pressed his lips together. *She'd heard rumors about the Reverend and the choir ladies?*

"When your article came out," Mrs. Boyle continued, "Harry saw it before I did." She hesitated and seemed to become lost in her own thoughts.

"Mr. Boyle saw my article?" Jack prodded. He was certain Mrs. Boyle had something important to say, and he hoped she wasn't having second thoughts about sharing it.

"At first, Harry thought it was funny. He couldn't stand Jonas—Reverend Breckinridge—and thought him running down the street naked was hysterical."

Jack told himself to be patient and let this woman tell her story at her own pace. From what Maggie had told him, she would do that anyway. He took another sip of coffee.

"Harry made fun of the husbands of the women who had been spending too much time with this good-looking young preacher. He couldn't understand how those men could have been so oblivious."

Mrs. Boyle bit her lip, and her face became tighter, more defensive. She removed her glasses. "And then it occurred to him that Reverend Breckinridge had been visiting *his* wife—me."

Mrs. Boyle took a sip of her coffee as if fortifying herself for what she was about to say. Or maybe, Jack thought, making a final decision about whether she would indeed say what happened next.

"Harry became enraged," she said. "He accused me of having an affair with Reverend Breckinridge. And then he hit me."

Jack hadn't anticipated that. "He hit you?"

"Yes. He slapped me with the back of his hand. Hard. He'd never done anything like that before and caught me off guard. I guess I staggered back a step or two and tripped over something—the cat, I suppose—and went down."

Jack jotted that in his notebook as Mrs. Boyle watched. When Jack looked up, she continued. "My nose was bleeding, and when I fell, I dropped the plate. It shattered and there was food everywhere."

Mrs. Boyle pulled a lace handkerchief from her pocket. "Harry seemed as surprised as I was. He said he was sorry, helped me to my feet, and told me to go clean myself up."

Jack scribbled into his notebook as quickly as he could, then looked up into Mrs. Boyle's eyes. They were tearing.

"I went to the bathroom and did what I could to get my nose to stop bleeding and to regain my composure. When I returned, I told Harry I wouldn't put up with him hitting me."

Mrs. Boyle paused while Jack wrote in his notebook.

"I told him I'd had such great hopes for him—for us. I thought one day he would be Governor, or maybe a Congressman. But with his drinking and his gangster friends and his whoring—I'd learned Harry was going to Greta's—I told him he was throwing away his future."

Jack watched the woman, expecting her to say more.

Mrs. Boyle sighed. "As you can imagine, we got into quite a row. He accused me again of having an affair with Reverend Breckinridge, and I told him he had to stop whoring and whatever he was doing with those hoodlums."

Mrs. Boyle stopped and once again seemed to become lost in her own private thoughts.

Jack caught up his notes, then returned his attention to Mrs. Boyle.

"Harry said we both needed time to calm down. He said he was going out and for me to take his plate. He would get something to eat wherever he went."

Mrs. Boyle wiped an invisible spot from her eyeglasses with her handkerchief. "I wasn't done, and I knew by the time Harry got back, he'd be boiled as an owl. I told him our marriage was over unless he stopped with the brothels and those mobsters."

Mrs. Boyle clutched the handkerchief tightly in her hands.

"How did he respond?"

"He scoffed and said, 'They'd ruin me.' Or something to that effect."

Jack scribbled that in his notebook.

"I told him it was just a matter of time until he got himself arrested or some reporter exposed him. 'One of these days,' I said, 'you will take Reverend Breckinridge's place on the front page of the newspapers, shaming yourself.'"

Jack glanced up from his notebook, surprised again to find himself, or at least his reporting, part of her story.

"Harry asked," Mrs. Boyle continued, "if the reporter who wrote the story about Reverend Breckinridge had contacted me. I told him no. He said it would be the end of us if I ever spoke with a reporter about his business."

"Do you remember his exact words?"

Mrs. Boyle nodded. "He said, 'If you do, you'll be a dead woman.'"

"He was threatening to kill you?"

Mrs. Boyle shrugged her shoulders. "I asked him, 'So, you're a killer now?' He said no, of course not, but I didn't know the men he was dealing with, how dangerous they were."

She glanced at Harrington, then continued. "Maybe he meant he could have them kill me, but I think he meant that if I interfered with whatever they were up to, they might act on their own."

Jack studied Mrs. Boyle. "Is that why you wanted to talk with me?"

"Yes," she said, nodding her head. "You cannot let people bully you." She put her glasses back on. "I'll feel safer with all this in the open."

"Anything else?" Jack asked.

"No, he just put on his jacket, swallowed the rest of his coffee, and left."

"Let me back up and ask you something I should have asked

earlier. I noticed your cast. When Mr. Boyle hit you and you fell, were you injured? Is that why you're wearing a cast?"

"I didn't realize it immediately, but I must have tried to brace my fall with my hand. The doctor said I had a hairline fracture of one of the bones in my wrist and another in my lower arm." She held up the plaster cast as if to illustrate the point.

Harrington opened the clasp on a manila envelope and removed several glossy, eight-by-ten, black-and-white photographs. "Agnes called me and asked me to meet her at the Emergency Room. I had a photographer make a record of the injuries Agnes sustained." Harrington glanced through the photos. "Of course," he added, "no photograph could show the full extent of what Agnes experienced." Harrington pushed the photographs and the envelope's other contents across the table to Jack. "The report from the Christ Hospital emergency room is in there too."

Jack glanced through the photos. They showed minor bruising, but no stitches or obviously broken bones. He set them aside to study later and looked up—but not at Agnes Boyle.

Jack's attention focused on the two manila envelopes still on the table in front of Harrington. He already had a solid scoop, but, like a child at Christmas, he couldn't help but wonder what else was under the tree.

"I advised Agnes," Harrington said, "that she was putting herself at risk if she went home by herself."

"Did you go home?" Jack asked Mrs. Boyle.

"Yes, but only to collect my belongings—clothes and things. I left before George got back." Mrs. Boyle looked at Harrington. "I called the woman who's our maid to help, and Duncan arranged for men with a truck."

Harrington looked at his well-manicured nails. "We placed a few calls to expedite things. We also arranged for security to be present." Harrington brushed some imaginary lint from his suit. "You could say, unfortunately, that we have experience in matters of this nature."

Jack glanced through his notes and back at Mrs. Boyle. "Mrs. Boyle, you say your husband accused you of sleeping with Reverend Breckinridge. I hate to ask this, but did you?" Jack hoped the question didn't end the interview.

Harrington cleared his throat. "Mr. O'Brien," he said, "that is not an appropriate question. Please ask something else."

Mrs. Boyle looked down, not making eye contact.

"How did you know Mr. Boyle was frequenting Greta's?"

"The short answer is," Mrs. Boyle said, "some nights he was coming home late, or not at all. But the answer you're looking for is this: some friends were at Greta's with business people from out-of-town, who wanted to get a glimpse of Northern Kentucky's underside. While they were having drinks, they saw Harry talk with some gangsters and then go upstairs with one of the women there who sell themselves."

"Who told you this?"

"A friend. I don't want to mention her name."

"Has anyone else seen him there?"

"Yes. After that, I asked the husbands of some other friends if they'd seen or heard anything. Some of them admitted they had heard rumors that Harry was a regular there." Mrs. Boyle pursed her lips. "And not just for the drinks and music."

"Did Two Penny Smith tell you that he'd seen Harry at Greta's?"

Mrs. Boyle looked surprised at the question. "Oh, my gosh, no. They wouldn't let a Negro into a place like that. Besides, I can't imagine Two Penny talking out of turn. It's just not like him."

Jack jotted down her answer in his notebook and tried not to react.

"Why do you ask?" Mrs. Boyle said. "Is there something I'm missing?"

"Two Penny had a full-time job working at Greta's. He was the janitor there."

Mrs. Boyle seemed surprised.

"A few days after you accused your husband of going to Greta's," Jack said, choosing his words carefully, "the police arrested Two Penny. I sat through the trial, and it looked like he was being framed for a crime that didn't happen."

Mrs. Boyle put her hand to her mouth. "Oh, dear. Do you think Harry blamed Two Penny for telling me? Did he have that poor man arrested?"

"Yes, ma'am, I do, but to be clear, I can't prove that. Not yet, anyway. And I'm having trouble finding someone who saw your husband at Greta's and will talk about it."

Mrs. Boyle looked to her attorney.

Harrington frowned. "Agnes, my advice," he said, "is that we keep certain things to ourselves."

Mrs. Boyle pursed her lips again and stared at the attorney. "Yes, well," she said, "I don't want to play that game. Let's see if we can convince Harry there's no point in fighting this."

"Very well." Harrington turned to Jack. "When Mrs. Boyle called me from the emergency room, I contacted the private investigators our firm uses. One of them witnessed Mr. Boyle leave Greta's. He said the thugs who work there had to help him out."

Harrington paused, apparently for effect. "These private investigators also observed Mr. Boyle visit Greta's on two additional occasions. They believe he met with a reputed crime figure. Someone named Roscoe Mascelli, who goes by the nickname 'Fats.'"

Harrington slid the second envelope from the stack of three across the table to Jack. "The reports are in there."

Jack glanced at the gumshoes' reports. He would read them later. "Are you are going to ask for a divorce?" he asked Mrs. Boyle.

"Yes," Harrington responded for his client. "We will also seek damages for assault and for forcing Mrs. Boyle to go into hiding."

"When?" Jack asked. He could feel his pulse quicken. "When are you filing?"

Harrington glanced at his client.

Mrs. Boyle nodded.

"Tomorrow, after Mrs. Boyle has finished her business and is safely out of town." Harrington picked up the third and final envelope. "This contains a copy of the suit we intend to file in the Kenton County Circuit Court. I can share it with you only on condition you do not disclose its contents until we file it with the court."

"Agreed," Jack said. "You have my word."

In an instant, Jack felt himself go from elated to deflated. "Mr. Harrington, the newspapers all routinely check the new filings basket in the Clerk's office. Once you file the petition, every paper in town will have the story."

For a long moment, Harrington frowned.

Jack wondered how much a Harrington frown cost a client.

Harrington stood. "Here's what we'll do," he said. "We will file with the court at the end of the day, just before the Clerk's office closes. If you're there, you'll be the only one to see it in time for the next morning's paper."

What Harrington suggested would work. Jack was glad Harrington anticipated—correctly—that he would need to confirm he had indeed filed the legal papers with the court. He couldn't have the *Tribune* run a story saying the Vice Mayor's wife had filed for divorce, only to learn that the lawyer had not filed the divorce petition.

Harrington came around the table to shake hands again and show Jack out.

Realizing the interview was over, Jack stood as well.

"By the way," Harrington said, "we will also arrange for an

emergency hearing with one of the judges. We intend to ask the judge to seal the file. If he grants our request, none of the other reporters will be able to see it."

Jack nodded that he understood and then turned to Mrs. Boyle. "Ma'am, I want to thank you again. And please, be safe."

"Mr. O'Brien," she replied, "I fear you have now taken this situation on yourself. I know you're young, and therefore, you're quite sure of your own invincibility, but please be careful. If they try to kill you again, you might not be so lucky."

On Jack's return to the office from his interview with Agnes Boyle, he called Vice Mayor Boyle's office. He couldn't get an appointment that day, but he convinced the secretary to give him an early morning appointment.

Jack looked forward to having another crack at the Vice Mayor, but he wasn't sure—appointment or not—the Vice Mayor would, in fact, agree to see him.

CHAPTER 29, TUESDAY, AUGUST 22

**REICH, RUSSIA PLAN PEACE PACT;
RIBBENTROP TO FLY TO MOSCOW**
TO BE SIGNED THIS WEEK

"Poland's Back Uncovered,"
Naxis Declare Clamly
As Europe Gasps
The Cincinnati Enquirer,
August 22, 1939

**ALL EUROPE IS STUNNED
BY HITLER-STALIN PACT**

THOUSANDS OF AMERICANS REPORTED
TO BE IN EUROPEAN DANGER
Cincinnati Times-Star, August 22, 1939

The next morning when Jack arrived at Boyle's office, it was obvious he was the first appointment of the day. His secretary appeared to have arrived only moments before. She showed Jack into Boyle's office.

"Mr. Boyle," Jack greeted the older man. "Good morning. Let me begin by saying that I'm afraid we haven't got off on the right foot. I'm glad you agreed to see me."

"I didn't, my secretary did," Boyle said. "I'm going to have a word with her." Boyle smiled.

Jack forced a smile.

Boyle folded shut the newspaper he was reading, but held it, as if he intended to resume reading it the moment he disposed of the interruption. "Are you okay?" he asked Jack. "I read about the attempt on your life."

"I'm fine," Jack said. "Thanks for asking." He was confident Boyle wouldn't have shed a tear had the attempt succeeded.

Boyle glanced at the newspaper before laying it on his desk. "Did you see the stories in the paper this morning about a Non-Aggression Pact between Germany and Russia?"

"Yes, sir."

"Does it mean what I think it means?" Boyle took a sip from his coffee mug.

"I don't know," Jack said, forcing another smile. "What do you think it means?"

"It means Germany is free to attack Poland. Russia won't go to war with Germany over this business."

"Yes, sir," Jack said. "That's how I understand it." He wondered if Boyle was processing the news or if this was going somewhere.

"Are you here about Patrolman Vance?" Boyle asked. His voice conveyed both suspicion and impatience.

"Not unless there's something new you'd like to share with me. The paper gave that to Driscoll, the crime reporter. I'm here about something else."

Boyle glanced at his watch. "What?"

"Before I get to that," Jack said, "there's something I need to say. In my business, when someone makes an accusation, we always try to contact the person affected and get his side of the story. I'm sure you wouldn't want the *Tribune* to print something that might put you in a bad light without giving you a chance to give your side of the story."

Boyle folded his arms. "You can put as much butter on your toast as you like, Mr. O'Brien, but don't try to butter me up."

Jack responded with a polite smile.

Boyle unfolded his arms and made a point of looking at his watch again. He asked, "So, why are you here?"

"I heard you and your wife separated," Jack said, "and that she might be planning to sue for divorce."

"No, we are not, and it wouldn't be any of your business if we were. She's just out of town, visiting friends. I think we're done here."

"Just one or two or more things, sir, if I can. I'll be quick."

Boyle stood. "What?"

"Is it true that you go to Greta's and consort with the women who work there on the upper floors?"

"I do not." Boyle's face colored. "Look, we've been through this before. Now, if you'll excuse me –"

Jack remained seated while he finished writing down what Boyle said. "Is it true, sir, that your wife is planning on suing you for divorce because she can't get you to stop going to brothels and hanging around with mobsters?"

"That is a damn lie. I don't go to brothels or hang around with mobsters, and my wife isn't suing me for divorce. Now, get the hell out of my office."

Jack finished writing that in his notebook, then looked up at Boyle and smiled. "Did you hit your wife because you suspected she had an affair with Reverend Breckinridge?"

Boyle puffed out his chest and doubled his fists. "If you print any of this crap, I swear to God, you'll regret it."

Jack stood. He locked eyes with Boyle but said nothing.

The air seemed to go out of the older man. Boyle sat back down and gestured for Jack to do the same. Evidently, Boyle realized that only Agnes or someone in whom she had confided could have known that.

"Did someone tell you this nonsense?" Boyle asked. "Or did you make it up?"

"You and I both know I didn't this make up."

"Your name's Jack, right?"

"Yes, sir."

"Look Jack, I'm a politician and a public figure. I can't have you trying to ruin my reputation. What do you want? What do I need to do so you and I can get along? What if I agree to take you under my wing, see that you get some real scoops, and you drop this horse crap?"

Jack rubbed his nose. "I *was* wondering what the City Commission will do with the trash collection contract."

"See," Boyle said. "I can make sure you know what the decision's going to be before it happens. You can have the scoop and plenty of others. That's the way things happen around here. You know, you scratch my back and all that."

"What I was wondering," Jack said, "was if someone has been scratching your back to make sure the Cleveland company gets the contract?"

Boyle sighed and shook his head. "Jack, the Mob doesn't own me or my vote. I do what I think is best for the city. If you knew me, you'd know that."

"So, for the record, no one from the Syndicate has talked to you about that contract, and you've not spoken to the Syndicate about it?"

"That's right. Jack, so you know, that's not who I am. I'm a politician and a city official. I talk with a lot of people. Maybe some of them aren't the best sort. But I don't knowingly talk with anyone connected with the Mob. I have nothing to do with the Mob. And I don't take bribes."

"Got it," Jack said when he finished scribbling that in his notebook.

"So, level with me," Boyle said. "Where do you come up this stuff? Is Maggie feeding you this?"

"I don't reveal my sources. But I expect the paper will run a story tomorrow saying your wife has left you and why—coupled with your denial, of course."

Boyle shook his head in disgust. "I swear, if you print that, you'll wish to God getting fired was the end of your problems."

"I'd ask if I need to check under my car for bombs," Jack said, "but I'm between cars at the moment."

Boyle jumped to his feet. "Get the hell out of my office, or I'll have the police remove you."

Jack stood and smiled. "It's always interesting talking with you, sir. And if you change your mind about any of what we just discussed, give me a call."

Boyle shook his head. "Get out of my sight."

***

When Jack entered the newsroom, he saw Rumble, the picture of pent-up frustration, standing by the door to his office. Jack headed straight to him.

When Jack got close enough, Rumble said, "In my office. NOW!"

Jack followed Rumble into his office and shut the door behind him.

"The Vice Mayor just called again. Do you plan to make a habit of antagonizing one of the most important officials in the city?"

Jack fought back the urge to make a smart aleck response. "The Vice Mayor's wife is about to sue him for divorce. I asked him about it, and he denied everything. He even denied his wife left him."

"What makes you so sure," Rumble asked, "that you know more about his marriage than he does?"

"I met with his wife and her attorney yesterday, and they laid it all out for me. I've got a copy of the divorce petition her attorneys are about to file."

Rumble sat and folded his arms. "She decided she wanted to make her dirty linen public and chose you to share it with?"

"I'd like to tell you I got this story because I'm a cracker-jack reporter, but the truth is, I imagine she has her own reasons. Maybe she wants her husband to settle. Maybe she wants revenge."

"And she chose the least experienced reporter on the paper to unburden herself to?"

"It had to do with the story I did on the naked preacher."

Rumble grunted.

"Mrs. Boyle is filing for divorce today," Jack said. "Her attorney agreed to hold off filing until just before the Clerk of Court's office closes, after the other reporters have done their last check of the day. Tomorrow morning, we should be the only paper with a story on the filing."

Rumble mulled over what Jack had just told him. "I'm not sure this is as big a story as you think it is. So, what if the Vice Mayor and his wife are getting divorced?"

"Boss, it's *why* she wants a divorce. She's going to allege that he broke her arm and that she's gone into hiding because she's afraid he or his Syndicate friends may try to kill her."

"She told you that?"

"Yes, and it's in the divorce petition her attorney is filing this afternoon. Like I said, he gave me a copy of the petition he's going to file."

"Boyle denies all this?"

"Yes, all of it."

"So, it's just her word against his?"

"Not quite," Jack said. "The attorney gave me photos of her injuries and the medical records from the hospital. She sustained fractures in her wrist and lower arm. And if you're worried about libel, we can just refer to the allegations in the legal filing."

"Why did he hit her?"

"She said if he didn't stop going to whorehouses and hanging around with his Syndicate pals, she would leave him. He's apparently a regular at Greta's. Remember my story about Two Penny, the colored guy who takes care of Boyle's yard, getting arrested and railroaded. That's where he worked."

Rumble rubbed behind his neck as if trying to soothe a headache that was forming. "We've been over that. You told me you had nothing solid tying Boyle to Greta's."

"That's the thing, boss. Mrs. Boyle's divorce attorney hired some private eyes, and the gumshoes saw the Vice Mayor leave Greta's the night he beat up Mrs. Boyle. And twice since then. I've got their reports."

Rumble picked up his unlit cigar from the ashtray on his desk and stared at it.

Jack was anxious to get to work adding his interview with Boyle to the article he'd already drafted. He wanted Rumble to say something instead of staring at his cigar like it was an oracle.

"Here's what we're going to do," Rumble said. "Go write this up, but don't put *anything* in your article you can't back up."

"Got it," Jack said.

"I want that on my desk by the time I get back from lunch."

Jack glanced at his watch. That would be tight.

"I will arrange for legal review. You know the drill. You're going to walk the lawyers through everything you've got. We're not printing anything they don't approve."

Jack nodded.

"If they sign off, I'll take this to the folks upstairs and see what they say."

Jack stood.

"And then, we'll see if Mrs. Boyle files for divorce this afternoon."

Jack nodded again.

"If I tell the Big Cheeses she's going to make these allegations in a divorce petition this afternoon," Rumble said, "you goddam well better be right about that."

***

Jack fed into the typewriter the cheap yellow paper the newspaper provided reporters.

Jack typed, "Vice Mayor's Wife Sues for Divorce, Alleges Adultery and Abuse." He added his byline and then glanced at the clock. He told himself to take a deep breath and focus. Rushing caused mistakes, and mistakes cost reporters their careers.

He began by retyping what he'd drafted the evening before:

> Mrs. Agnes Boyle, wife of Covington Vice Mayor Harry Boyle, filed suit for divorce Tuesday afternoon in Kenton County Circuit Court, charging her husband with adultery and physical abuse. Mrs. Boyle claims she fears that her husband or his contacts in organized crime may kill her. If proven, the explosive charges may dash any hopes the powerful local politician may have of running for higher office.

His lead covered the *who, what, when, where* and *why.* Now, he needed to flesh out the lead.

> Mrs. Boyle alleges that Vice Mayor Boyle struck her on the evening of Friday, July 21, after she accused him of frequenting a brothel and associating with gangsters. Mrs. Boyle's attorneys shared with the *Tribune* medical records from the Emergency Room at Christ Hospital dated the evening of the alleged attack. The records show that Mrs. Boyle

suffered fractures in her wrist and arm.

The medical records were a godsend. Still, Jack knew too many of the *Tribune*'s readers did not consider a husband hitting his wife a big deal, especially if the woman suffered only minor injuries.

Jack added Harry Boyle's denials.

> In an interview conducted hours be-
> fore Mrs. Boyle filed for divorce, Vice
> Mayor Boyle denied that his wife had
> left him or planned to file for divorce.
> He also denied that he struck his wife.
>
> Mrs. Boyle and her husband differ in
> their statements over other matters as
> well. In an interview, Mrs. Boyle told
> the *Tribune* she threatened to leave her
> husband if he did not stop going to
> Greta's Place and hanging around with
> people she believes are with the Syndi-
> cate.
>
> But when questioned by the *Tribune*,
> Mr. Boyle denied having ever been to
> Greta's or having met with underworld
> figures. "I don't go to brothels or hang
> around with mobsters," Mr. Boyle told
> the Tribune "and my wife isn't suing me
> for divorce." Mr. Boyle threatened to
> sue the *Tribune* if it reported his
> wife's claims.
>
> Countering those denials, Mrs.
> Boyle's attorney provided the *Tribune*
> with reports prepared by private inves-
> tigators, who describe seeing Mr. Boyle
> visiting Greta's on three occasions.
> According to those reports, on the even-
> ing he allegedly struck his wife, Mr.
> Boyle was ill or intoxicated and bounc-
> ers needed to help him out of Greta's.

Jack pulled the draft from the typewriter and read it. He had a terrific story, but he couldn't control how the paper's lawyers would react. Or whether Mrs. Boyle's attorney would file on time. He could feel the muscles in his shoulders tense.

Jack hoped Mrs. Boyle and her lawyers wouldn't change their minds or get to the courthouse too late to file. If they did, there was a good chance he'd lose more than a story. He would lose his credibility with Rumble and upper management—and maybe his shot at an overseas assignment. He called Harrington's office, but the lawyer was out, and his staff wouldn't say when he might return.

Rumble entered the newsroom, waving his cigar and barking orders at the reporters he encountered on his march to his office.

Jack took a deep breath and headed for Rumble's office.

***

The legal review with the *Tribune*'s attorneys was excruciating. For two hours, August Bearbeiter lectured Jack and Rumble on libel law. But in the end, relying on the photos, medical records, and the private investigators' reports, Bearbeiter approved Jack's story. He did so, however, contingent on Mrs. Boyle's attorney filing the suit, as promised, and on Jack or Rumble confirming with the P.I. firm that the reports of Boyle visiting Greta's were genuine.

Rumble left to get approval from his own higher-ups, and Jack called the P.I. firm. He got through to William Pierpoint, the head man himself. Pierpoint confirmed that the reports were genuine and that his firm stood behind them. Jack explained his plan for the evening. Pierpoint questioned Jack about the details. He also probed the gaps in Jack's plan. He said he would discuss the situation with Harrington. "I'll need to see what Mr. Harrington and his client want us to do." The gumshoe made no other commitment.

Jack dashed to the Kenton County courthouse.

***

Jack arrived twenty minutes before the Clerk's office's scheduled 5:00 p.m. closing time. He and three other reporters went through the wooden box that contained the afternoon's filings, looking for anything of interest. The legal papers were routine. He

368

and the other reporters finished their work and left. The other reporters, presumably, hurried back to their respective newsrooms to file their stories, check for messages, and call it a day.

Jack went to the ground floor, to the pay phone, and called Duncan Harrington. The attorney was out.

When Jack returned to the Clerk's office, it was ten minutes until the Clerk's office would close, and Harrington had still not arrived. Jack took a seat on one of the hard-backed wooden benches against the wall and waited.

With just five minutes before closing, Jack began pacing.

At three minutes before five, the door to the clerk's office swung open.

Jack turned, expecting to see Harrington. It wasn't. It was a young attorney there to make a last-minute filing. Jack hadn't seen this attorney before.

He sat back down.

The young attorney pulled papers from his briefcase. He, or a secretary, had clipped a neatly typed check and a summons to the pleading. The check would cover the filing fee. When the Sheriff's office served the summons, it would provide notice to the defendant that someone was suing him. It would also set the deadline for the defendant's response.

Jack stood and opened the door to the Clerk's office and looked down the hall. He did not see Harrington or anyone else in the hallway.

With one minute until the Clerk's office closed, the young attorney finished his business with the clerk, put the file-stamped copies of the papers in his briefcase, and snapped his briefcase shut.

Jack went to the counter and asked the clerk if a Mr. Harrington had filed a divorce petition on behalf of Agnes Boyle.

The clerk glanced at the young attorney.

"Hi, I'm Mark Christopolis. I'm with Mr. Harrington's firm. Are you O'Brien?"

"Yes," Jack said, "Did you file the divorce petition?"

Christopolis nodded. He pulled one of the time-stamped copies of the pleading from his briefcase and handed it to Jack.

"Any changes to the petition?" Jack asked.

"None," Christopolis confirmed.

"We're closing," the clerk said.

Jack followed the young attorney into the hallway. The clerk locked the door to the clerk's office behind them.

Jack shook hands with the attorney and asked him to repeat his name.

"Mark Christopolis," the attorney repeated. He dug a business card out of his suit pocket and gave it to Jack. "We drew Judge Chelone," he said. "I need to see if he will consider my motion to seal the file."

Jack waited in the hall outside the Judge's chambers.

Five minutes later, Christopolis emerged from the Judge's office.

"Did you get what you wanted?" Jack asked.

"Yes," Christopolis said. "He denied my request to seal the file. The complaint and related papers will remain public."

Jack scratched his head. "I thought you wanted the court to seal the file."

The young attorney smiled. "As soon as Mr. Boyle learns we filed, which I imagine will be tomorrow morning when he reads your story, he'll call his attorneys. They'll beat down the door to Judge Chelone's chambers, demanding that he seal the file."

"And the Judge will do that?"

The young attorney shrugged his shoulders. "You never know what a judge will do, but we asked for the court to seal the file, and he refused us. Given that, it will be harder for His Honor to grant Mr. Boyle's request." Christopolis flashed Jack a grin. "The Vice Mayor just may have to see this play out in public."

"How did you know Judge Chelone would deny your request?"

"We didn't, but we *knew* Judge Chelone hates lawyers from Cincinnati coming to this side of the river, even if they're licensed in Kentucky. He feels they're taking business away from the lawyers who practice in Kentucky. And, we *knew* he likes to make life miserable for young lawyers like me."

"So, you went in there like Brer Rabbit and begged him not to throw you into the briar patch?"

"Something like that," Christopolis said, still smiling. "I think Mrs. Boyle will be pleased."

Jack would have his scoop, but not an exclusive franchise. Once he broke the story, reporters from the other papers would be all over it, with their own follow-ups. It was good to get the scoop and to be out ahead on a story, but a potential problem if he were the only one reporting on the divorce. Boyle and his supporters would argue his newspaper was just out to sell newspapers by targeting a respected public official with salacious, unproven allegations.

***

Jack rushed back to the Tribune Building, his copy of the divorce petition in hand. But when he stepped into the building's lobby, he got a surprise. Woody was waiting for him.

"Day cough," Woody said.

"They gave you the day off?" Jack asked.

Woody nodded.

"That means Owl Polizzi is coming to town? They don't want you around in case you're feeding me information?"

Woody nodded again. "Dumb bass turds."

"I'll meet you at Scrivener's in an hour." Jack gave Woody some cash. "Take this in case something comes up and I don't make it."

Woody stepped closer to Jack and put his hand on Jack's shoulder. "You sure, you sure, snot whiz?"

It took Jack a moment to translate. Woody was asking if he was sure "about this."

Jack thought a moment and nodded his head *yes*. But he wasn't the only one whose life might never be the same. "You want out?" he asked Woody.

"Smell toe!" Woody said, his voice loud and clear, even if his message wasn't. "Pluck 'em!"

Upstairs, Jack swung by his desk on his way to Rumble's office. There was a note from Maggie. The note asked, "Are we on for tonight?"

Jack called Maggie, but Mrs. Hanover answered.

"May I speak with Maggie?" Jack asked.

"Jack, is this about tonight?"

"Yes, Maggie wanted to know if we're still on. I wanted to let her know we are."

"I'll tell her." Lillian Hanover hesitated. "I think that's best. George is… well, he's not happy about her seeing you again, and I don't want to aggravate him any more than he already is."

***

Vice Mayor Harry Boyle arrived at the Lookout House early for his meeting with Owl Polizzi. He was punctual as a matter of conviction and habit, but under the circumstances, he did not want to be late. The Cleveland mobster would likely be in an ugly mood and would take that as a sign of disrespect.

Besides, despite all that had happened, Boyle felt more confident about the contract than he had in some time. Fats Mascelli's attempt on O'Brien's life had been stupid. It could have killed any possibility of getting the trash contract re-directed to Polizzi's company—the news coverage had spooked his colleagues.

But the newspapers were playing up the car bomb as tied to O'Brien's confrontation with Fats—and to the possibility Fats' had a hand in framing Two Penny and the murder of Patrolman Vance. Boyle knew O'Brien had been trying to find a connection to the trash contract but had struck out. Nothing in any of his articles linked him to any of that.

With the newspapers' attention diverted from the trash collection contract, Commissioners Frank Vaske and Henry Meimann had given him their word they would vote with him to award the trash collection contract to the Cleveland company. Three votes were a majority. Barring something unexpected, at tomorrow afternoon's meeting, the Commission would award the trash contract to Polizzi's company.

But O'Brien had been making a habit of springing surprises on him just before the City Commission was about to award the trash contract. Which is what had made O'Brien's visit this morning so frustrating.

It sounded like Maggie had been feeding him information, but if all O'Brien had to go on was secondhand stuff from Maggie, the *Trib* wouldn't publish anything. Of course, if Agnes did eventually file for divorce, that would change things for him personally. *But even if she did, as long as Polizzi got the contract, that thug wouldn't give a damn about a divorce.*

Boyle took a sip from the whiskey he'd ordered and opened the *Kentucky Post*, one of the two evening newspapers. There was nothing in it about Agnes suing for divorce. He laid the *Post* aside and checked the *Times-Star*, the other evening paper. There was nothing in it either. That meant he was safe on that front for the time being. Even if Agnes filed for divorce in the morning, and he didn't think she would, the evening newspapers wouldn't come out until after tomorrow's City Commission meeting.

The newspapers had a bigger story to chew on than his marriage. The papers were full of coverage about the German-Soviet Non-Aggression Pact. Like the morning papers, the *Times-Star* headline writers had worked themselves into a fine lather about that. The news headlines suggested the deal likely meant the partition of Poland between Germany and Russia. The news stories quoted anyone willing to predict war.

Boyle grunted and took a long drag on his cigarette. It was just as likely, he thought, that Poland would see the handwriting on the wall and agree to a Reich "protectorate"—just as the Czechs, Hungarians, and Rumanians had. The newspapers led with the war angle because it would sell more papers.

Boyle checked the editorial page. He was about to take a sip from his drink when he saw the headline on the lead editorial. He almost spilled the drink on himself. The headline said, "Gangsters Get Together."

Boyle scanned the editorial. To his relief, it was not about Owl Polizzi and Fats Mascelli. It was more ink spilled on the Hitler-Stalin agreement.

He scoffed at the editorial's conclusion that, "the word of a Stalin or of a Hitler would seem to be worth about as much as that of a gangster." The editorial missed the point. When a gangster holds a gun to your head, it isn't the worth of his word you worry about.

***

George Hanover put his hands on his hips. "Maggie, I told you that you're not to see Jack."

Maggie gave her father *the look*.

"Yes, *I know*, he's a fine a young man," George said, "but what if the Mob tries to kill him again and you're with him? You don't know what those people are capable of."

Maggie turned so that her mother could help with a necklace. "Somebody has to stand up to them."

"You're a woman. It's not your place." George tapped a cigarette from a pack of Winstons.

"What if I had studied journalism?" Maggie asked. "What if I were a reporter? Then it would be my job."

"Hold still, so I can get this clasp," Lillian Hanover said. "There! Look at you! You look beautiful. Now, be a good girl and go get me some tea and let me talk to your father."

"Margaret Ann," George said, "you're not a reporter, and if you were, you would be writing for the society pages. I want to know why it's so important for you to see Jack tonight. You should be getting ready –"

"George, dear," Lillian Hanover said moving to where her husband was standing. She removed the cigarette from his hand and put it in the ashtray on the table. "It's Maggie's last night in town. If you want her to break up with Jack, you have to let her see him."

Maggie lingered at the dining room door.

"Can't she just call him or send him a letter?"

Lillian shook her head in mock disbelief, then pushed her hair back flirtatiously. "Is that how you broke up with your girl friends?"

George shook his head. "You know you're the only girl –"

Lillian gave George a wry smile. "What about Mary Ellen Depage? Is that how you broke up with her?"

"I don't know what –" George blustered.

"I've never heard about this," Maggie said, relishing the moment.

"Your father was dating both of us until –"

"Why can't Jack come here?" George interrupted, attempting to re-assert control. "She can tell him in the study."

"Tell him what?" Maggie asked.

"That you're breaking up with him," George said, "that you're—"

"Whatever are you talking about?" Maggie asked. "I think he's going to ask me to marry him."

"Now, listen here, young lady," George said.

"Maggie," Lillian said. "You're not helping."

Henrietta opened the door to the dining room. "Anybody need anything?" she asked.

"Could you get me some tea?" Lillian asked.

"Yes, ma'am," Henrietta said, but her attention had shifted to Maggie. "Lordy, Lordy, aren't you looking fine tonight, Miss Maggie! Why I bet that gentleman caller of yours will be begging you to marry him."

Lillian put her arms around her husband's waist. "Sweetie, don't let them get you riled up. Just let Maggie have her night."

George frowned and shook his head in resignation.

Lillian stood on her toes and kissed his forehead.

***

On a hill overlooking Covington, the Lookout House was a large, well-maintained building. It featured cocktail lounges, restaurants, and other amenities. But its claim to fame was its bustling casino, with slots and card tables. The casino's large picture windows gave patrons a sweeping view of Covington and the Cincinnati skyline. Upstairs, the Lookout House had a cocktail lounge and bar with its own panoramic view and several private rooms.

A little before nine, Jack escorted Maggie into the Lookout House, with Dick Watson in tow. Jack wore a freshly cleaned and pressed suit and his favorite bowtie. His shoes sported a new shine.

Maggie wore a Tulle Bowler hat with a silk flower, a stylish black-and-white dress, and high heels. Her entrance captured discreet attention from diners.

Flash carried a new camera. He had a fresh bulb in the flash attachment and a fresh cigarette between his lips.

The maître d' arched an eyebrow and noted that Jack's dining room reservation was for two. Jack explained the photographer was not joining them for dinner. It was a special occasion, and Flash was there to record it. Jack tipped the maître d' and explained where he wanted to sit.

When the maître d' led Jack and Maggie to their table, Flash left his camera with Jack and wandered off to look around.

A waiter materialized and took Jack and Maggie's drink orders.

Flash returned and nodded.

Jack checked his watch. It was a little past nine o'clock. He rose and moved to Maggie's side of the table. He knelt on one knee and produced a ring from his jacket pocket.

Flash moved into position. People at nearby tables interrupted their conversations to watch.

"Maggie," Jack said, "you're the smartest and most beautiful woman I've ever met, and I'm madly in love with you. Will you marry me?"

Maggie shook her head "yes," prompting applause from nearby tables. Jack slid his mother's ring onto Maggie's finger, wishing his mother were still alive. He was sure she would have liked Maggie.

Vice Mayor Harry Boyle and two other men, on their way out of the nightspot, paused and took in the romantic scene. As they did, Flash snapped a picture of Boyle and his companions. He turned and sprinted toward the door.

Boyle said something to one of the men with him. The man turned and gestured to the two beefy men behind him. Jack assumed they were bodyguards. The big guys hurried after Flash.

Jack took a deep breath and headed toward Vice Mayor Harry Boyle, Owl Polizzi, and Fats Mascelli.

***

Flash ran out the front door of the Lookout House. As he did, Woody, who had been sitting in the newspaper's "pool" car with the motor running, jumped out of the driver's seat, allowing Flash to take his place.

Flash squealed off. At the end of the driveway, Flash turned right onto the Dixie Highway and headed down the long, curving hill toward Covington.

The mobsters found the black Cadillac they had come in and sped off in the same direction.

A moment later, Maggie slipped out the front door and followed Woody to a waiting taxi. Maggie told the cabbie to take them to the *Tribune* building.

***

As Jack approached Boyle and his companion, he pulled out his notebook. "Mr. Polizzi," he said. "My name is Jack O'Brien, and I'm with the *Tribune*. I was wondering if you would care to comment on what business you have with Vice Mayor Boyle?"

"I'm a private citizen," Polizzi said. "Get out of my face."

"And Mr. Boyle is a public official. Were you discussing the Covington waste contract with Vice Mayor Boyle?"

Polizzi stepped forward and gave Jack a shove.

Jack stumbled backward but remained on his feet—propped up from behind by a patron whose table Jack's fall threatened to upset.

"How much are you paying to get the contract?" Jack asked when he regained his balance.

Before he had gotten that question completely out, Jimmy Brink and two bouncers arrived.

"Get him out of here," Brink said. The bouncers grabbed Jack and pushed him toward the door. When they had Jack outside, one held Jack's arms, while the other punched him in the stomach, knocking the wind out of him.

As the punch landed, a camera flashed. Two private investigators rushed out of the shadows, one carrying a camera. The other shouted, "Leave him alone."

The gangster gave Jack a hard shove, sending him to the pavement. He and his companion turned toward the private investigators.

The P.I. with the camera snapped another picture. The other P.I. raised his hand. It held a gun.

One of the bouncers reached inside his jacket.

"Don't," the P.I. with the gun said. "Hands where I can see them, or I shoot."

The bouncer slowly moved his hand from his jacket. He looked at his companion and said, "Let's go make sure the boss is okay."

The bouncers turned and went back inside the Lookout House.

The private investigator with the camera snapped another picture, this one of Jack on the pavement. The other gumshoe holstered his gun and helped Jack up.

***

Halfway down the hill, Flash rounded the sharp curve just before St. John's Church and pressed his horn hard. He hoped Jack's plan would work—the Cadillac was closing fast.

After Flash raced by, a Covington Waste Company garbage truck pulled out of a side street and stopped, blocking the highway.

The black Cadillac rounded the bend. The thick-necked driver saw the garbage truck, slammed on the brakes, and skidded to a stop just short of crashing into the truck.

Pulling a pistol from his shoulder holster, the big man on the passenger side of the Cadillac jumped out and ran forward to the truck. Standing on the truck's running board, he pointed the gun at the driver.

"Back this truck up," the gangster demanded, "and do it now." A neon light on a nearby business flashed on and off. Each time it flashed, it lit up the long scar that ran down the side of the gangster's face.

In the front seat of the garbage truck, Willis Smith nodded energetically, but didn't move the truck. "Yes, sir," he said. "I be moving this old truck anywhere you want. Just don't shoot me."

"I don't want to hear any of your shuck-and-jive," the gangster said. He kept his gun pointed at Willis.

The neon light flashed again.

"No, sir," Willis said. "I don't be giving no shuck-and-jive to nobody with a gun." He slowly put the truck into reverse. "No-o-o, sir!"

By the time Willis cleared the way, Flash was halfway to the *Tribune* building.

At the bottom of the hill, the black Cadillac gave up the chase, turned around, and headed back to the Lookout House.

***

When Flash Watson arrived at the newspaper, Rumble was standing in the doorway of his office, his hands clasped behind his back. Rumble's face had a strained expression—his lips pinched together, eyes squinted.

"Did they show?" Rumble demanded. "Did you get a photo for me?"

"They were there. I got the shot."

"Where's Jack?"

"Jack stayed behind to question Boyle and the hoodlums he was with."

"You left him there by himself?"

"He insisted."

Rumble shook his head. He paced first in one direction, then another.

"He'll be okay," Flash said, his voice more optimistic than confident.

Rumble waved his cigar at the cameraman. "Why aren't you in the darkroom? I can't wait all night for you."

"On my way."

***

The taxi pulled to a stop at the *Tribune* building. Woody paid the driver with the money Jack had given him and escorted Maggie into the *Tribune* Building. When Maggie was safely inside, Woody left and hustled on foot to the river and his shanty boat.

The security guard took Maggie to the newsroom. When she entered, Rumble looked Maggie up and down, removed his cigar from his mouth, and said, "And who are you?"

Maggie smiled. Jack had told her what to expect. "My name is Maggie Hanover. I was a decoy to help Mr. Watson get the photo."

"Then have a seat and try not to get in the way." Rumble returned his cigar to its rightful place and bit down on it.

"Jack was telling my father," Maggie said, giving Rumble a warm smile, "that you may be the best managing editor this part of the country has ever seen."

Rumble removed the cigar from his mouth and started to say something. Before he could, Maggie asked, "Do you know my father, George Hanover? He owns the brewery."

Maggie knew Rumble would understand she was referring less to her father than to the money his brewery spent on advertising.

Rumble nodded. "George Hanover is your father, huh?"

Maggie smiled. "He says that he's always heard the same thing about you. That you run a tight ship."

Rumble waved the cigar in a vague motion Maggie had trouble interpreting. *Thanks? A dismissal of the flattery?*

"Everyone's heard someone shout, 'hold the presses!'" Maggie said, "I mean in the movies. But I bet not many people have heard that in real life."

"Where's Jack, goddamnit?"

"He stayed behind to question Harry Boyle and those other men. It must be exciting to be a reporter like Jack." She gave Rumble an admiring look. "And it must be the top of the world to be an editor like you."

Rumble grunted and bit down on his cigar.

***

Ten minutes later, the newsroom door opened, and Jack entered the empty bullpen.

Maggie saw Rumble's face flash relief at the sight of Jack, but his expression quickly transformed into a scowl.

"I'm holding the presses for you, Mr. O'Brien. Nice of you to show up. Have you got a story for me?"

"Yes, sir," Jack said. "I see you've met Maggie. Give me ten minutes to get it written up."

"Five!" Rumble said, turning back toward his office.

Unbidden, Maggie followed Rumble into his office.

Rumble made a motion for Maggie to take a seat while he dialed a number on his phone. "Rumble," he said, identifying himself to whoever answered his call. "Naptime's over. Ten minutes."

Maggie suspected Rumble's comment was meant to impress her. Jack had explained what would happen. Normally, the printers would print section one, the local news section, and section two, the national news, simultaneously on the paper's two massive presses. But tonight, they were printing the national news section on both presses. Then, when his story was ready, they would print the local news section on both presses.

The process of running the national section first, then the local section was less efficient and would cause some delay, but not as much as would result if they waited for Jack's story to print both sections. The process meant that the men in the press room would be busier than usual, not idle as Rumble implied. But they would be idle soon if Jack took too long to write his story, or Rumble took too long to approve it.

Maggie pressed Rumble with questions about how the process worked. Rumble gave much the same explanation as Jack, but in more detail and in more colorful terms. It was obvious to Maggie the man loved the business of turning out a newspaper. "Cut Rumble," she remembered Jack saying, "and he'll bleed newspaper ink."

When Jack arrived with his story, Maggie excused herself but lingered just outside Rumble's office while he reviewed what Jack had written.

Two minutes later, with only minor revisions, Rumble pronounced himself satisfied and told Jack to check on Flash. Maggie followed Rumble to Typesetting, where he dropped off Jack's story. He then led Maggie to the ground floor where the printing presses were running. The printing "shop" was an area bigger than her high school's gymnasium, with most of the internal space taken up by the two huge presses. The noise was incredibly loud. Rumble shouted explanations of what was happening, but the presses drowned out most of what he said.

When the tour was over, Rumble gave Maggie a copy of the national news section of the next morning's edition and led her back to the newsroom. Maggie looked for Jack, but he was on the phone.

***

"Jack O'Brien here," he said, cradling the phone's receiver between his cheek and shoulder.

There was a pause at the other end of the line. "Jack, this is Harry Boyle."

"Yes, sir. How can I help you?"

"I'm calling to make sure you're not going to run a story linking me to whoever you think I was with this evening."

"Are you really going to claim you didn't meet with Owl Polizzi tonight to discuss the waste collection contract?"

"Jack," Boyle said. "I'm not sure you understand who you're dealing with." Boyle hesitated. "If I get mad at you, I might yell at you and shout obscenities. I might call the editor and complain. I might even make sure your competition gets access to stories before you do. Worst case scenario, I might file a libel suit."

Jack listened to what Boyle was saying, and to what he wasn't saying, and waited for the message he assumed Boyle called to deliver.

"But, Jack, these people from Cleveland aren't like you and me. They play rough."

Jack wrote those words in his notebook. He wanted the exact quote.

"Are you threatening me?" Jack asked.

"No, no," Boyle said. "You seem like a bright guy, someone who will probably have a great a career. I'm sure you will break lots of stories. I'm not threatening you. I'm trying to help you."

"But?" Jack said.

"But if you run a story implying someone from Cleveland is trying to influence the way the city awards contracts," Boyle said, choosing his words carefully, "someone in Cleveland, or their associates here, might take offense. It might not be your story that gets killed."

"Have you discussed that with Mr. Polizzi?" Jack asked.

Boyle did not respond immediately. Jack could picture Boyle shaking his head in frustration.

"Jack," Boyle said, "you need to work on your people skills. You need to learn to listen when people are trying to tell you something for your own good. If you don't, it could be… bad for your career."

"You're not the first person to tell me that," Jack said. "How many times have you met with Mr. Polizzi about the waste contract?"

"I don't know what you're talking about," Boyle said.

"Did you have Two Penny Smith framed?"

"It's been interesting, kid," Boyle said and hung up.

Jack went to look for Rumble. As he did, he hummed, "I'm just wild about Harry, and Harry's just wild about me."

***

Maggie sat at an empty desk, waiting for her father to come pick her up. She hadn't told Jack she called her father, but it was obvious Jack would be busy for some time.

As she waited, she did not read the next morning's national and international news, nor did she watch Jack work. Her attention focused on the engagement ring on her finger and her thoughts for the future. She had agreed to the proposal stunt in advance, and it had been fun, but she was in no hurry to remove the ring.

The security guard entered the now almost empty bull pen, looked around, and spotted Maggie. As he approached her, Jack jumped from his seat and hurried to Maggie.

"Your father's here, Miss," the guard said.

"Maggie, I could have taken you home," Jack said. "I, I…" He had trouble knowing what to say. "Mags, tell me, we're not done, that we will see each other again."

Maggie gave Jack a half smile. "I wish I could promise you that and know it would be true." She slid the ring off her finger and handed it to him.

Jack's face colored, and he held his breath for a moment. Slowly, he reached out his hand and let Maggie put the ring in his palm. He searched Maggie's face.

"Jack, I believe, I hope, we will meet again, but... who knows?" Maggie's eyes were tearing.

Jack stepped forward, put his arms around Maggie's waist, and pulled her close. He kissed her once, gently, tentatively, and then again with more feeling than he'd ever kissed a girl.

The security guard made a coughing sound.

Jack stepped back.

"Good luck!" Maggie said. "And congratulations on your scoop."

Maggie picked up the hat she had laid on the desk where she had been sitting, put it on and adjusted it, turned, and walked away.

***

When Woody reached his boat, he found the piece of pipe he'd set aside as a weapon. He set it in easy reach. Given what Jack had just pulled off and his own role in it, he figured the odds were better than even he'd get a visit from some Syndicate goons. He hoped to avoid that by pushing off and heading down river. He would meet up with Jack's friend, Ben Strasberg, who had found a job for him with the local public library.

Woody went ashore, unfastened the lines that held his boat in place, and climbed back aboard. He turned the motor over and headed out into the river. The river was quiet, and on the water, the air was more comfortable than it had been in the city. Woody glanced over his shoulder and saw car lights make their way slowly toward the spot where, for the past two decades, he had moored his boat. He guided the shanty out into mid-river and slowed the engine. A barge was coming up river toward him, but he wanted to give himself a moment to make out what was happening on shore.

The car lights stopped.

Woody could just make out two men leave the car and make their way to the riverbank. He turned the rudder to guide the boat closer to the far side.

Two shots echoed over the water. Woody ducked and looked back. At first, he saw nothing. Then, flames leaped from the shanty boat that had long been a fixture on the riverbank just behind his own. But that made no sense. He was sure Rizzi had checked him out and knew exactly where he kept his boat.

The barge was closing in. Woody moved still closer to the far shore and resumed heading down river. He willed himself to believe he would see Jack again.

CHAPTER 30, WEDNESDAY, AUGUST 23

**BRITAIN RENEWS GUARANTEE
OF AID TO POLAND**

RESERVES

CALLED BY PARIS

And London In Reply
To New Hitler Move

--

*The Cincinnati Enquirer,
August 23, 1939*

When the coffee began to percolate, Harry Boyle stepped out to get the morning paper. It was a beautiful morning. The sky was blue with not a cloud in sight. It would be hot and humid later, but for the moment, the air was comfortable.

As Boyle stepped from his porch, a blue jay sounded an alarm. A squirrel scampered across his lawn for the safety of the oak tree in his neighbor's yard. Down the street, caught up in its own concerns, a dog barked.

Boyle took in none of that. He picked up the morning paper, unfolded it, and scanned the front page. As he expected, there was a picture of him saying something to Owl Polizzi. The headline screamed:

WITH DECISION ON CONTRACT DUE,

VICE MAYOR MEETS WITH MOB BOSS

Boyle could feel himself tense. *It was a goddam nightmare.*

He glanced at the rest of the front page. A second story, beneath the fold, had its own headline:

HARRY BOYLE SUED FOR DIVORCE
FEARS FOR LIFE, WIFE ALLEGES

Standing where he picked up the paper, Boyle read the story, anger mounting as he did.

O'Brien had suckered him. He should have said Agnes was filing for divorce. Instead, the S.O.B. had baited him into claiming everything was fine between him and Agnes. On top of that, the damn story said nothing about Agnes and that preacher.

Without giving it conscious thought, Boyle rubbed a spot in the upper corner of his chest, below his left shoulder. He focused instead on the way the article quoted him. His denial that Agnes had left made him look like a liar. Coming after that, his denial of hitting his wife looked like just another lie.

O'Brien tricked me, he told himself. *This is all O'Brien's fault.*

Boyle switched his attention to the lead story, and as he did, he again rubbed the spot on his chest where the discomfort was.

The lead story was worse.

It not only described him leaving the Lookout House with Owl Polizzi and Fats Mascelli, it tied the meeting to the waste collection contract. Plus, it claimed private investigators had seen him at Greta's on three occasions. And that other, unnamed Lookout House customers had seen him there with Polizzi on at least one previous occasion.

Boyle rubbed his chest again but kept reading. "Assistant Commonwealth Attorney Leo Denton refused to say if the grand jury was investigating–"

"Mr. Boyle?" a voice said.

Boyle looked up from the paper. It was a Deputy Sheriff. So, he'd get to see the divorce papers for himself. "Good morning, officer, you have papers to serve?"

"Harry Boyle?" the officer asked.

"That's right. Let's see what you have."

"Here's your copy," the Deputy said, handing the paperwork to Boyle. "If you'll just sign this at the bottom."

"Do you have a pen?" Boyle asked, absently, as he scanned the paper. It wasn't what he expected. It was a grand jury subpoena. Boyle stiffened and coughed. As he signed the receipt, he could feel a headache developing.

Boyle handed the Deputy back the receipt and the pen.

"You have a wonderful day, Mr. Boyle," the officer said and hurried off.

Boyle was about to turn, to go into the house, when he saw a black sedan pull to the curb.

Two men from Greta's—Gus Panzer and another guy whose name Boyle didn't know—got out. Panzer held a manila envelope. Neither Panzer nor his companion waved or smiled or offered any greeting.

Waiting for the men, Boyle rubbed his chest—again, without giving it any thought. "Good morning, gents," Boyle said when the men closed.

"Let's go inside," Panzer said.

"Sure, I've got coffee brewing."

***

At the hotel, Jack had the bellman flag a cab for the short trip across the bridge to Covington. He had the taxi drop him off near the river bank where Woody kept his shanty boat. He needed to make sure Woody had kept his promise to head downriver to Louisville. And had gotten away safely.

Woody's shanty boat was not there. Jack looked around and saw no sign of Woody. That was a relief.

But gone too was the shanty boat next to where Woody had kept his boat. Charred scraps from the shanty littered the shore and floated in the water. Flames—and maybe an explosion—had consumed the boat. Police crime scene tape marked off the shore where the boat had been, but there were no police at the scene and not much of the boat.

Jack refused to think about what might have happened.

***

At the newsroom, before heading to the courthouse, Jack spent several minutes relishing his front-page scoops and collecting congratulations from his colleagues. On his return to the office, he found a note from Joe Dinklehaus on his desk. It said for Jack to see him.

Jack found Dinklehaus at the coffee stand, refilling his coffee mug.

"I can't find Vice Mayor Boyle," Dinklehaus said, "but I've canvassed the other members of City Commission and the Mayor. Thought you'd want to know. They all claim they're voting for Covington Waste to keep the trash collection contract. To hear them tell it, that's what they intended to do from the start."

"Joe, thanks for letting me know."

"Yeah, well, I don't believe a word of your story. I'm going to enjoy it when Boyle sues."

Rumble barked, "O'Brien!"

Jack looked up. As usual, Rumble had a scowl on his face and an unlit cigar clenched between the fingers of his right hand.

"If it's not too much trouble, Mr. O'Brien, I need to speak with you in my office."

Jack hurried to Rumble's office and took a seat. Letting Jack stew, Rumble walked across the newsroom to the coffee stand, emptied the dregs from his coffee mug, and refilled it. Reporters and others around the newsroom kept their heads down and did their best to appear busy.

Rumble returned to his office and slammed the door behind

himself. He sat his coffee down and lowered himself into his chair. "Jack, believe it or not," he said, "I used to be young once, and believe it or not, I was a damn good reporter. And, like you, I was a young man in a hurry."

Rumble tossed the cigar he had been chewing on into his waste can and rummaged through his desk drawer until he found a fresh cigar. He tore the wrapper off, but then laid the cigar down as if he had lost interest in it.

"When I see you in action, it gives me some sense of what I must have put my editors through." Rumble shook his head.

Jack smiled.

Rumble picked up the cigar again. He looked at it as if he didn't know where it had come from and stuck it in the pencil holder on his desk. "Promise me," he said, "that you won't slow down, that you won't let that fire in your belly go out."

"Yes, sir."

Rumble took a drink from his coffee but continued to stare at Jack over the rim of his cup with a fierceness that signaled he hadn't finished.

Not sure where Rumble was going with this, Jack waited and said nothing.

Rumble coughed, picked up his wastebasket, and spit the coffee into it. "Goddam, this stuff is awful," he said. His expression suggested that the sour-tasting coffee—like the state of the economy and the weather—might be Jack's fault. "It's probably rotting our stomachs and turning our brains to mush."

Jack tried to look repentant.

"But to get to the point, you don't need to concern yourself with our lousy coffee."

The point escaped Jack. He wondered if Rumble was firing him.

"While you were out, I got a call from headquarters," Rumble explained. "If you're still interested, they want to make a foreign correspondent out of you, *provided –*"

Jack jumped from his chair. A huge grin spread across his face. He wanted to give the gruff old bear a big hug.

"Hear me out," Rumble said, signaling for Jack to sit back down. "*Provided* you can leave tonight on the early train to New York."

Jack knew if he got the assignment, he would need to leave on short notice, but he never expected the notice to be *that* short. "To-night?"

"Oh, crab apples!" Rumble exploded. "Before I told you you've got the job, I was supposed to ask if you have a passport."

"Yes, I've got one. It's up to date."

Rumble nodded. "Good, because they want you to go to head-quarters in New York, fill out paperwork, and then leave the next morning for London."

"That's–." Jack struggled for the right word. "That's—."

"Herr Hitler refuses to put off his shenanigans until you're ready. So, if you want this assignment, you need to accommodate his schedule."

"I'll do it," Jack said. "Thanks."

"You're supposed to call this person in New York to get the details," Rumble said, handing Jack a handwritten note. "And to tell them you accept."

Jack glanced at the note.

"I'm sure they'll tell you," Rumble said, "but they'll have a train ticket waiting for you at Union Terminal in Cincinnati. The train leaves at five o'clock or around then."

"I'll call New York right away."

Rumble shook his head. "No, go home and call from there. I don't want a lot of commotion. When you leave my office, go to your desk, grab anything you need, and leave. Don't say anything."

"You want it to look like you fired me?"

"No, I want it to look like I sent you out on assignment. Editors do that, you know. I'll make an announcement when I'm sure you've made it out of town. Meanwhile, Jack, watch yourself. I'm afraid your stunt last night pissed off some dangerous people."

Jack shrugged.

Rumble's face reddened. "Jack, goddamnit, take this seriously! You won't be able to go to Europe and get your ass shot off if the Mob gets to you first." Rumble looked around his desk and found the cigar he'd stuck in the pencil holder. He picked it up and pointed it at Jack. "Watch your back, okay?"

"Yes, sir, and thanks." Jack stood and extended his hand to Rumble.

Rumble stood and shook Jack's hand. "Try not to get shot over there."

"I'll give it my best."

Rumble said, "And, one more thing."

"Yes, sir?"

"Wipe that shit-eating grin off your face."

Jack checked his desk. Aside from his notepad, there was nothing on top he wanted. In a desk drawer, he found the ten dollars from his bet with Dinklehaus. He tore a page from his notebook and wrote a quick note. He clipped the note to the money and tossed it into Dinklehaus' in-box on his way out of the newsroom.

The note said, "Use this to buy the office some decent coffee, Jack."

***

Jack left the newspaper building and walked the two blocks to the bank. He closed his account, put the cash in his wallet, and returned to the boarding house to pack.

Just in case Syndicate men were looking for him, he took a

roundabout way to his rooming house and entered by the service entrance in the back of the building. He crept up the stairs to the second floor, cringing every time the floorboards squeaked. He unlocked the door to his room, moved next to the wall, and pushed the door open. Nothing happened. He took a quick glance into the room and pulled back. He saw no one, and no one took a shot at him. He took a deep breath and entered the room. No one was there waiting for him.

Jack closed and locked his door and moved to the window. He pulled the curtain back enough to peak outside. No cars looked suspicious, and no one was milling around. He felt relief, but he suspected Syndicate men would be waiting for him later that evening when they would expect him to return from work.

By then, he'd be on the train.

From his pocket, Jack retrieved the note Rumble had given him and placed the call. The office manager at headquarters in New York confirmed what Rumble said. Jack should take the 5:10 p.m. red-eye train to New York, complete some paperwork, and meet a few key people. He would fly out the next morning to London. Jack jotted down the train number and departure time.

"Pack light," the New York office manager told him. "The airline's limit is seventy-seven pounds. If you need something, they have stores over there."

Jack spent the next hour packing—and fighting the urge to call his parents. They had been dead three-and-half months, but still, whenever something important happened, the urge to call and tell them about it returned.

Instead, Jack called Ben Strasberg and caught him at his desk at the *Courier Journal* in Louisville. "Ben," Jack greeted his friend.

"Before you say anything," Ben said, "I've got news."

"Okay."

"Well, first," Ben said, backpedaling, "I saw your articles on the wire service this morning. Great stuff! You nailed it. You got the big story."

"Thank you, thank you."

"Did Woody get away?" Ben asked.

"Yes, but I think it was a close call. His shanty wasn't there this morning. He promised me he'd go to Louisville and find you. He should be well on his way. What's your big news?"

"I think I've met the one, the girl I want to marry."

"Terrific! Who is she?"

"Sadie Auerbach Cohen."

"Ah, a nice Jewish girl. Your parents will be happy. Have you proposed?"

"Not yet, but soon, I think."

A funny thought occurred to Jack. "So, this time we turned the tables. I got the story, and you got the girl."

Ben didn't respond for a moment. "Has Maggie broken up with you?"

"That's why I called."

"Ah, oh."

"The newspaper—well, Overseas, its wire service—is sending me to London, and from there to Berlin."

"Congratulations!" Ben enthused. "That's what you wanted."

"Thank you. I'm excited."

"Have you told Maggie?" Ben asked.

"No. She's taken a position with an organization in New York that wants to convince art owners in Europe to loan their artworks to museums here for safekeeping."

"Jack, I don't know what to say."

"Then, just wish me luck. I'm leaving tonight for New York and tomorrow for London."

"Well then, good luck, and congratulations."

After he hung up, Jack placed one more call—for a cab. He took a last look around the room. He checked his pockets for his passport and wallet and assured himself he had everything he needed. He left and locked the door behind him. On the ground floor, he knocked on the door of the apartment of Mrs. Schickel.

When Mrs. Schickel answered the door, she was still in her pajamas and housecoat. Her hair stretched so tightly around the large, pink curlers, it seemed to tug her eyebrows up. Jack could not think of an encounter with the woman when she was not in her housecoat and her hair was not in curlers.

"Mrs. Schickel," he began.

"I'm not paying to have a plumber unplug your toilet," Mrs. Schickel interrupted. Her voice was too loud. A large cat circled around her thick ankles.

Jack reminded himself to speak louder. "I'm moving out and wanted to let you—"

"You have to give thirty days' notice," Mrs. Schickel snapped, "or you don't get your deposit back." With that, she slammed her door shut.

Even for Mrs. Schickel, that struck Jack as abrupt.

A moment later, Mrs. Schickel opened the door again, this time, clutching the cat in her arms. "Sorry," she said, "I didn't want Eleanor to escape."

Jack remembered that Eleanor was the cat.

Mrs. Schickel looked Jack's tall, thin frame up and down with undisguised disapproval. "When are you leaving?"

"Today. Now, actually. Something came up, and I've got to leave for—"

"Are you in trouble? The law after you?"

"No, ma'am. Like I said –"

"Well, I can't give you your deposit back."

"Mrs. Schickel," Jack said, speaking louder, "I'm leaving some things, clothes and other stuff, in my room, and —"

"I can't store your stuff for you," she interrupted. "God knows when you'll want them."

"I wanted you to know—"

"Nicht, Nein, Nebuchadnezzar!"

"… that you can have what I'm leaving behind. Sell it. Give it away. Anything you—."

"Did you get a girl in a family way?"

"No, ma'am," Jack said, shaking his head. "If you won't marry me, I will remain a bachelor."

Mrs. Schickel scoffed. "When are you leaving?"

"Now, ma'am, but first I need to ask you —"

"I don't give romantic advice," Mrs. Schickel said. "I'm not one to get involved in other people's business."

Jack nodded. "Have there been any strange men—"

"There's nothing strange about it. Just lock the door to your room and leave the key with me."

"Mrs. Schickel," Jack said, almost shouting, "have you seen any strangers hanging around the building? Gangsters? Anyone asking —"

"The bookies looking for you? Is that why you're leaving?"

Jack shrugged his shoulders. "Something like that." He reached out his hand. "Here's the key."

Mrs. Schickel put the cat down and, blocking the opening with her foot, and took the key. "If you're leaving without giving notice," she said, "I'm not giving you your deposit back."

Jack blew Mrs. Schickel a kiss, picked up his suitcase, and walked to the front door. He opened it a few inches and checked the street again, looking for signs of men with guns. He saw no one but felt a rush of adrenaline when he stepped out of the boarding house to the sidewalk.

***

Jack went to Scrivener's for lunch. If the Mob was looking for him, it was somewhere its men might well be waiting. But he felt more secure there, with lots of people around, than somewhere unfamiliar. Besides, he was hoping to see Flash and say good-by.

He found a booth in the back and scanned the menu.

"Jack," a voice familiar said.

Jack looked up and saw Sal Rizzi, and next to him the large, self-assured mobster he'd seen his first morning at the Bridge Café. He wondered if the two of them had been waiting for him.

"I'd like to introduce you to Gus Panzer," Rizzi said. Like usual, both men wore dark suits, dark shirts, and flashy, light-colored ties. Panzer had updated his wardrobe with a silk handkerchief in his jacket pocket.

Jack stood and extended his hand. "Mr. Panzer."

Panzer shook Jack's hand in a bone-crushing grasp. "May we join you?" Panzer's voice was heavy and bass, like it came from deep inside his body.

Jack nodded.

Panzer looked around, caught the waiter's eye, and signaled for coffees.

Jack sat. The two men slid into the opposite side of the booth.

"Sal says you're a square shooter," Panzer said.

Jack was uncomfortable with "shooter," but nodded.

Panzer pulled out a pack of cigarettes, tapped it on the tabletop, and offered Jack one.

Jack shook his head.

Panzer lit one for himself, taking his time.

Jack waited.

The waiter arrived with coffees and retreated without offering to take food orders.

"Fats is out at Greta's," Panzer said. "He sold his interest to me last night. He's… gone into retirement."

Jack asked, "How come?"

Panzer shrugged. "Maybe some folks didn't like how he was handling things, drawing too much attention to himself, putting the business in a bad light." Panzer stared at Jack. "Who knows? Maybe they don't like the way he swings a bat and wanted to trade him to another team."

Jack refused to show any reaction. He lifted his cup of coffee, blew on it, sat it back down.

Panzer blew cigarette smoke toward Jack. "The broads are out at Greta's too. It's all legitimate now—except for the slots, and nobody cares about those. You can come by and see for yourself."

Jack responded with a wry smile. "The Syndicate wants to buy the Lookout House from Jimmy Brink," he said. "And in the meanwhile, it doesn't need all this bad publicity."

Panzer returned Jack's smile. "I wouldn't know anything about that." He turned to Rizzi and said, "You told me he's smart."

"Mr. Panzer," Jack asked, "what do you want?"

"I wanted to clear the air and see if you and me can start fresh."

"Meaning what?"

Panzer drew deeply on the cigarette, held the smoke in for a moment, and then exhaled it slowly. "Can we reach an accommodation?"

"I'm not for sale. You can't buy me. Or my pen."

"Be a shame if something happened to a nice kid like you."

Jack stared Panzer in the eye. "Nothing to do with this, understand, but I've got an offer of a better job someplace else. Away from all this. I was thinking of taking it."

Panzer hesitated, sizing Jack up, weighing what he said, deciding if it met his needs.

"Problem is," Jack said, "I hate leaving loose ends. Things that might come back to haunt me later. You know the feeling?"

Panzer shook his head and laughed. "You got brass, kid. I'll give you that. What loose ends?"

"Is Two Penny in danger?"

"He kept his mouth shut, didn't he?"

"I tried to get him to talk, but he wouldn't. Told me what happened at Greta's wasn't my business."

"Two Penny's okay."

"I found Two Penny a job somewhere else. Is that going to be a problem?"

"It's a free country. Just tell him to keep his mouth shut."

"He knows."

Panzer stirred his coffee.

"Is Mrs. Boyle in danger?" Jack asked.

"Harry Boyle's wife?"

Jack nodded.

"She's okay, but she ain't getting that divorce."

That surprised Jack. "Why not?"

"We just heard on the radio. The Vice Mayor dropped dead this morning. Heart attack, indigestion, or something."

"Really?" Jack hadn't heard that.

Panzer gave Jack a sly smile. "Yeah. They said there were compromising photos on the table where he'd been sitting."

"Photos?"

"Rumor is, they showed the Vice Mayor in bed with some working girls. Chocolate ones."

Jack took a sip of his coffee. "What about me? Am I in danger?"

"You leaving town for good?"

"Yeah. I got a position as a foreign correspondent. I'm leaving next week."

Panzer crushed out his cigarette. "Can you keep your nose out of my business till then?"

Jack studied the big man. "I'm a reporter. If I smell a story, I follow my nose. Sometimes, that means I stick my nose in places where I'm not welcome."

"That's what they say about you."

"It sells newspapers."

Panzer shook his head and said to Rizzi, "Can you believe this guy?"

"I was just thinking," Jack said, "about something that might make for a nice story. Is Fats dead? Is he floating in the river? Buried in a farm? Taking a long nap in the trunk of a car somewhere?"

"Do you reporters protect your sources?"

"I do."

"A little birdie told me his Cadillac is down there by the river, a couple blocks from where those shanty boats were. I wouldn't know anything about it, but maybe, like you said, he's curled up in the trunk taking a long nap."

Jack said, "Thanks for the tip."

Panzer gave Jack a cold, hard stare. "Don't mention it."

The waiter approached.

Panzer stood and pulled a money clip from his pocket. Tossing a bill on the table, he said to the waiter, "His lunch is on me."

"Yes, sir."

Panzer turned and left without looking back.

Jack ordered a sandwich and looked at Rizzi.

Rizzi shook his head.

"Put a rush on it," Jack told the waiter. "And make it to go. I'm on a story, and I've got a deadline to meet."

The waiter shook his head. "Like I ain't never heard that before."

Rizzi tapped ash off his cigarette and let it fall into a little glass ashtray. "If you're headed down to the river, the shanty boat next to where Woody's used to be—"

Jack searched Rizzi's face. It showed no emotion.

"The folks at the store got themselves worked up last night," Rizzi said, "when they heard about Woody being at the Lookout House with you. They thought maybe Woody tipped you off."

Jack felt a chill. "What did they do?"

"He hadn't picked up his paycheck," Rizzi said. "They didn't want him to go without getting what he was due."

Jack could feel himself go numb. "Did you kill him?"

Rizzi studied the smoke coming off his cigarette. "No, he'd already left."

Jack breathed again.

Rizzi took a sip from his coffee. "But when that piece-of-shit shanty boat he lives in wasn't there, that other shanty boat got torched."

Jack searched Rizzi's face. He saw no emotion, no remorse. "Why are you telling me this?"

"I wanted you to know things could get ugly—for Woody, for me—if word got out that Woody went down river, and some other stiff got whacked. People might think I wanted it to look like Woody got rubbed out, so he could get away."

Jack wasn't sure what to say. "Thanks" didn't seem right.

Rizzi stared at Jack. "*Capiche?*"

Jack nodded.

Rizzi slid out of the booth and buttoned his suit jacket. "Don't take any wooden nickels, you hear?"

EPILOGUE

August 23, 1939 about 5:00 P.M.

Completed six years earlier, Union Terminal was the main train station for passenger traffic in and out of Cincinnati. An Art Deco masterpiece, the building's huge semi-dome dominated its surroundings. Bas-relief stone carvings marked either side of the entrance. Murals depicting local industries and companies decorated the central rotunda and concourse.

On another day, Jack's eyes might have wandered over the surroundings. But with only minutes to go before his train left, Jack hurried to the ticket booth and from there to his train. When he reached the boarding area, he scanned the crowd. Near the train, beside a porter, Maggie was kissing her parents goodbye.

Carrying his suitcase, Jack rushed forward.

Maggie spotted Jack. Her eyes widened.

George Hanover followed Maggie's gaze, spotted Jack, then his suitcase. His face hardened.

"I got it!" Jack called out to Maggie.

"Where do you think you're going?" George Hanover demanded.

"New York," Jack said, "and from there to London, and then, most likely, Berlin. I've got a position as a foreign correspondent."

Maggie broke into a broad grin.

The conductor shouted, "All aboard!"

"Maggie, you ready?" Jack asked.

Mrs. Hanover gave her a husband a nudge with her elbow.

"Jack," he said, "good luck over there."

"Thanks, sir," Jack said. "Mrs. Hanover."

Maggie waved at her parents and stepped onto the train.

Jack followed her. He'd gotten the big story and the assignment he'd dreamed of. But there was still an exclusive he wanted. He had the engagement ring in his pocket. That wasn't where it belonged.

HISTORICAL NOTES

The City of Covington, Kentucky, where this novel takes place, had its bookies and brothels, but in the year of Our Lord 1939, it was a model of rectitude compared with its sister city, Newport, which prided itself on the nickname "Sin City." Many citizens fought to keep organized crime out of Covington. Others saw no harm in compromises with Syndicate-supported activities.

But that year, a slate of "reform" candidates, led by Carl Kiger, ousted the old guard city commissioners. A year later, someone killed Kiger. Some believe the Syndicate murdered him; others blame his daughter. But Kiger had too much money hidden in his couch for his reputation to survive his death.

In that fateful summer, just before World War II broke out in Europe and changed the world forever, the New Deal remained *the* political issue of the day. Most people strongly supported the New Deal, but conservatives—and there were plenty of them—complained bitterly about the New Deal and programs like Social Security, which they regarded as socialism. Although the New Deal had helped boost employment and the economy significantly, conservative resistance prevented Roosevelt from expanding government spending enough—until the war—to pull the country completely out of the Depression.

In the South, including Kentucky, Jim Crow was very much the rule, and for many, its defense was even more important than the debate over the New Deal. The NAACP and others, for example, pushed for enactment of federal legislation making lynching a federal crime; Southern Congressmen prevented Congress from passing that or any other civil-rights legislation.

Many in the Evangelical community worried that Franklin Delano Roosevelt was the antichrist and that developments suggested that the End Times were upon us. See, e.g., Matthew Avery Sutton, *Was FDR the Antichrist? The Birth of Fundamentalist Antiliberalism in a Global Age*, J. Am. History (2012) 98(4): 1052- 1074.

When I set out to write this novel, I wanted to put a reporter in a situation in which he would need to confront the racism and corruption that were endemic at the time. Beyond that, I simply wanted to tell an engaging story, not re-litigate the municipal politics of the summer of 1939. I make this point to emphasize the usual disclaimer: Any resemblance to actual figures of that time is purely coincidental. The exceptions include: Mayor Knollman, City Commissioners Carl Kiger, Henry Meimann, Frank Vaske, and City Manager Theodore Kluemper. This novel uses them fictionally.

***

The Charity Day at Latonia Race Track was an actual event. After the 1939 meet, the Latonia Race Track never re-opened—at least not, in its original location. Most observers attribute its demise to low attendance due to the Depression.

The riot in the east Covington neighborhood of Austinburg is also an actual event but did not occur on the date indicated in this novel. That riot happened on August 30 when Andrew McIntosh and his wife moved into 421 Byrd Street. News reports at the time estimated that a crowd of about 3,000 whites milled around and that as many as 500 threw bricks and rocks at the home.

Jimmy Durante did perform at Devou Park on the date indicated. The local papers claimed the crowd size set a record for the Devou Park series. Following his Devou Park appearance, Durante performed at the Beverly Hills in Southgate—a town just south of Newport—for several weeks.

The controversy over the waste collection contract is pure invention on my part. The Mayfield Road Gang and Alfred "Owl" Polizzi were very real, but I have no reason to believe that "Owl"

Polizzi ever owned or controlled a trash collection company. This novel uses Alfred Polizzi fictionally. So too, the Mob lawyer, Charles Lester.

I know of no bar or brothel in Covington called Greta's Place. It is pure invention. There is, however, a beautiful old building at the location mentioned in this novel. Some prominent and successful lawyers occupy the building. I spent my career as an attorney. My appropriation of their building for my novel does not imply any criticism of the legal profession or the good folks at The Lawrence Firm. My thanks to them for permission to use their building in my novel.

And speaking of lawyers, the court did not appoint an attorney for Two Penney Smith in this novel, because the Supreme Court did not rule that the Sixth Amendment requires counsel for indigent defendants until *Gideon v. Wainwright*, 372 U.S. 335 (1963).

***

If you enjoyed this novel, please take a moment to post a brief review on Amazon or Good Reads.

ACKNOWLEDGMENTS

Thanks to local historian and writer Bob Schrage for reviewing a draft of this novel for the historical accuracy of the background events. And for not fretting over the literary license I took inventing the characters and incidents that make up the novel. His biography, *Carl Kiger: The Man Behind the Murder* (Covington, 2011), was indispensable reading.

For anyone interested in the period, I also recommend Alvena Stanfield's fictionalized account of Carl Kiger's murder, *A Covington Vice Mayor, an Anniversary and a Murder*, in Covington Writers Group, *Anthology 2015* (available on Amazon and elsewhere).

For insight into jazz in the 1930's in Covington, I drew from Nelson Burton and Simon Anderson, *Nelson Burton: My Life in Jazz*, Clifton Hills Press Inc. (2000).

Thanks to the Covington and Boone County Writers Groups for their feedback on sections of this novel and for their encouragement and suggestions. Special thanks to Alvena Stanfield for insisting I spend time doing research into the era. The time was well worth it.

Thanks to the Kenton County Public Library for its microfilm collection of local papers from the era and to the staff of the main branch in Covington for all their assistance.

Thanks to Karen Etling and the staff of the Baker Hunt Art & Cultural Center for providing background information and a tour of the center.

Thanks to Judy Clabes, the Editor and Publisher of the modern day *Northern Kentucky Tribune* and formerly, the editor of *The Kentucky Post*. Ms. Clabes was the first woman to serve as a Scripps

Howard editor. I first met Ms. Clabes when I edited my college newspaper and she was Editor of *The Kentucky Post*.

Thanks to the members of the Facebook group Old Photos of Northern Kentucky for their input. They reminded me how common bookies used to be in Covington, even as late as the 1950s and '60s.

Special thanks to Linda Schilling Mitchell for permission to use the cover photo.

Very special thanks to my beta readers. You know who you are. You contributed enormously to this project.

And my deepest thanks to L.N. Passmore for her editorial guidance and for being a great teacher.

CREDITS

Songs
"I'm Just Wild About Harry" (1921)
Lyrics by Noble Sissle
The music and lyrics are in the public domain.
"Till We Meet Again" (1918)
Lyrics by Raymond B. Egan
The music and lyrics are in the public domain.

Headlines
With thanks to:
The Cincinnati Enquirer
And to the Cincinnati Museum Center:
The Cincinnati Times-Star
The Kentucky Post

Biblical Verses
Bible verses are from the King James Version. The character who quotes Revelation, Chapter 16, verse 15, mangles it.

E.M. Forester
The quote from E. M. Forester is from *A Passage To India* (Harcourt 1924).

Cover Photo

Thanks to Linda Schilling Mitchell

Enjoy this book?

Your opinion is important! As an indie author, my success depends in large part on readers taking the time to post a constructive review on Amazon or GoodReads or wherever you purchased it.

Please take a moment and share your opinion with potential readers!

And if you enjoyed this novel, check out my other novel, *A Fatal Cell Phone Video*.

Gary Reed

20746561R00255

Made in the USA
Lexington, KY
06 December 2018